D0274986

The Longest Day

The Longest Day

Sara Hylton

PIATKUS

Visit the Piatkus website!

Piatkus publishes a wide range of bestselling fiction and non-fiction, including books on health, mind, body & spirit, sex, self-help, cookery, biography and the paranormal.

If you want to:
- read descriptions of our popular titles
- buy our books over the internet
- take advantage of our special offers
- enter our monthly competition
- learn more about your favourite Piatkus authors

VISIT OUR WEBSITE AT: www.piatkus.co.uk

Copyright © 2005 by Sara Hylton

First published in Great Britain in 2005 by
Piatkus Books Ltd
5 Windmill Street, London W1T 2JA
email: info@piatkus.co.uk

The moral right of the author has been asserted

A catalogue record for this book is available from the British Library

ISBN 0 7499 0737 1

Set in Times by
Action Publishing Technology Ltd, Gloucester

Printed and bound in Great Britain by
Mackays Ltd, Chatham, Kent

Chapter One

Perhaps that was when it all started, that hot sunny day in June when St Agnes on Rowansdale was alive with visitors because the longest day brought them in from all the surrounding towns. They came for the cricket match, to wander through the castle grounds and the old ruined keep, to enjoy the village shops and tea garden and then to climb the hill to Rowansdale Hall which Sir Robert and Lady Jarvis threw open to the public on this one day in the year.

It was a day when roses bloomed profusely in the gardens and tea was served in the long conservatory. A day when Major Robson marched his officer training cadets along the paths and put them through their paces on the terraces, a day when Commodore Watson hoisted his flag in front of his house at the top of Tremayne Hill and a day when young men in white flannels escorted girls in pretty silk dresses along the paths beside the river, or took them boating along its gentle meanderings.

Later in the evening there would be the dance in the village hall attended by those same young couples now changed into more formal attire, and when the day was over they would all congratulate themselves that it had been the best longest day ever. Why it was never held on Midsummer's Day nobody could understand, but for as long as the oldest villagers could remember this was how it had always been and none of them would think of changing it.

The visitors left in the early evening having spent an enjoyable day and as they walked back to the village down the slopes of Tremayne Hill they looked with admiration at the large houses surrounded by exquisitely kept lawns, waved enthusiastically at Commodore Watson standing next to his flagpole, and hurried on to spend whatever they had left in the village shops before they closed for the day.

As Major Robson marched his cadets out of the gates he encountered Lady Jarvis's sister riding her horse towards him and he beamed with delight, smoothed his moustache and encouraged the boys to step out a little.

Observing all this from his garden Commodore Watson smiled grimly to himself, and strolling over to where his wife sat underneath the trees he said acidly, 'The Major's eyeing up his chances. I doubt if he'll have much success in that quarter.'

'What quarter?'

'Lady Marcia's here apparently. They've exchanged pleasantries; that's all at the moment.'

'And that's all there will be. Elspeth keeps him on a tight rein.'

'Well, she's holed up with the bridge four, whether it's the longest day or not.'

'Of course, the only time they don't meet is if Tuesday falls on a Christmas Day. I expect Desmond was glad to get away.'

'Did you know Lady Marcia was visiting?'

'No, her sister once told me she came here in between husbands; how true that is I can't say.'

'There's probably something in it. How many at the last count?'

'Two that I'm sure of. I thought you'd be going down to the cricket match.'

'I might just do that. I saw Mrs Clarkson going off there a little while back. She'll be busy with the refreshments I've not doubt. You could come with me and help out.'

'Oh not today Andrew, it's far too hot and whenever I

2

go I seem to put the damper on things – either the team loses or the heavens open.'

'We don't pull our weight in the village, we could do more.'

'You could organise some sea cadets and vie with the Major. We have a river and we have a lake of sorts. Why don't you think about it?'

'I left all that behind me when I left the Navy,' he retorted and strode off towards the house, followed by his wife's mischievous smile. She supposed they could do more. She helped with the flowers at the church, she subscribed to prizes for the school and she had the occasional coffee morning in aid of charity. She did more than the newcomer Mrs Edgebaston.

Very little was known about Mrs Edgebaston. She'd alighted in the village three years ago after buying The Oaks, vacated a few months earlier when the Proctors decided to join their daughter in America. It had been a momentous decision for them to make but Mr Proctor hadn't been well for months and they thought the time had come for them to move on.

Mrs Edgebaston was something of a shock to the rest of the people living on Tremayne Hill. She informed them that she was a widow, but from the men coming and going she did not appear to be a very lonely one.

She had been seen trotting down to the cricket pavilion earlier that morning dressed as usual in a brightly coloured silk sundress and wearing a large hat decorated with floating ribbons. She favoured sunglasses that sat on her pert nose like a huge butterfly and she had smiled across the garden and waved her hand in the friendliest fashion.

The men thought she was very nice; the women thought she was too nice. Mrs Watson had learned from the other ladies that she was little help at the Cricket Club but preferred to sit under the trees chatting to any man who was available.

Lois Watson eased herself out of her chair and walked

3

towards the path to meet her husband coming out of the house.

'Decided to join me then?' he asked her.

'No. I'll walk to the gate with you. You look very nice dear, I like that panama hat.'

'Well, it's suitable for the day.'

As they reached the gate a young couple paused to smile at them before strolling along the road and the Commodore said, 'Pretty girl that, she'll turn a few heads and break a few hearts if I'm not mistaken.'

'Well, she seems quite happy with Councillor Stedman's lad, but aren't they a little young to be serious?'

'I can't help feeling the younger girl is missing out a bit, with her elder sister everybody's favourite. I rather like young Nancy, although she's a bit of a tomboy.'

'It reminds me of me and my sister. She was always the pretty one with the lovely voice while I had to take a back seat. Mother always said the blossoms that bloomed too early were the first to wilt.'

'Well, that's certainly true in Violet's case; as far as I'm concerned you were always the pretty one.'

She beamed, not displeased with his comments. They looked up the road towards the Clarksons' house where Nancy Clarkson could plainly be seen swinging on the gate and the Commodore said dryly, 'There doesn't seem to be much going for her today – parents at the Cricket Club and the sister out with her boyfriend.'

'Growing up can be pretty painful,' his wife said feelingly.

'Why don't you change your mind and come with me,' he persisted. 'You don't have to help in the pavilion. Mrs Edgebaston never does and you could join her if you want women's chitchat.'

'I don't think so, Andrew, in any case I'm quite sure Mrs Edgebaston prefers men's company.'

He decided it was no use to persist and she watched him striding off down the hill in the direction of the village.

4

After a few minutes she decided to stroll in the same direction stopping at the Clarksons' gate where Nancy favoured her with her usual cheeky grin.

'I thought you'd be out and about today, Nancy. Where are all your friends?' Lois asked her.

'Molly Peterson has to help her mother look after their visitors and the others have gone to watch the cricket. I hate cricket.'

'Isn't it a terrible thing for an English girl to say, but I hate it too. You could have helped your mother though, the ladies would have been glad of that.'

'Not really. I always manage to break something or it rains.'

'Will you be going to the dance?'

'My sister says I'm too young, and my dancing isn't good enough. We're having lessons now at school, so perhaps next year.'

'Well of course, you have plenty of time, my dear.'

As she sauntered back up the hill she met Major Robson on his way down. He had changed out of his officer's uniform and was similarly attired to Andrew with pristine white trousers and navy blue blazer, but without the panama hat.

He smiled brightly, asking, 'Andrew gone to the cricket club then?'

'Yes, a few minutes ago.'

'But you're not going, Lois?'

'No, not my idea of fun.'

'Shame on you, woman. Elspeth won't be there either, it's that damned bridge. There they are the four of them on a perfect summer's day when everybody with any sense is outside in the fresh air.'

'I don't suppose you really mind, you'll find plenty of people to talk to. Mrs Edgebaston is there, she'll greet you with open arms.'

'Now isn't that just like my wife, always going on about the woman.' He grinned mischievously. 'She could have

5

got hold of Andrew by the time I get there.'

'Oh, I rather think Andrew will be too staid for Mrs Edgebaston,' she replied.

'Don't be too complacent, my dear, some women prefer the strong silent types. I see the flag is hoisted, and I've been putting the lads through their paces.'

'So I believe. Andrew saw you chatting to Lady Marcia. I hadn't realised she was visiting.'

'We'll no doubt be hearing more about it, husband trouble probably. Actually I rather like her.'

Lois laughed. 'Of course you do, Desmond, you like all the ladies.'

She watched him striding out down the hill, a smart dapper figure pausing to chat briefly to Nancy, but not for long. Young Nancy Clarkson was a little too young to bring out the gallantry in him.

Lois sat back in her chair thinking how lucky she was to be sitting in her garden in the warm sunshine, with the scent of roses all around her and the joyful singing of the birds. In a world filled with trouble spots all the people around her needed to worry about was that their milk and daily newspapers arrived on time, whether the Vicar's sermon would be overlong and whether Mrs Edgebaston had had two gentleman callers the evening before or three.

She could hear the sound of women's voices calling their farewells and realised that Elspeth's bridge afternoon was coming to a close – earlier than usual, she thought, consulting her watch.

From the gateway a voice called out, 'How sensible, Lois, to enjoy your garden on such a lovely day.' It was Dorothy Spencer, the local chemist's wife and she called back, 'Do join me, Dorothy, if you're not in a hurry.'

She liked Dorothy Spencer and her husband and was glad when her friend opened the gate and walked across the lawn to join her. Taking the chair next to her Dorothy said, 'We left early because Grace was rather anxious about her

6

mother. She'd left her sitting in the sun and was afraid the old lady would be fretful.'

'Poor Grace, she doesn't have much of a life these days, does she?'

'No. It was different when her father was alive but her mother is so dependent on her and there's really no need for it.'

'She's not an invalid then?'

'By no means, but she likes to think she is.'

'I don't know the old lady, indeed I don't actually know Grace very well but she seems very pleasant.'

'You know, Lois, my husband always said you'd never settle here after Andrew's life in the Navy. He thought he'd hanker after some windswept moor within sound of the sea and that this place would only be temporary.'

'That's what I thought too – it was our son who persuaded his father to think of something else. I remember him saying, "You know, Dad, Mother's followed you about all over the globe, or sat at home waiting for you to take some leave, surely she has a right to some say in where you spend your retirement." I never thought Andrew would agree to it. Perhaps I don't really know him as well as I thought I did.'

'And he's happy here, Lois?'

'He hasn't said that he isn't happy.'

'Then he must be. Men don't suffer in silence, you'd have been aware of it. Did you know that Lady Marcia is here?'

'Yes, I saw her a little while ago.'

'This time she has her son with her. A very handsome boy. I'm not sure which husband is the father, the first or the second. He's around fifteen so it's probably the first.'

'A little bit too young for Erica Clarkson.'

Dorothy laughed. 'I'm afraid so. Do you think she'd dump the Stedman boy if something better came along?'

'Perhaps that is rather unkind, but she's quite a little minx, too pretty and too many people telling her so.'

7

'Perhaps it's as well Julian is away from her grasp then. I've no doubt she'll be around whenever he comes home on leave.

'I suppose I should call in at the cricket match, but no doubt they'll be having tea at this time.'

'How terribly remiss of me, Dorothy, why don't you join me for tea?'

'No really, dear, I'd better get off home. John's sister and her husband are coming round this evening and I still have things to do. Shall I see you at the church coffee morning?'

'Well yes, I did say I'd go. I'll walk to the gate with you.'

As they said their farewells at the gate they were suddenly aware of the flying figure of a girl coming towards them, apparently in some distress. Her pretty face was flushed and angry and stormy eyes filled with tears eyed them somewhat balefully as Dorothy Spencer said, 'Is something wrong, Erica? You look very upset.'

Fresh sobs took over and without a word Erica hurried down the road where her sister stood waiting for her.

'Well really,' Dorothy said, 'what can have brought that on. She was perfectly happy a couple of hours ago.'

'Young love,' Lois said quietly. 'Perhaps we've forgotten what it was like.'

'But to be so angry and tearful. Alec Stedman's a nice boy, hardly the sort to cause a rumpus like that. No doubt we'll be hearing more about it in due course.'

After her friend had gone Lois sauntered back to her seat under the trees reflecting on the girl's tear-filled eyes and angry expression. She hoped all would be forgiven before the dance in the village hall or there would be even more tears and very little forgiveness.

Nancy Clarkson followed her sister's mad charge towards the house and up to her bedroom, standing outside the slammed door before finding enough courage to open it and go inside.

8

Erica had thrown herself on the bed in a fit of weeping and the younger girl could only stand by to wait for the tears to subside.

Nancy loved her sister dearly even when she often envied her and wished she was more like her. She delighted in the fact that Erica was admired, made much of by teachers and pupils alike, envied the fact that she had a good figure, and was blondly beautiful with a doll-like porcelain face that had never had freckles or spots.

Erica was never short of boyfriends, who came and went as often as the summer storms. After the tears there was always some other boy, and she didn't suppose the present fracas would be any different.

She sat on the edge of her sister's bed and Erica said fretfully, 'Go away, I don't want to talk to anybody.'

Nancy did not go away but went to stand at the window and after a few minutes said, 'Alec's coming down the street, he's coming here.'

'Then I don't want to see him; tell him to go away.'

'Why don't you tell him. He looks upset.'

'So he should be, putting cricket before me, spending all afternoon there instead of boating on the river.'

Nancy was confused. Boating on the river was something she'd thought they were setting out to do, so why cricket? Perhaps her sister did have a problem after all.

'Why don't you do as I say and tell him to go away,' Erica stormed. 'I don't want to see him – but then come back here and tell me what he says.'

Nancy reached the door just as Alec was pressing the doorbell, and now face to face there was no disguising his worried expression.

'I want to speak to Erica, Nancy. Will you tell her?'

'She doesn't want to speak to you, Alec. What's happened?'

'We called in at the cricket match and they roped me in to play. Mr Prothero was not feeling well. I couldn't get out of it.'

9

'She wanted to go boating, that's why she's so furious.'

'I know, I'm sorry but it couldn't be helped.'

At that moment the door was flung open and Erica stood there, her face angry, her voice unusually vindictive. 'You could have said no, you could have told them you'd promised to go boating, but you had to show off in front of everybody, let them see how good you were, never mind about me.'

'Honestly, Erica, it wasn't like that, you heard them all persuading me. My father was there and said I had to play. I scored thirty runs, he was so pleased.'

'Well of course, but you've ruined my day.'

'You are going to the dance with me, Erica, you promised.'

'I have to think about it. I could go with the girls – there'll be plenty of boys to dance with.'

He stood looking at her with a dismal expression, and after a few minutes she said, 'Oh well, I suppose I will go or else everybody will be saying I've been spoiled and am silly. I'll see you later,' and with that remark she went back through the door, pulling her sister with her.

Alec turned dejectedly away. The evening ahead of them promised to be pretty dismal. He had no doubt that given time she'd forgive him but he was not looking forward to the early part of the evening.

He'd admired Erica Clarkson since the first day they'd met at junior school. He'd been a quiet studious boy who'd loved sport; she'd been an extrovert girl who'd hated sport, loved dancing and singing, and had been a leading light in every school concert of which there had been a great many. He'd seen how the other boys admired her, and when he went on to the boys' school he heard the others talking about the girls they admired making him think he had no chance with Erica when there were so many other boys with more going for them.

When his father became the Mayor of the town, somehow or other his popularity grew, and to his own

10

amazement he plucked up courage to invite Erica to the Mayor's Ball. They were both sixteen, and surprisingly they had remained something of a pair since then.

If he could be honest with himself he knew she was capable of transferring her affections should any other boy come along with greater credentials or more lucrative expectations, but he was besotted with her. The cricket had been a mistake. Erica should have come first, but his father had been so proud of him, particularly of the runs he had scored.

He'd make it up to her at the dance, tell her how beautiful she was looking, tell her there was no girl in the room who could hold a candle to her. Erica responded to flattery, and heaven knows, there'd been plenty of it from a number of other admirers.

Chapter Two

Janet Clarkson eyed her two daughters across the dining-room table with some misgiving. The eldest girl had a decidedly sulky look on her face and the younger one seemed ill at ease with her sister's mood.

'Do eat something, Erica,' she urged. 'It will be around ten o'clock before you get any food at the dance and you didn't get anything at the cricket match.'

'I didn't stay, Mother.'

'Why didn't you stay? Surely you watched Alec make his runs. He did very well.'

'No. I came home. We were supposed to be going on the river and we ended up at the wretched cricket match.'

'I wouldn't let your father hear all that if I were you.'

'Well it's true.'

'Have you seen Alec?'

'He called round.'

'You're going to the dance with him?'

'I suppose so. I don't want any more sandwiches. I'm going to sort out my dress for tonight.'

Both her mother and sister watched her leave the room with some uncertainty, and after a few minutes her mother said, 'Go up there, Nancy, and help her to get dressed. We're going to have to have a serious talk with Erica. She's being spoilt and unreasonable these days and needs bringing to her senses.'

Nancy found her sister throwing dresses out of her wardrobe some of which were from school dances, others from more recent civic parties to which Alec had invited her.

'Which will you wear?' she asked curiously.

'None of them are exactly new,' Erica snapped.

'The blue one's new.'

'I had it for the Mayor's Ball and that was in January; it's June now.'

'You have a lot more dresses than I ever get, it's ages since I had a party dress.'

'That's because I go to more functions than you do.'

'You look pretty in the blue one, Erica. Alec likes that one.'

'How do you know?'

'He told me.'

Slightly placated Erica said, 'Oh well, I probably will wear that anyway. I'm going to have a bath. Have a look around in that drawer for my undies, will you, and in the cupboard for my shoes, the silver ones.'

While Erica bathed Nancy hunted in the drawer and the cupboard, fascinated by the array of silken underwear and shoes for all occasions, comparing them to the items of school uniform she was expected to wear and the few exceptions for special occasions.

She sat on her sister's bed watching her dress for the dance, admiring her slender waist and blossoming curves, thinking and wishing she could be like her and harbouring the unhappy feeling that she never would be. As if she understood her sister's mood Erica said, 'When you grow out of that puppy fat and get something done about your teeth you could be quite pretty, Nancy. I was lucky, I never had puppy fat and my teeth never gave me any trouble.'

Sentiments that did nothing to restore Nancy's spirits.

Envy and admiration vied with each other as Nancy surveyed the finished product with its perfect combination of swirling skirt and shining blond hair – with the blue

13

chiffon stole she looked as beautiful as any movie star.

From downstairs they heard the sound of closing doors and men's voices. Erica said quickly, 'Heavens, it can't be Alec already, it's far too early.'

'It's Daddy, with somebody else, probably the Major.'

'Then we'll let the Major tell me how I look. He's always flattering every girl within sight, even the older women.'

'Well, he isn't young, is he?'

'No, but he's funny. Come on, let's go downstairs.'

But it was not the Major who had accompanied their father home, it was the Commodore and the Vicar, and they all sat round the dining table staring at each other with woebegone faces while their mother served them coffee.

'Oh Erica,' her mother cried, 'you've already changed. I'm sorry darling, but I doubt if there'll be any dancing this evening.'

'Why, what's wrong?' Erica asked.

'Mr Prothero died at the cricket match this afternoon. They found him sitting in his chair where they thought he was simply watching the match, but he was dead.'

Erica sat down weakly on the nearest chair, her face a picture of misery before she said, 'But he was old, Mother, so why does it have to spoil the dance for everybody?'

'You know very well Mr and Mrs Prothero have always provided a great many things for the dance and he has to be respected. The dance can take place another evening; it doesn't have to be tonight.'

'But it's the longest day.'

'That isn't important, there'll be other occasions.'

Jumping to her feet Erica favoured them with a long cold stare and ran out of the room.

Her mother was quick to say, 'She's disappointed and very young. She'll grow up.'

'He'll be sadly missed,' the Vicar said. 'Amelia is quite distraught. My wife is with her now but they were always such a close-knit couple, no children, just lived for each other.'

14

'Will she stay on here do you think, Vicar? The house is so large, all those antiques and they've done nothing to modernise it.'

'It's early days, Janet, but I doubt if Amelia'll up sticks, she's too fond of the house and St Agnes.'

'And of course she does have good gardeners and Edith Pinder. Oh I'm sure when she's got over the first shock she'll stay where she has so many good friends.'

'She does have a nephew, you know – Oliver Denton, her late brother's son. His mother lives abroad, on the Continent I think, but I've telephoned Oliver's college at Oxford so no doubt he'll be up here as soon as it's convenient.'

At that moment there was a ring on the front doorbell and Janet said, 'It's probably Alec calling for Erica. Will he know about Mr Prothero do you think?'

'Oh yes, I'm sure he will. He was at the match, and his father is aware of everything.'

It was obvious that Alec did know since he was still attired in his white flannels and blazer. David Clarkson said, 'Sit down Alec, have some coffee. This is a sad business, isn't it?'

'Yes sir. My father told me the dance has been cancelled. I liked Mr Prothero. I was only talking to him earlier this afternoon. He was pleased I was taking his place in the team.'

'Yes I know he was. Erica is upstairs taking off her glad rags, but she'll be down in a moment. You'll have to think of some other way to spend your evening. Those runs you scored made his last hours happy. He was devastated when he was unable to play.'

'Well, I'll need to get back to my wife at Amelia's,' the Vicar said. 'We shall need to talk about the funeral arrangements and I'm sure during the next few days you'll all rally round Amelia and show her what we all thought of Jethro. He'll be sadly missed both for his generosity and his humour. Perhaps we can try to persuade Amelia that she

15

can stay here surrounded by good friends. Sorry about the dance, Alec. You young people will no doubt all be disappointed but these things do happen, you know. Erica was all dressed up and ready to go. You'll be the one to console her, I'm sure.'

Alec favoured him with a wan smile and Janet said quickly, 'Run upstairs, Nancy, and tell Erica that Alec is here. They'll have to think of another way of spending the evening.'

Erica was wearing her everyday clothes and a sour expression.

'There's nothing I want to do,' she said sharply. 'The town will be empty, nobody boats on the river at night and everybody will have long faces because the dance is off.'

'Well, you have to go downstairs to see Alec.'

'Does he know the dance is off?'

'Yes, he hasn't changed.'

'A blazer and white flannels How ridiculous to expect me to spend an evening with a boy wearing something like that.'

'Oh well, please yourself. I've told you what Mother said. Are you coming or not?'

Erica realised there was no alternative, and as she met Alec's gaze from across the room she was well aware of his nervousness but seeing her father's frown she smiled at him.

Jethro Prothero's funeral was by any standards the most lavish spectacle the town could remember. The procession followed the black hearse pulled by four jet-black horses adorned with black plumes on their headgear; the procession itself consisted of the Major's cadets marching sombrely behind the mourners down the hill towards the churchyard and passing the Commodore's garden with his flag flying at half mast.

Children lined the road because Jethro had been a

16

governor of the two local schools, as well as a benefactor to every society in the town.

Standing beside her mother in the church Erica couldn't see why there had to be so much fuss. Mr Prothero was not a young man and his death had put a blight on the longest day festivities.

Amelia Prothero leaned heavily on the arm of a young man, evidently her nephew, and as he took his place in the pew beside her he turned briefly and smiled at the people sitting behind them.

He was tall and handsome and for the remainder of the funeral service Erica could not take her eyes off him. His was the sort of face she'd dreamed about, film star good looks with a figure to match them – her imagination began to speculate on how long he would be likely to remain in the town and if there was an occasion when they could meet.

Nancy was quick to see her sister's preoccupation with the young man sitting in front of them and she began to show more interest in the proceedings.

She didn't see why they'd been invited as guests to the funeral and would have preferred to be standing with others of her friends among the spectators lining the route. But her father had insisted and now with something new in the air perhaps it hadn't been a bad idea after all.

A lavish buffet meal had been laid on in the Town Hall and the funeral guests were doing justice to it, apart from Amelia Prothero who sat tearful and dejected surrounded by two elderly female mourners, her lawyer, Mr Henry Devenport and her nephew Oliver, who was trying his best to interest her in the food on the table and being charming to those around them who seemed intent on introducing themselves to him.

'Amelia's always doted on him,' Elspeth announced to her husband who had now managed to extricate himself from his cadets. 'He's awfully handsome,' she added, 'likely to break one or two hearts, and Erica Clarkson is vastly intrigued.'

17

'Nothing doin' there, old girl,' the Major said quickly. 'He's hoping to go into the diplomatic service, so he'll be quick to get back to Oxford as soon as possible.'

'It's my bet Amelia will keep him on here for as long as possible.'

Oliver Denton was well aware that he had captured the attention of the prettiest girl in the room but while she was intent on being beside him at the buffet table, he was more interested in talking to the older people in the vicinity.

Erica was furious, deciding that he was conceited and not worth a second's thought, until for a brief moment their eyes met and he smiled at her.

It was much later when they were leaving and her parents were saying their farewells that she was introduced to him. He took her hand and smiled into her eyes, then just as briefly turned to her younger sister with a similar smile and a few chosen words.

All the way back to the house she was quiet until her mother said, 'You look tired, Erica. I know funerals are not very uplifting but this is one we had to attend.'

The Vicar had largely acted as host throughout the proceedings and he was now standing at the door to the hall to say his farewells to departing guests. He spared a special smile for Grace Gantry.

Many years ago when he first came to St Agnes he had admired Grace. She was pretty, very nice, and he had in those days thought she would make an admirable vicar's wife. That had been before her father died, then suddenly everything changed.

Her mother suddenly became fragile, needing Grace to look after her day in and day out, and he'd known that he and Grace were never destined to become a couple.

He had married Molly Braithwaite who had made him an excellent wife. She had been a great asset to his work and the village church in general, was popular and although they hadn't been blessed with children, their life together had been happy.

18

Now today when he saw Grace shepherding her mother down the Town Hall steps he felt a momentary twinge of regret. In spite of the years between he still had thoughts for her, and on the many occasions that their eyes met he was sure she still had thoughts about him.

They had almost reached the bottom step when Mrs Edgebaston caught up with them, and smiling cheerfully said, 'Not too well today, Mrs Gantry? I thought you were looking so much better the other day when I saw you trotting down the road.'

Mrs Gantry favoured her with a haughty frown but oblivious to it Mrs Edgebaston merely smiled cheerfully and bade them good afternoon.

'What day was that mother?' Grace asked curiously. 'You didn't tell me you'd been out.'

'Really Grace, I didn't want to worry you. I'd had one of my turns and you were still at your bridge afternoon. I thought I'd just walk along the road to meet you, or perhaps call at the Robsons to say I wasn't feeling well.'

'You should have telephoned me, Mother'.

'I know, but it looks as if I'm always needing you, that you can't even move without me wanting you back. That woman's terribly nosey. How did she know how I was feeling, I only spoke a few words to her.'

'She was only being sociable, Mother. She's really quite nice.'

'There's a lot of gossip about her.'

'How do you know?'

'Well, Mrs Simpson tells me things. You can bet the daily helps know everything that's going on around here, and they gossip among themselves.'

'I'm sure they do, Mother, but that doesn't make them right.'

'Where does she come from anyway, is she a widow or is she divorced?'

'I really don't know, Mother.'

'She has a lot of men callers.'

19

'That's nobody's business but hers.'

'It gives rise to gossip.'

'Whatever Mrs Edgebaston does gives rise to gossip, Mother. It's probably because she's comparatively new to the town, people are suspicious and what she does is really none of their business.'

'It's more than that.'

'Because our daily says so?'

'She's quite often right about people, Grace.'

'Perhaps Mother, but then she's quite often wrong, isn't she?'

'What was it the Vicar was saying about the dance? I couldn't hear him very well,' Mrs Gantry asked.

'Only that it's to be held next Saturday evening and he hopes it will be well attended. He hopes some of the older residents in the village will attend.'

'Well I hope you're not thinking of going.'

'You don't want me to go, Mother?'

'Well, it is Saturday evening and we usually spend it together.'

'We spend every evening together, Mother. Why don't you and I go along, you'd have people to talk to and there will be refreshments laid on.'

'I don't think so, Grace. It's not really what I enjoy any more. If you want to go I'm sure I can manage without you.'

Grace knew that neither of them would be there. She wouldn't go without her mother and her mother would make every excuse under the sun not to be there. Besides, she was still having pangs of regret whenever she encountered the Vicar with his wife, regrets at what might have been, and with the realisation that she had little to look forward to.

'What would you like to do this afternoon, Mother?' Grace asked her.

'Oh I thought we'd sit in the conservatory. We can see the road from there and watch the people coming and going. I expect people will linger on at the Town Hall even though the affair is long since over.'

'Perhaps I'll go for a walk along the river bank,' Grace said gently.

'If you must, dear, but don't be too long, it's been a long day.'

No longer than any other day, Grace thought. Even a funeral had provided them with a little variety.

They paused at the gate to see Mrs Edgebaston being greeted by a gentleman stepping out of a large black car, raising his hat and favouring her with a warm smile and outstretched hand in greeting.

'Who do you think that is?' Mrs Gantry asked sharply.

'I have no idea, Mother. She has a great many friends.'

'All of them male I have no doubt,' her mother snapped, ignoring Grace's attempts to hurry her inside the garden.

Chapter Three

Amelia Prothero had insisted that the dance should take place the following Saturday, even when the Vicar had prevaricated that it was a little too soon after the funeral.

'Jethro would have wanted it,' she had argued, 'and I do think that Oliver should attend. He needn't stay all evening but it would show them that his uncle's death will not affect the enjoyment of the community any longer.'

Consequently it was an occasion for a gathering of older people and not simply for the young ones to enjoy themselves.

Oliver Denton put in an appearance just before the supper dance and as he stood gracefully in the doorway eyeing the dancers, every girl in the room hoped he would ask her to dance.

Oliver applied himself nobly to the occasion and Erica, watching from the sidelines, saw that he danced only once with the same girl; after taking the girl he had danced with back to her seat he smiled charmingly before moving on.

Of course he wouldn't ask her to dance, she obviously had a partner, and it was only later when they danced the Paul Jones that they came face to face and she melted into his arms.

He danced better than Alec, and when he smiled down into her eyes it felt as though there was only the two of them in the room. The music changed and they parted, then

22

as she marched round the room she was aware that he looked back at her and her heart raced alarmingly.

She had known so many boys but she'd never felt like this before, and as Alec went to the buffet table for their refreshments all she could see was Oliver helping several girls to whatever was on the table, the silly things clustering round him, flashing their eyes and chattering, while he stood listening to them; then once again their eyes met and she wished Alec and those silly girls were a hundred miles away.

Oliver Denton surveyed the hall with mixed feelings. He needed to get back to Oxford – his uncle's death couldn't have happened at a worse time as he wanted a good degree since he had set his heart on the diplomatic service.

He'd tried explaining to his aunt that perhaps she should think of staying with her two elderly cousins in Poole for a few weeks but she wouldn't hear of it. She wanted Oliver to stay as long as possible, and he knew how much she doted on him.

He'd never been a favourite with his uncle. He had always known that as far as Jethero was concerned he'd thought Oliver to be something of a charmer, too full of himself, and although he would never had admitted it to a living soul he'd been secretely relieved that his uncle had gone first and left his wife to handle their money, which was considerable.

His aunt had encouraged him to attend the village dance and although he hadn't been looking forward to it, he had to confess it hadn't really been so bad. Some of the girls were decidedly pretty, and the admiration he'd seen in their eyes had done much to restore his equilibrium.

There was one girl in particular, beautiful, with pale blond hair and blue eyes. Her figure was slender and although she was obviously with a partner she would not be reluctant to dispense with him.

He took good care not to allow his attraction to her to be too noticeable, and he was vastly amused that his interest

23

in the other girls there brought a frown to her pretty face.

Perhaps it might not be a bad idea to spend several weekends in St Agnes – Oliver Denton liked nothing more than a challenge. At that moment two girls came to chat to him and across the room he was well aware of the other girl's look of disdain.

He decided to leave before midnight and a great many young men at the dance were glad to see him go, while for some of the girls much of the glamour had gone out of the evening.

One friend of Alec's aired his feelings with some disgust. 'I can't think what they all see in him,' he said. 'He's conceited and fancies his chances no end. I'll be glad when he gets back to Oxford.'

'Getting on too well with Alice?' Erica snapped.

'Well, did you see them all, almost swooning when he asked them to dance?'

'You don't think too much of him then, Erica?' Alec said hopefully.

'I haven't even thought about it,' she replied, then added, 'I'm bored with this dance, it was better when only the younger people came, I'm ready to go home.'

'We can't go yet, Erica,' Alec protested. 'Our parents are still here; nobody leaves this early.'

'Nobody except Denton,' the other boy said feelingly. 'He seems to have turned the lights off.'

'We'll stay until it's over, I suppose,' Erica said ungraciously. 'Thank goodness it'll be over before twelve. When the dance is held on the longest day it can go on for much longer. Thank goodness it's Sunday tomorrow.'

'You've never wanted a dance to finish before,' Alec complained.

'It's been different before,'

'Oh well, come on, they're playing a waltz, your favourite.'

Alec was an adequate dancer but hardly Fred Astaire. She decided that Oliver Denton with all his charm would have made the waltz seem likc heaven.

Her parents watching from the sidelines smiled to one another. Her mother had thought several times that Erica seemed bored, not her usual sparkling self, except during the Paul Jones when she'd suddenly seemed to come alive.

Several other people had noticed it too. One of them had been Mrs Edgebaston, ever a connoisseur of other people's feelings, even the ones about herself.

She had arrived in the company of a bald, portly gentleman she had introduced as 'My friend from Cheshire, Nigel Hague. Nigel is a lawyer, we're friends of very long standing.'

Other people who had seen her gentleman caller of several days before were quick to observe that this was not the same man.

It had not taken Anthea Edgebaston long to sum up her neighbours and there were those she liked and those she didn't like. The Clarksons were nice, as was the Commodore and his wife. The Major was a silly flirt but his wife had him in hand and she liked Elspeth, but therc were many more whom she derived great pleasure in scandalising, like Mrs Gantry for instance, although she liked Grace. What a pity the poor girl had to be saddled with such a mother.

It was obvious to Anthea that the Vicar liked Grace – he could hide a lot of things from a lot of people, but not from a woman as sophisticated and worldly as Anthea Edgebaston.

She'd give the friendship between young Erica Clarkson and Alec a few more weeks at the most.

There was something to be said about living in a small town – one got to hear more, the petty intrigues that went on between neighbours, the jealousies. In a city, where she'd spent most of her life, unless you were directly involved you might as well be living on another planet.

There were those present who thought she had dressed

rather flamboyantly for what they considered a low-key affair so soon after a funeral.

Major Robson had been quick to tell her that her crimson dress had brought the party to light but she was well aware that her choice of colour had raised several eyebrows among the older ladies.

Erica and her partner danced by in silence, renewing her opinion that all was not well between them, and seeing the anxiety on Janet Clarkson's face she knew that her own thoughts were mirrored there.

A little while later she found Mrs Clarkson in the cloak-room looking decidedly worried, and she was prompted to ask if she wasn't feelings well.

'Oh it isn't me, it's Erica. She and Alec have gone home and it's only just after eleven. She was looking forward to the dance. I hope they haven't quarrelled.'

'Oh my dear, isn't that part and parcel of being young. How old is Erica?'

'Seventeen.'

'Oh well, there's your answer, my dear. Too young to be serious anyway.'

'I suppose so. But she's been spoiled by too much admiration. She's pretty and talented. It was always Erica who got the leading roles in school plays and concerts. I think it's gone to her head. I just hope she doesn't hurt Alec's feelings.'

'I wouldn't worry too much, my dear. She's out in the big wide world now, so there'll be more competition.'

Seeing that Janet's doubtful expression persisted she said, 'What does Erica intend to do with her life?'

'She's going to secretarial college; she's hoping to go into her father's firm, but one never really knows with Erica.'

'You can't have forgotten what it was like to be seventeen, Janet. Too many boys, little jealousies, tears about something and nothing. All forgotten in no time and hope-fully rarely remembered.'

26

'I'm sure you're right.'

Erica and Alec were walking home largely in silence. He didn't know why she'd wanted to leave the dance, didn't understand her silences or the sulky look on her face and in a strange way he was afraid to ask questions.

She would normally invite him in for coffee, but now she merely said, 'I'm tired Alec, I'm going straight to bed.'

'Is something wrong, Erica?'

'I didn't enjoy the dance, that's all.'

'Why didn't you? I thought it was good, other people were enjoying themselves.'

'All that fawning round Oliver Denton. Couldn't they see how bored he was?'

'Why should it bother you?'

'It doesn't.'

'When shall I see you again?'

'Well, I'm busy this week, telephone me towards next weekend.'

He had to be content with that, but couldn't help the feelings that things between Erica and himself were far from congenial. As he reached the hall he could hear the music and the sound of voices inside, and making up his mind suddenly he went up the steps and back inside. The first people he encountered were Erica's parents, and her mother said quickly, 'Isn't Erica with you?'

'No. She was tired, she said she hadn't enjoyed it.'

'Oh well,' Erica's father said, 'you go ahead and enjoy yourself, she can be very tiresome at times.'

As he sat watching the dancers Alec reflected that Erica hadn't always been tiresome. He'd liked her for a very long time, and she'd always seemed so nice; it was only recently that nothing he did was right for her. His father said she was a spoilt little brat, and his mother said he should look around for a more agreeable girl. Erica Clarkson was a spoilt little madam.

The girl sitting next to him smiled and he recognised her as one of Erica's friends. He couldn't remember her name

27

although he was sure he'd spoken to her before. When had he ever remembered any of the girls when the only girl he'd been interested in was Erica?

Her smile faded and she turned away. The last waltz was being announced, and tentatively he asked, 'Would you like to dance?' adding shyly, 'I'm sorry I don't remember your name.'

'Jenny Spencer. My father is the chemist; my parents are over there with your parents.'

Of course. He'd known the Spencers were friends of his parents, but when had he met Jenny? As if she knew what he was thinking she said, 'I met you at the end-of-term concert. I sang in the chorus – you were with Erica Clarkson.'

'Yes, I remember now. Are you at college with Erica?'

'Oh no. I'm working at the shop with Dad. One day I'm hoping to train to be a chemist; he'd like that.'

'Would you like me to walk home with you?' he asked politely.

'Well, I believe your parents have invited us round to your house after the dance,' she said with a smile, and Alec for the first time that evening felt that he was the one having fun, while Erica was missing out.

His parents seemed delighted with the arrangement but Mrs Clarkson watched them leaving the hall with certain misgivings. She wouldn't tell Erica. If Alec wanted to tell her that was his business, but she didn't want to upset her in case they'd had words.

Catching up with them in the foyer Anthea Edgebaston said cheerfully, 'Don't look so worried Janet, my father always said that if you missed one bus at seventeen, there would be another along in a very short time.'

'Oh, I'm not worried really. I just hope they haven't quarrelled.'

'Well, even if they have, dear, it won't be the end of the world.'

None of them were to know that evening that the last few

28

days had only been the start of the trauma that would affect the normality of a nice ordinary town and fundamentally decent people.

Erica pretended to be asleep when a little later her mother came into her room. She didn't want her asking questions, and she'd been glad that Nancy was staying with her friend instead of waiting for her in the house with all sorts of silly questions. Her mother sighed and went away, then she heard the closing of the living-room door and the quiet hum of their voices.

How could she possibly meet with Oliver Denton, where did he go when he wasn't with his aunt, and what did he look for in girls?

After the church service was over the following morning, Amelia was surrounded with well wishers and Oliver at his most charming was thanking them for the concern they had all shown at their sad bereavement.

At last he stood apart from the others and it was then Erica joined him, saying shyly, 'How wonderful it is for your aunt to have you to stay with her.'

'Thank you, and you are?'

'Erica Clarkson. Those are my parents speaking with your aunt now.'

'Of course, I met them at the dance last evening. I didn't see you after the Paul Jones.'

Coldly Erica said, 'I was there with my boyfriend. We left early.'

'Oh dear, does that mean you were not enjoying yourselves?'

'Not really. Did you stay until the end?'

'No, I left early too.'

He smiled down at her. Erica Clarkson was going to prove herself a worthy opponent and perhaps well worth the chase. With a smile he asked, 'So you have a boyfriend, Erica. A local boy, of course.'

29

'Alec is over there with his parents, Councillor Stedman and his wife.'

'Of course, I was introduced to them too.'

'Goodbye Mr Denton, we're going home now.'

Not displeased with her conversation with him Erica turned away. She'd been as condescending as he had been and she had not missed the gleam of interest in his eyes or the fact that he would have preferred her to remain in his company. Without a backward glance in his direction she followed her parents down the church path before turning to smile at Alec – his heart lifted as he really believed their romance was over.

Standing with her parents Jenny Spencer's heart sank. For years she'd cherished the hope that Alec Stedman would notice her – the evening before she'd thought it was all over between him and Erica, and they'd enjoyed each other's company. Now it would seem her hopes were to be dashed once again.

Oliver Denton had not missed any of it. He regarded the girls who had pranced around him, and the boys, as small-town kids, hardly in his league, but Erica Clarkson was somewhat different, and for the first time in days he considered that he was in no undue hurry to return to Oxford and his studies.

His change of plan delighted his aunt who was completely unconcerned with his academic qualifications – Amelia just needed him with her. For the first time since she had married Jethro Prothero she felt alone. Jethro had always been so supportive and for the first time in days Oliver had stopped encouraging her to move house.

She didn't want to move to Poole, where her elderly cousins lived. They were not to be compared to the friends in St Agnes, and in blissful ignorance Amelia determined to pursue her interests surrounded by her many friends.

Oliver set out to charm Erica. He stopped his car when she waited at the bus stop on her way home from college, and he met her in the library when he went to change his aunt's books. She found him charming and sophisticated; he found her beautiful and lively. His attention convinced her that she and Alec Stedman had come to the end of the road.

While Alec's parents were well pleased despite their son's apparent distress, Erica's parents were worried and cautioned her to be very careful. When Oliver returned to Oxford he would probably only return to see Amelia on rare occasions as he would have his studies to think about; and in any case his career would be geared to London or overseas, certainly not in St Agnes.

Erica didn't listen. She was in love, they were in love; she visualised living in London or overseas, and in those first few months Oliver returned to St Agnes frequently to see his aunt.

The Clarksons began to think that perhaps they had worried needlessly while Amelia knew nothing about Erica because Oliver never mentioned her. She thought he came back because he liked St Agnes and was very fond of her.

The Stedmans and the Spencers were delighted to announce the engagement of Alec and Jenny at Christmas, and Erica was among the first to wish them well.

Chapter Four

To Amelia's delight her nephew was awarded a first-class honours degree and she announced to her friends that she had been invited to Oxford to see him receive it. Erica waited in vain for the invitation to accompany her but it never came.

She sulked, and Oliver said reasonably, 'Darling, obviously Aunt Amelia has to be there, plus my mother and a host of other friends she's roped in. We haven't really known each other all that long, have we?'

'Have you told your aunt about me?' she demanded.

'Well of course, but she thinks you're really too young. Erica, time is on our side.'

'I'm older than Jenny Spencer and she's getting married in the summer.'

That was when warning bells began to ring in Oliver's head. She talked incessantly about marriage, where she would like to live, even have children one day. She showed him Christmas presents she'd received, ornaments and figurines, not the usual gifts for a young woman barely embarked upon life. He never enthused about the gifts and more and more Erica grew restless and impatient.

Alec and Jenny were married on the longest day with the town awash with visitors which merely gave the spectators an additional event to enjoy.

Most of their friends thought they were very young,

perhaps too young, but she looked radiantly happy and Alec every inch the proud bridegroom. Erica sat with her parents in church and watched her younger sister following Jenny down the aisle in her pale blue bridesmaid's dress, suddenly seeming prettier and grown up.

Nancy was enjoying herself. For the first time she was wearing a dress that reached her feet – blue organza adorned with white gardenias at the waist and in her hair – and everybody had told her she was looking lovely.

That her sister had sat for the most part in silence throughout lunch had not escaped Anthea Edgebaston, and later in the afternoon she made it her business to ask her if she had enjoyed the ceremony.

Erica said she had a headache and was ready to go home. Anthea thought that was pity, adding that Nancy was beginning to catch up in the beauty stakes.

Erica merely frowned and Anthea went on brightly, 'She's lived in your shadow for so long, Erica, it's nice to see her looking so pretty. I thought Oliver would have been here, but I suppose he's busy in London carving out his career.'

'Yes, he's going into the Foreign Office.'

'Really? His aunt told me he had received a first-class degree. I do think Amelia's looking so much better.'

Anthea smiled.

'She'll be delighted that he gets up here so often these days, thanks to you of course. Well, I must circulate. Lois Watson appears to be looking a little lost over there.'

Lois Watson was not lost, she was merely waiting for her husband to return with another glass of wine. Anthea joined her before he returned, saying with a sweet smile, 'You look lovely, Lois, that colour suits you. I wish I could wear it.'

The colour was beige, a colour far too dull for Anthea's taste, and eyeing her Lois wished she could wear something as flamboyant as the crimson dress Anthea was wearing and the huge black hat adorned with crimson roses.

33

'I've just been talking to Erica Clarkson,' she added. 'She doesn't appear to have enjoyed herself.'

'Nostalgia perhaps,' Lois said with a smile. 'Only last year Alec was her boyfriend.'

'Yes of course, but hardly destined to last, I think.'

'Didn't you think so?'

'Didn't you? Tantrums and tears – a boy who needed to grow up; a girl who had grown up too fast.'

'You're quite a student of human nature, Anthea.'

'Not really. I'm simply a woman who's been forced to grow up faster than most. I've been round too many corners, Lois. Now I can sit back and observe the passing show with something like amusement.'

'Perhaps getting old does have its compensations.'

'Of course, my dear, it has its compensations and its drawbacks. I like to make the most of one and ignore the others.' With a bright smile she added, 'Here comes your husband, Lois. Do come round one morning and join me for coffee. We can put the world to rights and engage in a little scandal-mongering.'

The Commodore handed Lois her wine, saying softly, 'What did Mrs Edgebaston have to say?'

'She was merely talking about the wedding, dear, and how pretty Nancy was looking.'

'Yes, didn't I tell you the girl would blossom later, just like you did?'

'Did you ever look at me before I blossomed?'

'Perhaps I suddenly became aware of it. I never looked at anybody else.'

'I'm worried about Erica, she seems unhappy. Perhaps it's because Oliver isn't here. Do you think Amelia knows about them?'

'Shouldn't think so or she'd have been talking to the girl.'

'I can remember what it was like to be young, all the insecurities, all the silly wishing you were older, prettier, whether any boy would ever look twice at you. Was it all worth it, do you think?'

34

'Are you telling me I haven't been worth it?'

'Oh no, Andrew, not you.'

She was saved from saying anything further because at that moment a young man was waving frantically to them from across the room, a tall handsome young man in naval officer's uniform, and Lois was rushing across the room to greet her son.

'Why didn't you tell us you were due some leave?' his father was asking, and Julian smiled saying, 'I thought I'd surprise you then when I got home I heard you were here at some wedding or other. I'm afraid I've gate-crashed it.'

'Don't worry, darling, we'll explain. I'm sure our friends would like to meet you. Come along and we'll introduce you.'

For perhaps the first time that afternoon Erica Clarkson smiled and Nancy fell in love with the most handsome man she'd ever seen or was likely to see.

He smiled down at her, seeing a little girl in a pretty dress looking up at him with adoring blue eyes, and then he moved on – there were so many girls that afternoon, he was hardly likely to remember one of them, and Julian Watson, like Oliver Denton, was not looking for love, but nor did he have Oliver's self-absorption.

In the days that followed the people on Tremayne Hill saw Julian out and about with his parents, or watching the cricket matches. In the early mornings he went riding over the downs and in the evenings they had supper parties in the gardens. With her usual perception Mrs Edgebaston viewed the months to come with a certain degree of anticipation.

All Oliver heard on his next visit was talk about the wedding, which bored him. Erica knew he was bored, but she couldn't stop herself – all she wanted was a little interest, a few words of encouragement to prove that they had some sort of future together.

Indeed it was Amelia who surprised him by asking if it was

true he had been seeing Erica Clarkson – it had been the Vicar himself who had told her and it would seem all her friends knew about it, so why hadn't he mentioned it to her?

'Because we're simply friends, Aunt Amelia,' he replied. 'You know, I have a lot of friends I was with at Oxford, but I'm too young to be serious about any one of them, and I do have a career to make.'

'All the same, dear, her parents are friends of mine, and she's a nice girl, a very beautiful girl. She comes from a nice family. Wouldn't she be right for you?'

'Perhaps in twenty years' time, Aunt Amelia.'

'Twenty years! Oliver, you'd be well into your forties. Why not now?'

'I've told you, Aunt Amelia, I'm not ready for marriage. You'll be the first to know when I am.'

'But what do I say to her parents, to my other friends?'

'Nothing at all, because you don't know anything. I've been thinking about this house, Aunt Amelia. It really is far too big for you. Round the corner from me in London they're building the most beautiful flats – one of them would be ideal for you. No garden to think about, everything modern and up to date, shops around the corner and lovely views of the river. Think about it.'

'I love this house, Oliver, your uncle loved it; and what about my furniture, my antiques? Where would I put them, who would want them?'

'Send them to Sotheby's and live on the proceeds. Think of all the cruises you could be going on, the South of France, wintering abroad, the prospects are endless.'

'Really Oliver. How can you be so insensitive? You know what they meant to Jethro, I can just see him sitting up there reproaching me for even thinking of selling them.'

'Well if there is an up there, Aunt Amelia, I'm sure he'll have more things on his mind than the fate of what he's left behind.'

'You're very cynical these days, Oliver, ready with your jibes on anything religious. You know, I don't like it.'

36

'And you know I don't mean it. I'm teasing, Aunt Amelia.'

'But you're not teasing about the house, Oliver?'

'No, I mean it. Even with good friends and neighbours, you and Edith rattle around in this place, and neither of you are getting any younger. She'd go with you to London, I'm sure.'

'And I'm sure she wouldn't. She had brothers and sisters here, nieces and nephews and a lot of friends. She'd hate it in London.'

'But she needs a job.'

'She's a treasure. I know a lot of people simply wishing she'd leave me for them. Don't say anything to Edith. I can't even think of leaving here, Oliver. I'm sure you'll visit me whenever you can, and there is Erica.'

Oliver knew he would have to be content with that for the time being, but he had sown the seeds and in the weeks to come he could only water them.

Erica decided that perhaps a little jealousy would help by going on about the attributes of Julian Watson who had been particularly attentive at the Stedman wedding.

'He's so handsome,' she enthused, 'and he was very nice to me. I really think he would have liked to have invited me out but his parents know about you and they'd evidently told him I was spoken for.'

'He's home on leave I take it?'

'Yes, from the Navy.'

'Of course, it couldn't be anything else. You should have encouraged him, Erica, you're the sort of girl he could have entertained the Mess with for months.'

'You mean you wouldn't have minded. That's horrible, I'd mind if you went out with another girl, I can't believe you said that.'

'Well you have been going on a bit about him, Erica. What are you trying to do, make me jealous?'

'No, of course not. I was just talking about things going on at the wedding, that's all.'

'Can we talk about something else besides the wedding,

Erica. It seems to be all we do talk about these days.'

'I talk about it because you know the people here. I don't know any of your friends in London.'

'Well perhaps this might interest you. My aunt is thinking of selling The Elms and going to live in London.'

She stared at him in disbelief, and he added quickly, 'It's all very hush hush at the moment so please, Erica, don't mention it to anybody, not even to your parents. It's our secret. She'll never sell it, that old dark old house with all those antiques. It needs gardeners and servants, young people certainly wouldn't want it.'

'Your aunt has gardeners and Edith as well as a daily.'

'You know as much as I do, Erica. She took me by surprise, I can tell you.'

'Why would she ever think of moving? After Mr Prothero died she told everybody she'd never move.'

'That was then, darling, now she's thinking about the times I won't be able to see her as often.'

In that brief moment she felt suddenly sick – it was as if he'd taken a sharp knife and thrust it into her heart. In sudden contrition he knew he'd spoken too soon and he was quick to say, 'She'll never sell it, Erica, at least not in the immediate future. It's a big, dark, old house that needs a lot of looking after. She'll change her mind when she realises the complications.'

'What did you mean when you said you might not be able to see her as often?'

'My job, Erica, the fact that I shall probably have to work abroad.'

So they drove in silence along the margin of the river and up into the hills beyond while Oliver used all his considerable charm to bring the smiles back to her face.

'Will you be here in the summer like you were last year?' she asked quietly.

Taken aback he said quickly, 'Well I shall have to go to France to see my mother sometime, and I'm not sure about holidays.'

'But you'll take some surely?'

'Well one hopes so, of course. Obviously I shall spend time with Aunt Amelia – got to keep the old dear happy. But at the moment I really don't know what is going to happen.'

'But it's June already Oliver,' she complained.

'Darling, you don't have my problems.'

'I didn't know your mother lived in France.'

'She descends on me from time to time, but for the most part she lives in France, Italy, Portugal, wherever the spirit moves her.'

'I saw her at your uncle's funeral but she didn't stay with your aunt. Don't they get on?'

'Not so you'd notice. My father was Aunt Amelia's favourite brother, that he married my mother was something she never got over. She regards my mother as a shallow, materialistic Jezebel, without either feelings or morals.'

'That must hurt you terribly Oliver.'

He smiled down at her. No, it didn't hurt him. When had he ever really known his mother with her fleeting visits to see him over the years. Never there for sports days at his school; never there for Christmas and birthday parties; occasionally whisking him away to spend weeks in the sunshine in some exotic villa near the sea, or in the snows of some equally expensive winter sports venue in Switzerland or France.

His mother would think Erica a sweet, pretty little thing and instantly dismiss her as inappropriate. Erica would think his mother entirely enchanting without ever knowing her.

Erica was quiet for the most part on their way back. She had been looking forward to the summer with Oliver, and had been convinced he would spend time with her in some holiday place; now it was seeming increasingly unlikely.

It was only when he parted with her at the front gate of the house that she said anxiously, 'Do you really think your

39

aunt will put her house on the market, Oliver?'

He shrugged his shoulders. 'Don't say a word to anybody, darling. I'm convinced she'll forget about it. Who would want it anyway?'

'Will you be here again soon?'

'I'm sure I will, you don't get rid of me that easily, darling.'

The sale of Mrs Prothero's house haunted her for days. She longed to ask her parents if they had heard anything about it but refrained for fear of starting a chain of neighbourly gossip. She found herself walking past it and staring up at the windows and the curving drive up to the front door, looking for signs that it was for sale, but all she saw were gardeners working in the flower beds, and occasionally Mrs Prothero sitting in the garden with some friend or other.

Her parents were talking about summer holidays and her father decided that they should go to Scotland for two weeks in August to see his younger brother and his family. Erica didn't want to go because surely Oliver would have something in mind and her parents were becoming frustrated with her lack of enthusiasm.

'Darling, you can't keep waiting for Oliver to invite you somewhere. You don't even know if he's coming here – actually, Erica, you know very little about him. Even his aunt isn't very sure when he'll be here again.'

'How do you know? Has she told you?'

'Well no, but he's got a job now and it won't be so easy for him to get here as often. Doesn't he write to you, doesn't he telephone?'

Erica didn't answer, instead she flounced out of the room causing her mother to say anxiously, 'I wish she'd find a local boy. I can't really see this friendship with Oliver Denton going anywhere.'

The summer passed and they went to Scotland where she went sailing and walking with her sister and their cousins,

40

and hated every minute of it. Her sister told her in no uncertain terms that she was being a complete pain and was stopping the rest of them from enjoying themselves, but Erica was unhappy – until she received a postcard from Oliver from France. He said he was staying with his mother and missing her terribly.

The rest of the party received her ecstatic news with cynical disbelief.

Chapter Five

The bridge four were sitting down to their usual Tuesday afternoon session. Grace was always the quiet one, preferring to listen to her friends as they gossiped about this and that before starting their game, but today she was the one who brought news that plainly astonished those sitting round the table.

They looked at her in amazement until Elspeth said, 'Are you absolutely sure, Grace, why Amelia was quite insistent that she would never ever move away from here?'

'Well, I'm only telling you what she told Mother. Apparently Oliver's been trying to persuade her for months now to buy some sort of flat near him in London – new flats they are – and I don't really think she's that keen, but apparently he is.'

'You're absolutely sure, Grace?'

'Well, I know Mother does often get things wrong but she is quite sure that Amelia said all that about the flat. She thought Amelia was bothered about it – she really doesn't want to leave St Agnes with all her memories of Jethro, but he's gone and all she's got is Oliver.'

'And what about Erica Clarkson? I rather thought they were seeing each other, apparently I was wrong,' Hilda Marks said.

'I was talking to Erica in the shop the other day and neither she nor her mother mentioned anything.'

'Maybe they don't know.'

'Oh surely they would. He'll have mentioned it to Erica.'

'Well, she's not seen much of him. When was he last here?'

'A couple of weeks ago.'

'Anyway, I don't think Erica knew. They were at the Simpsons' birthday party and he wasn't with them.'

'We'll just have to wait and see.'

Grace was wishing she hadn't said anything. Hilda Marks was an inveterate gossip who they only tolerated because she was a good bridge player and made up their four, but they were always most careful not to give her cause to pass on what she heard at the bridge table.

Now Grace felt sure Hilda would not miss an opportunity to discuss the matter with everybody she met, in the shops, on the high street or even at the church.

Indeed during the course of the afternoon Hilda referred to it constantly, particularly when they stopped for tea, and it was left to Elspeth to say firmly, 'I'm not going to say a word until Amelia tells me herself that her house is for sale. It's none of my business and I certainly don't think we should say anything to the Clarksons.'

'Well, they'll know if anybody does,' Hilda said sharply. 'Surely that young man Erica's been so friendly with must have told her.'

'I'm not so sure,' Elspeth said. 'Jethro never liked him, you know, even when Amelia doted on him. Personally I thought Erica should have stuck to local boys. He's too old for her, and lives too far away and in a different world.'

'Oh I do wish I hadn't said anything,' Grace exclaimed. 'Mother's sure to have got it all wrong and we're not ones to gossip.'

Hilda Marks didn't waste any time. She was curious, thought Erica Clarkson too full of herself by half and besides what was a titbit of gossip anyway? Nothing else was happening around the town – it was time there was something else to talk about.

The opportunity came several mornings later when she encountered Mrs Clarkson in the middle of the market stalls.

Hilda bided her time, and it was only when she was about to move on that she said, 'What do you think abut Amelia selling up and leaving?'

Janet Clarkson looked at her in utmost amazement.

'Leaving! You say Amelia's leaving?'

'Well yes. She told Grace's mother that she's off to live in London to be near her nephew – some new flat or other.'

'Are you sure, Hilda?'

'Oh absolutely. Apparently he's been trying to persuade her for some time. He can't get up here nearly as often, you see, and you know how she dotes on him.'

'Yes, but to move away. She said she'd never leave St Agnes – too many memories.'

'I know. Didn't Erica tell you about the move? She's been seeing a lot of the nephew. I'd have thought she'd have known.'

'No, she hasn't said anything.'

'Oh well, maybe they didn't want it to get around for a while. I wonder how long it'll take to sell it. Oh I know it's a fine old house but it's so dark and all those antiques – she'll have no room for those in a modern flat.'

'Perhaps she'll dispose of them.'

'Or perhaps the nephew will hang on to them. Jethro told me they'd fetch a mint and flats in London cost money. She'll need to keep solvent.'

Janet smiled doubtfully and Hilda went on, 'Well, I must get off. I'm calling in to see Grace and her mother. Perhaps the old lady will be able to tell me more about Amelia's decision to sell.'

Anybody seeing Janet Clarkson walking along the street that afternoon would have thought she was in something of a dream. She was certainly troubled. Her daughter was supposed to be involved with a young man who was obviously keeping secrets from her, and she felt sure that if Erica had been aware of Amelia Prothero's intended move she would have said so.

She was brought out of her reverie by a voice calling, 'Janet, Janet, where on earth were you?'

Dorothy Spencer stood outside the chemist's shop looking at her so curiously that Janet said immediately, 'I'm sorry, Dorothy, I was miles away.'

'Is something wrong, Janet? Aren't you well?'

'Yes of course. I was daydreaming, that's all.'

She was about to go on her way, then thinking better of it, she said, 'Dorothy, do you know anything about Amelia selling her house?'

'So Hilda has been talking to you, has she?'

'Well, she mentioned it in passing, that's all.'

'I'll bet she did. Didn't you know? Hasn't Erica said anything?'

'No, nothing. Surely it can't be right, she said she'd never leave.'

'Apparently the nephew's been trying to encourage her. She told Grace's mother he was here over the weekend doing his level best to persuade her.'

'He was here over the weekend?'

'Apparently so.'

'I didn't think he was up here over the weekend. Erica didn't say so.'

Dorothy was wishing she hadn't mentioned that item of gossip, and quick to distance herself she said, 'Well, you know what Grace's mother is like, she only half listens to anything you say, and she's probably quite wrong.'

'Yes, of course. Will you be at the Gardeners' for their silver wedding dinner?'

'Yes, of course, we'll see you then. Perhaps by that time we'll all know a bit more about Amelia and her move.'

Janet found her younger daughter chatting happily to the Commodore's wife and reflected that Nancy was becoming particularly friendly with the Watsons of late. Lois Watson enjoyed sitting in her garden and young Nancy had suddenly developed an interest in alpines and rockeries, followed by afternoon tea on the lawn. Lois had been quick to say that she enjoyed her company, that she was always full of fun and took a great interest in Commodore Watson's naval career.

Janet privately thought her daughter was more interested in learning a little more about their one son, since she'd never stopped talking about him since their one or two meetings.

Lois waved to her and invited her to have tea with them. Thinking that perhaps Mrs Watson might know something about Amelia's thoughts on moving house Janet accepted.

Lois Watson was not a gossip. She enjoyed the occasional light-hearted meander through the eccentricities of her neighbours, but she kept her own counsel and passed on nothing that she heard to anybody.

She quite liked Anthea Edgebaston, she wasn't fond of Hilda Marks and as for the rest of them, she considered them ordinary, pleasant and liveable with. Now to her surprise she found herself becoming quite concerned that one of the people she really did like was considering leaving the area.

Nancy listened to her mother with wide-eyed anticipation, and was quick to observe, 'Erica doesn't know or she'd have said.'

'Yes well, dear, perhaps we shouldn't say anything until we know a little more.'

So the conversation reverted to Julian, village activities and Anthea Edgebaston's latest gentleman caller. It was Commodore Watson returning from the golf club that broke up their little tea party and Janet and Nancy said their farewells.

The following Saturday afternoon Janet had not seen her other daughter since breakfast, and in the most casual voice she could muster she asked, 'Do you know if Oliver is here this weekend, Nancy?'

'I've no idea, she never tells me.'

'I was wondering if she will be in for tea.'

'I hope she doesn't bring him back for tea.'

'Why, don't you like him?'

'Not particularly. I think he's conceited.'

'You don't really know him, dear.'

'I know. None of us do, not even Erica.'

Privately Janet agreed with her. He was not the sort of young man who made himself at home around the dining-room table or in the rest of the house as other boys had done.

'Do you want me to help you get tea ready?' Nancy asked.

'No dear, take the dog out for half an hour. He's been shut in the kitchen all afternoon.'

She was busy in the kitchen when she heard the front door open and close, then footsteps hurrying along the hall and running up the stairs. Erica had come home.

There had been an urgency about those hurrying foot-steps, a sort of veiled anger, and Janet went about preparing tea until Nancy arrived back with the dog.

'Erica's in her room,' she said softly, 'run upstairs, dear, and tell her tea is almost ready.'

Erica was perched on the bed reading a magazine and could hardly be bothered to look up as her sister entered the room.

'Tea's ready,' Nancy said sharply.

'Isn't Dad home?'

'No, he's at the golf club. His match doesn't start until late. Where have you been? Is he here?'

'Who?'

'You know who I mean.'

'He does have a name.'

'Oliver then.'

'No, he isn't here. I was down near the river.'

'Before he came you used to go boating on the river, now nobody asks you. Nobody likes him.'

47

Erica threw her book across the room where it landed at her sister's feet. 'They don't like him because they're jealous of him, because he's better educated, better looking, has more money and better prospects. It doesn't bother me what they think of him.'

'You don't have fun any more, Erica. We used to laugh about all the fun you had, the boys you knew, where you went, what you did and now all I ever hear is Oliver – and it's ages since you've seen him.'

'It's only three weeks ago.'

'You didn't see him last week.'

'He wasn't here.'

'Oh yes he was.'

Erica leapt from the bed and took hold of her sister's arm saying angrily, 'You're lying, Nancy, he wasn't here. Who told you he was?'

'You're hurting me,' Nancy wailed. 'I heard somebody say they'd seen him. Perhaps they were wrong.'

She rubbed her arm ruefully where Erica's fingers had left a red mark. Erica had the grace to look ashamed and say quickly, 'I'm sorry, but you made me so mad. Don't let Mother see it. Who told you Oliver was here last weekend Nancy? You have to tell me.'

'I saw his car at the side of the house.'

'He doesn't leave his car at the side of the house. In any case how could you see it from the road?'

'Buster ran into the garden and I followed him to get him back. He was there, taking a suitcase out of the car.'

'Did he see you?'

'No, I hid behind one of the bushes.'

'Why didn't you speak to him?'

'Why should I? He never has much to say to me and besides, you'd told me he wasn't coming so I didn't think you'd want him to think I was spying on him.'

'Why would he come here and not come to see me?'

At that moment they heard their mother's voice calling from the hall to say that tea was ready and reluctantly Erica whispered, 'Don't say a word to Mother about Oliver being here. She'll only go on about it and I'm sure he has a very good reason.'

Janet could not help but be aware of the atmosphere as they sat down to their meal. Nancy was unusually silent while Erica's face clearly showed that her thoughts were miles away. This was not the carefree beautiful girl who had charmed their lives, whose dancing feet had endeared her to friends, teachers and all who knew her; this new Erica was somebody they didn't know – reclusive, fearful and strangely at odds with life.

They would have to talk to her about Oliver Denton, make her see that she was young and beautiful, that there could be some other man – after all she was only eighteen, with all of her life before her, and the man she was so besotted with was in another more adult world.

She'd talk to David about it. Together they would have to reassure her about the future, make her see that Oliver Denton was not the beginning or the end.

Later that evening they soon realised that Erica was not looking for reassurances about a future without Oliver. She had found the perfect human being she wanted to spend the rest of her life with. Of course, he'd met many other girls at Oxford and in London, but he'd told her she was the only one he cared for; at last in some despair her father said, 'You do realise, Erica, that if Mrs Prothero moves away he will not be coming here.'

'He'll still come to see me,' she affirmed steadily. 'Besides, Oliver says she'll never sell that old house – it's too big, too dark and she's got too many antiques. Young people would not be looking for a house that size – he says they'd never be able to afford it and it needs servants and gardeners.'

'And what about older people?' her father asked warily.

'Well, they wouldn't want it, would they. It needs a lot of money spending on it and an awful lot of work.'

'He appears to have got it all mapped out.'

'Of course he has, Daddy. Oliver's very intelligent about things like that. He thinks his aunt is absolutely stupid to even think about moving to London.'

'And yet I understand that he is the one who has been urging her to make this move.'

She stared at him with wide disbelieving eyes.

'No he hasn't, Daddy. Oliver told me he's been the one telling her to think again.'

'And yet the flats I believe are quite close to where he lives and he knows the area, she doesn't.'

'Oliver says she doesn't like to think of him so far away. Now that he has a job he won't be able to get here so often and if she lives near him that would solve the problem. I don't think he wants her there. Why should he be the one to look after her when she has so many friends here and servants.'

'I can see I'm flogging a dead horse, Erica. You don't want to listen to anything in the least detrimental about Oliver and it would seem nothing either I or your mother can say is going to alter your opinion.'

'I do know Oliver better than either of you, Daddy.'

'Probably, my dear, but if anything goes wrong with this friendship I want you to promise you'll confide in us, we're your parents and we care about you. One day when you have children of your own you might reflect on what I'm saying now.'

'Oh Daddy, you worry too much. I believe Oliver, she's not going to sell that house, and even if she does Oliver will still come to see me. He can stay with us, that way you'll all get to know him and like him.'

She was so sure, and they both knew they would have to be content with that. There would be either peace or trauma ahead but neither of them were pinning their hopes on peace. Erica was headstrong, and the vanity they had nurtured in her would not let her believe that life would disappoint her now.

Erica was so sure she was right. Oliver would explain his

visit to his aunt's house so satisfactorily she would have to believe him. In the end all would be well.

She was not to know that her younger sister had no such faith.

Nancy blamed Oliver Denton for changing the sister she had adored into a mean, malicious girl who nobody liked any more, and one day when she was married to Julian Watson they would all realise they'd been unable to see the wood for the trees. One day she'd be just as beautiful as Erica, and she'd be far more sensible in her judgement of potential suitors.

Chapter Six

Oliver Denton stood at his bedroom window looking out on the new flats going up almost directly opposite. He hated the fact that they were restricting his view over the river, and thought they were poky, with hardly enough room to swing a cat. He knew exactly what Aunt Amelia would think of them.

She loved her extensive garden, the orchard behind her house, the ordered paths and beds of flowers, and the village life that went on around her, as well as the friends who called to see her every single day.

London could be a lonely place, particularly for an elderly lady who had been brought up in the country and who would have nobody in London except himself.

A girl came out of his bathroom to stand beside him, eyeing the flats with the same sort of dejection as himself.

'They're getting on with them,' she commented.

'I suppose so.'

'She's not going to like them, is she?'

'No. Perhaps I should make her change her mind before it's too late.'

'What, and miss out on her money? Haven't you already talked to Sotheby's about her antiques?'

'Oh, there's nothing confirmed there.'

'What did your mother think about it?'

What had his mother thought about it? She'd been

predictably scathing, saying in her usual cynically amused voice, 'Really Oliver, having your aunt living here at all will be a disaster, but in those flats, after what she's been used to, you must have taken leave of your senses to allow her to think of them.'

'She's come to rely on me, Mother, and I can't go rushing up there every weekend. I have a job to think about, she's nobody apart from me.'

'She has an army of friends, or so she led me to believe.'

'Hardly the same thing as family.'

'Well, I'm family but we've never got on.'

'And you're out of the country, Mother. If I'm lucky I get to see you once a year, Aunt Amelia you never see.'

'No, except for funerals and weddings. I'll be seeing her at your wedding – didn't you have a girl in the village you were quite smitten with?'

'Nothing serious.'

'Really. You could talk of nobody else the last time we met.'

'She's beautiful, sweet, nice family background, but I'm not looking for anything permanent just yet. I've got ambition, Mother. There's no telling who I'm going to meet. Why tie myself down at this stage.'

She had sat curled up on the settee like some beautiful exotic cat, auburn-haired and green-eyed, wearing an animal print leisure suit in colours that only enhanced her feline appearance and brought out the impatience he always felt towards her.

'So, what are you going to do about the girl?' she'd asked astutely.

'Well, I'm here and she's there. When Aunt Amelia comes here I'm sure she'll see that we have to call it a day. Too many miles between us, too many differences.'

She'd had to be content with that. Now here was Cynthia Redman posing the same question.

He'd known Cynthia since they'd been at Oxford – different colleges, same crowd, similar interests. She was attractive, and was no more in love with him than he was with her.

He had given her the run of his house as she'd yet to find somewhere to live in London. Her parents lived in Singapore where her father was big in business although Cynthia had never elaborated on what sort of business he was in.

Her father had pulled strings to get her a job working for some foreign importers, apparently more lucrative than if she'd followed up her law degree.

He never really knew who she was with or where she went, money never appeared to be a problem since she dressed well and wore expensive jewellery, and although they'd enjoyed an intermittent affair neither of them was in love with the other.

She was attractive, sophisticated and intelligent, but Oliver needed to be loved even when he didn't think it altogether necessary that he should love in return.

That was the trouble with Erica – she loved too much, asked too much.

He looked down at Cynthia but she was absorbed with the building work going on opposite and after a few minutes she said, 'When your aunt moves in over there you'll want me out of here, I suppose. Wouldn't do to let the old lady think you're living a life of debauchery.'

'We're hardly doing that, are we? I don't know where you are half the time.'

She laughed. 'Doesn't all that add to the interest, darling?'

'There isn't any interest, Cynthia. You wouldn't like there to be and neither would I.'

'No. Well, I'm off now. Why aren't you visiting your aunt this weekend? Is it the love affair that's growing stale or are you becoming too involved?'

He grinned. 'Didn't you say you were leaving?' he said, and with a bright smile she left him.

He watched her leaving the house, walking briskly

towards the end of the street, and then he saw a bright red open sports car pull out from further up and stop for Cynthia to get into it.

London on a Saturday afternoon and he was bored. There were probably a thousand and one things to do, but he'd neglected his friends while he'd been visiting his aunt, and the girls he'd picked up and dropped to suit himself were hardly likely to welcome him with open arms.

He should have gone to St Agnes. Erica would have made her delight obvious, and he could have reassured his aunt that the flats were progressing, that they looked wonderful and that it was decision time.

He decided to telephone her, only to be told by her disgruntled servant that Mrs Prothero was having tea with the Vicar and his wife, and when enquiring what time she would be back received the laconic reply that she had no idea.

He did not fare much better when he tried to telephone Erica and received her young sister's cheerful message that Erica was at the tennis club and wouldn't be back home until late.

'Do they play in the dark in your neck of the woods?' he asked sarcastically, whereupon Nancy said brightly, 'Oh they can do. The courts *are* floodlit you know.'

After that he'd decided that next Saturday he would definitely visit Aunt Amelia – living in limbo did not suit him.

In St Agnes Nancy was feeling decidedly pleased with herself. Oliver's confident tones had seemed to her rather less confident when he said goodbye.

Erica was congratulating herself that she had handled the weekend perfectly. She had talked about other men who might admire her, not asked too many questions on the sale of Aunt Amelia's house, and Oliver had been at his most charming, making her feel loved and wanted.

It was only in the late afternoon when he was leaving for London that she said, 'Will I be seeing you soon, Oliver?'

55

'Hopefully, darling. My aunt's come to accept the fact that I can't get here so often, but you know I'll come whenever I can.'

'The college always have a reunion dance at the beginning of December. Will you be able to come up for that?'

'I'm not sure, darling, this is the first I've heard of it.'

'It's a great night, Oliver. Everybody dresses up for it and it's at the Trocadero. There's a wonderful buffet and we have the orchestra from the Palais de Dance. You would enjoy it, I know,'

'And what night is it to be held?'

'Oh, always on a Friday.'

'Then I'll do my very best to be here.'

In the weeks that followed she listened to the other girls talking about the dresses they would be wearing, the boys they would be bringing, but told them very little about her own arrangements. She would have a new dress to outshine anything the others could come up with, but her doubts about Oliver persisted.

She'd been relatively happy and contented until the afternoon her sister had dropped the bombshell.

Commodore Watson and the Major had been playing tennis watched by their wives and Nancy never missed an opportunity to chat to Mrs Watson. They had been joined by Aunt Amelia and in spite of her mother's warning glances Nancy had no hesitation in repeating the conversation word for word.

'Oh I'm so glad to find you both here,' Mrs Prothero began. ' You've probably heard a great many rumours but I can tell you that I have decided to move to London. I'm not looking forward to it. You both know how much I love St Agnes, but Oliver is the only relative I have and he's finally persuaded me to sell up and go to live near him.'

Both ladies voiced their surprise and even their doubts about the wisdom of such a move, but Mrs Prothero had simply said, 'Well, Oliver has a job at the Foreign Office and he's worked so hard for his career, I can't be the one to make problems for him now.'

'But doesn't he have a mother in London?' one of them asked, but Mrs Prothero shook her head impatiently saying, 'She's hardly ever in London and lives on the Continent. They've never really got on. I do have two elderly cousins in Poole, but Oliver is the only person I care about.'

'Have you put your house on the market?' Elspeth asked.

'The estate agent has it in hand. I'm not sure how soon I shall sell it, but the flats in London are almost ready. I'm going up to London next week to see them.'

There was more conversation about flats but by now Nancy felt she couldn't get home quickly enough – it was time for her sister to realise that Oliver Denton was a lying cheat. She was too young to understand the stress it would cause. So she was quite unprepared for Erica's despair, the anguished tears as she fled upstairs to her room and the slamming of the bedroom door.

Her mother had offered no chastisement, only the sad shaking of her head.

In the days that followed Erica haunted the area round Mrs Prothero's house looking for signs that the house was to be sold, and was rewarded for her vigil several days later when the 'For Sale' sign was put up at the front gate.

Oliver had told her he would not be able to spend time with his aunt for several weeks, but even so for several weekends she let herself out of the house in the early hours of the morning. She'd laid awake for hours until she felt sure the rest of the family were fast asleep, then she'd crept downstairs, shrugging herself into her coat over her pyjamas and then running frantically down the road.

At every car headlight that appeared along the road she had dived into the nearest driveway, then when the car had passed she'd run on. When there had been no sign of Oliver's car at the front of the house or at the side she'd gone home relieved and happy. He hadn't been lying to her after all, but

57

then on one occasion his car had been there and all weekend she'd waited for his telephone call to say they should meet, but he had returned to London without seeing her.

Mrs Prothero went to London to view the flats but on her return remained non-committal. She hadn't liked them, but decided her old neighbours shouldn't be aware of the fact.

Oliver had been sympathetic.

'They always look terrible while the building is still going on,' he'd said. 'When you move in with all your own furniture you'll see they look more like home. You'll have sufficient money to buy anything you want, Aunt Amelia, and you'll be able to travel, see the world.'

'And who will I do that with?' she'd asked him.

'Well, we can do some of it together...'

'And what about Erica?' she'd asked him.

'Erica?'

'Why yes. You never mention her, Oliver. You make me feel awfully guilty whenever I meet the Clarksons.'

'Why should you feel guilty. I've already told you that Erica and I are simply good friends, she's far too young and I have a career to think about.'

'And that girl I saw leaving your flat?'

'A girl I was at Oxford with, simply a friend. She already has a boyfriend.'

Amelia found herself thinking of all the derogatory things Jethro had said about Oliver, that he was too cock-sure, too conceited and too much like his mother.

She found herself wishing that she couldn't sell her house. Compared to other houses nearby hers seemed darker, more old-fashioned, and yet she loved it, loved her antiques, and even when Oliver told her they'd fetch a fortune, she would hate to see them go.

Jethro wouldn't have listened to him. Even the Vicar had advised her to think very carefully, but Oliver was all she had, her brother's son; somewhere in Oliver there must be some of Edwin.

The Clarksons were concerned that their beautiful daughter was looking pinched and miserable. It would seem that the once confident, sought-after girl had vanished into thin air.

Now it was Nancy who was blossoming. The boyish figure was developing curves, the eyes seemed bluer, the lips fuller and more provocative, and there was a new grace about her as she walked along the road.

Anthea Edgebaston noticed the transformation with interest. One sister was becoming interesting, the other was fading into insignificance – shouldn't her parents be concerned about her?

Her parents were very concerned but they were reluctant to mention anything. Erica was too volatile, in the clouds one minute and in the depths of despair the next.

The entire area was amazed to see the 'SOLD' sign going up at the end of November, and then Oliver's car was standing outside Amelia's house and he was inviting Erica out to lunch.

For the first time in weeks she was more like herself, choosing what she would wear, taking an interest in make-up, confident that he would be open and honest with her – the same Oliver, charming, handsome, caring.

'I'm absolutely amazed that the house has gone so quickly, darling. We both are, but it's not the end for us, you know. I'm not going to get here all that often but we're not a world apart and I'll telephone you often.'

'But surely she won't have to move out just yet.'

'Well yes, they want to move in as soon as possible. It's taken us by surprise, I can tell you. The flats are not quite ready so she'll have to move in with me for a week or so. By Christmas she'll be installed.'

'What about the dance in early December?'

'Well, obviously that might be a problem. I suppose I can get here and stay at the Royal Oak.'

'Oliver, you can stay with us. My parents would like that, and they would get to know you. My kid sister says she doesn't really know you at all.'

59

'That little brat. She's made up her mind she doesn't like me, I can tell.'

'Oh that's Nancy. She will like you, Oliver, I just know she will. Who are the people buying the house?'

'Up to now it's all really been done through the estate agent. My aunt's to meet them one day next week. They're called Mellor.'

'Where do they come from?'

'London. He's a musician, but I really don't know anything else. I believe they have one daughter, also an aspiring musician.'

'Oh Oliver, it's all happened so quickly. I thought your aunt would always be here and that you'd be here too. Now everything is changing. Why do London people want to live in the country? Why does your aunt want to live in London?'

'I know, darling. It's a rum old world, isn't it. But changes do happen. I've suffered a good number of those myself.'

'You mean your mother?'

'Yes.'

'Does she know about me?'

'She's not really interested in anything apart from herself, Erica. I stayed with her for two weeks – the usual round of cocktail parties and meetings with her friends, all very much like her, too blasé, too full of themselves. The next time she comes to England Aunt Amelia will be living in London. I doubt if they'll pass the time of day.'

Perhaps that was why Oliver was as he was. She found it easy to make excuses for him because she loved him. She would keep him, be all the things he expected of her, and in the end he would see for himself that there would never be anybody like her.

At least he had promised to be with her at the dance and all the other girls would be envious – she couldn't think of another boy who could hold a candle to Oliver.

She'd have a new dress, the most sophisticated ever, and

she'd ask for earrings and a necklace for Christmas so that she could wear them for the dance. To Erica on that afternoon the dark clouds had suddenly been swept away and ahead lay only sunlight and plain sailing.

Chapter Seven

It was all happening too quickly for Amelia – one moment she was contemplating the long lonely years ahead without Jethro, then suddenly she was being propelled into a new world where the only person she would know would be Oliver.

She was aware that Edith considered her very foolish to be taking such a step. She went about her household tasks with ill-disguised grumpiness, and she had no doubt that she aired her displeasure among her friends.

She had said quite adamantly that she would not accompany her to London, that she had friends and relatives in St Agnes – but what she said to her friends was a different matter.

She had little time Oliver Denton. She thought he was after his aunt's money, and had already decided what should be done with her antiques that Mr Prothero had prized so highly.

They listened to her and passed her remarks on to their associates, so that it was inevitable that in no time at all the families surrounding Amelia were made aware of Edith's misgivings.

Of the newcomers she knew precious little. They had viewed the house with the estate agent and decided it was what they wanted. Edith had been out at the time and Mrs Prothero had seemed to be in a bit of a trance about the whole thing.

All Erica was interested in was Oliver's assurance that he would accompany her to the dance, but her parents were less happy with the situation.

'David, I'm not sure,' Janet Clarkson said anxiously over the breakfast table. 'He seems nice enough whenever I've spoken to him, but we don't really know him do we.'

'No, and those that do are not exactly enthusiastic.'

'But Erica is so sure, David.'

'I know, that's what I'm afraid of.'

'She's asked him to stay with us when he comes up for the dance.'

'And will he, do you think?'

'Well, where else will he stay? Amelia will be in London and we really can't expect him to stay in some hotel or other.'

'It's some time off so perhaps we should wait a while to see how things develop.'

'If he lets her down I don't know what we'll do with her.'

'Well isn't Amelia having a farewell party? Surely he'll be there – when we've properly spoken to him we can make up our own minds up about whether he intends to stay with us or not.'

Amelia intended her farewell party to be a night for all her guests to remember so she chose the Town Hall for the venue and seemingly intended to invite everybody she knew in the town.

Oliver thought it was a waste of money – they were both on their way, so could simply have said their farewells to a few neighbours and disappeared quietly. After all they'd heaped generosity on the area for far too long, so why even more?

Nevertheless, as he stood with his aunt to welcome her guests he was at his most charming. Immaculate in his dinner jacket he wore his most welcoming smile, favoured them with his firmest handshake and remembered without being prompted who was recovering from some illness or other, who had recently enjoyed a holiday and told all of them how much his aunt would miss them and how much he would miss seeing them so often.

He favoured the Clarksons with special friendliness, and was rewarded by Erica's obvious delight, her parents' sociable acceptance and sister Nancy's aloof stare.

Oh well, he wouldn't have to put up with that for much longer.

All Nancy was aware of was that Julian was with his parents, looking splendid in his naval uniform. She had known he was home on leave and watched with some impatience while he spoke with her parents and Erica, then with a smile his mother said, 'And this is Nancy, Julian. She's happy to go to the shops for me and call in on her way home from school. I'm going to miss her when she leaves next summer.'

He smiled down at her. 'That's nice, Nancy,' he said. 'So kind of you to keep Mother company.'

Nancy blushed, and for the rest of the evening she never took her eyes off him, even when he didn't say another word to her.

People chatted, mingled and enjoyed the excellent buffet Amelia had provided, and whenever possible Erica spent time with Oliver. It was later in the evening however when Amelia said to her, 'You're going to miss Oliver coming here, Erica, but of course you have a great many friends and your mother tells me you'll soon be working for your father.'

Erica smiled. 'Oliver's promised to come for the dance in December; he's staying with us and we're so looking forward to it.'

Amelia stared at her uncertainly. 'Really, Erica, I didn't know, he hasn't told me.'

'He's probably forgotten, everything has happened so quickly, hasn't it. Mother is quite happy for him to stay with us, we'll all make him very welcome.'

'I'm sure you will, my dear.'

'Perhaps one day I'll be able to see you in London. Is the new flat nice?'

'Oh I do hope so, my dear. I hope one day it feels like home.'

Erica wasn't sure that she felt entirely happy with her conversation with Mrs Prothero. She hadn't said she'd be glad to see her in London, she'd asked no questions about the dance and she'd seemed so vague.

Later in the evening Amelia spoke with her mother and the first thing she said was, 'I believe Oliver is coming to stay with you for a weekend in December, Janet. He hasn't told me, Erica mentioned it.'

'Yes. It's the end-of-term dance which is the highlight of the year. They hold it at the Trocadero. They must have arranged it between them. I'm sure he'll be telling you all about it.'

'Yes well, they don't tell us everything, do they Janet? I'm sure you've discovered that for yourself.'

Janet smiled and decided to change the subject.

'I do hope you'll be happy in London, Amelia. Edith isn't going with you, is she.'

'No. Her roots are here. She doesn't even like the idea of going to London to see it.'

'She's set in her ways I suppose. But you like the flat?'

'Well it's modern, self-contained but really very nice. There wouldn't really be room for two of us. I have a balcony with a nice view of the river. If ever you're in London I hope you'll call to see me.'

'Yes, I'm sure we will.'

'I feel I'm leaving such good friends behind. Jethro loved St Agnes, whenever we went away he was itching to get back. He simply loved the cricket club, the river and even the old castle on the hill there.'

'Well, if you don't like it you can always come back here, we'll all receive you with open arms.'

The days before her departure went all too quickly and the

house didn't seem like home with all the crates and packages. All the shelves and ledges which had once displayed Jethro's antiques were empty now, and they seemed to stare back at her reproachfully.

Oliver constantly reassured her that they would bring in a great deal of money, but somehow money didn't seem important. Edith never addressed a word to Oliver, and although it didn't seem to bother him, it troubled Amelia. Unable to contain herself any longer she said, 'Edith, I do wish you wouldn't sulk, we've always got along together, now you're hardly able to pass the time of day.'

She had waited to chastise Edith until Oliver was out of the room, and now Edith snapped, 'It's him that's making you move and I don't see why when you've always been so happy here.'

'He's all I've got, Edith.'

'You've got good friends and you've got me. You're going to that big city when all you've got will still be him.'

'I'll write to you often, Edith, and tell you how I'm faring. I'll show you it's all working out.'

'And what about that girl he's been so friendly with? I suppose she'll be dumped too.'

'On the contrary, Edith, he's coming to stay with her parents so that they can attend some dance together.'

'That remains to be seen,' Edith murmured darkly. Amelia decided to change the subject. Edith would hear no good of her nephew and to be honest she too had reservations about the dance.

At the moment Oliver came back into the room to announce that he was slipping out for a moment and that she had visitors.

Mrs Gantry and Grace were full of apologies that they had come at an inopportune moment but Amelia was quick to say, 'Oh we're just dying for a cup of tea. I hope you can find somewhere to sit.'

It had been Grace's mother who had wanted to come, and as she sat eyeing the cluttered room Grace hoped she would keep the thoughts she had voiced over the past few days to herself.

Much to her consternation her mother said, 'I didn't expect you to be moving, although I did think you might have had a wedding in the family.'

'A wedding, Mrs Gantry?'

'Why yes. That Clarkson girl. Surely you knew about it, everybody else did.'

'Mother, they're simply friends, Erica has had a lot of boyfriends, she's very popular,' Grace said anxiously.

Mrs Gantry's eyes were beady with speculation while Grace was embarrassed. Her mother was well known for spiteful gossip. Most people ignored her, thinking it was because she was old, far from well and with not enough to do, but in some devious way she seemed to know more than people gave her credit for.

Grace felt uncomfortable and, looking across the room to where Edith was busy wrapping objects in newspaper, she could not miss the snide smile on her face.

Amelia decided to stop Mrs Gantry in her tracks.

'Oliver has a long way to go in his career, Mrs Gantry,' she said firmly. 'He's working for the Foreign Office and his career is very important to him. I'm sure one day he'll wish to get married when the right girl comes along. It may indeed be Erica, but she's very young and the distance between them is difficult.'

'She's been a bit high-handed with a good many of the young men in the area. I imagine she's been waiting for somebody like your nephew to come along.'

'Oh I don't know. I rather suspect Oliver is just one more young man she will cut her teeth on. Anyway, we'll all have to wait and see, won't we.'

Grace smiled at her uncertainly. Surely her mother would leave matters alone after that remark, but Mrs Gantry was determined to have the last word.

'I always thought she'd have married Councillor Stedman's lad but she led him a pretty dance by all accounts, and then he married somebody else. Too big an opinion of herself, and you know, Amelia, it doesn't always work out. Perhaps she needs taking down a peg or two. Was Mrs Edgebaston at your party the other night?'

'Why yes, everybody in the area was invited.'

'I suppose she brought some man or other?'

'Yes, a very nice gentleman. Gordon I think she called him. A very nice gentleman. Accountant, I think.'

'Well I wouldn't know, sometimes they leave their cars at the front of the house, sometimes behind or at the side. I suppose it depends what time they leave.'

'Perhaps we should go now, Mother. I'm sure Mrs Prothero still has a lot to do,' Grace said anxiously, 'I've brought you a little farewell gift, a tea cloth that I've embroidered. I do hope you like it.'

Amelia spread it out across her knee exclaiming how much she admired it, and Grace said softly, 'I was always very good at embroidery but precious little else. I hope it will be one more thing to remind you of us.'

'I shall never forget a single one of you, Grace. I'd like you to visit me in London.'

'My travelling days are over,' Mrs Gantry said sharply, 'and Grace prefers the country.'

Amelia smiled gently and Grace reflected somewhat bitterly that she had never disclosed a preference for the country and that her mother as usual was speaking for her.

As Amelia helped Grace's mother to another cup of tea she found herself longing to say that it would be nice for Grace to spend time looking at the shops in London, visiting the theatres and the many parks, but she decided it was better to say nothing at all. The old lady was self-opinionated and Grace had been too long under her thumb. She was rather hoping they would go before Oliver got back – Mrs Gantry wouldn't be against questioning him on some aspect of his future life and Oliver could be caustic.

Edith on the other hand was wishing they would stay. It would be amusing to see how he would respond to the old woman's sharp tongue, but Grace had had enough and was gently reminding her mother that they must get home before the gardeners left in case something was needed for the garden on their next visit.

As Edith collected the tea tray Amelia said, 'I always feel rather sorry for Grace, she's such a nice person and her mother can be difficult.'

'What a pity it was that she didn't marry the Vicar, she'd have made a great vicar's wife.'

'The vicar already has a good wife, Edith.'

'I know, but he liked Grace before she came on the scene. Pity her father died, she'd have got away with it and her mother'd 'ave 'ad to make the best of things like most other women have to do.'

'That was all a long time ago, Edith. The vicar and his wife are very compatible and very happy together. I'm sure Grace realises that.'

'I was only saying that things could 'ave been a lot different if she 'adn't lost her father.'

'I know what you mean, Edith. If I hadn't lost Jethro I wouldn't be leaving this house, selling my furniture and moving into a flat.'

Nor would you have been brain-washed into doing anything so stupid, Edith longed to say, but decided for once to keep her thoughts to herself.

Oliver returned in high good humour and Amelia asked gently, 'Have you seen Erica?'

'Yes, we had lunch at The White Eagle, they put a very nice lunch on, Aunt Amelia.'

'So I believe. So you've said your farewells until you come here for the dance?'

'The dance?'

'Why yes. Her mother told me you'd be staying with them, in December isn't it?'

'Well, I've only half promised, it's a few weeks away and no telling what will be happening with my job. Erica knows the score.'

69

'Are you quite sure about that Oliver?'

'Yes of course. Aunt Amelia, we're not engaged, we're simply friends and there are a good few miles between us. If nothing changes between now and December I shall be here for the dance, but how can any of us forecast what tomorrow is going to bring?'

'How indeed,' his aunt murmured. Oliver shrugged his shoulders and left her alone.

As he packed his few belongings he wished they could be on their way, hoping there would be no more visitors to detain them in a house that was like a barn now with just a few chairs and the odd small table. Edith would take them although his aunt had already given her a load of things. Some of the farewell gifts his aunt had handed out to her friends would have been better cared for in the hands of Sotheby's.

He found his aunt and Edith making their last tour of the house, his aunt in tears, Edith with a glum look on her face and reproach in her eyes.

'Time to go, Aunt Amelia,' he said cheerfully, 'we've a long journey ahead.'

'Yes dear, I'm ready. The estate agent has asked Edith to be here to meet the new people tomorrow.'

'They're not wasting any time.'

'No. Apparently Mr Mellor is in London so he won't be with them tomorrow. I don't know who is coming, his wife presumably and maybe some others.'

'Perhaps she'll offer you a job, Edith,' Oliver said brightly.

Edith didn't think that remark required an answer and Amelia said softly, 'I don't think she's looking for work at the moment, Oliver. At least that's what she's said. Don't provoke her, she's very upset.'

'Well come along then, I've loaded your things into the car. You can take your last look at St Agnes.'

Her friends had come out into their gardens waving to them as they left, and as they drove past the Clarksons

Erica stood on the pavement. She was clutching a bunch of flowers so Oliver slowed the car to let her place them in his aunt's hands. Amelia smiled tremulously, but as he watched the tears rolling slowly down Erica's cheeks, it was difficult to ascertain who was the most distressed.

'Poor child,' Amelia croaked, 'she really is very fond of you.'

'Yes, well. I'm really very fond of Erica. We'll have to wait and see, Aunt Amelia. Rome wasn't built in a day.'

Chapter Eight

Edith was tired of rambling round the empty rooms, trying to picture what it had been like. She hadn't really liked the antiques, merely thinking of them as dust collectors, but she'd seen Jethro stroking them, a look on his face that she'd noticed on the face of her brother when he stroked his beloved dog.

Where the pictures had been there were now huge white squares on the darker wallpaper, and the sheen of brass and copper had gone from corners they had helped to brighten.

She made her way upstairs. The bedroom she had slept in for years was devoid of furniture, and she was none too happy that it was now in her sister's little bedroom. She really didn't want to be there, nor did they want her if they'd be honest enough to admit it, but it had all been so sudden and where else could she could have gone at such short notice.

In the room that Oliver had occupied she could still smell cigarette smoke and she opened the window quickly. It wouldn't do for the new people to smell it – not everybody enjoyed cigarettes.

On the window ledge was a small pile of envelopes and other rubbish, and she sniffed disdainfully – that was Oliver, couldn't be bothered to burn them. She picked them up idly. They were empty, but there was a snapshot and she looked at it more closely. It was of Erica Clarkson sitting on an upturned boat on the banks of Loch Maree in Scotland during

72

her summer holiday – a pretty girl, wistful and lonely. Turning it over she read: 'I'm missing you so much, Oliver. The sun is shining, the loch is lovely but without you there's nothing. I do want to see you very soon.'

There was sadness in her eyes as she slipped the photograph into her pocket before turning away.

The estate agent had advised her to arrive early, but he hadn't said when the new people would be arriving and she was hating this lonely vigil in a house with too many memories. Why did they need her anyway? They'd already looked over the house and her sister'd be grumbling that she'd left her house without unpacking some of her belongings.

From the front window of Amelia's room she saw the car arriving followed by the estate agent's car and a very large removal van. They were here.

Two women were sitting in the front of the car and as it stopped at the door the back door of the car opened and a young girl jumped out onto the drive. One of the women was tall and thin, dressed severely in a dark suit, and as she looked up at the house Edith stared down at a plain cold face and spectacles.

The other woman was smaller, hatless and wearing a beige raincoat, but it was the girl who looked up at that moment and Edith found herself looking at a face of indescribable beauty; pale blond hair and azure blue eyes only enhanced her delicate features, but as she followed the two women into the house there was a grace about her movements that only a dancer could have emulated.

Edith decided it was time to go downstairs to meet them.

The taller woman stood in the centre of the hall. As Edith walked down the stairs their eyes met and the estate agent came forward with a smile saying, 'This is Miss Edith Pinder, she worked here for Mrs Prothero for a great many years and also lived here. Edith, this is Miss Mellor, Mr Mellor's sister, and this is Mrs Mellor and her daughter Miss Joyce Mellor.'

73

The girl smiled and held out her hand, then her mother came forward with a swift smile. The other woman merely said, 'We have a lot to do, so we'd better decide where we want the furniture to go. Are you here to help us, Miss Pinder?'

Edith looked at the estate agent doubtfully, and he said quickly, 'I'm sure if you require some help Miss Pinder wouldn't mind obliging.'

'That would be very kind,' Mrs Mellor said softly.

'Which is the drawing room? I seem to remember there are two rooms at the front of the house, one larger than the other,' Miss Mellor said briskly.

'Yes, Mrs Prothero called one the Drawing Room, the other the Morning Room.'

'Well, our concern is the piano – the largest room I think.'

'Mrs Prothero kept her piano in the morning room as it gets the morning sun,' Edith told them.

'I wasn't aware she had a piano. I don't remember it when we came round, do you Margaret?'

'Oh yes, a small piano. Rosewood I think.'

'This is a grand piano, Miss Pinder. My brother and his daughter are musicians.'

'Sorry, I didn't know.'

'Tell the men in the first van we'll get the piano installed first in the drawing room. There's not going to be room for very much else. I told Arthur he should have thought about extending this hall or looking again at the house in Slough.'

'Oh not Slough, Aunt Edna. I love this house and the town. I wanted to come here, didn't you, Mummy?' Joyce carolled.

Mummy decided to stay out of it.

It was early afternoon when they paused for a cup of tea and Edith decided that in all the long years she had worked for Mrs Prothero she had never felt as tired and worn out.

74

The grand piano was installed in the largest room in the house leaving little room for anything else. The Steinway gleamed in pristine walnut, and Edith stared at it in amazement, finding it impossible to reconcile this majestic creation with Amelia's much-loved upright piano. The rest of their furniture paled into insignificance.

None of it was new, but neither was it memorable. Much of it was scratched, very ordinary and certainly not in the same league as Amelia's beloved antique pieces.

Joyce helped her to set out the tea tray in the kitchen and even there she found herself comparing the white, gold-rimmed china with Amelia's Wedgwood and Royal Doulton.

'Will ye be goin' to school here?' Edith asked, feeling that she really needed to know something about the Mellors.

'Yes, but it's so long since I've been to a proper school. I went to music college in London.'

'So you'll not be doin' music any more?'

Joyce laughed. 'Oh yes, my father is going to teach me. He says music college couldn't teach me any more than he can.'

'But doesn't your father work in London?'

'Yes, but he's decided to retire and spend it all with me. I'll be fifteen next year so I'd be leaving school in a couple of years.'

'Ye don't want to be a secretary or work in a shop then.'

'Gracious no, I wouldn't be any good at that sort of thing.'

By this time Edith had formed her own opinion of the new occupants. The sister was overbearing and altogether bossy; the daughter was beautiful and very nice; Mrs Mellor was a mouse.

By the time the removal men had left the house was more or less in order Edith decided it was time to put on her coat and hat and head for her sister's house on the other side of the town. Meeting Miss Mellor in the hall she said, 'I'm

75

off home now, Miss Mellor. It's nigh on five o'clock and I 'ave some way to walk.'

'I need to pay you for your services today, Miss Pinder. How much would Mrs Prothero have been paying you?'

'I worked for Mrs Prothero, Miss Mellor. I don't really work for you.'

'My sister will be needing somebody here – would you be willing to work for her?'

'Well, I don't really know, it's something I'll 'ave to think about.'

'She's easy to get along with. My brother is rather more exacting but I can assure you he won't interfere with the running of the house as long as it doesn't interfere with his music. I'm sure he'll be willing to pay the same as whatever Mrs Prothero gave you.'

Edith didn't immediately reply so Miss Mellor said sharply, 'You don't have a job, Miss Pinder. Surely my offer has great advantages.'

'Well yes,' Edith said, still doubtful, then making up her mind, 'I'll give it a try. We can always part company if we don't get on together.'

'Right. Well we'll be seeing you in the morning then.'

'Will you be wanting me to live in, or come as a daily?'

'I really don't think my brother would like anybody living in, they've always had a daily.'

'Won't Mrs Mellor need to speak to me about it?'

Miss Mellor stared at her in some dismay. 'No, of course not. I'll tell her what's been decided. You'll be here in the morning – what time?'

'Isn't that up to you? Will you want me before Miss Joyce goes to school?'

'We can talk about that in the morning. Good night Miss Pinder.'

Edith marched down the road in deep thought. It was cold and frosty for early December and she was soon feeling decidedly unhappy about the new arrangements. She'd had her own room with Mrs Prothero, so there'd been no turning out on a cold rainy morning, it had been home for a long time, and now she was relegated to the same job Ellie Entwistle had had for years and grumbled incessantly about, trudging through snow-laden streets before it was properly light.

Her sister didn't exactly agree with the idea either.

'Why couldn't ye just think about it, our Edith. You could have got a job anywhere, with the doctor or with the Major, and ye know Mrs Robson said they'd be wanting somebody at the Scouts hut soon.'

'Well, she took me by surprise, and I do love that house. I know every cranny of it and I don't think I'll 'ave any trouble from Mrs Mellor, the poor woman looks as if she can't say boo to a goose. That sister of 'er 'usband's took complete charge, but she won't be moving' in with 'em.'

'Well I suppose you knows best. Are you goin' to be comfortable in that small bedroom? Ye could be lookin' round for somethin' of yer own, I suppose.'

'Perhaps I might do that. A little flat perhaps, and I do 'ave some furniture, a few bits and pieces our mother left me and the things Mrs Prothero gave me. As it is they're cluttering up your attic and some o' the garage.'

Halfway through the next morning Edith was regretting her decision. Mrs Mellor was nice, receiving her with a smile and nothing else, while Miss Mellor laid down the instructions on how the rooms should be cleaned, what times meals should be taken, while Joyce looked on with an uneasy smile.

'How long does your aunt intend to stay?' she asked Joyce during one of the rare moments when they were alone together.

'She's leaving in the morning. She works in a bank and has to be back there tomorrow.'

With a sigh of relief Edith said, 'I need to have a word with your mother about what she expects of me.'

'I'm glad you're staying, Edith,' Joyce said quietly.

'Mummy hasn't been well and I'll be at school next week. I'm not sure how we could have coped on our own.'

'Your aunt didn't live with you in London then?'

'No, but she came nearly every day. Father relies on her very much.'

Later in the afternoon Miss Mellor said sharply, 'I've told my sister-in-law that I've spoken to you with full instructions about the running of things. She won't change anything.'

'But I'll need to speak to her,' Edith persisted.

'If you feel you must, but she won't change anything. You'll be responsible for the housework. She's keeping one of the gardeners on, I'm sure she won't need two.'

'Won't Mr Mellor decide about the garden?'

'My brother isn't interested in gardening just as long as it's kept neat and tidy.'

'Mr Prothero loved his garden. Even though he'd two gardeners he liked to do things for himself. He always looked after the rose bushes and the things in the green-house.'

'Really. Well when you've met my brother, Miss Pinder, you'll realise perhaps that the only thing he is interested in is music, to the exclusion of everything else.'

'It's a good thing his daughter is musical then.'

Miss Mellor stared at her haughtily. 'Yes it is. I'm sure she will repay him for all the time he's going to spend on her.'

Grimly Edith thought, what if she doesn't, what if she rebels like so many young people rebel, most of it brought on by parents who expect too much?

Life at the Mellors' house was the sole topic of conversation around the table that evening, and by this time there were quite a few others in the area who knew what was going on in what had been known as the Prothero House.

'I wonder how long you'll stay there,' Edith's sister said astutely.

'It's early days. When the Mellor woman's gone, it might be different.'

78

'But will it be any better.'

'I don't know. I like the girl, but I've yet to get to know the mother.'

'And the father?'

'I know.'

'I saw Ellie Entwistle this morning in the newsagents and I was telling 'er a bit about your problem. She said she knows of one or two people who are disappointed you're stayin' on there.'

Edith knew her sister was a gossip and perhaps it would be wise to say little during the weeks ahead. It was early days with the Mellors – perhaps she wasn't destined to stay with them but she didn't want Gladys to influence her either one way or another.

The girls' high school across the park received Joyce with open arms. Since Erica Clarkson had left the school there had been a decided gap in what the school had to offer the parents at the end-of-term concerts. Erica had sung prettily, danced charmingly and was a good actress in the school plays. True the school orchestra could always be depended upon to entertain an audience under the expert tuition of the music master, but Erica had been sorely missed.

Now here was Joyce, undeniably pretty, musical and the fact that her father played the violin with one of the most prestigious orchestras in the country was surely an added bonus.

Nancy Clarkson couldn't get home fast enough to inform the family that the new girl was nice, talented and likely to fill her sister's place most adequately.

Erica listened without comment. What did it matter that a new girl had stepped into her shoes? She'd moved on and had better things to look forward to, like the dance at the Trocadero and Oliver's visit to her home.

Her mother anxiously asked her what sort of things he liked to eat, whether he liked a cooked breakfast, which of the spare bedrooms he would prefer and exactly how long he would be staying.

'Oh Mummy, don't fuss so,' Erica exclaimed. 'Oliver will fit in – ask him all those questions when he gets here.'

Nancy was the only member of the family who doubted that Oliver would ever arrive, but she kept her thoughts to herself. She wanted to be wrong. She loved her sister and there'd been so many times of late when she'd found her in tears over something Oliver hadn't done. Why couldn't she find somebody else and forget about Oliver Denton?

Nancy entertained the Commodore and his wife with the news of the end-of-term concert which promised to be as good as anything they'd put on before. This year Major Robson had decided the Cadets' Band would play some military music for them, the school choir would sing carols, the orchestra would play classical music and Joyce Mellor would play the piano and the violin.

'Then we must certainly ask if we can have tickets,' Mrs Watson said. 'Julian will be home on leave, we hope, and it will be one evening when we don't have to entertain him.'

Julian would be home, and she'd be tucked away in the middle of the school choir so that he'd never notice her. Why did Erica have all the talent? It wasn't fair – surely just a little bit of it wouldn't have been asking too much.

Nancy reflected that her sister had not been too popular at school. Jealousy, she decided, but now she wasn't so sure since her new friend Joyce Mellor seemed very popular indeed.

Joyce had all Erica's acumen, but she didn't have an ounce of conceit in her, being almost diffident about her accomplishments. Boys who might have been overawed by Erica approached Joyce as friends. Girls who had been ready to accuse her of taking over where Erica had left off were now anxious to make friends with her, but because they lived in the same area it was Nancy she walked to school with and home again in the late afternoon.

On one such afternoon Nancy introduced her new friend to Mrs Watson and after they had left her Joyce said, 'She's awfully nice. Is her husband the Commodore?'

'Yes, how did you know?'

'Edith told me a little about the people nearby. She told me he hoists his flag to celebrate old naval battles.'

Nancy laughed. 'Yes he does. Their son Julian is in the Navy and will be home on leave at Christmas. He's awfully handsome.'

Joyce smiled. 'You like him, Nancy. Does he like you?'

'I doubt he'd recognise me if he met me on the street.'

'Perhaps not now, but one day perhaps when you're older.'

'They're coming to the school concert and I'll be tucked away in that horrible uniform in the middle of the choir. He won't even see me.'

'Well, perhaps you'll see him afterwards.'

'You're the one he'll notice, just like my sister was always noticed. Isn't there some boy you like?'

Joyce didn't speak for several seconds, and then in a quiet almost distant voice she said, 'There aren't any boys, Nancy, there won't be any for a long long time.'

'How do you know?'

'I know my father. Heavens, it's starting to rain. I'll see you in the morning, Nancy.'

The next moment she was darting across the road and Nancy took to her heels and ran though the sudden shower of hail.

Chapter Nine

The people living closest to the Mellors debated among themselves if they should call on their new neighbours, having learned from Edith that Mrs Mellor was a shy, retiring woman who kept herself to herself, even though many of them had met her daughter and found her quite delightful.

Mrs Gantry however was not to be put off, and consequently the week after the Mellors moved in she announced her intention of calling on Mrs Mellor in the company of her daughter Grace.

Edith announced their arrival and did not miss the look of alarm on Mrs Mellor's face as she said quickly, 'Who are they, Edith? I don't know anybody round here.'

'They live in the house next to the church, a widow lady and her daughter. I think they've just called out of politeness. It would be nice for you to get to know your neighbours.'

'They were friends of Mrs Prothero then?'

'Well yes, Mrs Prothero knew everybody, she was a very sociable lady.'

By this time Mrs Mellor was smoothing her hair and looking anxiously in the mirror, then with a nervous smile she said, 'Ask them to come in, Edith. I suppose I should offer them tea.'

'That's up to you, ma'am. If ye don't want them to stay ye can allus say you were goin' out.'

'Yes, I suppose so.'

They were invited to sit down and neither Edith nor her employer missed Mrs Gantry's astonishment at the sight of the grand piano. Edith decided it had been a mistake not to have taken them into the morning room.

Grace was the first to break the ice by saying, 'Are you settling in, Mrs Mellor? The first few weeks are sure to be dreadful.'

'Yes I think so. Joyce has started school and is happy there.'

'It's a lovely town. Of course nothing looks quite so nice in winter, but come spring you'll see how pretty it can be.'

'Yes of course.'

'You'll find a lot to do here, Mrs Mellor. The church organises so many things, and the schools. Concerts and the like, then there's the longest day. I'm sure you've heard about that.'

'The longest day? No, what is that?'

'Something that is celebrated here for some reason nobody's quite sure about. By the time it comes around you'll feel you've never lived anywhere else.'

Mrs Mellor permitted herself a bleak smile and Mrs Gantry said, 'It's plain to see you have a musician in the family – your husband I believe.'

'My husband and my daughter.'

'They'll be made very welcome, particularly your daughter for the school concerts.'

Mrs Mellor smiled again, and looked up with relief as Edith arrived carrying the tea tray.

As Grace assisted her at the small table Mrs Gantry said, 'Grace was musical. Her father and I always hoped she'd do something with her music but she was more interested in other things.'

'I wasn't very good, Mother. I would never have made a pianist.'

'Rubbish, you never practised. You were always at the

tennis club or with those friends from the Old Girls' Society.'

Grace decided to say nothing more and hoped fervently that her mother wouldn't labour the subject. She was relieved when Mrs Mellor said quietly, 'Joyce has settled down well at the school. I'm so pleased about that.'

'Your husband works in London, I believe,' Mrs Gantry said. 'A musician, isn't he?'

'Yes.'

'So he's still in London?'

'Yes. I'm not sure when he'll be joining us.'

Edith came in to collect the tea tray and Mrs Mellor's discomfort was not lost on her. Conversation and long silences had been difficult, and Grace said brightly, 'Well, Mother, perhaps we should get off now. It's Tuesday, you know, my bridge day.'

'And of course that has to come before anything else,' her mother snapped. 'Do you play bridge, Mrs Mellor?'

'No, I'm afraid not.'

'Perhaps it's as well, or Mrs Robson and the others would have been roping you in when one or other of them can't play.'

By this time Grace had helped her mother to her feet and a relieved Mrs Mellor smiled, thanked them for visiting and hoped to see them again.

Edith saw them out, and as they walked down the drive she smiled grimly as she heard Mrs Gantry say, 'She's not much to say for herself, has she. Hardly likely to shed much lustre on the life of the community.'

Back in the kitchen Mrs Mellor said, 'The young lady seemed very nice; it was kind of them to call.'

'Yes. I'll get off home now, Mrs Mellor. Me sister's wantin' me to go shopping with her this afternoon and I think I've finished here.'

'Oh yes, Edith, thank you. I'll see you in the morning.'

Margaret Mellor was glad to have the house to herself. In London she'd had a daily woman who had got on with her work, had had no conversation and they'd had no neighbours to speak of – at least, no neighbours who found it necessary to call on them.

She didn't really need Edith. She'd nothing else to do so why couldn't she have done all the housework herself? Why had her sister-in-law deemed it necessary to think they should employ Edith? Here she was with nothing to do for the rest of the afternoon. She could go to the library and change one of the books Joyce had brought home for her but she didn't want to meet any of her neighbours. She didn't know them, she didn't want to know them and she felt sure they would all be as intrusive as Mrs Gantry.

She decided to polish the brasses. Edith had already done them but in damp December the lustre would soon wear off.

Although Joyce would come home in raptures about the school concert and her role in it, Margaret was worried that Arthur wouldn't like it. He'd said they mustn't talk to anybody about the future he'd planned for his daughter – it would be years before she'd be ready to face the world as a concert pianist, and until then she had to practise, so no boys, no parties, no outside disruptions of any sort. Now here she was already playing at the school concert before people they didn't know.

Arthur had said he was unlikely to be home for Christmas as the orchestra was playing here there and everywhere. When they next saw him he'd have resigned and would be ready to devote himself entirely to his daughter's future.

As she rubbed her brass ornaments they became the pivot of all her frustrations until she sat back exhausted by her efforts.

Further up the road another woman was setting out her frustrations in front of her equally anxious husband.

'David, I'm getting absolutely nowhere about Oliver's arrival for the dance next Friday. I've asked her time and

85

again if she's heard definitely from him but all I get is "Stop worrying, Mother. Of course he's coming, so stop worrying about the food, we'll probably want to eat out anyway."'

Voicing her anxieties to her younger daughter she was met with Nancy's uncompromising stare and the words, 'He won't come, Mother. I'm sure he won't.'

Janet had prepared the spare bedroom, arranged a set of menus, and hoped she'd included the favourite foods Erica had told her he liked. Now all she wanted to know was when he hoped to arrive and if it was definite that he was coming.

Erica had spoken to him on the telephone but he'd said he was under a lot of pressure at the office and was also busy helping his aunt settle in. He'd be in touch nearer the weekend. She had to be content with that and each morning she rushed to retrieve the morning mail, scanning it anxiously before laying it on the hall table. She was so sure he would come, but as the days passed her anxiety grew and when she tried to telephone him there was no answer.

On the Friday morning the post had not arrived when it was time for her to leave for the college; later in the morning her mother looked at the envelope addressed to her daughter with some misgiving. She wanted to open it but had no faith that its contents contained the news that Erica wanted, so she had to wait until the afternoon when Erica snatched it out of her hand and ran immediately up to her room.

She sat on the edge of her bed staring down at it. There was no need for a letter if he intended to come, and even as she opened it she knew what it contained.

He was sorrowful and bitterly disappointed, but he was being sent abroad at short notice and there was absolutely nothing he could do about it. Hadn't he always said this might happen? He would think about her, never forget her

86

and hope that one day in the not-too-distant future they might meet again.

She didn't believe a word of it and moments later she laid it on the table in front of her mother, who didn't believe it either.

When her father read the letter he said dryly, 'He's encouraged his aunt to sell her house and move to London, and now he's going abroad – either he's let his aunt down very badly or it's all a pack of lies.'

They had expected tears from Erica and were singularly unprepared for her cold hard expression worthy of the face of a woman twice her age. It would seem that overnight Erica had become old and bitter. Her mother said anxiously, 'He has apologised for any trouble he's put us through darling, that's big of him.'

When Erica didn't answer her mother went on quickly, 'You'll go to the dance, darling. You know so many people there, you have girlfriends and you'll have a wonderful time. After all, Erica, you've always been popular so you don't really need Oliver Denton to take you. Your father will run you to the Trocadero and call for you when the dance is over.'

'I'll get a taxi, Mother, and share with some of the others.'

'Well, if you're sure, dear, I'll help you to get ready. Are you absolutely sure about the taxi home?'

'Yes of course. Don't fuss, Mother.'

Erica had only been at the dance for just over an hour when she realised that it had been a mistake to come.

The old Erica had always been the girl everybody envied for her beauty, her prowess on the dance floor and her escort, but not tonight. Tonight she didn't have an escort, and although her dress was beautiful that once enchanting face seemed cold and hard. The boys who had once fantasised over having the courage to ask her out had moved on to other girls less intimidating.

87

The girls were surprised that she was alone, that the man she had drooled over for months, the man they'd expected her to be with, was not there; and boys who at one time would have longed to dance with her were now showing off their current girlfriends.

In the ladies' cloakroom one girl decided to ask why she was alone, and with a shrug of her shoulders Erica said coldly, 'He's had to go abroad. He did warn me this could happen.'

'Oh dear, and at the last minute too.'

'Yes, these things happen.'

'So you may not see him again.'

'I don't know.'

Word got round quickly, and although some of the girls felt sorry for her, others thought it served her right. The boys did not ask her to dance and long before supper Erica wanted to go home. She waited until the dancing had started again then ran upstairs to the cloakroom to collect her coat.

She hung about the stairs until she felt she could leave unobserved, then flew out of the building into the damp misery of the night. It was half-past ten, too early to go home and admit to her parents that the dance had been a disaster, and in any case the taxi rank was empty.

She found a scarf in her coat pocket which she put over her head, but she was soon aware that the hem of her dress was damp and her satin shoes were wet through. She didn't want to meet anybody who might recognise her, so she walked quickly towards the river, taking the steps that led down from the bridge to the path below.

The river seemed weird and eerie under the lamps along the path and was unusually high for early December. The cold damp mist swirled round her and she paused at the river bank to look across the expanse of water towards the weir. The swirl of the water had a strange hypnotic effect on her and she allowed her misery to wash over her as insidiously as the puddles drenching her feet.

She thought about the girl who had thrown herself over

88

the bridge and who all the town had talked about a few years ago, a girl from another part of town. A girl some married man had been seeing, it was said, a girl who was pregnant – all the people in the neighbourhood had said what a terrible waste it had been.

Erica and her friends had talked about it and decided such a fate would never be for any one of them. No man would ever use them in that way, but now as she stood in the damp swirling mist she understood that girl. She knew what it was like to be forsaken and she took another unwitting step towards the river.

Across from the river Mrs Edgebaston was leaving her front door in the company of a man who said solicitously, 'It's a cold damp night, Anthea. I hope you're not intending to walk too far.'

'No, but Benjie has to go out, so you get off, Nigel. I'll see you when you're next in St Agnes.'

He kissed her on both cheeks and she walked towards the gate while he went to his car, but then he turned and hurried after her. 'I'm coming with you, Anthea. I don't want you walking alone on such a night, you don't know who's lurking about.'

'Oh Nigel, I do this walk most nights. I never meet a soul.'

'Well I'll keep you company. Where is it to be?'

'The top road from the bridge is the path I usually take.'

The Yorkshire terrier was not too happy to be out on such a night and walked with his ears laid back making Anthea laugh. 'He's not enjoying himself; we'll just walk to the next lamp then we'll go back. You should be getting off, Nigel.'

As they walked along the road she looked down to where the river swirled against the reeds, then paused in surprise at the sight of a figure standing too close to the water's edge, a female figure with a gleam of satin under the short jacket she was wearing.

They watched for a moment before walking on but Anthea

was strangely troubled. Anxiously she said, 'Nigel, I have to go back. Just hang on to Benjie, I'll not be a moment.'

She hurried back until she reached the steps leading down to the path below, careful not to fall as they were slippery from the damp, and stepped onto the path with some relief. Then she recognised the girl standing as if in a dream staring down into the river's dark depths.

Softly, trying not to startle the girl, she called out, 'Erica, what are you doing here in all this mist.'

Erica looked at her uncomprehendingly, like a sleep-walker. Anthea went to her and took hold of her arm.

'Come along with me, we're going back to the house to have a cup of coffee. Why aren't you at the dance?'

Erica didn't answer. By now they were walking along the path and up the steps towards where Nigel waited with the dog.

'Everything all right?' he asked softly.

'Yes, we're going back to the house for coffee.'

He looked in some amazement at Erica's soaked dress and shoes, but a brief glance from Anthea warned him to ask no questions.

Once in the house she told Erica to sit in front of the fire, and said she would find a dressing gown for her to wear while her dress dried out. Out in the kitchen she said to Nigel, 'Something's gone wrong, perhaps she'll tell me, perhaps not, but in any case she's in no fit state to go home yet.'

'Do you know her?'

'Yes, Erica Clarkson, they live across the road.'

'She's obviously upset about something, probably some boy or other.'

She smiled cynically. 'You've obviously deduced that, Nigel. You get off now, I'll see you when you're next in the area.'

'You can cope?'

'Of course I can cope. What could you do anyway?'

Erica was sitting where she had left her, in front of the

90

fire, shivering in her damp coat. Anthea said sharply, 'I've brought you a dressing gown, Erica. Get undressed while I make coffee.' But Erica continued to sit staring into the fire so she went to pull her to her feet.

'Erica, you can't go home looking like this. You need to pull yourself together. We'll talk and you'll find I'm a very good listener – I have been told I'm blessed with a great deal of common sense.'

Wrapped up at last in Anthea's dressing gown some semblance of warmth seemed to permeate through the damp chill of her body.

Chapter Ten

Anthea had listened to it all, the disappointments and the bitterness, the evening's disaster when nobody had asked her to dance, when the boys had snubbed her and the girls had gloated, the preparations her mother had made for a man who hadn't come, and the last-minute excuses she hadn't believed in. In the end they simply stared at one another in silence until Anthea said, 'Do you feel a lot better for having told me?'

'I don't know. It's always going to be like this, I'll never want to go to another dance and I'll never see him again.'

'Do you want to see him again?'

'I was in love with him.'

'Yes, before he let you down so badly, but do you love him now?'

'I don't know.'

'So many girls have this sort of thing happen to them, boys too. It comes with growing up. There'll be other boys, other dances, perhaps in the end disappointments can be good for you, they help you understand more, be a better person.'

Erica stared at her before saying, 'Did it ever happen to you?'

'You think it couldn't have happened to me?'

'Well, you're always so assured, so confident. You always have a lot of men friends, so can't possibly know what it's like to feel as wretched as I feel.'

'I can promise you, Erica that one day, perhaps one day soon, you'll be able to smile about your memories of tonight. Ask yourself this, my dear: did you never let some boy down? Were you always kind and generous to some boy who really cared about you?'

She was rewarded by seeing the blood colour Erica's cheeks and how quickly she averted her eyes.

That beautiful, spoilt Erica had hurt a good few boys and girls as she had shown off her popularity and acumen, and never in a million years would she have expected that one day some man would do it to her.

Erica didn't want to think about the hurts she might have inflicted, and Anthea was glad. She didn't want to think or talk about things she had spent the last twenty years forgetting. She'd moved on, and now it was time for the girl sitting opposite her to do the same thing.

In an endeavour to change the subject she said, 'You'll be leaving college at Christmas, Erica. I believe you're going to work for your father's firm.'

Erica's eyes opened in dismay, she'd forgotten it would be so soon and suddenly she didn't want to work for her father – same old town, same people, same to and from the office with her father, no new people. She said quickly, 'I don't know what I'm going to do yet. I think I might want to get away from St Agnes and into something new.'

'I'm sorry, I understood from your mother that that's what you would be doing.'

'Yes, it's what they want, but it's not what I want, not any more.'

'Not after tonight, do you mean?'

'I suppose so.'

Before tonight she had been going to work for her father until she married Oliver and moved to London, now there would be no London and no Oliver, and there'd be no more working in some boring solicitor's office either. Anthea Edgebaston read the signs well.

The girl was looking at her for some sort of understanding

that she might agree with her desire to free herself of familiar things. It was the moment when Anthea might have talked about herself but she let it pass.

Instead she said, 'I must see if your shoes and dress have dried out. It will be terribly stained, Erica. Will your parents be waiting up for you?'

'I suppose so, but I don't want to talk to them tonight. They'll want to talk about the dance, whether I had a good time or not, and I don't want to talk about it to them ever.'

The shoes and the dress were dry but there were green stains round the hem of the dress and tears welled into Erica's eyes as she remembered how beautiful she had looked earlier in the evening.

The dress had been expensive and had been meant to make every girl at the dance envious of her attire and her partner. Now all the talk would be of her having no partner and being the wallflower of the evening.

'I'll walk home with you,' Anthea said. 'It's still raining, I'm afraid, but it isn't far.'

'You don't need to walk home with me, Mrs Edgebaston. You've been very kind, but please, you won't say anything about tonight to my mother, will you?'

'Of course not. It's our secret, Erica, and forget Oliver Denton, he really isn't important any more. Relegate him to the past where he belongs.'

Erica looked at her with wide tear-filled eyes before she said, 'You'd never have made mistakes like I've made, you're always so confident. I'm going to be like you – a lot of men friends and none of them too important.'

Anthea smiled. She was well aware that this was how everybody saw her – overconfident, unconcerned by public opinion, morally unsound and obviously rich. It would have been so easy to enlighten Erica Clarkson so that she could pass it on to her mother, and to the rest of her neighbours, but Anthea's past was not something she wanted to talk about to anybody.

She had seen Erica looking curiously at a range of

94

photographs on the mantelpiece and at one in particular of
a plain girl with straight fair hair and wearing spectacles.
But Erica had asked no questions – she had been too
absorbed with her own misery.

Now Anthea picked up the photograph and stared down
at it. She'd been seventeen when it was taken. Since then
she'd made herself indifferent to those early years, telling
herself that they no longer mattered, that they were unim-
portant. But somehow tonight another girl's misery brought
the past back all too poignantly.

Her grandmother had liked her to dress in shirt blouses and
dark skirts, with straight, unattractive hairstyles and
wearing the glasses she'd hated. Her grandmother had been
so afraid that she would grow up like her mother, but
Anthea couldn't remember her mother who had disappeared
out of their lives when she had been two years old. Her
beautiful mercurial mother, who hated her humble background in the small North of England town, hated her
respectable dull parents and the man who had abandoned
her when she told him she was pregnant. She was just
sixteen.

Anthea had grown up thinking that her grandmother was
her mother, and she hadn't thought fit to enlighten her until
she asked permission to attend her first dance in the village
hall. Rules were laid down. She had to promise to be home
no later than ten-thirty, and when Anthea objected that the
dance wasn't over until twelve o'clock, her grandmother
had made her sit down and listen to what she had to say.

She had sat wide-eyed and disbelieving, that the women
she called Mother was in fact her grandmother, and that her
mother had been a wilful stupid girl who had become pregnant at sixteen by a man she had met at one such dance.
There would be no repetition of that disaster.

All Anthea could think about was that her mother had not
wanted her, had seen fit to abandon her and that everybody
in the town must know about her.

95

She attended the dance and was home by ten-thirty, but it was the last dance she ever went to. Instead she attended evening classes for shorthand and typing, and while most of the girls she knew went to work in the mills, she set her sights on office work.

Whereas her grandmother was proud of her, her grandfather was a dim, shady figure who paid her little attention and was content with a life centred round his allotment and his darts matches in the local pub.

When Anthea stated her intention of applying for a job at one of the large mills in the nearest big town her grandmother didn't think it was a good idea.

'You'll have to go in by train, which'll cost a lot and it'll be late by the time you get home in the evening. I think ye should stay local. I don't like the idea of ye workin' in some big place.'

Her words had little effect on Anthea. She had managed to save a little money which she spent on business-like attire, and although her grandmother looked at her with jaundiced criticism, she couldn't really compare her with her pretty mother with her frilly dresses and powdered face.

The Edgebaston family owned three of the largest mills in Sleaton and Anthea found a junior position in one of them. The pay wasn't great and travelling took a great deal of it, but she listened and she learned, and the efficient, quiet girl who worked on the switchboard in the general office soon came to the attention of the Sales Director who thought he had a place for her in his secretarial section.

With her new job came an increase in salary but none of her colleagues thought they had anything to fear from the quiet, unobtrusive young woman who had no interest in any of the men and attended to her duties efficiently and quietly.

She decided she wouldn't attend the office party that Christmas and when she said as much to one of the other girls she was told, 'But it's the highlight of the year,

Anthea. Everybody goes. The boss will be surprised if you don't turn up.'

'Well, I live out of town, so it isn't really convenient.'

'You can stay with me that evening. My mother won't mind. Surely you can do that.'

Her grandmother wasn't sure that it was a good idea, but Anthea merely said, 'I don't want to be the only one not there, Grandmother, and Molly Peters is really a very nice girl. I don't want to offend her.'

Anthea knew what they would all expect to see – a young woman in something circumspect, dark and probably unflattering. Perhaps it was time at last for her to emerge from her shell.

She spent a great deal of her savings on a blue crêpe-de-chine gown, exquisitely cut to fit her good figure.

The mere fact that Molly Peters stared at her in amazement reassured her that this was the new Anthea – when they arrived at the venue for the party the looks and whispering really started.

Most of the girls had boyfriends on the staff so Anthea found herself sitting with the older members, most of them talking shop and none of them interested in dancing.

She was bored, tried to think of a reason to leave and wished she still had the money she'd spent on the dress. The Sales Director's wife was feeling rather sorry for her and leaning forward asked, 'Haven't you worked very long for the firm?'

'No, since the summer.'

'I remember my husband telling me he had a new girl on the staff. So you don't really know any of the directors?'

'No.'

'Oh well, there they are on the top table. Mr John Edgebaston is the Managing Director, the owner you might say, then there is Mr Ernest and Mr Godfrey, his two brothers, and Mr Ernest's son Colin. I'm not sure about the two ladies, which one belongs to which gentleman, you know.'

97

Anthea smiled, looked more closely at the people on the top table and found that the younger man was looking at her with a half smile on his face. The next moment he had crossed the floor and was inviting her to dance.

She was aware that all around her the conversation had momentarily stopped as Colin Edgebaston guided her expertly around the dance floor.

That had been the start of it. Intimate dinners and drives into the country in his open sports car soon followed. Everybody knew about it – the girls envious, the men cautious. They didn't particularly like Colin Edgebaston, who was considered conceited and flirtatious. They thought it highly unlikely that he would be serious about a young member of staff and were not afraid to say so. Most of the girls hoped they were right, but Anthea didn't believe any of it.

Her grandmother didn't like the young man who would arrive at the garden gate in his rakish car, blow the horn, but never come up the path – and her warnings too went ignored.

For the next twelve months Anthea believed she was in love and that Colin was in love with her, then came the next office party and he seemed strangely diffident. She thought he would invite her to sit with him, that they would be together, but he simply said the family had invited guests, directors of one of the other mills in the town, and of course it would be expected that he would sit with them.

She bought another dress, more sophisticated than the last one, and once again Molly Peters invited her to spend the night. As they got ready for the party Molly said, 'Will you be with Colin Edgebaston, Anthea, or will you be sitting with us?'

Anthea explained the situation, aware of the doubts in Molly's eyes, and found herself asking, 'Do you think there's something wrong in that, Molly?'

'Well, there's talk.'

'What sort of talk?'

'Oh, it's probably nothing. Bob Marley works for the Jenkinsons and said Colin Edgebaston was friendly with Angela Jenkinson.'

'If he was he can't have seen very much of her recently as he's been with me.'

Molly deemed it wiser to say no more but when they sat down to dinner Anthea was aware of those sitting at the top table and that beside Colin sat a dark-haired girl, sophisticated and very pretty.

The people sitting near her were quick to inform her that the girl was Angela Jenkinson, and as the evening progressed she sat staring in front of her while Colin opened the dancing with Miss Jenkinson as his partner.

He danced a great many times with Angela Jenkinson while Anthea danced with a few of the young men she worked with. She felt that they were sorry for her as Colin was behaving like a cad and she was unhappy. She even wished she could go home but Molly was having a good time and she couldn't leave without her.

It was very late in the evening when Colin finally invited her to dance with him, which they did in silence as she had nothing to say to him.

It was almost eleven o'clock when Mr Ernest stood to his feet and knocked loudly on the table in front of him. He thanked everybody for being there, spoke warmly of the loyalty of the workforce and for the successful year the firm had enjoyed, then said he had a very happy announcement to make – the engagement of his son Colin to Miss Angela Jenkinson, which would bring together the town's most successful and distinguished business enterprises.

After the applause Anthea was only aware that people were not looking at her, but chattering amongst themselves, although some of the younger element stared at her in disbelief.

They wanted her to burst into tears, scream with rage, anything except this stony-faced calm which tried to say

99

that she didn't care, but to more discerning company could only mean that she cared too much.

In the weeks that followed whenever she met Colin in the office corridors, she ignored him and he looked away in embarrassed silence.

She felt utterly wretched and betrayed, the face she showed to the world giving no indication of the misery she felt inside. But time changed many things, it made her harder, it made her fiercely ambitious and she gave herself up exclusively to moving onward and upward.

There were no more men in her life even though a great many tried to take Colin Edgebaston's place. She was polite to them, a good friend, listening to their insecurities but telling them little of her own. In the end she was put forward as assistant secretary to John Edgebaston himself, and when his secretary became pregnant and left the firm she was offered her job.

She became the rock on whom John Edgebaston leaned. He liked this girl with her quiet charm and her business acumen, and because of her closeness to him she quickly became a power to be reckoned with.

Now she sat with the directors at the office party, and although she found it easy to ignore Colin with his new wife, she found she could be pleasant to Angela now that the hurt had gone.

John Edgebaston was a bachelor with no intention of marrying anybody. He was incredibly rich and had two brothers with children who desperately hoped he would never marry so that his money would be equally divided between them. They did not approve of his dependence on his secretary and thought her too ambitious by half, but there was nothing they could do about it.

When he was forty-nine John Edgebaston decided to think about semi-retirement. He would still be the figure-head, but there were other things he wanted to do with his life outside the mills – he would travel more, play more golf, spend some of his money instead of ploughing it all back into the business – and get married.

Marriage was not something he had contemplated, although from time to time there had been women in his life, none of whom he had wanted to marry. Now for the first time he found himself rapt in admiration for his efficient and attractive secretary, whilst knowing all about his nephew's treatment of her.

Some people were astonished, some were intrigued, members of his family were chagrined, but John Edgebaston and Anthea were married in early spring and immediately set off on their travels – America and the Far East, South Africa and Europe – then Anthea was entrusted with the renovation of the vast house in Sleaton.

From its dour bachelor appearance she turned it into a house people came to marvel at and enjoy the garden parties they indulged in, while the rest of the Edgebaston family began to wonder if there would be any money left for them.

Chapter Eleven

Anthea laid the photograph back on the mantelpiece and picked up another one which she looked at with a tender smile on her face. It was the portrait of a man with a kind pleasant face framed by silver hair. Searching grey eyes looked at her from under straight brows and her own eyes became misted with tears.

She had not been in love with John Edgebaston but she had loved him dearly and deeply until he died at the age of sixty.

Twelve years was all they had but they had been happy years – then had come the years of wrangling with his family over the mills, the house and the money.

John had envisaged that this would happen, and his will had been concise and unalterable. His private fortune and the house would go to Anthea, who would also be paid an income from the business. Any interest he had had in the mills would be equally divided between his two brothers. This hadn't been enough for them, but this too John had envisaged so his will instructed his solicitor, Nigel Hague, and his accountant, Gordon Stedman, to take charge of all his wife's affairs.

In Sleaton Anthea was portrayed as the devious scheming wife who had robbed the family unmercifully, and even Anthea's grandmother saw fit to distance herself.

She wished she could have loved her grandmother more.

She had brought her up, fed and clothed her, but the love that should have been there had always been strangely absent. When Anthea wished to buy them a small bungalow on the coast, something they had always wanted, her grandmother had said scathingly, 'Ye married him for his money, Anthea. A young woman in her twenties and a man goin' on fifty, ye were as bad as yer mother. We don't want anythin' from ye. It's bad money, that's what it is.'

So for the next few years Anthea travelled the world. She took long cruises on exotic liners, spending time in Madeira and Egypt, the Greek Islands and Italy, but whenever she returned to Sleaton the family were always waiting for her with their usual venom, having made sure that the rest of the town's community were made aware of what she had done to them.

She had two good friends, Gordon Stedman and Nigel Hague. Gordon was a widower and Nigel a bachelor, and between them they offered Anthea advice that she should think of moving away, either abroad or elsewhere in England. It was Nigel who had told her about the property in St Agnes.

'But I won't know anybody,' she'd objected. 'I've never been there – at least on a cruise ship I can make friends.'

'But you have no roots, Anthea,' Nigel protested. 'At least with your own home you could take an interest in the town and make new friends you could spend years with.'

'I have a home here, Nigel, and no friends.'

'Nor will you have if the family have anything to do with it.'

'Why do the people here believe everything they say?'

'Because most of them are employed at the mills – it's their bread and butter, my dear.'

'Oh Nigel, I don't know. Perhaps I should take a look at St Agnes.'

So she went with Nigel and again with Gordon, and liked what she saw. The house she looked at would have fitted

103

into a small corner of the one at Sleaton, but what did she want with a house that size anyway?

As they drove around St Agnes she was intrigued by the Commodore in pristine white flannels hoisting his flag in the garden of his house, by the dapper figure of the Major marching with some of his cadets, and by the sight of young men and girls boating on the river. They had afternoon tea in the gardens of Rowandale Hall where Anthea said with some surprise, 'The place seems alive with visitors, is it something special, Nigel?'

'It's the longest day, my dear.'

'Well, I know it is, but what's the relevance?'

'Nobody seems to know, but apparently it's been observed here for centuries. Some time way back something must have happened here to warrant it continuing to be celebrated.'

'I liked the house, but will the people round here like me, do you think?'

'Why wouldn't they. Anthea, that house is far too big for you, and they'll never leave you alone. Are you thinking that John would have minded you moving out?'

'Perhaps a little.'

'He would have hated what his family are doing to you.'

'I know. Perhaps I'll sleep on it for a while.'

'By which time the house could have gone.'

'Then I wouldn't have been meant to have it.'

'Not as simple as that, Anthea. Look, you're a rich woman. If you don't like it here you'll still have your cruise ships, your holidays abroad, but it's my bet you will like it here. I'll come and visit and so will Nigel – it'll give the neighbours something to talk about.'

'And that's before I've even moved in.'

'Come on, let's take another look at the house, then if you like it we can see the estate agent tomorrow.'

She had given the family one last reason to hate her and that had been the house. She didn't want any one of them to have it, and John wouldn't have wanted them to have it either, so instead she gave it to Sleaton as a place to hold art exhibitions, musical concerts, wedding functions and so on. The house would earn money for the town, and the gardens would be kept in good repair and remain an asset to be admired.

The evening she faced John's two brothers and their wives, Colin looked at everybody in the room except her.

They accused her of treachery, that the house should have been offered to one of them, that they were his brothers, that one day Colin would be the master. Colin was the new generation, the one who had every right to say what should happen to the house.

She had looked round the table with calm unwavering eyes, then she looked directly at Colin saying, 'I was John's wife, the house was left to me to do what I liked with it and it is my wish that the town should have it.'

When at last Colin looked at her she said quietly, 'I had thought I would enjoy this moment but strangely enough I am not feeling any pleasure. Yet I feel I am doing the right thing. If the town have this house they will remember John Edgebaston as a benefactor, a man who gave employment to half the town and left them something to enjoy and remember him by. Now, if you will excuse me I am very busy so there is nothing more to say.'

She had watched them leaving from her bedroom. They were angry, that much was apparent by the way they stormed across the drive to their cars, and as Colin held the car door open for his wife he looked up into her eyes. His face was dark with anger, an anger that years before would have caused her terrible pain; now she felt nothing, not even the satisfaction of revenge.

She put her husband's portrait back on the mantelpiece and, looking at the clock, saw that it was after two o'clock and the fire had died low. She went to the window and looked across the road to where the Clarksons' house stood in darkness and thought that in the days to come their lives too

105

could be irreparably changed. Perhaps Erica would regret having talked to her, after all she was a bit of a mystery to half the population, but she had no doubt that in the days to come she would learn more about the future of Erica Clarkson.

Although the lights were out one member of the family was still wide awake. All night Erica had tossed and turned as memories of the dance came to plague her, and more and more she came to the conclusion that she would move away from St Agnes and the neighbourhood. She would not go to work in her father's office where she knew everybody and where they all knew her.

She'd soon find out how well she'd done in her exams – there were other offices, other jobs. Milly Johnson had gone to work in the office of a large group of manufacturing chemists where they had a sports club and a rugby team. They played tennis and in the winter they held dances there. Milly had said there were more young men than they knew what to do with, young men from the city, and Milly had moved in with three other girls in a fairly big house turned into flats.

She'd liked Mrs Edgebaston. She'd always thought her smart and attractive, she knew how to dress, and she'd been very kind – perhaps one day she'd talk to her again when she'd made up her mind what she was going to do.

Talk of the dance was a nine-day wonder, but Erica was aware that it had been talked about wherever there were girls who had once envied her, girls who perhaps she hadn't been very nice to.

Her mother received sympathetic glances from Hilda Marks, and at her bridge afternoons she felt sure the dance, Oliver Denton and her daughter's disastrous love affair would be the sole topic of conversation.

Erica had said little to the family, who were more concerned with her decision not to work at her father's office and intention to seek employment elsewhere.

David had told Janet to leave matters alone – either Erica

106

would come to her senses or they would have to accept it. She was nineteen, determined to go her own way and in the end there would be little they could do about it.

Other matters took the place of the dance, and now the town was talking about the concert at the girls' school where Joyce Mellor was to be the main event of the evening.

The concert was on for two nights, the first evening for parents, the second for guests. The Clarksons went to both and as Erica sat between her parents she could only think about those times when she had been the star of the evening.

Now there was quiet in the vast hall while Joyce took her place at the piano. From the choir sitting above the stage Nancy Clarkson looked to where Julian Watson sat with his parents.

They had spoken briefly in the early part of the evening. He had also been introduced to Joyce but as yet hadn't heard her play. Nancy felt very sure that when he did he would be so filled with admiration she wouldn't stand a chance.

Joyce played Chopin nocturnes and waltzes, and then with the girls' orchestra and the choir sang 'Jerusalem', the song which always closed the concert.

The applause was overwhelming, everybody congratulated the headmistress and the music master that it had been one of the best concerts ever, and as Nancy looked along the centre aisle she was aware that Julian was looking down at Joyce Mellor with considerable interest.

Erica smiled and agreed with everybody that the concert had been wonderful. They had a new star and she'd soon be forgotten – even more quickly when she moved away, she thought to herself.

Joyce joined her mother who had been sitting next to the music master, and noticed the tears in her eyes.

'Did you enjoy it, Mother?' she asked anxiously.

'Yes Joyce, very much. Are we ready to go home now?'

107

The music master was quick to say, 'But surely you'll stay for refreshments, Mrs Mellor. I can assure you they're excellent and as you're new to these parts people will want to meet you and congratulate your daughter.'

'Thank you, Mr Catlow, you're very kind but I do think we should be getting off home. I've so much to do before Christmas.'

He didn't try to persuade her. She'd been rather heavy going throughout the evening, and he had quickly realised that Joyce was nothing like her mother. Joyce was outgoing and friendly, whereas her mother was withdrawn, with little conversation.

A great many people tried to talk to them on their way out but they were all met by Mrs Mellor's swift but shy smile and Joyce's anxious desire to hurry her mother away.

Meeting Mr Catlow in the refreshment hall the headmistress said, 'Aren't Mrs Mellor and her daughter joining us then?'

'No, Mrs Mellor was rather anxious to get off home.'

'But she enjoyed the concert, surely?'

'Oh yes, very much. She's rather a shy person, not much conversation, but she did assure me that she'd enjoyed the evening.'

The headmistress moved on to greet others and Mr Catlow was quickly surrounded by a crowd of people wishing to congratulate him.

Nancy joined her parents where they were chatting to the Commodore and Julian, and, smiling down at her, Julian said, 'Excellent concert, Nancy. You were well and truly tucked away up there in the choir stalls.'

'Yes, well, I'm not much good at anything. It was the only place they could put me.'

'I can't believe that.'

'It's true. But Joyce was marvellous, wasn't she?'

'Yes indeed. It's going to be her profession, I believe.'

'Yes.'

108

Just then Erica joined them and Julian said with a smile, 'Night of nostalgia for you, Erica?'

'I was never a pianist.'

'But you were very good, or people have been lying to me.'

She smiled.

'How is Oliver?'

'I don't know, he's moved away.'

Somewhat uncomfortably Julian said, 'Oh I'm sorry, I didn't know, but then I'm hardly ever here, am I?'

Erica moved away and then she saw Mrs Edgebaston and the man who had been with her that awful night of the dance. Did she really want to speak to them? The man had left them alone and Mrs Edgebaston had been very kind, but she wanted to forget that evening – Mrs Edgebaston was worldly and probably thinking her a bit of an idiot.

Mrs Edgebaston read the signs well – young pride, so easily damaged, so vulnerable. She smiled briefly at Erica and turned away so that Nigel said, 'Wasn't that the girl you took home that wet night, the one you found on the river bank?'

'Yes. I think she wants to forget that evening.'

'Obviously.'

'Do you want another coffee, Nigel, or shall we get off home?'

'I rather wanted to have a quiet word about the house at Sleaton. Colin Edgebaston's got himself on the Council and he's now having too much to say about the letting of the hall for functions.'

'You mean he's suggesting them or turning them down?'

'A little of both, I think. We all know why he's doing it – you've given the hall to the town, but he's on the Council and is wanting to say how it's used.'

'And there is a clause in the deeds, Nigel, to say that I have a say in how it's used and by whom. What exactly is he objecting to?'

'Mrs Silverstone's hundredth birthday party. He says it's

quite ridiculous to hold a private family party at the hall – it is meant for things rather more luxurious and expensive than a gathering of old people.'

'Mrs Silverstone has a very extensive family, and I'm sure she wouldn't have asked for the hall if she couldn't pay for it.'

'Mrs Silverstone has had very little to do with it. Her family have requested it.'

'This is Colin being vindictive, Nigel. What do you think?'

'Well, the Silverstone family are very nice. I think they will be very hurt if they can't have the hall.'

'Then tell them they shall have it. I thought when I moved away, Nigel, that all the bitterness could be put behind me. I didn't want to see any of them or cross swords with a single one of them, not even Colin. Now here we are again just when I'd begun to feel safe.'

'Leave it with me, Anthea. Colin Edgebaston hasn't really got a leg to stand on, but he'll keep trying.'

As they moved into the main hall Erica came towards them, her face flushed and not a little embarrassed. Nigel said quickly, 'I'll look for somewhere to sit, Anthea, then we'll think of something to eat.'

Erica said breathlessly, 'Mrs Edgebaston, I'm so sorry, I should have called to see you. You were so kind to me the other evening.'

'There was really no need, Erica. Everything all right now?'

'Yes. I've told my dad I'm not going to work for him. I don't think he's too happy about it, but I've made up my mind.'

'I'm sure he'll accept it in time. Did you enjoy the concert?'

'Oh yes. Joyce Mellor was marvellous, wasn't she?'

'Yes she was. I hope you and your family have a nice Christmas, Erica.'

'Oh yes, and you too. Thanks again.'

110

Nigel waved to her from across the room where he had found seats, but as she made her way there she was accosted by Hilda Marks who said coyly. 'Lovely concert Mrs Edgebaston, and how lucky you are to have such a charming escort. But then you have more than one, don't you?'

Anthea smiled. 'Variety *is* the spice of life, isn't it, Mrs Marks?' she said softly.

They smiled and moved on, and it was only when she reached Nigel that the annoyance evaporated and her sense of humour reasserted itself.

She looked around the room with interest. The Major was flirting with Lady Jarvis's sister, who was obviously spending Christmas in St Agnes, while Mrs Robson was also obviously irritated by her husband's philandering.

The Vicar was assisting Grace Gantry with the selection of food from the buffet table while her mother sat frowning. That Grace had got her mother there at all was something very unusual.

The Commodore's handsome son was chatting to the Clarksons while Nancy looked up at him with obvious admiration. When he smiled and walked away, she seemed somehow lost.

Anthea Edgebaston had thought St Agnes would be pristine and perhaps boring, but she was beginning to realise that underneath the respectable face it showed to the world there could be the same sort of undercurrents she'd grown up with.

One never really knew what was in store, but no doubt in the months to come one or another of them would surface.

Chapter Twelve

All over breakfast Margaret Mellor had listened to her daughter's enthusiasm for the concert the evening before. She had loved every minute of it, the applause, the acclaim and now she was saying, 'Mother, why didn't you want to stay? Everybody was asking after you, they wanted to meet you.'

'Well, I hadn't done anything, so why would they want to meet me?'

'Because you're my mother, because we're new here.'

'Well dear, I thought I should get home and warm the house up before you came home. I knew you'd want to stay on. Who brought you home?'

'Mr and Mrs Clarkson, Mother. I should have asked them in but I wasn't sure you'd want me to.'

'No dear. It was late and I don't really know them, do I?'

'Mother, you'll never really know them if you don't make an effort.'

'Joyce, you know what your father's like. He prefers us to keep ourselves to ourselves, and he won't want people expecting him to talk about his music or play for them.'

'They were so kind, Mother. He's not going to stop me from playing for them, is he? After all, the music master is talking about the next concert.'

'We'll have to wait and see, dear. He'll be home early in the New Year.'

'Will Aunt Edna be here for Christmas?'

'I'm not sure, did she say?'

'Mr and Mrs Clarkson said we should go round one evening and one or two other people asked if we'd like to visit them. We should go, Mother, or Christmas is going to be so awful with just the two of us.'

'And possibly Aunt Edna, dear.'

'Well yes, but they would include her, surely.'

'Let's just wait and see. I think perhaps I should have a chat with Edith. I'm not sure what she wants to do about Christmas.'

She found Edith sitting at the kitchen table with a letter in her hand and a disturbed look on her face. She quickly folded up the letter and laid it aside as Mrs Mellor said, 'I thought I'd ask about Christmas, Edith. When you'll be able to come to us or if you want some time with your family.'

'Well, it depends on you, Mrs Mellor. Will ye want me here?'

'My sister-in-law might be coming, but my husband isn't until the New Year. Will you think about it and let me know.'

'I'll do that, Mrs Mellor.'

Edith opened the letter again and stared down at it gloomily as Mrs Mellor said hesitantly, 'I hope you haven't had bad news, Edith. You look a little upset.'

'It's from Mrs Prothero. She's not very happy in London and wishin' she was back 'ere. The nephew who wanted her to move there is workin' abroad and there she is not knowin' anybody and feeling lonely. She should never 'ave gone there, and but for 'im she'd still be 'ere.'

'I'm sorry. What does she want you to do?'

'She'd like me to join her but there's no way I'm goin' to London. London's right enough if ye knows it, but I don't. I've never even bin there and besides the flat's only quarter the size of this 'ouse, so she doesn't need a servant.'

113

'I'm sorry, Edith. You'll let me know about Christmas?'

'Yes, I'll talk to me sister.'

Margaret Mellor didn't really care whether Edith spent time with them or not – she wasn't even sure that Arthur would want her working for them at all.

She was glad that Joyce was happy with her new school, glad that she'd found friends, although Joyce didn't realise how quickly their lives would change when her father came home permanently. Arthur was not an easy person to live with.

Margaret had always felt inferior and between them Arthur and his sister Edna had fostered this belief.

She had no musical talent. Being an only child of rather old-fashioned parents she'd led a very sheltered life, until at the age of twenty-seven she'd met Arthur Mellor at a small hotel in Scotland. She was on holiday with her parents, he with his sister. She was just the type of woman he was looking for, somebody who would idolise him because of his talent, his job and his prospects; his sister agreed that she would always be the one to put him first, agree with whatever he suggested and never step out of line.

Edna had long grown tired of being at her brother's beck and call, and wanted her own life. Consequently she encouraged his thoughts of marriage, and Margaret's unworldly parents believed their daughter had captured a young man entirely suitable.

Margaret both loved and hated him. She also feared him. That their one daughter had taken after her father musically made her believe that in this at least she not failed him, but in everything else she believed she had.

Arthur idolised his daughter. She was the one bright spark in his life, a girl who was going to accomplish all the things he'd never been able to. It hadn't been in Arthur Mellor to rise to the top, to be a solo artist, to be the first violin even, and to the other members of the orchestra he was something of a loner, a quiet, remote man.

114

None of them had been surprised when he decided to retire to devote himself to tutoring his daughter. They liked Joyce and wished her well, but in their hearts they had reservations as to whether her father was doing the right thing by her.

Edith went about her work listening to the sound of the piano and later in the day she would inform her sister that the music Joyce played was the only thing that really made her day.

She had listened to Mrs Prothero playing pretty pieces from musical comedies but she recognised that the music she was hearing played now was more classical and far superior. She had heard all about the concert at the girls' school and how Joyce had excelled herself – somehow or other it gave Edith a sort of glamour to be associated with such talent.

Mrs Prothero might hope that she would join her in London but it wasn't to be. She really didn't need to stay at home over Christmas – the Mellors would need her, particularly if the sister-in-law was coming, and besides, she'd most likely hear more about when the master of the house was expected.

Edna Mellor decided to stay at home and attend the last concerts in which her brother would play in the orchestra. In St Agnes her sister-in-law and Joyce heaved sighs of relief.

Christmas was all around them, in the shops and the town market. A large Christmas tree had been erected in the main square and every night it shimmered and gleamed with innumerable fairy lights.

Joyce had listened to her friends chattering about what they hoped to be doing over Christmas, the parties they would go to, the visits they would be paying, the visitors they would be having, so when they asked her what she would be doing she invented all sorts of activities.

Many of them invited her to coffee mornings and afternoon tea parties, and always with the plea that she take her mother along, but Joyce knew that her mother would never go and became good at making excuses.

Her mother was painfully shy and yet when she did make an effort she could be so nice, like with Edith, for example – at first they'd had little to say, now they chatted like old friends.

They spent Christmas Eve listening to the wireless. Her mother said she'd got a very nice book from the library and while she read Joyce looked round the room with something like despair.

All along the road, indeed throughout the town, Christmas trees gleamed in almost every window – while in this room the only sign that it was Christmas was a bowl of holly in the centre of the table. When Joyce had suggested that they buy a small tree from the market her mother had said adamantly that her father would think it was a waste of money since it would only have to be thrown away in the New Year.

Her father didn't like fripperies as he called them; he liked the rooms to be uncluttered and pristine neat. There were times when Joyce wondered what he would have to say about Edith. She liked Edith as she brought an earthy sense of humour into the house and knew everybody and everything that was going on around her.

'We are going to church in the morning, Mother. Nancy says the service will be lovely with all the carols and simply everybody will be there.'

'Oh I don't know, dear, perhaps next year when we'll know more people.'

'Mother, if we don't mix with them we'll never get to know them.'

'I'm sure they'll all be anxious to get back to their homes on Christmas morning, Joyce. They won't want to spend time chatting after the service.'

'I want to go, Mother, it's the only thing we shall be doing all over Christmas. Please Mother, I told Nancy we'd be there.'

'Well, she'll be with her family, won't she?'

'Of course, and I'll be with you. Mother, please, we must be there.'

'They'll all be so fashionable, darling, what shall I wear? I've never been a fashion plate.'

'Mother, you always look very nice. Wear that brown coat with the fur collar, I like you in that.'

So her mother wore the brown coat and hat and Joyce wore the only coat she had that wasn't school uniform. It was beige tweed which she wore with a brown tam-o'-shanter but then she looked pretty in anything, thought her mother as Joyce waited for her at the door.

It seemed most of St Agnes was at the church that morning and the Vicar looked down at his congregation with a warm smile.

Sitting with her parents and Nancy, Erica reflected that this would be the last Christmas she would spend sitting in the family pew singing carols. Next year she'd be away from St Agnes, a high flier sharing a flat with some other successful girls.

Erica had visions of what her future would be like. Her college diplomas had been good, her teachers had told her that she could land a job as secretary in some vast organisation and she'd believed them. Her father was less enthusiastic and reckoned she was in for a period of re-adjustment.

Nancy looked across the aisle to where Julian sat with his parents. He had favoured her with a warm smile, but at that particular moment his eyes were on Joyce and her mother who were being ushered into a pew just in front of them.

The Major's cadets marched sedately along the centre aisle to their usual places above the choir stalls, and the Major himself saluted smartly as they passed the family pew of Sir Robert and Lady Jarvis sitting with Lady Marcia and her young son. As always Lady Marcia was very eye-catching in a rich sable coat and hat and there was great conjecture as to who the man might be sitting

117

next to her. Could he possibly be lined up as her third husband?

Mrs Gantry and Grace sat in the front pew and as the Vicar's wife took her place opposite them Mrs Gantry gave her a friendly smile, then in a whisper she said, 'She looks very nice this morning, Grace. She's the one you should be friendly with, not the Vicar.'

Grace ignored the remark. She'd heard it all the evening before when her mother had accused her of flirting with the Vicar after the get-together in the church hall after the evening service. Mortified, Grace had said she would not attend church in the morning if that was what she was being accused of, and her mother had said, 'And what are they all going to think if you stay away, that there's something going on? Really Grace, all the time he was speaking to you you were simpering away like a schoolgirl. He's a married man – whatever he thought about you at one time is now forgotten by him and should be by you.'

Grace had thought her mother's sentiments unworthy of a reply but there had been an atmosphere between them all morning. She would now find it difficult to behave naturally whenever she met the Vicar and remained silent so that she could hear his wife's rich contralto from across the centre aisle.

He was waiting at the church door to shake hands with his parishioners as they left the church, friendly, charming and with a word for every one of them.

Grace was aware of her mother standing next to her as she stood with her hand clasped in his and was glad to move away so quickly that his eyes followed her curiously. Her mother silently congratulated herself that she had stepped in before matters got any worse.

Walking out of the church with Mrs Clarkson Hilda Marks muttered, 'Who do you suppose the man with Lady Marcia is?'

'I've no idea, a family friend probably.'

'I haven't seen Mrs Edgebaston. Isn't she here?'

118

'Yes, there she is with Mrs Robson. She always looks so smart.'

'Well, I'm not too sure. I always think her hats a bit outré.'

'I think they're lovely, that one particularly.'

Indeed the large black hat with its attractive curve of feathers along the side of her face seemed entirely flattering.

Approaching the Major's wife Hilda Marks said somewhat dourly, 'It would seem Mrs Edgebaston is alone for Christmas – at least there's nobody with her this morning.'

Elspeth was unconcerned about Mrs Edgebaston, but she was worried that her husband was giving her neighbours something to talk about. Why on earth did he find Lady Marcia so engrossing, especially as she appeared to have a man in tow?

Meeting Mrs Edgebaston's calm gaze she said, 'I wonder if he's destined to be the next husband.'

'Who can say.'

'Are you on your own this Christmas, Mrs Edgebaston?' Hilda Marks said coyly.

'Well, I'm surrounded with people at the moment, Mrs Marks, but I like to spend some time alone, it makes a pleasant change.'

Elspeth Robson smiled. Trust Anthea Edgebaston to be a match for anything Hilda might say.

They looked to where Joyce was shepherding her mother towards the doorway and Elspeth said, 'Mrs Mellor seems very shy, they seem to be leaving already.'

'Perhaps I should go too,' Mrs Edgebaston said. 'Enjoy your Christmas.'

'She won't be on her own long,' Hilda said sharply. 'It's my bet one or another of her men friends will be on their way.'

'Why not,' Elspeth said. 'She's a free agent.'

'Like Lady Marcia,' Hilda said sharply. 'Such women are dangerous.'

'Only when men are such fools,' Elspeth answered pointedly.

As other people made their way home Joyce and her mother could hear their laughter, with smiles and good wishes being exchanged.

Joyce said happily, 'People are nice, Mother. Have you enjoyed it?'

'Yes dear, it's been very nice.'

'There's another service on New Year's Eve and on New Year's Day, perhaps we should come.'

'Oh I don't think so, dear, your father will be coming home soon after. There's a lot to do – we have to get ready for him.'

'But Mother, the house is perfect, and we do have Edith.'

'I know dear, I'm not very sure how your father is going to take to that.'

'Well Aunt Edna asked her to stay with us – he never argues with Aunt Edna.'

'Aunt Edna isn't paying her wages, dear.'

'I know, but Father is well paid, you always said so, so did Aunt Edna.'

'Yes he is, but he's always been careful with his money and now when he retires his salary will stop and it'll be a long time before you're earning anything, dear.'

'Mother, don't you think that perhaps Father is expecting too much of me? I know that I'm musical and I love playing the piano, but am I good enough? Suppose he's wrong about me, suppose I don't make the grade after he's devoted so much time and money to me.'

'You mustn't think like that, Joyce. Your father is right, you are going to be good and very famous one day.'

Joyce's face was thoughtful as she entered the house. She had just another year at school surrounded by girls who would go out into the world to work in offices or go to university. They talked already about boyfriends and a future with nice homes and children, but none of that would be for her.

120

Her father had already stressed that she had to forget the things other girls were taking for granted. Not for Joyce an array of boyfriends until the right one came along; not for Joyce the dances and picnics, boating on the river and visits to the cinema and theatres – they would all come later when she was the famous Joyce Mellor the world was waiting to listen to.

Her mother went to bed early that Christmas Day saying that she had a headache.

'Play the piano if you want to, dear, you won't disturb me,' she said, but somehow Joyce didn't want to play the piano; instead she sat curled up on the settee in front of the fire listening to the wireless. The programme was light-hearted nonsense until later in the evening when a young man played classical music and she fell asleep listening to Chopin.

Chapter Thirteen

Joyce was glad to be back at school, listening to the girls talking about all they had done for Christmas, and she found herself inventing pleasures she had read about but never experienced.

Her mother had been irritable and morose for most of the holiday, so much so that even Edith had asked, 'Isn't your mother well, luv, she seems in a bit of a dream these days?'

'She's been having a lot of headaches. I expect she's worried about when Father is coming home.'

'But it'll be soon, won't it?'

'Oh yes, any day now.'

Two days later a taxi arrived at the front door and Edith watched a tall, thin man alighting from it from the kitchen window. His luggage followed, one strange-shaped item of which she surmised contained some musical instrument or other, and together the driver and the tall man she assumed to be Mr Mellor carried everything to the front door.

Edith hurried to open it and found two stony grey eyes looking at her with some surprise as she said, 'Good morning, sir.'

'And who might you be?' he asked her.

'I'm Edith Pinder, I work here.'

'Do you indeed. Since when?'

122

'Since the last thirty-five years, Mr Mellor, and your wife asked me to stay on.'

'My wife?'

'Well, perhaps it were Miss Mellor, sir, yes that's who it were, your sister.'

Edith watched husband and wife greet one another without an embrace – instead he put his arm lightly around her shoulder saying, 'Edith and I have introduced ourselves to each other. You didn't tell me about her, Margaret.'

'No Arthur, Edna asked Edith to stay on with us as she worked for Mrs Prothero and hadn't found a new post.'

'You remember what I've always said about servants. She's not living in, I hope.'

'No, but Edna thought it was a good idea to keep her on.'

All this was said in front of Edith who immediately began to feel that she had no right to be there. She didn't like Mr Mellor, but she'd have a lot to tell her sister when she got home.

She returned to the kitchen and several minutes later Mrs Mellor appeared with an apologetic smile on her face and asking if they could have tea 'and those shortbread biscuits, Edith.' Without answering Edith started to set a tray out. Faced with her grim expression Mrs Mellor said, 'My husband is feeling very tired, Edith. He was playing with the orchestra last night, and then travelling today with all his luggage hasn't improved his temper. I'm sure he didn't mean anything, so please forget it.'

Edith sniffed. Let them think she'd forgotten it by all means, but she wasn't going to take any nonsense from Mr Mellor. Oliver Denton had tried it on and she'd been a match for him.

Back in the drawing room Margaret found him staring down at the piano, picking up a piece of music and studying it carefully. 'Chopin?' he enquired.

'Well yes, dear, for the school concert.'

He raised his eyebrows in disbelief. 'School concert? What have I been missing?'

'Arthur, it was wonderful, everybody was there, two full evenings and everybody enjoyed it so much, the applause was deafening. The school orchestra played, one little girl sang and there was the school choir – when Joyce played everybody thought she was wonderful.'

'Joyce played?'

'Why yes. She played Chopin, which I can recognise, then she played something else. As you know, I'm not really musical, Arthur, although I do enjoy listening to it.'

'If you'd been musical, Margaret, you wouldn't have allowed Joyce to play in some school concert. You know I would never let her play in those concerts in London, she's destined for something better.'

'But Arthur, Joyce was so happy to be there, and what you're talking about is a long way off.'

'And I don't want her to be playing here, there and everywhere. I want her to erupt like a meteor, not a damp squib. I intend to have words with the headmistress and the music master at the school.'

Neither of them had heard the door opening or seen Joyce standing in the doorway, her face filled with concern. She turned away quickly and went into the kitchen where she met Edith's intense gaze and her eyes filled with tears.

As long as she could remember it had been like this – her father's intransigence, her mother's docile acceptance and the long lectures when he'd driven into her the fact that she was not like other girls. She was special, with a unique talent that would thrill the world, a blessed God-given talent denied to others. Her thanks for it would be to work and learn; nothing else was important.

Her mother followed her into the kitchen and, putting her arm round her shoulder, she said gently, 'He's tired, darling, he's had a long journey home and he's giving up so much. It'll be all right, just wait and see.'

Joyce turned away and in a flat empty voice said, 'It's always going to be like this, Mother. Father won't change. For just a few weeks I've been like every other girl, but

124

from now on I'll be different. I'll be old, Mother, old and empty.'

'But in the end, Joyce, you'll be brilliant and they'll be ordinary.'

Joyce shook her head and her mother said, 'Go to him, dear, tell him how nice it is to have him home, tell him about school.'

'About school, Mother, yes I'll tell him about that, but not about the concert.'

After Joyce had gone Edith felt uncomfortable. Mrs Mellor knew she had heard every word but began to set out a tea tray without once looking at her. In desperation Edith said, 'Mr Mellor seemed surprised to see me 'ere, Mrs Mellor. I 'opes I'm not intruding.'

'Well of course not, Edith. We had a full-time daily before, after all.

'If that's what he'd rather 'ave, Mrs Mellor, you only 'ave to say so. I'll never be short of work in this town.'

'Oh Edith, I'm sure it won't come to that.'

No, but it'll change, thought Edith, and not for the better. Edith Pinder was not a particularly intelligent woman but she had a crafty streak in her that most people who knew her recognised. After only a few words with Mr Mellor she had decided that she didn't like him. He was a cold distant man who despised his wife, dominated his daughter and objected to any changes to his home. She began to believe that her days in the Mellor household were numbered.

Joyce's father brought up the subject of the school concert by asking about it.

'What did you play?' he asked her. 'Have they any other talent? Who got you into it?'

On Monday morning Arthur Mellor faced the school's headmistress and music master, and it did not take him long to make his displeasure felt.

125

They had both eulogised over the event but now he was telling them that his daughter would appear in no more such enterprises, that from now on, after school had finished for the day and in school holidays, she would work hard at her music. That would be her life, there would be time for other things later, when she had erupted like a flash of light onto the world's stage.

He did not wait for their comments, but left them abruptly, staring after him with angry astonishment.

'Enterprises indeed,' the music master said. 'Most fathers would have been ecstatic about their daughter's performance and its reception. What kind of man is he?'

The headmistress was thoughtful.

'I think perhaps we should be feeling rather sorry for Joyce Mellor. It may be that she will struggle against the sort of life he has planned for her.'

'He's not going to be a very popular man in the town.'

'I don't think that will trouble him in the slightest, Mr Catlow.'

'Well, I think it's tragic. We had so many things planned for next year and I feel so sorry for the girl.'

'Yes. It could be what she wants, on the other hand I have had a few weeks to study her and have liked what I've seen. She has enjoyed being with the other girls, entering into their games, their conversations, as keenly and enthusiastically as the next one.'

'She's been particularly friendly with Nancy Clarkson and we all know what Nancy's like, don't we? A bit of a tomboy, outspoken and friendly. How will she react if her friend is forced into being something of a recluse?'

'How will the town react when they learn Joyce will appear in no more enterprises, as her father calls them?'

'We must be very discreet, Mr Catlow, and must not give Mr Mellor reason to think that we have discussed his attitude with anybody.'

*

126

Nancy aired her views over the evening meal several days after the school reopened its doors.

'Joyce isn't coming to music lessons any more,' she said, 'she's doing theory instead, and she's not taking part in the concert at Easter.'

'I'm sure she will when the time comes,' her mother said. 'After all it's some time to Easter.'

'But she's told me, Mother, there's to be no more concerts, and she's not doing games.'

'That's odd,' her father said, 'what's wrong with games?'

'She's afraid of injuring her hands – she has to look after them.'

'When did all this start?'

'After her father came home. Mrs Watson said Mrs Mellor had told her he's devoting all his time to Joyce and her music.'

When her parents didn't continue this discussion Nancy knew instinctively that the time was not right – they had other things on their minds, largely Erica.

Erica had got a job as a Junior Secretary with Clevesons, the large industrial chemists in the city, and was living in a house with three other girls who had found employment with the same firm. Together with three other parents, her father had bought a large old house on the outskirts of the city and all of them were convinced it wasn't a good thing. The girls would need subsidising to pay for the house, and although they kept in touch by telephone because rail fares were expensive, even though their parents had offered to pay for them to come home for weekends, they were worried what the four of them might be doing when they didn't come home.

Erica had assured her parents over the telephone that she loved her job, that she had made new friends and that the prospects were very good indeed, but her father was unconvinced.

'She'd have had a decent job with us,' he said.

'Obviously she'd have had to start at the bottom and make her way up, but why this hankering after city life? Clevesons is an enormous concern and she'll be a small cog in a very large wheel.'

Meanwhile Nancy couldn't understand why they couldn't be a little more interested in her problems. She'd really liked Joyce Mellor and thought they'd be friends for years – now all she saw of her was when they were in the classroom. Immediately class was over Joyce took off on her own, running home as though she was being pursued by a pack of hounds.

Joyce had been popular, but now she was always alone. Even the music master seemed disinterested in her and she'd let the school down badly by not taking part in the next concert.

Joyce always ran home because she didn't want to talk to Nancy. Nancy was astute, she would ask questions about things she didn't want to talk about and would suggest they do things together over the weekend, but Joyce knew her father would never allow it.

She had to look after her hands, so no ball games, no climbing stiles or sauntering by the river. The paths were slippy, she might fall, but worst of all she was not allowed to play the music she loved, with melodies and tunes people knew.

Now there were scales and arpeggios, and only very occasionally duets with her father when he chose what they should play.

Her mother pottered about the house wishing she could shut her ears to the same sounds every single day, and in the kitchen Edith felt like screaming.

In the evening she talked to her sister about all she had to endure during the day, and her sister simply said, 'Why don't you leave then? You know there's half a dozen families who'd jump at you, so why stay where you're miserable?'

Edith knew that her sister was right, but she was curious, sensing that she was living on top of some sort of volcano and that one day it would erupt changing the lives of all of them. How long would Mrs Mellor tolerate her husband's sarcastic jibes, and would young Joyce go on forever playing those ridiculous scales with him standing over her like some ghastly dragon?

The Clarksons welcome Erica home for Easter and sat listening to her tales of office life, the shops in the city and the latest film she'd seen. When she talked of the house and some boy who was doing some decorating for them, her mother asked sharply, 'Is he your friend, Erica?'

'No Mother, he's simply a boy who works at the office. He offered to do some painting for us so we said he could.'

'Then I hope you're all paying for the paint and anything else he needs.'

'His father's a painter and decorator so he gets the paint from him.'

'It still needs to be paid for, dear.'

'Oh Mother, you worry too much. Do you ever get to chat to Mrs Edgebaston?'

'When we meet in the town, dear.'

'Does she ever ask about me?'

'Well, she has asked if you like your job. In fact, most of our neighbours have asked about you, dear, so if you get the chance you could call round and see them.'

'Oh I don't think so, Mother, the weekend's too short.'

The opportunity to meet most of them came after church on Easter Sunday and Mrs Edgebaston arrived in the company of two gentlemen. She did not linger around the churchyard to chat but left in a large black car, much to the speculation of those left behind.

Anthea Edgebaston had expected Erica to be talking enthusiastically about her new job to anybody prepared to listen, but she'd been very quiet, standing back from the groups around her, merely giving Anthea a swift smile when their eyes met.

Why did Erica remind her so much of the girl she had

been, and why, when she met her on the road the next morning, did Erica hurry up the garden path as though she didn't wish to talk to her?

The next afternoon Erica couldn't avoid her when they met face to face while exercising their dogs. Erica would have hurried on but Anthea said quickly, 'I'm sorry I hadn't time to speak to you at the church, Erica, but we were going out to lunch. Have you settled down to your new job?'

'Oh yes, I think so. It's very nice.'

How banal it sounded. Quite obviously something was amiss but she wouldn't ask – if Erica wished to tell her that would be different.

'And I believe you have a house with three other girls,' she said.

'Oh yes, we're having it decorated.'

'That's nice.'

'You didn't tell Mother about seeing me near the river, Mrs Edgebaston? I was hoping you wouldn't.'

Anthea smiled. 'My dear Erica, I know I'm the subject of considerable gossip around here, but I myself don't indulge in it. Did you think that I would?'

'I didn't know.'

'So you're going back to the city in the morning?'

'Yes.'

'Well, I hope everything goes well for you, my dear. Oh dear, it's started to rain, we'd better get inside. Would you like to come in for a cup of tea?'

'No thank you, I'm busy packing for tomorrow. I'll be leaving on the early train.'

Anthea smiled and, picking Benjie up in her arms, she said quickly, 'He does so hate the rain. Goodbye Erica.'

Erica smiled briefly and hurried on towards her gate, then making up her mind suddenly she turned and hurried back after Anthea who had paused at her front door and was watching her with some surprise.

'Mrs Edgebaston, I'm sorry but I really do need to talk

130

to somebody and I can't talk to my parents. They wouldn't understand.'

'Are you quite sure about that, my dear?'

'Oh yes I am, very sure. Will you be in this evening? I don't really want to go with them to the Spencers', so I could make an excuse and come round to see you – that's if you're not going out.'

'No, I'm not going out. Come round whenever you like.'

'Oh thank you, around half past seven then. You're very kind.'

As she went into the kitchen and started to rub the dog's wet coat she asked herself why Erica Clarkson would suddenly need someone to talk to. She no longer had Oliver Denton to worry about, so what could be her latest problem?

Chapter Fourteen

Erica could see immediately that it was a beautiful room with soft lamps and the firelight shining on rich velour and dark polished walnut. She had never seen a Chinese carpet quite so large, and there were huge bowls of flowers on small oriental tables set in discreet niches.

'The flowers are lovely,' she said.

'Yes, Easter presents,' Anthea said with a smile.

Anthea served coffee and Erica admired the rich rose-coloured velvet housecoat she was wearing. She knew for a fact that not another woman in St Agnes would be wearing something as glamorous – they'd still be wearing the clothes they'd worn for their evening meal. But Mrs Edgebaston looked so right with her rich auburn hair and slender figure in the flowing robe. As she came to place the coffee on the small table near Erica's chair she said with a smile, 'Why don't you call me Anthea, Erica. Mrs Edgebaston sounds so formal and we are friends, aren't we?'

'Oh yes. You wouldn't mind?'

'No, of course not. Everybody around here call me Mrs Egdebaston and I've lived here some time now. I can't think why, can you?'

'Well, you're not quite like the others, are you?'

'Why am I so different?'

'They're all like Mother, terribly genteel and ordinary.

You're always so fashionable and you're not married but you do have men friends.'

Anthea threw back her head and laughed. 'I'm a widow, my dear. I had a lovely husband who died and left me all alone. I do have men friends – one of them is my solicitor, the other my accountant, and fortunately they are both single. One of them is a widower and the other is a bachelor who intends his condition to be permanent.'

'You don't want to marry either of them?'

'No, and I doubt if they'd want to marry me.'

For several minutes they sat in silence drinking their coffee. Anthea looked at Erica's pretty face staring into the fire and deemed it wise to wait until she told her why she had felt the need to talk to her.

She was surprised when Erica said, 'This is a lovely room. I'd love my mother to see this colour scheme – she's so fond of greens and beiges. They're always the same.'

'She might think this colour reflects my personality, a little flamboyant perhaps.'

'Oh no, it's lovely.'

'Why were you so anxious to talk to me, Erica? Nothing to do with Oliver Denton, I hope. Hasn't he been relegated to the past?'

'For now, perhaps.'

'For ever, I hope.'

'I don't suppose I'll ever see him again.'

'Then what is worrying you now Erica?'

For what seemed an age Erica sat staring down at her hands, twisting her ring round her finger. Anthea waited patiently until at last she looked up saying, 'It's my job. I've been so stupid. I should never have gone there.'

'But you've only been there a few weeks. It takes time. What's wrong with it?'

'They told me at college I'd be a secretary to some director, that I was fit to be a secretary, but it's not like that at all – I'm just a general dogsbody, I run errands and answer the telephone. I've never even seen the Director.

133

All I see are a load of other women and junior staff.'

Anthea looked at her pretty, disgruntled face and pictured her arriving at her first job, beautifully dressed, exquisitely made up and expecting to be received with some sort of enthusiasm.

'Haven't you made friends there?'

'Not really. Most of the women have never worked anywhere else and never went to secretarial college. They simply went to evening classes and picked the work up day by day.'

'Has it never occurred to you that you knew absolutely nothing about the workings of the firm while these women had probably been there years and knew the job backwards. If you arrived expecting the earth it is natural they would resent you.'

'Miss Carter is the worst. She's the Director's secretary; I was supposed to be her junior. She's a spinster, middle aged and terribly dowdy.'

'Dowdy?'

'Why yes. She always wears dark skirts and shirt blouses. She has spectacles and hardly any make-up, and when I told her I wasn't there to run errands she said I had an awful lot to learn.'

'And you don't think you have?'

Erica bit her lip and remained silent.

'You've made a bad start, Erica. Perhaps you should look around for something else and not expect quite so much too soon.'

'But I don't know what I've done wrong. Why are they so distant? Why don't they like me?'

'Perhaps they do like you, Erica, but you seem to have made all the mistakes I made and it takes a long time to recover from something like that. You know, you don't have to be overglamorous, they'd have liked you better if you'd arrived looking rather less alluring but considerably more intelligent and eager to learn.'

'But learn what? I knew how to type and how to take

notes – that's what Miss Carter was doing most of the time.'

'But would you have understood the notes, Erica?'

Erica looked at her doubtfully before saying, 'I suppose not. Perhaps I have been stupid after all.'

'Try not to worry too much. You're in the big city now, there are a great many jobs there and one disaster doesn't have to ruin your life, so learn from it.'

'Please don't say anything to Mother?'

'Of course not, I won't even tell her you've been here.'

'I'm a nuisance, aren't I?'

'No you're not. I wish I'd had somebody to talk to when I was your age.'

'Didn't you have a mother, a family?'

'I had a grandmother who was totally unworldly, even if she was a good woman. I think she despaired of me a great many times. We never understood each other.'

'But you fell in love and married. What was your husband like?'

'He was a wonderful man, kind and generous. I loved him very dearly.'

Anthea didn't tell her that she had never fallen in love with him, that falling in love and loving were two very different things.

'I suppose I'd better go. I'm going back to the city in the morning and I have some packing to do. Dad will take me to the station. Thank you for letting me talk to you. I realise I have to think about where I go from here, and I have to change a lot of things about me.'

Anthea smiled. 'I doubt if it will be easy, my dear, but it'll be worth it in the end.'

She was in her garden next morning when Erica and her father drove down the road, both of them favouring her with a wave of their hands and a smile. At the same time she saw Major Robson marching down the road in his uniform, obviously on his way to meet his cadets.

135

Touching his cap with his stick he said, 'I see Erica's going back to the city, likely to set it alight, do you think?'

'Possibly.'

'Summer's on its way, Anthea. Got anything planned?'

'Not at the moment, and you?'

'I'd like to go to Portugal but Elspeth fancies the Rhine. I'm not so sure – the last time we were in Germany the Hitler Youth were making themselves felt.'

'I rather fancy Italy myself.'

'Where you have the Fascist Youth – not much to choose between them.'

'Perhaps it's the military in you that's making you so distrustful.'

'That's what Elspeth says, but I was talking to the Commodore the other morning and he thinks like I do, that there's trouble afoot.'

'There you are then, two ex-servicemen together.'

He laughed. 'Perhaps you're right, one never really moves on. And which of your attentive gentlemen friends will be going with you to Italy?'

'Neither, Desmond. One of them prefers walking in Scotland, the other golf or sailing.'

'And there isn't a third?'

'That would really set people's tongues wagging, wouldn't it. No Desmond, there isn't a third.'

'As usual Elspeth's got her bridge four today. For some reason Grace couldn't play but Hilda Marks has found a stand-in. You know, Anthea, bridge isn't a game, it's a disease.'

She laughed at his expression as he smiled and raised his hand in greeting to a woman hurrying along the road. 'I wonder where she's off to at this time of the morning,' he said curiously. 'I don't think our vicar's wife's been looking too well recently – she does too much. I'll have to have a word with him.'

'She seems to enjoy being involved in everything.'

'All the same, she's looking decidedly peaky to me.'

136

'You're lucky the cadets keep you occupied on Tuesday afternoons, Desmond. Elspeth wouldn't want you around.'

'Certainly not, and I wouldn't want to be around. Seen anything of the Mellors?'

'No, they keep themselves to themselves.'

'That they do, but it's not much of a life for the wife or the daughter. She was as happy as a sandboy at that concert, now it's all had to end. They never have visitors and only the mother goes to church. What sort of life is that?'

'You know, Desmond, when I came to live in St Agnes I thought it would be terribly boring and strait-laced, and all the people incredibly proper, and oh so ordinary – now I've found that the entire place is like the world in miniature. Gentility waiting to erupt into chaos, respectability tottering on the edge of catastrophe.'

'Steady on, old girl. All St Agnes will have to offer are a few home-grown scandals, when the women meet for morning coffee, round the bridge table or at the market stalls. You have to go into the cities to find real trauma.'

'I'm not so sure.'

He laughed. 'Well, there's always Lady Marcia – third husband's gone off with some trollop he met at a race meeting and I believe her sister's given her an ultimatum: either settle down to respectability or stay away from St Agnes.'

'You know that for sure, Desmond?'

'From Lady Marcia herself.'

With a bright smile he raised his hat, gave her a knowing wink and walked away.

For a little while she pottered round her garden. Easter was really too early this year to expect too much life from it, although the crocuses were flowering and there were new leaves on the azaleas.

As she walked back to the house she could see the Vicar's wife hurrying back to the vicarage with her eyes to the ground as if she was hardly expecting to see anybody at

137

such an early hour. She had always found Mrs Tremayne very nice, totally dedicated to her husband and his work in the Parish; she always seemed terribly busy with all and sundry but with no special friend.

Perhaps a vicar's wife didn't need special friends, perhaps all the community was special. Major Robson was right, there had been an air of weariness about the way she was walking – it was not her usual brisk stride as if she hadn't a minute to spare.

By this time Erica would be on the train on her way back to the city and she wondered if she would have given any thought to their conversation of the evening before.

She thought of Erica as being like herself, but it wasn't entirely true. Erica Clarkson was a product of wealth and small-town respectability. She was a beautiful girl with monied parents and surrounded by men and women who had been prepared to spoil and pamper her.

She thought about her own upbringing when there had never been enough money, with a grandmother who was hard and unyielding, and a grandfather who was never there, a mother she had never known and a man who had used her but never loved her.

Then there had been John. John, who had been good, kind and able to give – she still wished fervently that she had loved him more. Her life seemed at times to be burdened with regrets, but they were all too late, and all that was left was the irrelevance of what she was left with.

Molly Tremayne let herself into the vicarage and went immediately into the kitchen where Mary her daily help was washing up the breakfast things.

'The Vicar's had to go out, Mrs Tremayne,' Mary said. 'It's old Mrs Holt again. He's left this note for ye.'

She took the note and looked at it with a frown. It was a list of all his calls and a plea that she would not forget that the Mothers' Union meeting had been brought forward to that afternoon.

Molly sat down wearily at the kitchen table and Mary said, 'Ye look tired. I'll make ye a cup of tea. Easter's too much for anybody, what with all the services and the calls he's 'ad to make, and you too. Ye could do with a good curate.'

Molly didn't answer. She felt exhausted and yet she'd only walked as far as Mrs Proffit's, half a mile away.

She'd always enjoyed her work – the meetings, the organisation that went into summer fetes and Christmas parties. She'd always felt so lucky that she had a good husband who was kind and cheerful, and who appreciated all she did for the Parish. It was only recently that she'd felt so tired. Now instead of looking forward to things she'd come to dread them.

They'd brought the Mothers' Union meeting forward and it was going to be all about the longest day, even though it was more than two months away. She longed to ask somebody else to take over but Paul would ask questions and she didn't want to worry him – he had enough to worry about without her state of health.

She'd been so lucky to have married Paul Tremayne because she'd fancied him as long as she'd been old enough to fancy anybody.

At one time she thought he would have married Grace, and even now whenever they met Grace she had the distinct feeling that he still felt something for her.

Grace had been the one he'd danced with, invited to church functions, and they'd always seemed so happy together, at least when Grace's father had been alive, but after he had died somehow everything changed.

Grace's mother was very demanding and in some strange intangible way Grace changed from the pretty, friendly girl into a woman who was too remote, too wrapped up in herself.

When she'd said as much to Paul he simply said, 'I don't think Grace has really changed, Molly, I think she's pleasing her mother. The old lady wants her to be like that.'

139

'But why?'

'She wants Grace to remain with her, no men friends, no diversions. All she has now is bridge on Tuesday afternoons.'

Molly became aware that Mary was looking at her with a worried frown. 'Why don't ye rest up for the day? That meetin' tonight will go on a bit and ye really don't look at all well.'

'There's notes to be made, Mary, and questions to be answered. I've got to be ready for the likes of Mrs Marks.'

'Maybe she won't be there. Isn't it their bridge afternoon? I saw her with some other woman this mornin' in the butcher's. She was telling Mrs Banks that they were playin' this afternoon. Obviously Miss Gantry can't play.'

How typical of St Agnes when everybody seemed to know everybody else's business. By this time tomorrow the neighbours would know that she wasn't feeling well. There was the meeting, of course she couldn't rest up for the day, besides what would she tell Paul, he had enough worries on his shoulders without her starting.

Mary placed the teapot at her elbow and started to pour out the tea. She was a good, kind soul who had served them loyally for a great many years; now she sat opposite her with every intention of imparting some local knowledge.

'I saw Edith Pinder on her way to work this mornin'. She's none too happy at the Mellors'. Mrs Mellor's alright, but she doesn't care for 'im and she thinks her days there are numbered.'

'Oh surely not, the house is quite large and she was with Mrs Prothero such a long time, I thought that was why they kept her on.'

'She says he's arrogant, that he lays the law down all the time and is a bit of a penny pincher.'

'Well, he's given up his job to devote all his time to Joyce. There probably isn't nearly as much money coming in.'

'Far be it from me to gossip about people I don't know

much about, but the girl doesn't look happy and when anybody sees Mrs Mellor in the shops she puts 'er 'ead down and hurries away.'

'I've spoken to her at the church and she seemed very nice. She must be very shy.'

'Shy or browbeaten.'

'Mary, we don't know that. I do wish people wouldn't gossip so much.'

'Well, you'll never stop 'em. Makes a change from Mrs Edgebaston.'

'Yes, and I've always found Mrs Edgebaston quite charming. She's a pretty woman and very smart.'

Getting up from the table, Mary said philosophically, 'P'raps that's the trouble, ma'am,' and Molly stared after her with a wry smile.

Chapter Fifteen

Joyce closed the door behind her and hurried down the path. There were so few days left when she could go out of the house of her own free will. In just three months she'd be seventeen and leaving day school behind her, but she wouldn't be like any of the other girls who would be looking forward to college, university or their first job. She was the one destined to stay at home playing the piano every single day, with her father standing over her like some omnipotent god.

The tension over the breakfast table had been almost tangible, with her father staring down at his plate in silence and her mother plucking nervously at the tablecloth.

Edith had looked at her sympathetically when she met her in the hall, and she guessed that even now her parents would be having words about some quite ridiculous matter.

A voice hailed her from the Clarksons' garden and she saw Nancy hurrying towards the gate calling, 'Joyce, wait for me.'

She normally tried to avoid Nancy these days because Nancy couldn't understand why they could never go to places together, not even to the river or the park, but this morning she waited for her. To keep the subject away from herself Joyce said brightly, 'I saw your sister was home for Easter, Nancy.'

'Yes, she went back on Tuesday.'

'Is she happy in the city?'

'She didn't say much about it which suggests to me that it's not all that it was cracked up to be.'

'She's awfully pretty.'

'Yes, I used to wish I was like her, but I know I never shall be.'

'You'll be just as pretty.'

Not displeased, Nancy said, 'Well, I've got those wretched braces off my teeth at last but I'll never be blond like Erica.'

'You have very attractive hair, Nancy. I think you're every bit as pretty, different perhaps, but just as pretty.'

'And you're the nicest person, Joyce. Have you been swotting for the exams?'

'Some of the time, but Father says my music is more important, so these exams are not for me.'

'Really. I thought they were important to all of us.'

'He doesn't think so. Arithmetic and English won't improve my piano playing.'

'I suppose not.'

'What are you going to do, Nancy? What do you want to be?'

'You mean where do I want to work, or do I want to go to college?'

'Yes.'

'I suppose I'll have to think about it. All I really want is to meet some nice man and make him a good wife.'

'Preferably Commodore Watson's son.'

Nancy blushed, then laughing she said, 'I'll never look at anybody else – never. But he doesn't know I'm alive. Oh, he chats to me, thanks me for being nice to his mother and helping his father and the gardener with the weeding, but he doesn't really see me. I'm just the kid up the road and one day his mother's going to tell me that he's engaged to some gorgeous girl he's met somewhere.'

'Maybe you give up too easily, Nancy.'

'You're lucky that there's nobody you fancy.'

143

'Yes I am. If there was somebody I'd have to forget about him anyway as my father'd never allow it. For me there's only music and more music.'

Margaret Mellor hated it now that Joyce had had to return to school. There were so few days like this left, and she knew Joyce was loving them and dreading the fact that all too soon they would have to end.

Her husband was already wondering what to do with himself for the rest of the day. He would spend it sitting in what they now called the music room, surrounded by old programmes of his time with the orchestra, selecting over and over again the music that one day Joyce would play to convince her mentors at the very best music college that she was the best, the one truly destined to hold the world enthralled.

The clatter of Edith's pail and brushes could be heard as she mopped the tiles in the hall. Irritably Arthur said, 'Do we really need that woman, Margaret?'

'Well, it is a big house, my dear, and your sister thought we needed her.'

'She interferes too much.'

'You've always allowed it; you always listen to her more than you ever listened to me.'

'Because she was more intelligent than you, Margaret. She's always held down a good job, is more worldly and better at arranging things.'

'She did arrange for us to have Edith.'

'And that is the worst move I've known her make. How much are we paying her? You know that money is tighter now.'

'We can cut down on other things perhaps. I don't want to get rid of her, the neighbours would talk.'

'The neighbours – what do I care about them?'

'Well, they're very nice people. Edith's sister lives in the town and everybody knew her when she worked for Mrs Prothero.'

144

'Mrs Prothero's long gone. We're here now, and I don't see why we have to live in the past. Will you get rid of her or shall I?'

She looked at him with anguished eyes. 'Oh Arthur, not today. Let's just think about it. All our neighbours have dailies, most of them more than one. I don't want them thinking we're mean or unkind.'

'What is mean or unkind in getting rid of a woman we don't need? You've nothing else to do apart from housework. You don't even bother to read the papers, all you do read are those trashy novels from the library. And you don't even bother to go to church most Sundays now.'

'Because we don't mix, they don't know me. They asked questions about why Joyce had dropped out of rehearsals for school concerts, and I had nothing to say to them.'

'It was none of their business.'

'My books are not trashy, Arthur, they've been recommended by that nice young lady at the library.'

'Well, they're trashy to me.'

At that moment there came a loud noise from the hall and, jumping to his feet, Arthur said, 'That's all I need. If that had happened when Joyce was practising it would have completely thrown her. She's leaving today, and I'll be the one to tell her.'

He stormed out of the room and all she could do was watch, with the tears streaming down her face. At that moment she hated her husband and she hated her life, she hated St Agnes and she hated a future which offered no gleam of light in her cold grey world.

She heard the sound of their voices in the hall and suddenly the kitchen door was thrown open as Edith appeared red-faced and obviously upset. Without a word she laid her cleaning utensils on the kitchen sink and took off he apron. Margaret said anxiously, 'Edith, I'm so sorry. My husband isn't very well, he has so many problems at the moment.'

145

'Don't bother, Mrs Mellor, I wasn't aimin' to stay anyway.'

'Has my husband paid your wage?'

'No.'

'Well, I'll ask him for the money if you just sit down for a moment.'

'Perhaps you'd rather I called round for it. He isn't in the mood to be askin' him for money just now.'

'Yes, perhaps that would be for the best, Edith. Tomorrow morning perhaps, or I could ask Joyce to call at your sister's on her way home from school.'

'Yes. I'd like to say goodbye to her, and I don't really want to see Mr Mellor again.'

'I'm sorry, Edith.'

'I've no doubt you'll find somebody else.'

'I don't think we shall be looking for anybody.'

'Then you're goin' to 'ave your hands full. This house is bigger than it looks.'

Margaret smiled feebly as Edith finished buttoning up her coat and with a swift smile let herself out of the back door into the cold wet morning.

She was not sorry to be leaving the Mellors, and it was true that she'd more or less made up her mind to leave them. She knew she'd soon get another job – there was the Doctor's surgery, Mrs Prescott's and a stream of people her sister said had been asking about her, but she'd never expected to be sacked from her job and in such a peevish, vindictive way.

She'd liked Mrs Mellor, there'd been nothing to dislike about the woman, indeed she'd felt sorry for her because she was such a mouse. The poor soul was utterly browbeaten. Why hadn't she stuck up for herself years ago?

As she rounded the corner near the bus stop she met Miss Gantry trying to hold up her umbrella in the strong wind and Edith took hold of her arm to steady her.

Thanking her Grace said, 'You're leaving early today, Edith?'

146

'And I'm never going' back. I've got me cards.'

'Really Edith, whatever for?'

'It's 'im. I don't like him and 'e's never liked me.'

'What will Mrs Mellor do without you?'

'That's up to them, Miss Gantry. No bridge this afternoon then?'

'No, Mother wasn't well.' She smiled and started to walk way, then turning suddenly she said, 'Edith, would you like to work for us? We've got Jenny but she's getting married in June and going to live out of town. We shall need somebody to replace her.'

'Well, I'll think about it, Miss Gantry. I'll need a job but I'm not too sure I want housework again. I've been asked to work at the Surgery. I thought that might suit me.'

'Think about it, Edith, and let me know.'

Sitting in the bus on the way home she thought about Grace's offer, but did she really want to work for Mrs Gantry? The daughter was nice, a real lady, but the mother could be difficult as all who knew her could testify.

Mr Mellor and Mrs Gantry she could do without, but she didn't have a husband behind her, she needed the money and her sister would be the first one to tell her so.

Poor Mrs Mellor and poor Joyce. They didn't have much going for them.

Joyce came home from school to find her mother in tears and her father morose and tetchy.

'I don't want you pestering your mother while she's getting the meal ready,' he said sharply. 'She needs to concentrate. She was getting too used to servants.'

Margaret didn't speak and Joyce followed him into the Music Room, well aware of the tension.

'Why is Mother crying?' she asked him.

'She's upset. I've had to get rid of Edith, we didn't need her anyway and she was making so much noise this morning I couldn't hear myself think.'

147

'You've got rid of Edith?'

'I have, and I'll have no impudence from you, young lady. This is my house, I pay the bills and I decide who and what we need.'

'But Edith was nice. How will Mummy manage without her?'

'Your mother hasn't been brought up to have servants. She needs something to do or she gets dejected and miserable. Looking after the house and doing the cooking will give her an incentive in life.'

'Aunt Edna asked Edith to stay on.'

'Well, Aunt Edna doesn't live here, does she, and she'd no right to employ her without asking my permission. Now let's have done with all this. You need to practise before we have something to eat. I'll be glad when you finish school and we can really work.'

The meal was eaten in silence. Her mother was still tearful, her father impatient and the meal indifferent. As they washed the dishes afterwards her mother said, 'I'll want you to call round at Edith's sister's tomorrow after school, Joyce, with her money. Can you do that?'

'Yes Mother, but I'll feel so embarrassed.'

'There's no need, dear, Edith knows you're not to blame.'

Ever since she could remember her mother had said that her father was a good man who wanted the best for her, and that one day when she was famous she'd understand all he had done for her. Joyce only knew that other girls' fathers were different. Whereas they were friends with their children, she had never been able to look upon her father as a friend.

Edith received her money with a bleak smile as Joyce said, 'I'm so sorry, Edith. I'm going to miss you.'

'Yes, well, I'll hear about you from people around and I'll always be wishin' you well, you and your mother.'

'Thank you, Edith. What are you going to do? Will you get another job?'

'So I will. I've already 'ad people askin' for me. Now all I've got to do is make me mind up where I want to go.'

'That's good, Edith.'

'Yes. Tell your mother not to worry about me, I'll be fine. She needs to worry about herself more.'

Joyce didn't pass on Edith's sentiments. Her mother would worry – worry about the house and the meals, worry that her father was moody and hardly grateful for anything she did. But it was best that they forget about Edith. No point in upsetting her father needlessly.

At least there were three months before she left school for good, three months to feel like the other girls, make the most of what was left before it all began to change. There were times when she longed to confide in Nancy, but Nancy was worried about her exams, her appearance and her feelings for Julian, so better to keep her problems to herself – they would either make or break her.

Margaret concentrated on the running of the house, trying to remember Edith's routines, hating the times when her husband ran his finger along a ledge or window bottom, inspecting it for any trace of dust.

She pored over cookery books she had had for years and used recipes that never seemed to turn out right.

In the evenings she sat alone in the small sitting room knitting jumpers she would never wear. She dropped stitches and lost count of rows that formed a shape, so that in the end she discarded her work to the waste bin until one day her husband found it and then came the long chastisement that she was wasting money on wool that she never used to finish anything.

After that there seemed nothing to do. He did not allow her to use the wireless because it might have interfered with Joyce's piano practice, but she couldn't understand how it would do that since all she seemed to hear were endless scales.

Her mind dwelled constantly on the time when Joyce

would leave them to pursue her career – but leave them to what?

Whenever she ventured out she was afraid to meet people, afraid of their criticism that they had dispensed with Edith, afraid of question about Joyce. What would any of them make of a woman who had no answers?

For the first time she began to wish that Edna would visit. Edna could handle Arthur and would talk about London. Edna went to museums and exhibitions, at least it would make a change from the emptiness that was her life.

Whenever Joyce was in the same room she made herself smile and hum to herself so that Joyce would not know that she was miserable – it would depress her and put her off her music.

She was sure in her heart that Arthur Mellor had never loved her. He believed she'd trapped him into marriage by being too willing, too worshipping, and she believed that was how his family had always seen her.

Arthur's father was a respected clergyman who ruled his wife and son with a rod of iron. In Margaret he had recognised a young woman who would be eternally grateful that she had captured such a prize as he, a talented man from a praiseworthy family.

The one really good thing she had done was to produce Joyce, but over the years she had come to learn that Arthur had regretted everything else about their marriage and she would be condemned into accepting her inferiority and everything that went with it.

Joyce had been her redeeming light. She had talent, all the potential her father had been born with, and that was the only reason they had stayed together. Now she felt they had reached the point of no return.

Edith would have lost no time in telling the people she knew that all was not well in the Mellor household. She knew that Edith was not a troublemaker but she had been dismissed from her job and would feel the need to justify herself.

150

Edith in the meantime was wondering what to do about the offers she had received for employment.

She decided the Gantrys were not for her. She liked Grace but not her mother. The Doctor's surgery was her favourite until the morning her sister told her Mrs Edgebaston's daily was leaving the area for family reasons and she was looking for a replacement.

Edith decided that if she was suitable for Mrs Edgebaston that was where she would like to be. All the town gossiped about the lady – her style, her money, her gentlemen friends – and she'd have first-hand knowledge of them, not that she'd ever discuss them with a soul.

Anything was better than working for the Mellors and Mrs Edgebaston would be generous with her money, she felt sure about that. Mrs Prothero had given her very good references and she'd no doubt Mrs Mellor would speak well of her if she was asked. Well why not?

Chapter Sixteen

David Clarkson sat in his office listening to his daughter at the other end of the telephone with the utmost amazement.

'I don't understand you, Erica,' he said sharply. ' I thought you were happy in your job, you enthused about it all over Easter.'

'I know, Daddy, I only did it to keep Mummy happy.'

'Why would you do that?'

'Well, you know what she's like. Daddy, I hate the job and I hate the people I work with. It's not a bit like I thought it would be.'

'But you haven't been there very long – you have to settle in, learn about things. What do you want me to do? Do you want to leave?'

'Yes I do.'

'I'm afraid the position I was hoping you'd fill here has gone.'

'I don't want to work for you, Daddy.'

'Then what do you want?'

'I've heard of another job, something that would suit me and with no other girls telling me what to do.'

'And where is that? What can I do?'

'You know him, Daddy. I've heard you talk about him from Rotary, Mr Stevenson, the Conservative Agent. You know the MP too, Daddy.'

'You say he's looking for a secretary. How do you know?'

'I heard some of the girls talking about it on the way to work. Two of them are thinking of applying, but I thought with you knowing people I'd stand a better chance.'

'Not if he thinks you're leaving a job after only a few months. He'll be looking for somebody older and with considerably more experience.'

'My college results were good, I worked very hard for them.'

'But Erica, you're in the big wide world now, forget your college results.'

'That's what Mrs Edgebaston said.'

'When did you discuss matters with her?'

'Oh, one evening. She was asking me if I liked my new job. She said new jobs were always the most difficult, particularly working with women who'd been there for years.'

'Yes, I would think she's a pretty good idea of what she was talking about.'

'I didn't know you liked her.'

'I hardly know her, but I don't dislike her. Now what is all this, Erica? I am rather busy and we need to talk a lot more about this.'

'When will you be in town?'

'I'm at the Law Courts on Tuesday, but you'll be at your job.'

'I have a very bad cold, I can get time off.'

'Telephone me in the morning, and Erica, you need to think long and hard about this. I'm not at all sure that this sort of work would suit you.'

'Bye Daddy, I'll ring you Tuesday morning.'

He was frowning as he put the telephone down. What was there about Erica that caused so many problems? He'd known Jason Stevenson for years – his wife and Stevenson's wife were friends, went to the same functions, but he didn't really know much about his job except that he

153

was the agent for the Party and close to the city's MP. He'd met the MP and thought he seemed a decent enough sort of chap but he didn't know much else about him, whether he was married or not.

He looked round Erica's home on the outskirts of the city and failed to understand why she had exchanged it for home in St Agnes. Seeing his cynical expression she grinned and said, 'I know what you're thinking, Daddy, it's not up to much compared to your place but I wanted to move on. What was there for me in St Agnes?'

Wisely he decided not to argue with her; instead he said, 'Are you still determined to change your job?' You haven't been there five minutes.'

'Five minutes too long.'

'It's what you wanted.'

'I thought it was what I wanted, now I know I was wrong.'

'What is so wrong with it?'

'I don't want to work with older women who think they are so superior. I want to make my way in life without them telling me to do this and that, and treating me like some ignoramus who's about five years old.'

'And what makes you think a job in the Conservative Agent's office will suit you any better?'

'I know Mr Stevenson and he's nice. He'll be fair and I'll not let him down. Please, Daddy, will you talk to him, tell him that my results at college were good, tell him I worked really hard for them, tell him why I'm leaving my present job, he'll understand.'

'I'm not so sure that he will. His present secretary has been with him a great many years and knows the job inside out. I'm not sure that he'll take to some young girl taking over and I'm not sure his wife will like it either.'

'Gracious, I'm not interested in him, only in the job.'

'Wives have heard all that before.'

'And you're being ridiculous.'

154

'I rather think the MP has a hand in what goes on in his constituency.'

'Well, you know him. I've heard you say you like him. You vote for his lot anyway.'

'I'll put a few feelers out. I can't promise to do any more. Don't build your hopes up, Erica. I know what you're like when you get a bee in your bonnet.'

She grinned. There had never been a time when she couldn't twist her father round her finger. She'd always been his little girl – even when he'd been most cross with her she'd been able to charm him with her smiles and her beauty. Today was no exception. He left her promising to do what he could, but not to be too disappointed if it came to nothing.

His opportunity to talk to Jason Stevenson came several days later at a Rotary meeting. The meeting was over and they met in the bar when Jason said, 'I saw you in the city the other morning, David, but you disappeared before I could have a word with you.'

'Yes, I was going to see my daughter. She's living there now.'

'Really, I thought she was still at school.'

'No. The younger one's still at school. Erica was at business college, but left a few months ago.'

'Time flies, doesn't it. I hadn't realised she was old enough to work.'

'Well, actually she's none too happy with what she's doing at Clevesons. She really doesn't like working with a crowd of other women. She'd really like something quieter, something where she can work on her own or with a small staff at least.'

'I'm losing my secretary very soon. I thought she'd stay on until retirement but she's decided to go out to Australia to live with her brother. I'm going to miss her.'

'Have you a replacement in mind or will you have to advertise?'

'I don't have a staff of girls. There's just been Miss

155

Foster and myself so I shall have to advertise.'

'Would you mind if Erica applies? I know she's young but she got excellent reports from her business college and she's keen. Of course, she may not be suitable and I don't want you to think I'm pushing her because we know each other – it wouldn't be fair on you or Erica either.'

'Tell her to apply by all means, David. No hard feelings though if I can't give her the job?'

'Of course not.'

Erica was told the extent of their conversation but she had never been one to look on the dark side. Of course she would get the job. Her mother would reassure Mrs Stevenson several days later. Erica was all a daughter should be, with ambitions to be a good secretary, make something of her life and she decided it would be a very different Erica Clarkson Mr Stevenson would interview than the one the directors of Clevesons first met.

She was wearing a dark clerical grey suit and white silk shirt blouse. The blond curls she had been so proud of had been replaced by smooth shingled hair; black leather court shoes with medium heels and plain black leather handbag completed the ensemble.

As she sat in a small ante room in the company of six other girls she felt she could hold her own with any one of them even though she was probably the youngest.

Her father had given her instructions as to how she should conduct herself. 'You don't know it all, Erica, but you are anxious to learn. You think a great deal about the Party and you want to do the best you can for it – after that it's up to Stevenson. Above all, dear, don't be too upset if you don't get the job, it's not the end of the world and there will be other opportunities.'

Three days later Erica heard that she had got the job and that weekend people in St Agnes were aware that there were celebrations at the Clarkson household.

156

She left Clevesons with few regrets and few friends, but to her credit she did set out to learn everything she could in the few weeks Miss Foster remained at the office, and in the end she could only tell Mr Stevenson that he had made the right decision.

Alistair Greavson was the MP and almost every weekend he came to what he called his surgery to attend to his constituents. These were the times Erica liked best. She liked showing off in front of the men and women who sat waiting to see him, treating them to warm smiles and consideration as to who should occupy seats nearest the fire, and on which chairs, and how she needed to speak to them before escorting them down the long corridor and into his room.

She liked making morning coffee and taking it into them, to be favoured by smiles of gratitude, and she decided she liked Alistair Greavson, and wished she knew more about him.

It was the elderly lady she opened the door to one morning who said, 'What a nice man the MP is, wouldn't you think he'd be married?'

So over a working lunch the following week she said innocently, 'I didn't know Mr Greavson wasn't married.'

'By choice, I feel sure. He doesn't seem to lack for admirers at any of the functions here, and I expect there are even more at Westminster.'

'My father thinks all MPs should be married.'

'Does he indeed. I'll pass those sentiments on to Alistair and see what he thinks.'

'Oh please no. I don't want him to think I've said anything.'

Mr Stevenson smiled. 'I believe he's been engaged but it didn't last, and he has a secretary in London who keeps pretty close to him.'

Erica didn't pursue the conversation. Rome wasn't built in a day.

*

She sat with her parents at the Annual Party dinner and could see that her father and the MP got along very well. When she asked him later what they talked about he simply said, 'All sorts of things, my dear, oh and he did say you're shaping up very well.'

Alistair Greavson was well aware that a great many of his constituents wished he was married. Bachelors could be flighty, the bait of too many predatory women, making it too easy for the opposite camp to dream up scandal when none existed.

Alistair had never given them cause to identify any scandal, but all the same, a wife and family would stop it before it got started. He was forty-two years old, good-looking and well heeled – surely in all of London there must be some woman he fancied.

'I've heard a lot about that longest day tradition you have in St Agnes,' he was saying to David Clarkson. 'I've thought one of these days I might just take a look around.'

'Well yes, why don't you? We'd be delighted if you came for lunch and spend the day.'

'But what's it all for? I can understand Midsummer's Day but not this one.'

'Locked away in obscurity, I believe.'

'But what do they do?'

'Sir Robert and his wife throw open the Hall gardens for the afternoon. There's a dance in the evening and the two schools hold concerts. The Major marches his cadets and the Commodore hoists his flag, other than that we're inundated with visitors and the shops do a thriving trade.'

'Sounds fun.'

'Most of us are glad when it comes to an end.'

'Well, I might just take you up on that offer one of these days. I've driven through St Agnes. I liked the look of the place – somehow dreamy – and it left me feeling strangely nostalgic.'

'Yes, that's the effect it has on a lot of people.'

'And this year it poured with rain all day, I believe.'

158

'Heavens yes. I don't ever remember it being washed out like it was this year, even the Major had to contain himself.'

'And the flag?'

'Drooped like never before.'

They all laughed and Erica wondered what they would all be doing on the next longest day, before reflecting that at least they were all still there. It was as if the longest day put a curse on them all.

'So what's the next occasion St Agnes has to look forward to?' Alistair asked.

'We'll think of something,' David said with a smile.

Janet was thinking to herself that they had so much to think about. Nancy would be going to college and as yet she'd no idea what she wanted to do with her life.

They'd always known what Erica wanted – the best of everything, the best job, the richest boy, the most beautiful face and fashionable wardrobe – but Nancy never said what she wanted.

Nancy had always been the child, the young one with the brightest smile and the sharpest wit, the dancing feet that had never learned to saunter.

They always thought that Erica was the one most likely to be hurt because she was vulnerable and asked too much of life. Nancy had never said what she wanted of life, had smiled defiantly at such problems and got on with things.

It seemed almost overnight that Nancy had changed from the sometimes boisterous young girl into a graceful and thoughtful young woman. She could still find time to smile and make fun of life, but beneath it there was another Nancy who they had yet to discover.

Unlike Erica, Nancy had never been keen on any particular boy. She was popular, but strangely uncaring of the boys who invited her to tennis or boating on the river. When Janet chided her for being a little too uncaring she simply smiled and said, 'He's nice, Mother, we're friends, but that's all.'

159

'I hope when you do meet somebody special, Nancy, you'll be a little more enthusiastic.'

She laughed. 'I shall be, Mummy, I shall be.'

Erica had given up on her.

'I don't understand her at all,' she complained. 'When I was her age I had dozens of boys, they hung around like flies.'

Nobody felt inclined to tell her that she had been less than kind to many of the boys, nobody except Nancy who both loved and hated her.

Seeing Mrs Edgebaston in her garden one morning David decided to wander over to ask if she knew that Erica had found another job. He agreed with most men in the village that she was a very attractive woman, but nobody seemed to know much about where she'd come from.

'Doing a spot of gardening then?' he asked with a smile.

'Yes, I thought I'd take advantage of the weather.'

'Of course. I just wondered if you'd heard that Erica has left Clevesons.'

'I didn't know, but she wasn't very happy there. She did tell me.'

'She's working for the Conservative Agent. I wouldn't have thought it would be her choice but she seems happy enough.'

'I'm glad.'

At that moment the door opened and Edith Pinder stood there saying, 'You're wanted on the telephone, Mrs Edgebaston,' and with a smile and a quick word of apology she turned to go back into the house.

Calling out to Edith Mr Clarkson said, 'So here you are, Edith. My wife was wondering where you were going next.'

'I started on Monday. It was either 'ere or the surgery.'

'I'm sure you'll settle in very well.'

When he told his wife that she was now in Mrs Edgebaston's service all Janet could say was, 'I'm rather surprised. I'd have thought she'd want somebody more like Mrs Prothero.'

160

'You mean less glamorous and nowhere near as mysterious. Why all you women seem to think there's a hint of infamy about the poor woman I can't understand,' he said.

'Oh David, we don't. It's just that none of us really know much about her. I'm sure she's really very nice.'

He decided not to tell her that Erica had confided in her, but he had no doubt that now Edith Pinder was working for her Mrs Edgebaston would become considerably less mysterious.

Chapter Seventeen

It was a glorious afternoon in summer when the only sounds that could be heard were the sounds of lawnmowers and steady clipping of hedges. It was a day for the savouring of gardens, the cutting of flowers and the soft hum of voices from all around.

Nancy Clarkson was on her way home from school and, looking over the Commodore's gate, she could see Mrs Watson sitting on the lawn underneath a huge sunshade so she decided to join her.

Smiling, Mrs Watson said, 'Bring over another chair, Nancy, I'm afraid the tea will be cold but if you go to the kitchen Polly will give you some lemonade.'

'No, really Mrs Watson, I don't want anything. We had something at school and Mother will be making tea.'

'And how is school? Only a week to go and you'll be moving on.'

Nancy nodded. Mrs Watson decided she looked a little glum.

'Aren't you happy about leaving school, Nancy, most girls can't get away quick enough.'

'I really don't know what I want to do. I know it will probably be college and the same sort of thing Erica did, but I don't know if it's for me.'

'Then what else is there?'

'That's it, I don't know.'

'Your mother was telling me that Erica seems to have settled into her new job very well – but you're not sure.'

'No. We're busy at school with the usual concert to mark the end of term. A lot of the girls will be leaving for good.'

'And what is to be your role in the concert then?'

Nancy laughed. 'The usual. I'll be in the choir, probably in the back row. I won't be taking any sort of leading part.'

'I'm sure you'll look very pretty and sing very sweetly. You're still feeling a little overshadowed by Erica, Nancy, but really there's no need.'

'She was always so pretty. I used to watch her getting ready for the school concerts. The dresses always fitted so well, and while she was always the fairy queen I was destined to be the ugly duckling.'

'My dear, you were only a child, but now you're growing up and very beautiful. My mother always told me I'd grow up one day to be as pretty as my older sister. I never believed her but I do now. When I see my sister I know she was right, you ask my husband.'

Nancy laughed. 'But Erica could sing, and she could dance while I had four feet. Oh, I know I'm not bad now, but when she showed potential she was sent to dancing and singing lessons. I never wanted to go because I was so resentful.'

'You'll see, my dear, one day you'll have just as much as Erica. All you need when the time is right is the right sort of young man. He'll come along, I'm sure.'

Nancy smiled. She would have liked to ask Mrs Watson so many things. When Julian would be coming home on leave, whether he was interested in any particular girl, had he ever said that he liked her even though she felt sure he hadn't.

Mrs Watson's face was pensive, her thoughts miles away – suddenly smiling she said, 'Forgive me Nancy, but I was thinking about Julian. My husband is very unhappy about the state of things in Europe. He thinks we're heading for some sort of conflict. He keeps going on and on about

163

Hitler and that Italian dictator. I have to admit I'm not happy with the news either.'

'He thinks there might be war?'

'Well yes. He says it's looking that way, but then all those years in the Navy have conditioned him to expect the worst. Elspeth says her husband is on the same wavelength.'

'I wonder if that's the reason we're singing so many patriotic songs this year? Oh surely there can't be a war. Would Julian be in terrible danger?'

'A great many young men, and women too, will be in danger if it comes to that.'

'I wouldn't be thinking about a job, would I? I'd be told what I must do.'

'Well, it's a beautiful summer afternoon and we shouldn't be thinking about war, Nancy. Here comes my husband – he mustn't even think we've been discussing anything so terrible.'

The Commodore greeted Nancy warmly. He liked the girl, she was bright and cheerful, and she did his wife good just to talk to her. Mrs Watson said quickly, 'Has Joyce Mellor decided to take part in the concert, Nancy?'

'I wouldn't think so, her father says she can't.'

'And Joyce has no say in the matter?'

'I don't think so.'

'Can't say I like the fella,' the Commodore said shortly. 'Never actually spoken to him but he shows no sign of wanting to know any of us. Doesn't come to the Cricket Club, doesn't play golf and his wife's even stopped coming to church – it's as if they don't want to have anything to do with any of us.'

Nancy decided it was time to go home. Somehow or other the talk of war was uppermost in her mind. What would war mean to St Agnes and what about Julian? What would it do to Julian? One thing was certain, it wouldn't bring him any closer to her.

She was also worried about Joyce. The music master was

164

urging her to do something on her own at the concert, particularly as she would be leaving the school and it would be something for St Agnes to remember her by.

Joyce had been quiet on their way home and when Nancy asked her if it was because of the concert she said anxiously, 'My father won't allow it, Nancy. I wish he wouldn't keep asking me to do something. If I tell my father he'll be furious and will no doubt come to the school to confront him.'

'Why would your father mind so much, Joyce? It'll be the last time and then you'll be leaving. Surely just for once he won't object.'

Joyce remained silent before parting from Nancy with a shake of her head and a doubtful frown.

Why does the house still looked so unlived in? Joyce wondered as she opened the gate. The garden looked unkempt and even the few shrubs seemed dejected. Her father had no interest in gardening, and although her mother normally pottered around digging up weeds she was singularly disinterested in anything these days.

She'd passed houses where people sat enjoying the sunshine, where there had been laughter and the clinking of glasses. They had smiled at her tentatively but she knew that they all speculated about her way of life and that of her parents.

Her mother was in the kitchen preparing the evening meal and looked up with a vague smile, saying 'Your father's gone to the post office, he'll be back in a few minutes.'

'Can I help you, Mother?'

'No dear, perhaps you'd better let your father see you're practising your music.'

But Joyce sat at the kitchen table staring morosely through the window, causing her mother to ask anxiously, 'Is something wrong, dear? You seem a little troubled.'

Joyce smiled bleakly and remained silent.

Margaret Mellor already knew that her husband was in a

165

fractious mood. He hadn't said a word to her over the breakfast table but had sat reading his newspaper, ignoring any comments she'd made. Surely there wouldn't be any confrontation today. She had a headache and they were becoming more and more frequent.

Joyce got up from the chair and started to lay the table. They normally ate in the kitchen as her father had said that the dining room was a waste of time. More and more she began to ask herself why her parents had even considered buying the house.

In an attempt to make conversation her mother asked, 'Is your friend Nancy looking forward to leaving school?'

'Not really, Mother, we all love it there.'

'What is she going to do?'

'She's not sure.'

'Not like you, with all your aspirations, dear.'

'Mother, can't you talk to Father and ask him if I can do something at the end-of-term concert. They're all asking me at school and I hate telling them it isn't possible.'

Alarmed, her mother looked at her anxiously, saying, 'Darling, you know it isn't possible. Please don't antagonise him by asking – you know what he's like.'

Joyce knew she would get no help from her mother, but some strange feeling of defiance was making itself felt, and when her father entered the room he too was aware of the atmosphere – from his wife's frightened look and his daughter's heightened colour.

Before Joyce could speak her father said, 'I've seen that music teacher of yours in the post office. He didn't even pass the time of day.'

'That's because you won't let me take part in anything at the school,' Joyce replied.

'As a musician surely he can understand why.'

'No he can't, Father. He's been trying to get me to do something at the end-of-term concert. It'll be the last time so surely just this once you can allow it.'

'No, I will not allow it. I've already said my piece when

166

I saw him at the school. That will be the end of it.'

'But it isn't fair. You're not the one who has to face all of them. You should be proud that they want to hear me play. Other fathers want to listen to their children – you're always telling me that I'm the best, and yet you won't let anybody listen to me.'

'Because you're not ready for it yet.'

'All I ever do is play scales, endless scales, hardly ever a tune, and just when I have the opportunity to entertain other people you put a stop to it.'

'And I won't listen to any more of this young lady. While you live in my house at my expense you'll do as I say. And you can forget food, I don't want any.'

He stormed out of the kitchen and they could hear the slamming of the music room door behind him.

'Oh Joyce, you shouldn't have spoken to you father like that,' her mother said miserably. 'I've cooked a meal and now he's gone off in a temper and the meal will be ruined. He only wants what's best for you, dear, do remember that.'

'No Mother, he wants to control me, just like he controls you. I don't care what he says, I'm going to play in that concert. He can't stop me.'

'But he can, Joyce. He'll go to the school and cause a scene. We'll be the talk of the town and everybody will ignore us just like your music master's ignored your father. Go to him, Joyce, and apologise. Tell him he's right, that you didn't mean any of it.'

'But I did mean it, Mother. I'm going in there to tell him I meant it. I've got to make him see that I want to take part in that concert, it'll be the last time. After that he can have his own way with me.'

Margaret sat at the kitchen table listening to the sound of their voices, her husband angry, Joyce tearful at first, then pleading and finally angry too.

She became aware suddenly of the smell of burning and realised that it came from the meal in the oven, now probably ruined, and she went quickly to turn it off.

She heard the sound of Joyce's footsteps running up the stairs. Their argument was obviously over, but it would drag on until Joyce's days at school were over, and she didn't think she could bear it.

There was nothing for them in St Agnes and she had so loved it on that first afternoon when she and Joyce had walked along the path beside the river. It had seemed so peaceful. She had loved the gentle meandering river with the wild iris growing among the reeds – the young people boating on it had seemed so happy and carefree. She had thought that perhaps one day Joyce would enjoy it in the company of some nice boy, but it had been a pipe dream, nothing more.

There would be no boys for Joyce. There would be nothing and nobody in her life to interfere with what her father had planned for her. He would not allow Joyce to fall in love because he had never experienced love himself.

She had seen the river in its darker moods, a mood so in keeping with her own life, and even now, when she went to the water's edge to feed the mallards, its tranquillity seemed to mock her troubled heart.

He came back into the kitchen while she was disposing of the burnt meal, his expression dour. 'More expense,' he grumbled. 'Were we expected to eat that?'

'It was alright until you had your argument. I'd forgotten I'd left the oven on and you said you didn't want anything.'

'You forget most things these days, Margaret. Between you and the girl I don't know whether I'm coming or going.'

'I'm sorry.'

'I suppose she's in her room sulking.'

'Actually she's very upset.'

'I'm upset. I get no thanks for what I'm doing for her. All she cares about is showing off in front of the rest of the school and when she does make something of herself they'll remember how inept she was.'

'They wouldn't be asking her to play for them if they thought she wasn't good enough.'

'She's good enough for the school hall; my plans are for the concert hall.'

Exasperated, he watched the tears rolling down his wife's face. It didn't take much to make her cry – she was too emotional by half and his mother'd been like that, ready to cry at the drop of a hat. It was true his father had always been an unreasonable man, but he wasn't going to stand for it from Margaret.

'Pull yourself together, woman,' he snapped. 'I've had it from the girl, I'm not having it from you.'

Looking at him piteously she said, 'Arthur, just for once, can't you allow her to take part in the concert at school? She'll be leaving very soon and it will be for the last time.'

'And let her see she's won?'

'No, it isn't that. We have to live in this town, we don't want to be the people that nobody speaks to, nobody likes.'

'It doesn't bother me. Who are they anyway?'

'It bothers me. They're nice people. Couldn't we go to the concert, listen to her play, be part of them, then when it's all over forget about it?'

'And you'd be there smiling at everybody, trying to be one of them, chivvying me into be being one of them, making me out to be the nicest person in the world, instead of a father with his daughter's best interests at heart.'

'If you're not very careful, Arthur, she could end up hating you, blaming you that she hasn't any friends, that when she walks out of the door nobody wants to speak to her. Is that really what you want?'

For a long time he remained staring through the window, his expression moody. At last he turned, saying abruptly, 'I can't fight both of you about this. When she decides to come down send her to me in the music room. I'm not going chasing after her.'

She stood trembling, hardly daring to believe that he

169

might reconsider anything. But maybe there was hope. Perhaps for the very first time she had made him listen to her. She'd ask Joyce to come downstairs, talk to her father, and then she'd have to think about a meal, something decent that might improve Arthur's temper.

Joyce was sitting on the edge of her bed, still angry, still defiant. Her mother said gently, 'Do go to him, dear, he's coming round, so try not to make him cross again.'

'Mother, he won't change his mind.'

'Just try darling, be nice to him. I remember your granny telling me that your grandfather was difficult, but sometimes by being specially nice to him she got her own way.'

'And I've seen Granny in tears and very unhappy.'

'I know, dear. The dinner was spoilt and I've had to throw it away, so I'll have to think of something else. You can imagine he wasn't too happy about that. Do it for my sake, dear.'

So Joyce went downstairs, swallowing her anger and her pride. She remembered her grandmother doing the same thing when she was most hurt, so now she told her father she understood all he wanted of her, that she would never ever argue with him again or attempt to disobey him, but just for the last time would he please allow her to join in the school's performance.

'And what will you play?' he asked sourly.

'I'd like you to choose it for me. You know what music you like and which I can play best. I'll tell the music master you have to be the one to choose as you know best.'

Later that afternoon they sat down to tinned salmon and salad, something that had been easy to prepare, and with some semblance of normality restored.

Joyce was to be allowed to perform in the school concert, playing the music her father would select, but after that both Joyce and her mother knew that Arthur Mellor would dominate both their lives.

170

Chapter Eighteen

The concert was well under way. The hall was crowded with proud parents and the school choir had sung the patriotic songs so favoured that year by the music master. The school's orchestra was well rehearsed and had been well received, now it was Joyce's turn to play the music her father had chosen – Schubert, not her favourite composer.

She was playing mechanically, without panache, her thoughts a long way from the crowded hall or her music. She was thinking of her mother's anguished face as she had stood in the hall doorway watching them drive away.

Her mother had been wearing a new silk dress in lilac which Joyce had chosen for her. Normally her mother would wear black or beige, colours that did little for her colouring, but she had looked so pretty and she had stood smiling in the hall waiting for her husband's approval – instead he had looked at her dourly and said, 'I don't want you to come with us to the school, Margaret.'

They had both stared at him in dismay as he went on quickly, 'I don't want you drooling over the affair or our daughter's accomplishments. I don't want you smiling at all and sundry and kowtowing to the teachers. After tonight they're history.

'We'll come back as soon as the concert is over, and I don't want you weeping and wailing while we're gone, think about my feelings for a change.'

171

He had literally dragged Joyce out of the house so that her last sight of her had been her dismayed face. She felt a deep anger in her own heart.

She was glad of her lacklustre performance, glad of the occasional wrong note knowing that it would embarrass her father, glad that the applause was tinged with misgivings that the girl who had played for them tonight was not the same girl who had captivated them months before.

They drove home in silence. Her father had stormed out of the school without speaking to anyone and she had followed him with an apologetic smile at the music master. No doubt they would be the topic of conversation amongst those remaining.

The house was in darkness when they drove up the drive flanked by rhododendron bushes; he slammed the door of the car and strode off towards the house without a backward glance.

Joyce looked up at the dark windows anxiously. Her mother had probably gone to bed and was lying there miserably aware of his cruelty. Because of her performance that evening there was likely to be much more of it.

The kitchen table was set for breakfast next morning, something her mother always did the night before. Her father was evidently in the music room nursing his shattered pride. Joyce decided to make her mother a cup of tea and do all she could to comfort her.

Her mother's bedroom was empty. The lilac dress lay across the coverlets, the new shoes she had been wearing near the chair.

Joyce looked round her with dismay. Her mother never went out at night, she had nowhere to go to. Many of their neighbours had been at the school and in any case her mother hardly knew them. She went to the wardrobe and looked at the clothes hung there but was unable to think what her mother could be wearing.

She had obviously changed into a skirt and blouse.

172

Looking in the hall wardrobe she could see that her mother's old fawn mac was missing.

Where would her mother have gone?. There was the church, but the Vicar and his wife had been at the school, and in any case why would her mother go to the church when she rarely went on Sundays these days?

It was almost ten o'clock and still light outside, the sky tinged with pink over the western hills. Joyce hurried along the path and out into the road.

It was very quiet. There would be laughter and chatter in the school hall where they would be enjoying the buffet supper, and as she hurried towards the church she didn't meet a soul. There were no lights on when she got there but she could see the sexton walking towards her so she hurried forward to meet him.

'Is there anybody in the church, Mr Barlow?' she asked him.

'Nay lass, not at this time. I've just been to lock up.'

'I don't suppose you've seen my mother here this evening?'

'Why no. That would be Mrs Mellor, wouldn't it?'

'Yes.'

'She's not been round here, miss. Gone walking has she?'

'She's not at home, so I thought she might be here. Perhaps she's walking near the river.'

'I shouldn't think so, love, folks try to avoid the river path at this time of the evening. It's getting dark now. I'm sure she'll be at home when you get back.'

Joyce smiled and thanked him before hurrying towards the river. She met only one other person, a lady walking her dog, and recognised her as the lady who lived opposite the Clarksons. Mrs Edgebaston they called her, a lady who smiled and wished her good evening.

Joyce paused only briefly to look over the wall towards the dark river with only the occasional lamp reflected in its swirling water. The path was empty, even of the couples

173

she had often seen there. Making up her mind suddenly she ran back until she caught up with Mrs Edgebaston.

'Did you see my mother somewhere on your walk?' she asked quickly, as Mrs Edgebaston paused.

'No, I didn't meet a soul. I thought it was unusually quiet tonight, but everyone's probably at the school.'

Joyce fell into step beside her and Anthea said, 'I thought you were performing in the concert this evening.'

'Yes I did, we left early.'

'Wasn't your mother with you?'

'No, she didn't want to come,' Joyce lied.

'She's probably at home waiting for you to get back. Did the concert go well?'

'I suppose so.'

'What did you play?'

'Schubert, my father chose it.'

'And it wasn't your choice?'

'Not really.'

'I hear you practising the piano when I'm out walking my dog. An awful lot of commitment is demanded of you, I think.'

'Yes. Well, I must get home. I do hope she's back by now.'

As she let herself into her house Mrs Edgebaston was aware of a strange feeling of disquiet. She had felt it on the night she'd seen Erica standing too close to the water's edge, a feeling that something was terribly wrong, and she felt it now. The girl's face had been too anxious, her eyes filled with fear, and as on that other night she felt there was more to come.

Joyce entered the house in hopeful anticipation but her mother had not returned, and when she went into the music room she found her father asleep in his chair, a bottle of whisky on the floor, an empty glass on the table. She knew that her father often drank long after she and her mother had gone to bed because she heard his lumbering footsteps passing her door as he made his way to his bedroom.

174

Her parents had occupied separate bedrooms for several years, her mother saying it was because his comings and goings were unpredictable, but she'd known it was more than that.

He would be no use to her now, and once again she left the house and wandered towards the river. It was the river that frightened her most, even on a warm August night when the leaves hardly stirred in the branches over her head, and she felt strangely alone in that empty silent place.

Anthea Edgebaston too was unable to sleep. She hoped Margaret Mellor had returned home, but it was her daughter's frightened face that bothered her most. She knew very little about them, only the odd bits of gossip Edith had indulged in and she hadn't encouraged her to say more.

She was up and in her garden before seven o'clock and when Edith arrived at eight o'clock she was dressed and eating her breakfast when normally she would be pottering around in her dressing gown.

Edith smiled. 'You're up early. It's going to be nice, I think.'

'Yes, that's what I thought. Did you pass the Prothero House?'

They still called it that, even though Mrs Prothero had been gone some time.

'Yes. No sign of life there.'

They didn't know that Joyce was already out and wandering round the town. Her mother had not been home and now she was desperately worried, made more so by her father's lack of concern. He had simply said that her mother was probably sulking and this was her way of paying him back for not allowing her to go to the concert.

Furious Joyce had said, 'Mother wouldn't do that, how can you even think it?'

He had laughed, told her not to be such a little fool and gone on eating his breakfast.

She was on her way back to the house when she again

175

met Mrs Edgebaston walking her dog – there was no way she could avoid her much as she wanted to.

'Did you find your mother?' Mrs Edgebaston asked gently.

Joyce immediately burst into tears and Anthea said, 'I'm so sorry, I do hope nothing is wrong.'

'She didn't come home and I don't know what to do.'

'Is there nowhere she could have gone to? Friends, relatives?'

'We don't have relatives here, we don't have many friends.'

'Then we really should so something about it, Joyce. What has your father said?'

'He's not very well. I don't want to worry him.'

'Well, somebody has to be worried. You're friendly with Nancy Clarkson, aren't you? Why don't you call on them – perhaps David Clarkson will be able to help.'

'Mother won't want a fuss, she'll not want people knowing she's been out all night.'

'My dear, she could be ill somewhere. Don't you think it's time to get some sort of help?'

'Oh I don't know, my mother wouldn't like anyone to know. My father will be angry.'

'And your mother might have been taken ill somewhere and be badly in need of help. Really, my dear, something should be done and done quickly.'

Joyce looked at her in silence then, making up her mind suddenly she said, 'Yes, I'll go to Nancy's. Perhaps her father will help, he's very nice.'

So they walked back together and at Anthea's gate Joyce said, 'You won't tell anybody, will you. I'm sure Mother's alright. She hates people knowing our business.'

'Hurry Joyce, there's Mr Clarkson in his garden.'

In all the time Joyce and Nancy had been friends neither of them had visited each other's homes. Although Nancy had invited Joyce many times she had never accepted the invitations; Joyce had never invited Nancy to visit her.

176

David Clarkson therefore regarded the girl walking up his garden path with some surprise. As she drew nearer he could see her pale worried face was streaked with tears and he said anxiously, 'Hello Joyce, is something wrong?'

Joyce started to cry, and taking hold of her arm he said quickly, 'Come inside, tell me what's wrong over a cup of tea.'

Both Nancy and her mother sat at the breakfast table and they waited in silence until Joyce was able to control her crying and tell them her fears. Afterwards David said, 'I think we should inform the police, Joyce, obviously something is wrong. If your mother has been taken ill somewhere she needs assistance, but in any case we have to find her.'

'Oh surely not the police,' Joyce cried. 'Mother would hate it. Can't we all look for her?'

'I suspect you're spent most of the night looking for her.' David said reasonably.

'Yes, but there's only been me. If you were to come with me we could look further.'

'Joyce, you really should inform the police. Your mother could be ill somewhere and very frightened. They can do this better than any of us and there would be no prying eyes wondering what they are doing. I'll go with you to the Police Station and we'll tell them together what has happened.'

'Mother will be frightened by the police.'

'She will also be very grateful to them. Now come along and have some breakfast, then we'll go down together. What about your father? Will he come with us?'

'No, he isn't well.'

'Then perhaps he should stay at home in case she comes back.'

David had no illusions that her father would want to go with them. He didn't know the man, but what he did know of him hadn't exactly endeared Arthur Mellor to him.

The police sergeant on the desk was sympathetic, assur-

177

ing them that no time would be lost in looking for Mrs Mellor, and advising Joyce to go home and await results.

So Joyce declined David's offer to go home with her, as well as his invitation for her to stay with them. Instead she went home to tell her father that the police were now involved.

'Then until your mother comes to her senses I suggest we get on with your music. It's what she would want.'

Joyce stared at him incredulously before saying, 'I'm not playing the piano again until my mother comes home, and if she doesn't come home I shall never play again.'

It was two o'clock in the afternoon when police informed them that Margaret Mellor's body had been found floating in the reeds above the weir.

The entire town was shocked into disbelief, another suicide to add to the one so many years before. It was true that unfortunate accidents had happened when the river was in full flood, usually in the early spring when adventurous youths had accidentally fallen into the swirling waters, but there was no way Mrs Mellor could have fallen into the river on a calm August night when the Rowan was at its most peaceable.

Neighbours wrote letters of condolence, but they did not visit, largely because the doors of the Mellors' house remained adamantly closed, and neither Mr Mellor nor his daughter emerged from its portals.

When the Vicar went to make enquiries about the funeral he was met by Arthur Mellor's sister, who told him that her brother had left all the arrangements in her hands and they wished the funeral to be very private.

There would just be the three of them at the service and they did not wish anybody in the town to attend, the entire time had been stressful for all of them, and they simply wanted to be alone in their grief, and left to recover on their own.

The Vicar passed their wishes on to his congregation, but

he had worries of his own. His wife was unwell and adamantly refusing to see her doctor, telling him that she was simply out of sorts and that it would all pass over if they could get away for a few days' rest.

The Vicar obeyed Arthur Mellor's instructions to the letter. He had never conducted such a spartan funeral before as the Mellors were the only people in the church and at the graveside before departing straight home.

He was however determined that a memorial service should be held the following Sunday and although the Mellor family were not there it was well attended by the rest of his parishioners.

There was no denying the deep sadness prevailing over the ceremony – many people were also aware that he kept looking anxiously at his wife sitting in her pew. She was pale and hardly her usual cheerful self, and though some people put it down to the sadness of the occasion, others thought she had not looked herself for some time.

None of the congregation thought it strange that a For Sale sign went up outside the Mellors' house shortly afterwards – they were hardly people likely to tell others what they were up to.

Nancy said she should call round to see Joyce but her father thought it wiser not to. 'Let Joyce grieve for her mother in her own way,' he advised. 'I'm sure she'll call to see you before they move away.'

'I wonder if Mrs Prothero will come back,' her mother said.

'Why would she?' David asked.

'Well, her nephew went abroad, didn't he, and she's in London on her own, probably not knowing anybody. London can be a very lonely place.'

'I doubt if she'll come back.'

'I'm not so sure.'

David stared down at his newspaper reflectively. London could soon become a very dangerous place. He didn't believe in the 'peace in our time' theory that the Prime

Minister was promising, particularly when gas masks were being issued and meetings mustered to discuss how they should be used. There was also much talk about taking in evacuees from the large cities and Nancy Clarkson was hinting that she was going into the WRNS instead of secretarial college.

The entire area was speculating on how long it would take to sell the Prothero House and what part Joyce's music would play in a world that was becoming increasingly dangerous.

Chapter Nineteen

Mrs Prothero was delighted to welcome the Clarksons and the Robsons to her flat in London. The sitting room was pleasant but very small and with five people in it there wasn't much room for anything else.

They duly admired the flat, but Mrs Prothero said, 'I suppose it's very nice for just me, but Oliver is abroad and I know few people around here. One of the girls he knew calls to see me, but she's only here for a few minutes and she's gone.'

She was interested in all that had happened in St Agnes since she'd left – Margaret Mellor's suicide and the fact that the Vicar's wife was terminally ill, Lady Marcia's third divorce and Erica's job in political circles. Then Mrs Robson asked the question uppermost in all their minds.

'Is there any chance that you might come back to St Agnes?'

They were reassured by her lack of surprise at the question.

'Oh I'd love to, but it would be too much bother and I don't have Oliver here to advise me.'

They decided not to labour the issue, but her response gave them something to think about on their way home.

The house had been on the market for a month but it was a sign of the times that there didn't seem to be much interest from potential buyers. Mr Mellor's sister had returned to London and both Joyce and her father were seldom seen. This worried Nancy considerably until the morning she saw Joyce furtively walking across the garden and she rushed inside the gate to catch her before she could enter the house.

She was well aware that Joyce would have preferred not to have seen her, but Nancy was determined they should talk.

Not very long ago all the town had remarked on Joyce's beauty, but today she seemed strangely colourless and she was thinner, as though she didn't care any more.

'Do you have to move away?' Nancy asked plaintively.

'Yes, I don't want to live here any more, nor does my father.'

'But nothing that has happened is your fault, Joyce. Everybody understands.'

'We haven't sold the house yet, but there are some people interested in it.'

'But where are you going?'

'My father has seen a house in Derbyshire. Aunt Edna said it is a sort of farmhouse surrounded by the Peaks.'

'You'll have nothing but your music.'

'So nothing will have changed, will it Nancy? I think there will be a war. If there is everything will change. What will you do?'

'I want to go into the WRNS. Couldn't you come with me?'

Joyce merely smiled. It was a dismissive smile and, deciding to drop the subject, Nancy said, 'I don't suppose I'll ever see you again when you move to Derbyshire, but you could always come to us for holidays. I'm sure Mother would be delighted.'

'Thank you, Nancy, but we can't really make any plans for the future can we, everything is too uncertain.'

'I suppose so.'

'I must go now, Nancy, there's so much to do. If I don't see you again before we leave I'll think of you a lot.'

Nancy joined Mrs Watson in her garden and related her conversation with Joyce to her.

'It all sounded so final,' she said sadly. 'How can you be friends with somebody, then simply go away without even intending to meet again?'

'I rather think you can if you are Joyce Mellor, Nancy. Something quite terrible happened to her and her father is obviously a difficult man. You on the other hand have a lot of friends, my dear, and a happy family life. What of you sister Erica these days?'

'Oh she likes her job. She goes on and on about the MP's surgery visits, what a lot she has to do and how nice he is. It's not something I would like to do.'

'What would you like to do?'

'I'm going into the WRNS. If there's a war I'll be called up anyway.'

'Probably.'

'Do you ever hear from Julian? Aren't you very worried?'

'Very. I went through the last war with his father, now it's our son's turn. Yes Nancy, I am very worried.'

'Isn't he due any leave soon?'

Mrs Watson's face brightened considerably. 'Yes, this next weekend for a few days. Both his father and I are so looking forward to it. Andrew thinks it might be the last one for some time.'

'Perhaps I'll see him.'

'Well of course, dear. He knows all about the girl who keeps me company in the garden and runs errands for me. You must call, Nancy.'

She had every intention of calling, even though Julian Watson would be polite and charming, would thank her for being kind to his mother and then forget her immediately.

Erica sat in her office listening to the hum of conversation from next door. The MP and his agent had been closeted together for most of the morning and it wasn't simply business.

As they both came through to her office together Erica said, 'I've sorted all the letters out in date order, Mr Greavson. I think you'll find they're all there.'

'Thank you, Erica, I'm sure I shall. Are you coming to the surgery with me now, Jason?'

'No, I've one or two things to see to first. I'll join you later.'

'Right. I'll expect you then.'

After the MP had left Jason perched on the end of her desk and started to read through his correspondence, then with a brief smile he said, 'We're running late this morning, Erica. He was decidedly out of sorts this morning.'

'Isn't he well?' she asked.

'He's losing his secretary in London. She's been with him a good many years. Taken him by surprise, I suppose.'

'Why is she leaving?'

'To get married.' He smiled. 'Tired of waiting I think, so she's marrying a gentleman farmer from Hertford. Nothing to do with politics or politicians.'

'Oh dear,' was all she permitted herself to say, and Jason said, 'Well, I'll be off now, Erica. He's likely to need some help this morning.'

After he had gone she sat thinking about what little she knew about the MP and his secretary. She gathered from bits of conversation she'd heard that they'd been together long enough for speculation to have arisen about their future as an item, but somehow or other he hadn't been able to make up his mind and now it would appear he'd lost her.

What would it be like working in Westminster, living in London? Of course, he'd want somebody older, more experienced, more sophisticated. When he came to meet his constituents he was invariably charming, helpful and considerate, but to work for him every day, what would it be like?

184

However pampered she'd felt in St Agnes when she'd been with Oliver Denton he'd always made her feel that she was countrified, hardly a match for the city girls he knew.

She got up from her chair and went to look out of the window. In the city she was just one of a million other girls who came in from the suburbs every morning and went home again in the evening, faceless, except to the families they went home to.

She shared a house with two other girls who talked about the same things: boys and clothes and office parties, and how one day they'd meet the boy they'd want to marry. Then it would be semi-detached houses in quiet avenues, mortgages and schools for their children – at that moment Erica wanted none of it.

She was lucky. Her father had a good position and money, but neither his position nor his money had been enough for Oliver. Oliver had seen what he wanted in London and compared to that she'd been a nonentity.

She felt restless, recognising it as the feeling she'd always had when things seemed mundane and something more adventurous loomed on the horizon.

There was no harm in seeking information about the vacant post in London, he could only say no. But she knew that her father would not help her as both parents would object to her even thinking about London.

When the MP had returned to London she mentioned it to Jason Stevenson who immediately said, 'You want to leave me already, Erica?'

'Oh, it isn't that. I'm ambitious, I want to spread my wings. I've always been like that and I suppose I always will be.'

'Nothing wrong with that, my dear, but would your parents approve? Let me see, how old are you?'

'I'm twenty, I suppose I'm too young to even think about it.'

'And he might already have somebody in mind.'

'Yes, of course.'

'Well, let me sleep on it, Erica, and if I think it's worth a shot I'll have a word with Greavson when I next talk to him.'

The next few days dragged by. She was expectant and fearful in turns, and whenever she heard the telephone ringing next door she waited anxiously for him to tell her that that was the call. Every time he came into her office she looked up anxiously until one day he said, 'He's in Paris, Erica, at some conference or other. I haven't forgotten.'

She was getting ready to leave the office several days later when he said, 'I've spoken to Alistair, Erica. He's told me to tell you to apply in the usual manner, and you'll be considered along with others.'

'Will there be many, do you think?'

'I don't know. Perhaps some aspiring young woman who is anxious to take over where Celia left off. Maybe they all think he intends his condition to be permanent, and somebody your age would prefer a younger man anyway.'

'It's the job I want, Mr Stevenson, not a husband.'

When she told her parents they were horrified. To move to London would be foolish, particularly with war threatening. Who did she know, where would she live?

The girls who worked with Celia had sympathised with her over a great many years. She had cared deeply for Alistair, but although he had thought a great deal of her somehow or other it had never been enough. Now her job was vacant and there were girls in the pipeline who admired him, thought he would be good to work for but didn't want to fall in love with him.

Alistair too had reservations. Someone new, he thought. Someone with no knowledge of the past and who did not know Celia.

Erica fitted the category well. She was young, probably had a dozen boyfriends of her own age, and she'd worked well at the constituency office. She couldn't believe her

186

luck when he offered her the job – and then began her battle with her parents.

They were against it, not the job but the move to London. Then suddenly, out of the blue, Amelia Prothero was on her way back to St Agnes. She'd never really settled in to her flat, and her old house was empty and up for grabs. Arthur Mellor was asking far more than she had sold it to him for but Amelia said she could afford it. She was feeling happier and more contented than she'd felt since Jethro died.

Erica persuaded her father to make an offer for the flat. She would find some other girl who would be prepared to share it with her, and since it wasn't in the centre of London the danger would not be as great if there was a war. Her persuasions were too much for both her parents and in the end she got her own way.

While the Clarksons felt that they were losing both their daughters there were also problems at Mrs Edgebaston's house.

Edith Pinder liked working for her. She was generous, always giving her clothes, handbags and the like – indeed Edith's sister had declared there wasn't enough space for all the ornaments she brought home – but now Mrs Prothero was coming back and Edith was feeling some sort of apprehension about it. She had worked happily for Mrs Prothero for many years and so she might well expect her to return to her.

It would be nice but it would be dull. Mrs Edgebaston was amusing and it was a bonus being close to the woman the town liked to speculate about. If she went back to Mrs Prothero it would be like before – respectable gentility until they were both in their dotage. At least Oliver Denton wouldn't be there to issue orders and keep an eye on his aunt's spending

Indeed it was Mrs Edgebaston who raised the issue when she found Edith staring pensively through the kitchen window.

'Is something worrying you, Edith? You're not been yourself for several days,' she asked.

'I've 'eard Mrs Prothero's comin' back to St Agnes. Bought the old 'ouse, she has, and I'm thinkin' she'll expect me to go back to her.'

'Is that what you want, Edith?'

'Oh I like workin' for you Mrs Edgebaston, I really do, but I liked Mrs Prothero too. She was allus very nice, both her and her husband.'

'Edith, if you feel you should return to Mrs Prothero then I shall quite understand. You have a little time to think very carefully about it.'

Edith nodded. 'I never thought she'd come back, he was so keen for her to go.'

'But I believe he went abroad and she was all alone there, at least that's what I've heard,' Mrs Edgebaston said.

'That's right. You know, I never did like 'im very much but she doted on 'im. I reckon he didn't treat that Clarkson girl very well, but then she was always a proper little madam.'

Anthea smiled and decided not to take any further part in the discussion. Erica and Oliver Denton had been a topic of conversation for some time. Scandal was never really forgotten, she was well aware of that.

Changing the subject she asked, 'Have you heard how the Vicar's wife is, Edith? He's looking decidedly miserable these days so I don't suppose the news is good.'

'No. She's gone into a nursing home. He's so busy what with one thing and another, and it's what she wanted, I've heard.'

'I'm so sorry, she's a very nice person.'

'Yes, and a vicar needs a wife.'

So thought Grace Gantry as she laid flowers on her father's grave in the churchyard and the Vicar spoke to her absent-mindedly as he walked along the path towards the church.

Normally when he did so she felt there was something

special between them, even after all these years, but not that morning. He was thinking about his wife and it was right that he should do so. In the months to come there would be all sorts of speculation, but none of it would concern her, not while her mother was with her. Grace's life was like an open book.

On her way home she met Major Robson, dapper as usual, but strangely reflective. Crossing the road beside her he said bleakly, 'Bad news this morning, Grace. Hitler's invaded Poland. We'll be in it before you can say Jack Robinson.'

'You really think so?'

'Absolutely certain.'

For some time they walked in silence. For weeks there'd been meetings in the village hall on what should be done when war came as they'd all believed it was inevitable. Now the Major said dolefully, 'Some of those young lads I've been involved with will be called up for sterner duties than anything I've been concerned with. They're good lads, all of 'em. We'll be losing a few familiar faces, Grace.'

'Yes, I expect we will.'

'The young Clarkson girl's going in the WRNS. I like young Nancy and will miss her cheeky grin whenever I pass their garden.'

'What about Erica?'

'I've heard a rumour that she's moving to London to work for Alistair Greavson, the MP. I haven't seen any of them to ask if it's true, but I expect it is. It has to be something unusual to suit Erica.'

'And Mrs Prothero is coming back to St Agnes.'

'By Jove yes, that's something we didn't expect. I wonder what's going to happen to that Mellor family. Disastrous state of affairs that was, and that girl – right beauty she was when she came here, then almost overnight she seemed to change. No wonder though with a father like that and that terrible problem with her mother.'

'It seems strange that there should be so many awful

189

things that seem to have happened overnight. Once this town was so circumspect and normal.'

'Funny you should say that, Grace. I've heard it from Anthea Edgebaston. She said she came here thinking it would be so normal – dull but normal – and it's been anything but.

'It's not the town, is it Grace, it's the people in it, all of 'em different, all of 'em somethin' they're not perhaps.'

'I wonder if Edith will go back to Mrs Prothero,' Grace said.

The Major shook his head. 'There goes the Commodore. They'll be thinking of Julian at this time. I'd like to have a word with him. See you soon, Grace, probably next Tuesday at your bridge afternoon.'

She watched him striding across the road while the Commodore waited for him and guessed that all their talk would be of war and its aftermath. It was something they were both familiar with.

Chapter Twenty

A few months, a few days even, is long enough to change an entire lifetime, thought Joyce Mellor as she stood at the downstairs window of the stone house overlooking the bleak Derbyshire hills.

Her father had settled down remarkably well. He had been welcomed into the community as a musician who had played the violin in a famous orchestra, and now often played at concerts in Buxton and other towns proud of their musical background.

It was at one of these concerts where he had met Mrs Cameron who seemed to be the Secretary for every event the town staged. She was a widow with a son who had recently been called up into the Army and it quickly became apparent that Arthur Mellor was exactly the sort of man she had been looking for.

She was a constant visitor at the old stone house and more and more Joyce began to realise that Mrs Cameron was taking over the running of the house and her father's life.

Between Joyce and her father there was an uneasy peace. She had failed him by not becoming the musician he had wanted, and she held him responsible for her mother's death.

The grand piano stood forgotten in a room where it took over all the available space and her father kept the room locked. He did not want Joyce in there, did not want to hear her play the piano and Joyce felt sure that Mrs Cameron was well aware of the bitterness that existed between them.

Joyce had elected to join the Women's Land Army. They were surrounded by farmland and the days were long and arduous. Three sisters owned the farm where she worked – it seemed like there was no other life since her day started before it was light and ended long after the sun had set.

'Your father tells me you were a good pianist,' Mrs Cameron asked one evening when she arrived home exhausted to find them enjoying a drink in the sitting room.

Joyce smiled but offered no comment.

'What a pity to have given it up, and that beautiful instrument lying idle next door.'

When Joyce remained silent she went on, 'Doesn't it worry you, Joyce, that your father is so talented and you've simply let it slip through your fingers?'

'Perhaps I was never meant to be the sort of pianist my father expected me to be. Perhaps I changed with the world.'

'And to work at that farm with those awful women. They were never popular in the village nearby, you know, they seldom went to church and when the brother was at home they let him do all the rough work.'

'I didn't know they had a brother.'

'Oh yes. Roger is his name. Good-looking boy, if you like the rough type. He's in the Army, so no doubt you'll meet him if he gets leave.'

'They never mention him.'

'Do you have any conversation with them at all? I didn't think they could string two words together.'

It was true that conversation was rare between them. They regarded Joyce as a general dogsbody, somebody to work from dawn to sunset, but they abhorred her cut-glass accent and were doubly hard on her because of it.

It seemed to Joyce that her life was all bed and work.

192

She retired exhausted, and yet she was glad of it because it gave her little time to think about St Agnes and all that had happened there.

She thought about it a lot, particularly Nancy who was somewhere in the WRNS, and Mrs Edgebaston who had been kind to her. She thought about Edith who had stood outside the church on the day of her mother's funeral, and she remembered the singing from within on the day of the memorial service.

It had been a nice town with good people and it could all have been so different.

She was baling the hay on the day Roger Blackstock arrived home on leave, and he walked across the field with a pronounced swagger, a smile on his good-looking, rugged face.

He was a tall robust figure in khaki, broad-shouldered and with a shock of red-brown hair.

He grinned at her as he asked, 'They're puttin' ye through it then?'

She smiled in return and taking up a pitchfork he joined her. 'What's your name then?' he asked.

'Joyce, Joyce Mellor.'

'I'm Roger Blackstock, the brother.'

'You're home on leave?'

'That's right, four days. Long enough for you and me to get to know one another.'

She smiled.

'How are ye gettin' on with me sisters?'

'Well, I get on with my work, I don't really have much to do with them.'

'This'll be my farm one day – they'll treat ye alright while I'm here.'

'I have no complaints, Mr Blackstock.'

He threw back his head and laughed loudly. 'Roger, if ye please, I wants no Mr Blackstock from you.'

In the days that followed she saw a lot of Roger Blackstock.

He was there when she arrived in the morning and he walked with her to the stile when she left to go home.

It was his last day of leave when he waited for her to arrive and, strutting forward to meet her with his usual cheeky grin, he said, 'I've told me sisters you're leavin' early this evenin'. You and me are goin' to have a drink in the Black Bull.'

'I don't know, Roger, my father will be expecting me.'

'Oh come on, all the village knows you and yer father don't 'it it off.'

'How, how do you know?'

'Well, 'e's friendly with that Mrs Cameron, isn't he, and she knows everything and everybody.'

Joyce didn't dispute it, and he went on, 'Have ye never been in the Black Bull since ye got 'ere?'

'No.'

'Well then, ye'll enjoy it. Ye can go home first and put yer glad rags on then I'll walk ye 'ome when we leave. It's time ye met some o' the people fro' round 'ere. Me sisters have you workin' all hours.'

'It's my job.'

'Where 'ave ye come from with that posh accent, London?'

'I lived there for a time, then St Agnes.'

'Where's that then?'

'Devon, on the banks of the Rowan.'

'Never 'eard of it. Did ye like it there?'

'Oh yes, I liked it. I liked the river and the peace there. I would have liked to have stayed there.'

'Then why did ye leave?'

'My mother died and nothing was the same after that. Now it seems a lifetime away.'

He stared at her. He'd never met a girl like Joyce before. The girls he'd met were earthy, they didn't lapse into a sort of poetry or stand staring into space as if they could see something he couldn't.

She was a stunner though. The fresh country air and the

194

sun had brought the colour back into her checks and her body had a supple grace. Not the stalwart shoulders and broad hips of his sisters, but the contours of a dancer. Roger Blackstock could afford to get lyrical about this strange addition to his life.

Her father was out when she went home to change into a dress for the evening ahead, and Roger beamed with delight at her dainty figure in its pretty silk dress and camel coat.

There'd be nobody in the Black Bull to hold a candle to her, he thought with deep satisfaction. There'd be girls there he'd dallied with in the past, most of them village girls, but this one was different. It never entered his head that he was no match for her – he'd always been aware that he was a farmer with his own farm; that he shared it with three sisters was irrelevant. He bore his father's name and his sisters were there to help him run the place, nothing more.

The men drinking in the Black Bull were impressed with Joyce. They'd seen her working on the land, but her high-falutin accent merely puzzled them, and when she told them she had lived in London and St Agnes on Rowansdale they decided among themselves that her time with Roger Blackstock was in no way long term.

Some of them had met her father in the company of Mrs Cameron, and they didn't quite know what to make of Joyce or her father. On the other hand the girls drinking in the pub decided they didn't like her – she was not one of them and never likely to be.

On their way home he walked with his arm around her and she didn't object. England lay in darkness, lit only by a pale new moon – in the distance the deadly throb of German bombers was the only sound.

'Sounds as if they're goin' for Manchester tonight,' Roger commented, 'either that or the RAF place out yonder.'

'When will you get leave again?'

'God knows. I reckon we'll be movin' out soon, but ye'll be 'ere when I get back, Joyce, they'll keep ye workin' on the land until they all get back – at least the ones that are comin' back, that is.'

They could see the house now and Joyce said anxiously, 'Don't come any further, Roger, my father will be home. Thank you for a lovely evening.'

He pulled her quickly into the side of the road. The arms that held her were like a vice and at first she struggled and turned her face away from his searching mouth, then with a laugh he said, 'Yer not frightened of me are you, what's a little kiss?'

'I have to go, Roger, it's late.'

She couldn't avoid his kiss. It aroused no response in her, but when he released her he laughed, asking, 'There's more to come, love, next time I'm home. You and me are going to be a twosome.'

She ran unsteadily towards the house followed by his laughter and as she put her key into the lock she was trembling. She had experienced her first kiss. She had often dreamed about it – a tall handsome young man who would be charming and tender, in a moonlit garden or conservatory, with the sound of music from the ballroom. Never a country lane under dark old trees with the wind whistling through the branches, coarse gnarled hands holding her like a vice and the smell of beer from the mouth pressing hard against hers.

As she ran up the stairs she could see the light creeping through the bottom of the living-room door, and in the next moment it was flung open to reveal her father standing against the light.

'Where have you been, girl? It's well after eleven,' he snarled.

She turned and walked slowly down the stairs and stood on the bottom step where they could look at each other, his face hard and stern, hers anxiously aware of the strictures to come.

'You've been with some lad or other, haven't you?' he snapped.

'I went to the inn with Roger Blackstock. It's the last day of his leave.'

'So a night out with some farm lad is better than all those plans I'd made for you?'

'Father, I would have had to do some sort of war work. Being a would-be concert pianist wouldn't have let me off that.'

'I could have pulled strings, I could have got you off war work, but no, you're too much like your mother. You're the price I paid for marrying her.'

'Perhaps you shouldn't have married her, Father. Mother and I would have survived somehow. Have you forgotten the price she was asked to pay?'

With a long look she walked slowly up the stairs and had almost reached the top step when he caught up with her, spinning her round to face him. With a muttered curse he struck her, sending her flying against the wall where she fell heavily against the door of her bedroom.

Without a word he went down the stairs and dimly through her pain she heard the living-room door slam shut.

Slowly she pulled herself to her feet, aware of the excruciating pain in her shoulder and her back. She limped painfully into her bedroom and sat weakly on the side of her bed.

Sleep did not come easily that long cold night, and in the early morning she limped painfully along the rutted lane on her way to the farmhouse where Mary Blackstock stared at her in some dismay. 'What's happened to you, then?' she snapped, 'ye look as though ye've 'ad a fall.'

'Yes, I fell in the lane. I've hurt my shoulder.'

'Well there's work to be done and I've got me hands full. P'raps yer'd 'ave been better goin' off 'ome last night instead of spendin' it with our Roger in the Black Bull.'

Joyce didn't reply, but she knew where her duties lay and Mary said, 'Winter's comin' on earlier that usual, it's cold and there's things to be done. Me brother's goin' back this mornin', so he'll be no help.'

'Shouldn't you be asking for more help on the farm?' Joyce ventured to ask.

'We'll not get it. All the farms round 'ere need more help. If ye'd bin bought up to farmin' you'd know more about it.'

She was right, but as Joyce made her weary way back to the fields she was hailed by a shout from the farmyard and Roger came running towards her, a broad smile on his face. She paused and then his smile faded as he asked, 'Why are ye limpin'?'

'I fell in the lane and have hurt my shoulder.'

He put out a hand and touched her shoulder gently. When she winced with pain he said, 'Ye didn't fall, Joyce, ye've no mud on your coat and it's bin rainin'. Did yer father do this to ye?'

Her eyes filled with tears and she looked away quickly, but he spun her round to face him, hurting her shoulder as he did so, making her cry out with pain. 'Why should you think that, Roger, it has nothing to do with you,' she whispered, shaking herself free.

'I've heard about 'im. I've heard that 'e's bin swankin' about ye in the town, the daughter who was goin' to be famous. He's only got you and you're workin' at the farm. What's he on about?'

'Oh Roger, it would take too long to tell you. He's been hurt and I've been hurt, there's a lot more but I can't tell you and now I've got to get on with my work. Your sister is watching me and has already had something to say.'

'Take no notice of 'er. I'm goin' back this mornin', Joyce, but when it's all over, if not before, I'll be seein' you. You and me'll be all right. Ye won't ever have to bother about yer father again, I'll sort 'im out.'

She smiled tremulously at him. Somehow at that moment, for the first time in her life she felt that she had a champion. He was not her knight in shining armour, not

198

the charmer who swept her into his arms on the ballroom floor, but a rough young farmer who was going back to the war, and she was unsure if they would ever meet again.

She stood on the hillside after he had left her and thought dismally of the months ahead. Winter was coming and her early life had not prepared her for life in the shadow of the Pennine hills, but she would work hard at it. She had heard it too often that she was like her mother, scared of life, living on her insecurities, fearful of every new day, but not even Joyce was prepared for the day her father informed her he intended to marry Mrs Cameron and that she would be moving in – no doubt making a great many alterations to the house and their life.

The real bone of contention was the grand piano, and Mrs Cameron said one evening, 'There's so much more we could do with this house if only we could get rid of the piano. It simply takes over, you never play it, Joyce never plays it. I've got furniture and nowhere to put it because of the piano. Do think about it, darling.'

So Arthur thought about it, but Joyce was not consulted. On a cold morning a month later Joyce watched the price-less Steinway being loaded onto the back of a lorry, its pristine woodwork scratched in several places, and with only a coarse rug thrown over it to shield it from the sleet falling from leaden skies.

She wept that morning, for the dreams that had faded, for the music that seemed to have gone out of her life forever, and for the beautiful instrument that she would never see again.

She asked no questions about it, but several days later Mrs Cameron said, 'Your father's been paid for the piano, not nearly as much as he would have got in peacetime, but it will recarpet the sitting room and a great many other improvements to the house. I hope you're not expecting any money from it, Joyce. After all, your father bought it. You're the one who refused to play it.'

Joyce didn't answer, and after a few minutes Mrs

Cameron said, 'I shan't expect you to call me mother or anything like that, Joyce. My name is Janet. You can call me that if you like. My son's name is Ian, after his father. You might meet him after the war, but he and I never got along. He hated it when I left Scotland and he'll no doubt go back there.'

'Does he have a wife?'

'A fiancée. Also Scottish.'

'Will you always want to live around here?'

'I shouldn't think so. We'll get you off our hands. No doubt, when the war is over, you will move on. Isn't that what all young people do?'

Chapter Twenty-One

Five months in Arbroath had not conditioned Nancy for the bleak journey up to the Scottish coast to Aberdeen, and as she stood wet and miserable waiting for the ferry that would take her to the Orkneys she could only think that there was worse to come.

The building was crowded with sailors and soldiers and there was nowhere to sit down. They jostled and jested among themselves, but to Nancy it seemed like a sort of bravado between men and women who were trying to make the best of things even when they expected the worst.

She was joined by a girl who came to stare through the window at the teeming docks below. Turning to Nancy she said, 'Are you waiting for the ferry?'

Nancy smiled and nodded. 'Are you?' she asked.

'Yes. God, what a day. Are you a driver?'

'I'm hoping to be.'

'Me too. I'm going up there to learn about the workings of anything on wheels and then I'll be fit to drive huge things wherever they decide to send me. I'm aiming to be driving nothing larger than an Admiral in some posh car. What about you?'

'I doubt that our wishes will be taken into consideration. We'll get what we're given.'

'But there's no harm in dreaming, I suppose. What's your name?'

'Nancy Clarkson.'

'I'm Louise Barcroft. Where do you come from?'

'St Agnes on Rowandale. I don't suppose you've ever heard of it, it's in Devon.'

'No I haven't. I'm from Cheshire, on the borders with Derbyshire. Ever been there?'

'No. I had a friend who has gone to live in Derbyshire but I'm afraid we've lost touch.'

'Very rural. Why did you join the WRNS?'

'No special reason really. I knew I'd be called up if the war started so I volunteered.'

'So did I. Better chance of getting a commission, I think. You know the ATS and the Air Force girls have to wear whatever they're issued with, whereas the WRNS can wear their own things. That's why I opted for them.'

'Really, I didn't know.'

'Do you have a boyfriend in the Navy?'

'No. Do you?'

'One in the Navy, one in the Army. But I'm not settling for either one of them, after all we don't know who we might meet, do we?'

'No. Particularly if you've set your sights on an Admiral.'

Louise laughed. 'He'd be far too old, well he's bound to be, isn't he. I say, it would be nice if we could get together, wouldn't it. I expect there'll be a bunch of us.'

Nancy decided that she liked her. She was brash and funny but fun was not something to be despised in a world that was crumbling.

They were herded at last onto the ferry and the voyage was uneventful until they reached the Pentland Firth which they crossed in a howling gale – neither of them could have cared whether they lived or died. When at last they reached their destination all on board left the ferry like a herd of zombies hardly able to believe that they had arrived unscathed from their ordeal.

They were received by a petty officer who eyed them

202

with jaundiced disbelief, a bevy of girls miserable and bedraggled. Most of them were still suffering from seasickness, and their resentment was very apparent.

'Stick close by me,' Louise mumbled. 'We're not going to get much joy out of her.'

As she sat at last on the side of her bed Nancy couldn't believe that they were here in a tin hut in the company of eight other girls. Ten beds and a stove that smoked, filling the air with an acrid smell. A small cupboard beside each bed and a narrow wardrobe between two of them was the extent of what passed as furniture.

They had been told where to find the sick bay, the dining hall and the ablutions. Although none of them were interested in food, they were soon faced with two petty officers who ordered them to eat. Lights were to be out by ten o'clock and they would be woken at six in the morning, after which they favoured the girls with a cool 'I am to be obeyed' stare before leaving the room.

The first few weeks were the worst. Nancy dreamed about motor engines, and when she had the time she wrote home about vehicles her father had never heard of, let alone the workings of them.

The Commodore and his wife read her letters with delight, particularly the Commodore who said she was undoubtedly turning out to be an asset in the right place. Major Robson thought she'd have done better to have gone into the Army.

They were all delighted when she received her commission after eighteen months of hard graft, and the Clarksons lived in hope that she would be soon returning to more hospitable shores.

Summer had come to the Orkneys, people smiled more, the sun shone out of a clear blue sky and on the hillside heather bloomed in profusion. Summer was something that did not last long, and to people who were used to high winds and storm clouds it was a blessing to be cherished.

Nancy and Louise sat on the hillside from where they could look down on Scapa Flow and the conglomeration of warships that were moored there. Two destroyers were just limping into the harbour, and it was evident that somewhere at sea they had been engaged in some sort of battle.

Nancy was thinking about Julian. She had no idea what sort of vessel he was serving on, and on the occasions when they ventured into the Officers' Mess she always looked around quickly in the mistaken hope that she would find him there.

Mostly they sat around and chatted, now and again there was dancing, but most of the men whose ships lay at anchor in Scapa Flow had been embroiled in the battle of the Atlantic, and they were either anxious to get back there, or were not in the mood for something more light-hearted.

They sat listening to the news bulletins which were not good. The war that they hoped would be over quickly was dragging on interminably and at that moment the Allies were not winning it. Germany occupied all of Europe and across the Atlantic America seethed and anguished that she could do little beyond arming England as best she could.

It was Captain Burrows' birthday on midsummer's day and he decided that war or no war he was going to celebrate it; as a result he invited all and sundry to join him in the Ward Room for dinner and dancing, and woe betide anybody who was able to attend but declined the invitation.

'I'd love to get out of this uniform if only for the one night,' Louise sighed. 'What about you? Do you have a dress?'

'No. When would I ever wear one?'

'I could wear my nightie, I suppose. I'm more covered up in that than my swimming costume. Would anybody mind?'

'You know they would. You'd be up before the Commander first thing in the morning and accused of indecency.'

'I suppose so. I wonder if there'll be any new faces. There are new ships in the Flow, surely they'll come to the Captain's party.'

There was no dearth of junior officers on the dance floor and neither of the girls lacked for partners. Nancy had always lived in her sister's shadow and even now found it hard to believe that young men would admire her. She often looked in the mirror and tried to reconcile the new Nancy with the impish tomboy she had been. Now in her officer's uniform she somehow seemed to have acquired a beauty she had never thought she would possess, from her pale auburn hair to the maturing grace of her body.

They were happily surrounded by a bevy of young men when a group of older officers arrived in the company of more senior WRNS. She stared at Julian Watson in some sort of panic. She had hoped to meet him one day, but she had been totally unprepared to do so in the company of a young and very pretty woman.

They were obviously happy in each other's company, dancing and staying together throughout the evening; just once her eyes met his and Nancy smiled. He did not recognise her which she could see at once from the seconds that elapsed before he returned her smile, purely out of politeness.

She was quiet on the way back to their quarters and Louise said, 'Haven't you enjoyed it, Nancy? You seem very subdued. Got a headache?'

'No. Perhaps I'm tired, I had an early start this morning.'

'Darling, we have early starts every morning. It was that officer who came in with the blond, wasn't it? Did you know him?'

'Slightly.'

'I knew her slightly. She's the sister of a girl I went to school with. A very rich family actually. They seemed keen on each other. Does it worry you?'

'Like I said, I only knew him slightly. We lived near his parents in St Agnes.'

'He's the Captain of one of the destroyers that came in yesterday. I danced with a boy who's a junior officer on the same ship. They'd had some sort of spat in the North Sea and they're in for repairs. You'll see him again, I feel sure.'

The next time she saw Julian was at Church Parade the following Sunday when the congregation stood around outside the church in the bright sunlight after the service was over. Julian stood in the company of several others and when their eyes met he responded to her smile with one that was faintly puzzled. As she drew level with him she said, 'Good morning sir, how are you?'

'Do I know you from somewhere?' he asked evenly, and with a swift smile Nancy said, 'I lived near your parents in St Agnes.'

Suddenly his face cleared and his smile became warmer. 'Of course, Nancy, the girl who kept my mother company in the garden. Didn't you have a sister?'

'Yes. Erica.'

'I remember her, and you had a friend, a pianist and very good. I heard her play at some concert.'

'Yes, that was Joyce Mellor.'

He said nothing more about either Erica or Joyce, and Nancy wondered if his parents had told him anything about the tragedy of her mother's death.

As she smiled and turned to move on he fell into step beside her.

'You've come a long way from St Agnes,' he said gently.

'Yes, and you.'

'Ah, but I was never a St Agnes boy. Whenever I came on leave I expected to find that my parents had elected to move, but I was glad that they hadn't. My mother liked it there, although I was never very sure about Dad.'

'I never heard him complain.'

'No, that rather surprises me. I wouldn't have expected

206

him to suffer in silence. When I was at school in England and they were both miles away, I thought that sailors should never marry.'

'And are you still of that opinion?'

He laughed. 'And if I said I was I feel pretty sure you'd enlighten my mother when next you meet. I should be very careful what I say to you, young Nancy.'

At that moment a staff car pulled up at the kerb and Julian said, 'Well, here is the young lady who is picking me up. Next time we smile at each other, Nancy, I shall remember who you are.'

The blond officer of the evening before looked at her curiously, and with a brief smile at Julian Nancy walked away.

He had called her 'young Nancy' and that was probably all she would ever be to him – the tomboy kid his parents had taken to. It was time for her to move on. At that moment a young midshipman passed her, smiling in warm admiration, and Nancy told herself sharply that Julian Watson was not the only man in the world.

He would be entertaining his pretty Wren, telling her he'd just met a girl who knew his parents in order to satisfy her curiosity, and that she was so engrossed with her memory of their conversation that she failed to see Louise rushing down the road to meet her, waving a piece of paper in her hand.

'Nancy, we're being moved on, here's yours,' she cried. 'I'm for Cyprus. Oh I do hope we're posted together.'

As Nancy wrestled with the envelope Louise stood impatiently beside her until they could read the posting together. Then they stared at each other in dismay and Nancy cried, 'Alexandria, but why there?'

'Why anywhere?' Louise said. 'Oh why couldn't they have posted us together. We might have known they'd not be so accommodating – we might never be together again.'

They stood looking morosely at the warships moored across Scapa Flow and Louise said, 'There's his destroyer,

207

waiting to go into the repair yard. That Wren he was with last night is a staff driver. She's got the sort of job I was hoping for, driving some senior officer around, looking pretty in pristine uniform driving some single divine man who's looking for a wife.'

'Probably some long-married man with a brood of children, you mean,' Nancy said laughing. 'But right now she's driving Julian around and he isn't married.'

'And in a couple of weeks he'll be off into the blue and she'll be concentrating on the next one.'

She saw Julian only once before she left the Orkneys. She was sitting in the Officers' Mess with a group of young officers, both male and female, enjoying each others' company.

Julian came in with another officer, but was soon joined by two Wrens, one of them his companion of the other evening. He had already smiled across the room at Nancy and her friends but it was later in the evening when he took the opportunity to speak to her. Out of politeness the others in her group took to the dance floor and sitting next to her Julian said, 'You're moving out, I believe?'

She didn't ask him how he knew but simply said, 'Yes, I have four days' leave, then I've got my posting.'

'I won't ask where you're going, but I take it you'll be spending your leave in St Agnes.'

'Yes. Can I give a message to your parents?'

'Only to tell them that I'm OK. I don't suppose Dad will be satisfied with that so you can tell him we've been in a bit of a spat but nothing to worry about. I've no idea when I shall see them.'

'Your mother won't be satisfied with that. She'll want to know how you look, who you're with and if it's serious.'

He laughed. 'And you, young Nancy, can tell her you don't know.'

She looked into his laughing eyes and knew she would learn nothing more. She felt furious with herself, hating his

208

amusement, but there was no resentment, and she was quick to say, 'I don't intend to tell them anything, after all it's none of my business who you're with.' Then she hated herself even more for appearing to sound childish and immature.

Julian got to his feet to return to his table, saying, 'Well, good luck, Nancy. Who knows, we might meet up again before it's all over.'

'If we do meet again I might not be "young Nancy" any more.'

He looked down at her with gentle irony, placing his hand on her shoulder and saying, 'Cherish the young bit while you may, my dear girl. It isn't a very happy world you're growing up in.'

She watched him walk across the floor, saw the welcoming smile on his companion's face and her heart ached dismally. Perhaps in Alexandria she might forget Julian – after all, schoolgirl crushes never came to anything, or so she'd been told.

She passed on Julian's message to his parents and as she had forecast his mother asked, 'Was he with a girl, Nancy? He never tells us anything. Daughters confide readily with their parents, sons seldom do. They think it's part of being grown up and manly.'

'He was with a Wren who was very pretty. I really don't know very much about her.'

'Did he seem serious about her?'

'Honestly, I couldn't tell. If he is I'm sure you'll hear.'

His father was more interested in the conflict that had brought him to Scapa Flow, but of that Nancy knew very little.

Her parents were very concerned about Erica living in a London that suffered bombings every night, even though she reassured them that she was perfectly safe and enjoying her work.

'Has she met up with Oliver Denton in London?' Nancy asked, and saw the look that passed between her parents.

'I believe they have met,' her mother said diffidently, but seemed indisposed to say anything else.

She went with her mother to visit Mrs Prothero and the house was exactly the same as when she had lived in it before moving to London. It was as though the Mellors had never set foot in it – or in a town that preferred to forget them.

Edith Pinder served them with afternoon tea and Nancy said, 'I often wondered if you'd come back here, Edith, but you were happy with Mrs Edgebaston, weren't you?'

'Oh yes, nice lady she was. She 'ad no difficulty in gettin' somebody else, and in the end I thought I should come back 'ere with Mrs Prothero.'

Nancy smiled and looked through the window. An old man was tying up the dahlias and Mrs Prothero said, 'Young Joe and Ned who used to do my garden have been called up. Charlie does his best but he's well into his seventies. I love the autumn, the trees are just beginning to turn.'

So there are changes in St Agnes, Nancy thought. On the surface nothing had changed, but underneath things were different, and in the end perhaps not even St Agnes would remain unscathed by what was happening in the world.

Chapter Twenty-Two

Oliver Denton stood in the hallway of his flat surrounded by a mountain of luggage. He was weary. The flight from Bombay had experienced several delays and he was feeling isolated and irritable.

On the journey across London he had stared in disbelief at the bomb damage to the city's squares and buildings, and at a people hurrying through the streets only too aware of the trauma the night ahead would bring.

This was not the London he remembered, not the sort of London he had hoped to return to. It was late afternoon and already the winter sky across the river was touched with crimson; all too soon night would come.

He frowned as his eyes fell on the block of flats where he had hoped to find his aunt living. He had visualised a warm welcome from her, tea and toast before the fire, her expressions of joy at his homecoming, but instead there had been a brief letter received just before he left India which had told him very little.

She was going back to St Agnes and people she knew. She was frightened in London and she had the opportunity of selling her flat. She would write again in greater detail when it was all sorted out. He was still waiting for that letter.

There was nothing to eat in the flat so he would have to go out, then in the morning he'd have to see about getting another daily woman. When would there ever be time to do all he needed to do? He'd never been one to like sudden changes in his life and usually there'd been someone to sort things out for him. Where was his mother in all this? Somewhere on the continent in some country overrun by Nazis.

The small restaurant he had often dined at was still there but it looked decidedly run down and the food was inferior. As he ate his solitary meal a woman with a small dog came into the restaurant and he recognised her immediately as someone who lived in the flats where his aunt had lived.

When she looked across the room he smiled, and then suddenly recognising him she got up from her chair and made her way towards him.

'It is Oliver?' she said with a warm smile.

'Yes, you're Mrs Walsh. Do join me.'

'When did you get back, Oliver? Your aunt will be so sorry that she isn't here to welcome you.'

'I only got back this afternoon. I'm still trying to get used to seeing London like this. You must feel very afraid living here on your own.'

'Well, we go down to the air-raid shelters when the sirens start – they don't come every night which is a blessing. Your aunt and I used to go together, she was such a nice lady and I have missed her.'

'She was lucky to sell her flat at such a time.'

'Oh yes, very lucky. It all happened so quickly, one minute she was here then she was going home, as she called it.'

'Who bought the flat?'

'That's the strangest thing. Some girl who lived in St Agnes and who is now working in London. Working for an MP at Westminster, a very pretty girl. Your aunt knew her quite well, and her parents.'

'Then it's possible I might know her.'

'Oh yes, I'm sure you will. Your aunt said you knew her.'

Oliver wracked his brains to think of any girl in St Agnes who was likely to be working in London. Not for a single moment did he think it might be Erica.

Erica had been a small-town girl, cossetted and pampered by being thought to be somebody in a small world – she would never settle for being nobody in a larger world.

He allowed Mrs Walsh to chatter on about the changes she had experienced, the lack of food in the shops, the rationing and the disastrous news that filled the newspapers every morning, and it was only when she finally said, 'I think Monty and I should be getting back, he gets so upset when the sirens go and everybody is rushing about.'

'I'll walk with you to the flats, Mrs Walsh, perhaps one day I'll call at my aunt's flat to see if I know the young lady who's moved in there.'

'Oh yes, do that, Oliver. She's out quite a lot, but she's very nice. Her parents have been to see her and they were very friendly. They told me your aunt had settled back in as though she'd never really been away. She was so delighted to be going back.'

Oliver could well imagine her delight. He'd been the one pressing her to move.

He couldn't see the entrance door to the flats from his window so he couldn't really see the people moving in and out of them, but several days later he sauntered casually across the road from where he could see some of the residents leaving. Although some of them were young he didn't recognise a single one of them. That was the moment he decided he should call.

As he stood at the door he could hear the sound of music from inside so he knocked a little harder. Then to his utmost amazement he was staring into Erica's eyes and she was saying in a calm voice, 'Hello Oliver, when did you get back?'

Of the two of them he was the more disconcerted. Warning bells were already beginning to sound in his ears.

213

Had she chased him to London? Was it all going to start again with the advantage on her side?

He looked round the flat with interest, recognising several pictures and articles of furniture that had belonged to his aunt, and seeing him staring at one of them Erica said, 'Your aunt was awfully generous, Oliver. She said she had enough things in store to fill the house in St Agnes without taking any of these, so she gave them to me. Wasn't that generous of her?'

'Very,' Oliver said dryly.

'My father said he would willingly buy anything she wished to dispose of but she wouldn't allow it. Of course, if you think any of these things should be yours I shall be quite happy to hand them over.'

This was hardly the old Erica who had been only too happy always to fall in with his wishes, to please him at all times. This Erica had a sophistication that was veiled by a cynicism he didn't remember and he wondered how many sides to her he had never discovered. He thought about the people in St Agnes who had compared the Erica he knew with the Erica they remembered.

'Would you like a drink, Oliver?' she asked him. 'I'm afraid sherry is all I have, but we could have coffee.'

'Sherry will do very nicely, Erica. What are you doing in London, particularly wartime London?'

'I work here. I'm PA to Alistair Greavson. Do you know him?'

'Alistair Greavson, the name rings a bell.'

'MP. I work at Westminster.'

'That Alistair Greavson! Destined to go far, ministerial material, I believe.'

'So you do know him?'

'Well, I've been out of the country for some time but yes, I do know something of him.'

She was amused by his puzzled expression and knew what he was thinking. How had small-town girl Erica Clarkson found a job at Westminster, working for a

Member of Parliament who was destined to go far?

It was just like Oliver to ask no questions at that time; they would no doubt come later.

Wasn't all this what she had wanted, schemed for, promised herself, to be with Oliver and make him see that she was all the things he wanted.

It was inevitable that they picked up their romance where they had left off. They met in the evening and he took her to the theatre and the ballet, they dined in exclusive restaurants and spent hours in air-raid shelters with the drone of planes overhead. Surrounded by other young people they found gaiety in those crowded shelters and thought nothing of walking through the deserted city streets still shaking from the aftermath of the night before, but weary and unbowed as the All Clear sounded over a city coming to life in the first pale streaks of dawn.

Erica was aware that they had both changed. Oliver was kinder, more considerate, she more unconcerned. She no longer talked about friends who were getting married in the hope of spurring him on.

Oliver told himself that this was the Erica he had wanted, a girl who was content to make the most of today and let tomorrow take care of itself. No doubt they would drift into something more positive, but for now it was one day at a time.

Alistair Greavson came into his office one evening to find Erica still at her desk and in response to her smile he said, 'You're working late, Erica. Is there any need for it?'

'Well yes. I don't want to leave anything undone. I'd like to get off a little early on Friday as I'm hoping to spend a weekend in St Agnes.'

'To see your parents?'

'Yes.'

'And how long do you intend to work tonight?'

'I'm almost finished.'

He smiled and sat down at his desk to leaf through some

papers, but he was disconcerted by her presence.

Celia had been a fixture, in his life and in his job, and he'd been complacent enough to think it would always be like that. She'd been pretty and intelligent, and he'd thought he was in love with her, but he knew now that what he'd felt for Celia had not been love, it had been the selfish preoccupation of a man well satisfied with his life and not wanting change.

He watched Erica placing the cover on her typewriter and reaching in her drawer for her handbag, then surprised himself by saying, 'Have you eaten, Erica? It's quite late.'

'Oh, I'll get something on the way home.'

'Why don't I take you out for dinner, unless you have another engagement?'

'I haven't but these are my working clothes.'

'Mine too. I don't propose to take you anywhere glamorous.'

As they were shown to their table in the restaurant he had chosen she felt that she had known it would be like this. Men in dark suits dining at tables under subdued lighting, one or two ladies elegant and none of them in their first youth, but all the same it was refined and gracious.

He consulted her about the wine and the food, and when it came it was exquisitely cooked and served. Alistair said, 'I dine here often as it's reliable, even in these uncertain times.'

She felt strangely shy with this older sophisticated man who knew how to be charming whilst doing his best to entertain her. He talked of his travels overseas and asked her about her life in St Agnes – while he talked Erica said a little prayer that he would not be bored by her.

Alistair watched the expressions flitting across her face as they talked and became increasingly aware of its beauty.

Before the evening was over she had told him about Oliver, how they had met up again, and that she had promised to go to St Agnes with him over the weekend.

216

'To recapture what you missed before,' he prompted with a smile.

'Oh no, I don't think I could ever do that. I'm different and Oliver too is different.'

'Perhaps you've both grown up.'

'Perhaps. He was already grown up, but I don't think I was.'

He deemed it wise to change the subject but in the taxi he had put her into for the drive home she found herself thinking that the evening she had just spent had been vastly different to any she had spent with Oliver. Oliver talked about himself, Alistair had been more interested in her.

Next day Oliver was anxious to make arrangements for the weekend at St Agnes.

'I've written to tell Aunt Amelia that I'll be with her around eight o'clock. It's going to be impossible to drive there, Erica. Petrol's at a premium if one is lucky enough to get hold of any. There's a train at 5.30 – I'll wait for you at the station.'

She nodded. 'Does your aunt know I'll be with you?'

'I probably told her. In any case it won't make any difference as you'll be with your parents.'

As she packed her weekend case on Friday morning she was dismayed to find she had little enthusiasm for the weekend they had planned. Her parents would question the wisdom of her being back with Oliver, although they would be nice to him. Aunt Amelia would be gracious and welcoming, but there would be a few raised eyebrows elsewhere.

She was still at her desk at half past four in the afternoon and knew she had to leave if she was going to get to the station on time. She visualised Oliver striding up and down impatiently waiting for her, and as she jumped to her feet and rushed headlong towards the door she almost knocked Alistair Greavson off his feet. He stared down at her in

217

surprise, at the weekend case lying on its side and the panic in her eyes.

Before he could say a word she burst into tears and, closing the door swiftly he said, 'What's all this about? Shouldn't you be going for your train?'

'I don't want to go.'

'Not to see your parents?'

'Not to be with Oliver and my parents. Nothing's the same, I'd thought it would be different this time but it never will be.'

'What time is your train?'

'Half past five, I'll never make it.'

'No, I don't think you will. Is there no way you can let him know?'

'No, he'll already be at the station. I'll have to telephone my parents this evening.'

'And how about him?'

'I can telephone his aunt.'

'And say what?'

'That I couldn't make it.'

'Not good enough, Erica. He'll want more than that.'

'I wanted more than that, but he went away, didn't he, so I got nothing more.'

'And is this your punishment?'

Her eyes opened wide. 'Oh no, I never wanted it to be like this. It was only this afternoon when I realised it has to be over. I don't want him any more.'

'I've finished for the day. I'll take you home and we'll talk. It might do you good to get it out of your system.'

So she made coffee and sandwiches and they sat in front of the fire and it seemed miraculous that that night the German bombers stayed away.

She telephoned her mother to say something had cropped up to prevent her coming; she would write and explain. And then she telephoned Aunt Amelia and Oliver's crisp, annoyed voice asked, 'What made you miss the train, Erica?'

'I'm sorry, Oliver, I couldn't get away, it was work. I

really am very sorry, I hope you have a good journey. How is your aunt?'

'Quite well. disappointed not to be seeing you, as I am sure your parents will be.'

'Yes, I'm sure they are. I really am very sorry, Oliver.' She repeated.

She heard him replace the receiver then she looked up to find Alistair staring at her with a new intensity.

'Well, I know its not work, Erica.' He mused. 'Did you not want to meet him?'

'I realised I didn't want to go, I want to put Oliver behind me, going to St. Agnes with him would have meant people were thinking of us as a couple again. Did you ever feel like that?'

'No, but I knew a girl who did. I kept her waiting like you waited, Erica, but for a great deal longer. I thought I was in love with her and that one day there'd be something more but she grew tired of waiting and found somebody else, just like you will.'

She smiled tremulously and nodded. He's nice, she thought, handsome too even if he is so much older. She didn't want a young man, somebody too full of himself, obsessed with too many conquests.

Alistair knew what she was thinking. Celia had once looked at him like that and her thoughts had been the same as Erica's, but at least they had been compatible. This girl was too young for him. He needed a woman of his own age, a woman who would understand his job, climb with him into the future, not this wide-eyed girl with ambitions above her years.

He thought about her on the way back to his flat. In the morning he'd go home to Cheltenham to see his mother, who'd been sad when Celia married somebody else. She'd liked her, told Alistair he didn't deserve her and should have made up his mind years before. What she'd think of some young twenty year old working for him he couldn't begin to guess.

How would a girl like Erica affect his career? Would there be raised eyebrows and snide remarks about his intelligence, or would there be a degree of envy that a man in his forties could attract a nubile young woman?

He smiled to himself. Of course it was ridiculous. She'd patch it up with the boyfriend – he'd seen it all before.

Chapter Twenty-Three

It was like no other longest day they could remember. For one thing most of the young people were in uniform, a great many of them foreigners from the airfield several miles away – Polish and French, and now a bevy of other young men who had at last come to Britain's aid. Light-hearted young Americans searching the streets for fun, marching to the beat of a boastful song with all the bands playing 'Over there, over there, Send the word, send the word to beware'. To the people standing on the pavement there was suddenly hope that it was the beginning of the end.

They were heard in the shops speaking an English totally alien from the one spoken in St Agnes. 'Call that stuff coffee? Gee, take it away.' 'Oh for a drink of iced water, they think nut sundae's a day.' 'Say, is this chicken feed money?' 'Why does everyone drive on the wrong side of the road?'

Nobody minded what they said, there was only joy that they were here. The local girls were treated to nylon stockings and boxes of American chocolates, and the English boys were saying caustically that they were over-sexed and over here.

Major Robson smoothed his moustache, put on his cap and viewed himself in the hall mirror with satisfaction. All right, there'd been better longest days, but he had to make the best of it. In any case he was glad to get out of the house as the women would be gathering to play bridge.

Once his wife would have spent all morning making cakes for the occasion, but now they had to make do with biscuits and all contributed something. Dorothy Spencer could be relied upon for shortbread, Hilda Marks for something with currants in it and his wife saved her chocolate ration. They were waiting for Grace who would arrive full of apologies without actually saying why she was late, although they all knew that her mother had probably been troublesome.

The Major went in to say his farewell, kissing his wife's cheek and saying brightly, 'Well girls, here you are again when you could be out in the sunshine watching the American capers.'

'What time will you be home?' his wife asked.

'The usual time. How long do you intend to play?'

'Well, Grace isn't here yet so we're not sure when we can start. If you meet her on the road do hurry her up, dear.'

Hilda Marks was in no hurry to get started. She liked the gossip that came first and this afternoon she had a rather spicy bit to impart.

'Did you know that Mrs Edgebaston entertained the American Colonel to dinner last evening, as well as her two men friends?' she asked.

'I suppose they're glad of a bit of socialising,' Dorothy Spencer said.

'Well of course, but so soon. Apparently she was introduced to them at the church parade last Sunday, so it didn't take her long to climb on the band wagon.'

'And no doubt he was happy to accept,' Elspeth said.

Sometimes she wondered why they tolerated Hilda but if she didn't play who else could they get? Lois Watson said she played when she was younger but was out of practice, Anthea Edgebaston said she'd never played and Amelia Prothero said she'd never been any good.

'Wouldn't you think Grace would have made an effort to get here a little early today. She knows it's always busy on this day of all days,' Hilda said, realising that she was getting nowhere with talk of Mrs Edgebaston.

'She'll be here,' Dorothy said. 'She would have let us know if she couldn't make it.'

'Perhaps she's met the vicar,' Hilda said shortly.

'What difference should that make?' Elspeth asked.

'She never really got over him, did she?'

'Well, I don't know that there's anything going on.'

'There's been some talk—'

Her words were cut short by the opening of the front door and Grace calling out, 'It's Grace, Elspeth, I'll put the catch on the door.'

She was blushing as she entered the room, evidently flustered at being late, and Elspeth said, 'Don't worry, Grace, we've been chatting. Is it very busy out there?'

'Oh yes. The Americans are putting a show on at the playing fields and the Major is joining them with his cadets.'

'Has the Commodore hoisted his flag as usual?'

'Yes, I came past Amelia's house and she was sitting in the garden with her nephew, Oliver Denton. Isn't he the young man who came to live with her after Jethro died?'

'Not to live with her, dear, just to stay over the weekends. He got her to move to London then went abroad.'

'And wasn't he very friendly with Erica Clarkson? He's obviously not with her in London or they'd have visited here together,' Hilda said.

'Oh, I rather think that was over years ago,' Dorothy said.

'I do think the vicar's looking much brighter these days,' Hilda said. 'He seems to be getting over his wife's death, but he must have missed her terribly.'

Warning glances were thrown in Hilda's direction, but she went blithely on.

'I saw him chatting to you last Sunday, Grace. He

223

seemed so much brighter and he was actually laughing. Of course, you were very good friends at one time, weren't you?'

'A long time ago,' Grace murmured.

'Well, he's on his own again now, you're both reasonably young, what would your mother have to say?'

'About what?' Grace said quietly.

'You know, dear, life goes on, doesn't it?'

'Are we playing bridge or not?' Elspeth snapped. This time Hilda got the message and Elspeth dealt the cards.

Grace seemed miles away, although she was actually thinking about the row with her mother after church on the Sunday morning. It was true she and the vicar had chatted for a little while but her mother had rounded on her vindictively as soon as they arrived home.

'It's disgraceful the way you're flirting with him,' she accused her. 'Everybody was looking at you and they'll all no doubt be talking about you. His wife hasn't been dead five minutes and here you are making a spectacle of yourselves.'

She had stared at her mother in disbelief, then not answering her she had gone into the cloakroom to take off her hat. Her mother followed her saying, 'Well, what have you to say for yourself?'

'Nothing Mother. I'm allowed to pass the time of day with an old friend, and he is an old friend.'

'An old friend who is no doubt looking for a wife, and you're making yourself very available.'

'I don't intend to answer that, Mother. I think you're being cruel and unkind, so perhaps when you've had a rest you'll realise you've been ridiculous.'

Grace had spent Sunday afternoon in the garden and her mother stayed indoors, but after their evening meal Mrs Gantry said sharply, 'I'm not going to church – once is enough to see my daughter behaving like a harlot.'

So neither of them went to church, and after her mother

224

retired at eight o'clock Grace spent a miserable evening just thinking about their quarrel.

Of course she loved Paul – she'd never fallen out of love with him – but she'd been glad to see him happy with Molly and had done her share of weeping when she died. Now Paul was free again and there was that hidden spark between them that refused to go away.

It would never be any good. She had her mother and her mother would never accept that she had a life of her own. Her mother was old, but she was not seriously ill and could in fact live for many years. She could never leave her mother, and the intransigent old lady would never live with Grace and a husband.

She had thought it was over until her mother said acidly at breakfast, 'I couldn't sleep last night for thinking about you and the Vicar. You're going to be as talked about as that Mrs Edgebaston. It's not taken her long to get hold of that American officer.'

Grace didn't answer but she was thinking about Mrs Edgebaston and wishing she was like her. Mrs Edgebaston had looked beautiful in church on Sunday in a deep azure silk gown and hat, wearing heels three inches high, slender as a young girl but twice as sophisticated.

The officer had looked enchanted. They had walked down the road together, oblivious of the glances thrown in their direction by all and sundry.

Mrs Edgebaston wouldn't care – why should she? She was a free agent with enough money to please herself what she did, and the means to make any man admire her. That her mother should compare her with Mrs Edgebaston was ludicrous.

She knew she was playing bridge very badly, and at last Elspeth said, 'You're not with us today, Grace, that's twice you've revoked.'

'I'm so sorry, perhaps I shouldn't have come today. Mother was fretful and it doesn't take much to make me lose track. Isn't there somebody else you can get to join you?'

225

'We wouldn't dream of it, dear. You'll get over it,' Dorothy said.

As she walked home later she blamed herself for the somewhat disastrous afternoon they had spent. When she met the Major on his way home he said, 'Finished so soon then? Did you enjoy it?'

'Not really, Major, and it was my fault. I mustn't have been in the mood, and of course I was late.'

'Shouldn't worry about that, my dear. You'd have done better to have spent the afternoon at the field there – the Yanks put on a first-class show and there were a lot of spectators.'

'I'd like to have been there.'

'Your mother was there with Amelia Prothero. Did you know she was going?'

'No.'

Did her mother know about the display? she asked herself. Her mother wanted to know everything that happened in her life but seemed unprepared to tell her what went on in her own. Her mother's visit to the playing field had probably been a last-minute invitation from Mrs Prothero.

People had not looked forward to the longest day this year. For the last two years there had been calls from a great many people to scrap it until the war was over, but this year they'd decided to hold it because of the Americans nearby. They'd done their best with the rations they were allowed and the American base had helped considerably with everything they had. Then there would be the usual dance in the evening to which the girls were looking forward and to which the Americans had been invited.

Grace's mother didn't want to talk or read about the war, believing it would go away like a summer storm, and she thought that letting loose young foreigners with English girls was a disaster waiting to happen.

'There they are,' she complained. 'Throwing themselves at those young Americans and Poles – they've probably got wives and girls at home.'

As Grace looked towards the playing field she could see that there were still a great many people there. The American band was playing and there was dancing around the bandstand. She could hear the laughter and as she turned into the garden she could see her mother standing at the window staring out morosely.

When she went in her mother said, 'Did you pass the vicarage on the way home?'

'No Mother, I came past the playing field.'

'I see the Bishop and his wife have arrived. Their daughter Phoebe is with them. I've never seen her here before on the longest day. It's probably to keep the Vicar company at the dance.'

Grace didn't reply. She had never met the Bishop's daughter and couldn't think how her mother knew her.

'She's a teacher in some very good girls' boarding school near London,' her mother enlightened her. 'She's about the Vicar's age and she isn't married.'

'How do you know all this, Mother?'

'Amelia Prothero told me. She's quite good-looking and she'll be the sort of wife the Vicar should have.'

'Do you think he's looking for a wife, Mother?'

'Probably not, but he should have one. Molly was right for him, she was always nice and a hard worker. You'd never have been right for him, Grace. I said that to your father years ago when you two were friendly.'

'Why would I have been so wrong for him?'

'Well, you can be flighty, and too fond of enjoying yourself.'

Grace sighed. What constituted enjoyment in her mother's eyes? Without referring to it she asked, 'Have you had tea, Mother? I can get you something now.'

'I thought we got something at the dance.'

'So you do intend to go then? You always said it was for young people, not older people with more sense.'

'A lot of the young people are away now and Amelia's going. She said we should help to make it a success.'

Grace smiled to herself. Her mother wouldn't make a success of anything. She'd go and complain about it later, and curiously she asked, 'What will you wear? You haven't been to something like that for years.'

'Nobody is going to be interested in what I'm wearing. How about you? I don't like you in that green thing you bought for Amelia's party; you look better in maroon.'

The maroon that she'd had for at least eight years, Grace reflected.

She knew what her mother was about. She was frightened because the only man her daughter had ever really loved was now a widower and some spark still lingered for both of them. Now the Bishop's daughter had come to stifle any hopes Grace might have had, and in case she didn't she should dress dowdily for when they would meet.

Grace felt a sudden overwhelming pity for her. At the same time some rare feeling of rebellion made her ignore the maroon dress with its old-fashioned style and outmoded hemline. It was true the green wasn't exactly fashionable but her one gold necklace and earrings brightened it up and the colour did suit her.

Her mother regarded the dress with some distaste, and Grace said, 'The maroon is very old-fashioned, Mother, and is years old. Are you able to walk to the village hall or shall I call a taxi?'

'I can walk. Taxis are expensive and they're hard to get because of the petrol problem. I wonder if Amelia's nephew will be there.'

'No Mother, he went back to London on Sunday evening.'

'How do you know?'

'Major Robson told me.'

'Oh well, he knows everything, doesn't he?'

Grace settled her mother well away from the band since she invariably complained about the noise, and when Mrs Prothero joined her Grace said, 'I'll help with the refreshments, Mother. I'm sure they can use all the help they can get.'

228

'Come back here when you've finished,' her mother said sharply, and Mrs Prothero said, 'Don't worry, Grace, your mother and I are quite all right here.'

As Grace looked along the length of the buffet table where they had set everything out she thought it was miraculous that it looked so well. It seemed that every family had donated something to the success of the evening and the young Americans had arrived bringing a mountain of goodies they had received from home.

They were having a wonderful time with the local girls, while the local boys stood around scowling, yet as the evening progressed somehow the spirit of camaraderie spread and they were jiving to American dance music while the waltzes and foxtrots of other years were forgotten.

Across the room the Bishop and his wife were being escorted round the room by the Vicar and for the first time Grace caught a glimpse of the Bishop's daughter, a tall slim woman in a black crêpe-de-Chine dress, who later greeted Grace with a charming smile and Grace's heart sank.

Later the Vicar told her that Phoebe had recently lost her husband at sea when the merchant ship of which he had been the Captain had been lost.

'My mother said she was teaching somewhere in London,' Grace said. 'Will she continue there?'

'Yes, I'm sure she will. Molly and I met her years ago at some religious function. She's a strong woman and she's already accustomed to spending a great deal of time alone. Do you feel like dancing, Grace?'

'Well, I certain don't know how to dance this one, Paul.'

'Nor I. We'll make our way to the bar and wait for something a little more melodious. I see your mother is at the other end of the hall.'

'Yes, she hated the noise.'

He looked down at her with some degree of concern before saying, 'Things don't change much for you, do they Grace?'

'My life do you mean?'

229

'Yes. Have you never learned to assert yourself?'

'There never seemed much to assert myself for, at least at the time my father died.'

'No, that made it difficult for you, I know. But life moves on, you know. Don't let it slip through your fingers a second time, Grace.'

He was looking down at her very intently, and across the room she felt her mother's eyes on them. When they got home she knew she would feel the brunt of her mother's anger. Suddenly her eyes filled with tears, and Paul took hold of her hand, saying gently, 'I know, Grace, but you have a life too, you know. Don't throw it away.'

Chapter Twenty-Four

Grace felt sorry for her mother because she was afraid, afraid that the world she had fashioned for herself was crumbling. The man her daughter had loved for a long time no longer had a wife, and Grace seemed to be taking no notice of all the obstacles she was putting in the way of their renewed friendship.

The Bishop's daughter appeared not to be looking for a husband and Grace seemed to be ignoring her strictures.

Now people were beginning to talk. Mrs Marks for instance had cornered her mother coming out of church the previous Sunday while Grace chatted to the Vicar.

'How nice,' she'd said. 'They do seem to be getting along very well, don't they, and a man really needs somebody. I think he and Grace will be so good together.'

She'd looked at Hilda Marks with the utmost disdain before saying, 'Grace has known the Vicar since he first came here – she's not the only one he chats to.'

'Well of course not, Mrs Gantry, but she's the only one available, isn't she. I'm sure you must be delighted, after all you're not getting any younger and Grace needs somebody like we all do.'

She'd told Grace about her conversation with Mrs Marks thinking Grace would have some answer to it, but Grace had simply smiled and said, 'Hilda is an inveterate gossip, Mother. We all know what she's like.'

'And you and the Vicar are feeding gossip like that.'

'I don't see why, Mother. Now what would you like for tea?'

Mrs Prothero thought it would be wonderful if they found romance. 'She's been such a good daughter and I know if she was my daughter I'd be hoping and praying they'd get together,' she'd said.

'Well yes,' Mrs Gantry had agreed, 'but what about me? They won't want me living with them, I'm too old to live on my own. They'd put me in some home somewhere and I've heard no good opinions about those.'

'But so many of them are wonderful. I have a friend who moved into one in North Wales when her son got married again and she's absolutely delighted with it.'

'Well, I wouldn't be. I'd think it was time for me to die and leave them to it.'

Unable to stand the uncertainty any longer Mrs Gantry decided it was time Grace put her cards on the table, so she chose a very inopportune moment to ask questions when Grace was leaving the house on Tuesday afternoon.

'Grace, I want you to tell me exactly what is going on between you and the Vicar. Something's obviously going on, you've always got your heads together, and I need to know where I stand. Has he asked you to marry him?'

Grace sat down weakly on the nearest chair.

'Not in so many words, Mother. Can't it wait until I get home later on?'

'No. I want answers now.'

'I'm sure he loves me, Mother, and I think he would like to marry me, but he's not sure of my answer. Neither of us are sure how it would work out.'

'Because of me do you mean?'

'Mother, I don't know. I don't know if you'd be pleased or sorry. Obviously our lives would change, but I really don't know what the changes would be.'

'I'll tell you exactly how they'll be. I'll stay here and get a housekeeper. You'll move into the vicarage and that will that.'

'I can't leave you here, Mother, housekeeper or no housekeeper.'

That was the answer Mrs Gantry had been waiting for. If she refused to budge, then there'd be no marriage.

Grace went off to her bridge afternoon highly troubled and the other three members of the bridge four wished she'd stayed at home. She was upset and couldn't concentrate until in the end Hilda Marks snapped, 'Really Grace, you're miles away. I'm your partner and I don't know what you're doing.'

Grace promptly burst into tears and Elspeth and Dorothy Spencer looked at her helplessly. It was Elspeth who said, 'We'll not play any more, obviously Grace isn't in the mood. Let's have a cup of tea and talk about whatever is troubling you – four heads are better than one.'

Grace had known they would be on her side, after all none of them had had her problems and they regarded her mother as something of a tyrant. In the end Grace said gently, 'It's hard for Paul and me, but it's hard for Mother too. How can I marry him and leave her on her own?'

'You should have married him years ago,' Hilda said sharply. 'You should have realised that every year you and your mother stayed together would make it harder for you to get away.'

They all knew she was right.

'But do you have to leave her?' Elspeth asked logically. 'The vicarage is a big house. She could live with you surely, have some sort of flat of her own in it.'

They all agreed it was the best answer they'd come up with, but Grace knew her mother better than any of them, and besides, the idea of accommodating her mother might not go down too well with Paul.

Grace decided to leave early and after she'd gone the other three talked it over between themselves.

'She's surely not going to let him slip through her fingers a second time,' Hilda said acidly.

'She will if her mother's anything to do with it,' Elspeth replied. 'Oh, can't we talk about something else, the whole thing is too depressing for words. Haven't we any more scandal in the offing?'

Hilda could be relied upon to rise to the occasion and somewhat relieved to be finished with Grace and her problems, she said, 'I saw Janet Clarkson in the chemist's yesterday – apparently Erica is seeing Oliver Denton in London.'

'You mean the affair is on again?' Dorothy asked.

'Well, I'm not quite sure about that, but he lives close by because she's in his aunt's flat – weren't they supposed to be close to each other?'

'He was here the other weekend and she didn't come with him.'

'No, her mother said she had to work.'

'What do the Clarksons feel about it?'

'Janet doesn't give much away. When I tried to draw her out on it she started to talk about Nancy. She's in Alexandria, so the next bit of scandal could concern her. We don't know what these girls are getting up to, do we?'

'I always liked Nancy. Erica was the unpredictable one.'

'The Commodore and his wife are not seeing much of their son. Lois says he's been promoted to Commander, and of course they've no idea where he's serving. Funny if he was to meet up with Nancy. Her eyes used to light up whenever he was anywhere near.'

They laughed. Nancy was always the sort of girl they could laugh about. Erica brought trauma, Grace brought problems, but then there was Anthea Edgebaston.

'I saw the American Colonel walking home with her after the church service,' Hilda Marks said caustically. 'I wonder what her two Englishmen think about it?'

'Well, we don't really know what relationship they have with her, do we?' Dorothy said.

234

'No, and she doesn't exactly give much away, does she. How much do we really know about her? Only that she's got money to burn, she's fashionable and is nice enough to talk to, but that's the end of it. What do we know about her husband? Does she have any family? They were chatting away on Sunday as though they'd known each other for years, and he seemed mightily smitten.'

'I rather like her,' Elspeth said. 'She knows she's being talked about but she doesn't care a fig. I admire her for that – after all, why should she? She's never harmed any of us.'

They laughed. 'Edith Pinder liked working for her,' Dorothy said. 'She said she was very generous and she never tittle-tattled. It's my bet she's finding it a little dull working for Amelia after Mrs E.'

'I wonder if Mrs Prothero knows anything about Erica and her nephew. I know she doesn't go in for gossip much but he is all she's got – she's sure to be interested.'

'I asked Janet if she knew when Erica would be coming home for a visit but she didn't seem to know. It can't be very pleasant living in London now with all the bombs and everything. Janet told me Erica is working for Alistair Greavson at Westminster. I must say, she's done rather well for herself.'

For a few moments there was silence as Elspeth poured out a second cup of tea, and several minutes later said, 'I wonder what happened to Mr Mellor and his daughter after they moved away? Did anybody around here get in touch with them?'

'They never really made friends in the area. Nancy Clarkson was friendly with the girl, but even that seemed to fizzle out. She was a beautiful girl, and so talented.'

They all agreed on that score and it was Hilda again who said, 'The mother was on edge all the time, even when we were speaking about normal everyday things. She talked about Joyce but closed up like a clam whenever her husband was mentioned.'

'I can't believe they were happy together,' Dorothy said.

'Desmond spoke to him once in the post office. He said he was very brusque and not very communicative. I never said a word to him. Desmond's a pretty good judge of character and didn't think much of Arthur Mellor.'

At that moment they heard the front door opening and Dorothy said, 'That must be Desmond looking forward to his evening meal. I think it's time we made ourselves scarce.'

The door opened and Desmond put his head round it saying, 'Finished, girls? Good afternoon's bridge?'

'Not really,' Hilda said. 'Grace wasn't in the mood for it.'

'Other things to think about, has she?'

'Did you spend all afternoon with the cadets, dear?' Elspeth asked.

'No, they're busy with exams. I've been chatting to Lady Marcia, she tells me one of her sons has joined the RAF. The other is hoping to go into the Blues.'

'I didn't think they were old enough.'

'Apparently so.'

'And the husband?'

'Never mentioned him. I'm not like you women, I didn't pry.'

'You seem to get to know most things,' Elspeth said pointedly.

'Well, between Lady Marcia and Mrs Edgebaston you've all certainly had a go.'

'What do you know about the Colonel, the American Colonel?' Hilda asked.

'Nice chap. Home's in Vermont, and that's as much as I know.'

'You don't know if he's married or not?'

'Never asked him.'

'At his age he probably is, although it won't be the only scandal to erupt before this war's over,' Hilda said sharply. 'They've all probably got wives and girls at home, and our girls are making themselves too available.'

The Major grinned. 'And none of us really know whether we'll be here tomorrow or not,' he said. 'But back to Anthea Edgebaston – I like her, she's straight and she doesn't indulge in some of the backbiting other women find attractive.'

'I hear the Commodore's son has been promoted to Commander,' Elspeth said. 'They'll be pleased about that.'

'Of course, but they'd like to see him again, if only for a day or two. Young Nancy said she'd met up with him in Scotland.'

'That would be a thrill for Nancy.'

'He was with a Wren officer.'

'Oh well, isn't that the way of things these days? There'll be a good many romances in the offing before the last All Clear.'

The Major and his wife were largely silent over their evening meal. The Major liked to eat undisturbed and Elspeth was busy thinking about the goings-on in a town totally unprepared for change.

What would be the outcome of Erica Clarkson's renewed friendship with Oliver Denton, and what of Grace and her mother? Would Grace have the courage to make the most of her life and would her mother be able to accept it if she did?

Then there was Mrs Edgebaston. To young people a broken romance was quickly forgotten – there was always somebody else. But it wasn't so easy once the first flush of youth had gone.

Suppose Anthea fell in love with her American, and he was married? After the war he would go home to America and pick up the threads he had left behind, but could Anthea do the same? Elspeth suspected there had been a good few threads Anthea had needed to pick up in her life, and it would get harder as the years passed.

She looked across the table at her husband complacently enjoying his meal. He grumbled incessantly about food

237

rationing but when his meal was put before him he invariably accepted it without complaint.

She'd thought many times over the years that she would like to have had children, even when they had been denied her. Now if they'd had children they would most likely have been away from home so that every day she and Desmond would have been sick with worry about them. As it was they enjoyed a comfortable life in a pretty town. They had friends and pastimes they both enjoyed, and altogether their lives were comfortable and ordered. Not bad when so many people's lives were being turned upside down.

After dinner they listened to the news on the radio as usual and Desmond said, 'I don't know why we bother, it's never good news these days.' Later they took their usual walk along the river with their dog.

Desmond's bull terrier Sadie was getting old now and she didn't like to walk too far; consequently as they reached the church with its square tower standing above the path they turned back and headed for home.

It was then that they saw the Vicar standing pensively in his garden and Desmond called out to him. 'Care for a drink at our place, Paul? Bit of company wouldn't come amiss surely.'

Paul smiled. 'Thanks, I'd love to. Hold on a minute and I'll get my coat. Do you mind if I bring Bruce, I think they'll get along all right.'

'By all means, the old girl's too long in the tooth to flirt with him. We'll wait for you.'

'What made you suddenly invite him?' asked Elspeth.

'Didn't you think he looked a bit lonely, just standing in his garden staring into space?'

'I suppose so.'

'It'll do him good to talk about things.'

'What sort of things?'

'It's my guess he's worried about Grace Gantry and that mother of hers. Can you see any way out of it?'

'We've been talking about it this afternoon. What do you

238

think about a separate flat at the vicarage for the old lady?'

'To have the old girl move in with them, do you mean?'

'Can you think of anything else?'

'Yes I can. I can think the old girl should move into a home. There's plenty of them about even in wartime, and Grace could visit her as often as she liked. At least she wouldn't be making life miserable for the pair of them.'

'Desmond, I don't think Mrs Gantry will go into a home, and I don't think Grace will let her.'

'Then she should stay where she is and get a decent housekeeper.'

A man would think like that, Elspeth reflected. Everything cut and dried. How would the Vicar view Desmond's reasoning?

Paul was glad to have somebody to talk to about his predicament.

'I love Grace and I want to marry her. But she's been too long with her mother in her mother's home. Now she's forgotten any other life and while I'm talking to her about our life her mother's talking to her about theirs.'

'But she loves you, Paul?' Elspeth asked gently.

'Yes, I really believe she does, but her loyalties are so divided.'

'What do you say about her own flat at the vicarage? It's a very big house, there's room for one.'

He looked at her in some surprise and it was obvious neither he nor Grace had discussed such a suggestion.

'Do you think it would work?' he asked hopefully.

'Well, I think you could mention it to Grace and see how she feels.'

'What do you think, Desmond?' Paul asked.

'My wife knows what I think – get as far away from the old girl as possible, that's what I think.'

'Oh Desmond, it doesn't always work like black and white,' his wife said sharply. 'We're talking about Grace's mother, and whatever we think about the old lady isn't important.'

Paul nodded his head. 'I agree, Elspeth. When I see Grace tomorrow I'll see what she thinks about a flat. I don't think her mother dislikes me, she just doesn't want anything in her life to change. I think she's frightened.'

This time Desmond didn't speak, and later when the Vicar decided it was time to go home they accompanied him to the door and waited while he put the dog's lead on before walking down the path.

'I told you your dog would be all right with old Sadie. A pity human beings can't behave so sensibly. Sadie's old, but she's practical. She takes life as it comes and never ever upsets the apple cart. Mrs Gantry could do with taking a leaf out of Sadie's book,' Desmond said and the Vicar chuckled as he walked down the path.

Chapter Twenty-Five

Erica had not seen Oliver since he returned from visiting his aunt in St Agnes although she knew he was sulking. But she didn't care.

He had every right to feel aggrieved, although what she had done to him was no different to what he had done to her and wasn't this what it had all been about? Revenge.

She hadn't wanted it to be like that. The old Erica had wanted to meet him in London and hoped that they would both realise something remained of their old feelings for each other. The new Erica had discovered the Oliver he really was. She no longer loved blindly, recognised his conceit and his arrogance, and no longer wanted him to love her.

Two weeks passed before she met him on the road outside her flat, and even then he favoured her with a distant smile and a carefree attitude.

'Did you enjoy your weekend with your aunt?' she asked him calmly.

'Yes. I found her looking very well and pleased to see me.'

'I'm glad. Did you meet any of her friends?'

'Well no, there wasn't any time. She's busy with things in aid of the war effort and with the church, and she's got Edith Pinder living with her again.'

'That's good. I'm sorry I wasn't able to go with you, Oliver. It was work, something I couldn't get out of.'

'Did you try, Erica?'

'Yes of course. You must know what it's like.'

'I'll give you a ring sometime, perhaps we could have dinner.'

'Yes of course.'

That had been that and he was in no hurry to ring her.

She had found friends among the secretarial staff at Westminster and from them she had learned something of Alistair Greavson's long-standing association with her predecessor.

She learned the Celia had been popular and had cared desperately for the man she worked for. Everybody had been amazed when she said she was leaving to marry somebody else – there were those who thought even at that late stage that if Alistair decided he wanted her she would have willingly gone back to him.

He had cared for her and was unhappy to lose her, but it hadn't been enough to make him want her back.

There had been several occasions when he had invited Erica out to dinner, usually when she had worked late, and he tended to treat her like a father figure, listening to her tales of the boys she had known, and particularly her affair with Oliver Denton.

They dined in obscure restaurants, left early before the bombing started, and he would put her in a taxi and send her off home with a grave smile and a casual farewell.

The girls at Westminster were intrigued. They thought there was never likely to be anything in it as she was far too young, even though she was decidedly pretty and dressed well.

She gradually developed a new sophistication. She had always been a sassy girl with a high opinion of herself, but now it reflected in the clothes she chose to wear. Back in St Agnes her father was loud in his condemnation of the money she was demanding, saying that the flat was expensive, London was expensive and she really did need to keep up appearances for her job.

As always she got her own way. Nancy was off their hands in distant Alexandria and they were afraid of losing both their daughters which made it easier to give in to Erica's demands.

Oliver kept his promise to telephone her and took her to an Italian bistro near their flats. He talked about his time abroad, his job and himself, and she asked him what he intended to do with his life when the war was over.

'I hope it's overseas,' he replied. 'I intend to be a diplomat, it's what Oxford conditioned me for and let's hope it's somewhere exotic in the sun.'

The old Erica would have longed to ask if any of it concerned her but the new Erica allowed his words to pass over her head and smiling briefly she said, 'I suppose you'll be hoping it's somewhere like Bermuda or Singapore.'

'Anywhere, darling, as long as it isn't London in the winter, listening to them rebuilding the city, shivering in the mist. Are you looking forward to that?'

'I don't know what I'm looking forward to. The war isn't over yet, many things could happen.'

'You could go back to country living in dear old St Agnes. I expect your parents would like that.'

'I never realised it before, Oliver, but you can be very patronising.'

'I didn't mean to be, Erica, but you did ask me about my future.'

'I don't mean about your future, Oliver, about mine.'

'Well, what do you want to do?'

'I want to marry a nice man, live in a lovely house with a nice garden, have two children and a couple of dogs. I want to stay in this country, so you see, Oliver, you have absolutely nothing to fear. God, I must have bored you with all that talk about settling down. I'm not surprised you decided to cut and run.'

He was disconcerted by her. This new Erica seemed to

243

have moved on too fast. He had been afraid of the old Erica who had been too clinging, too pushy, but he was becoming more afraid of the new Erica because she hurt his vanity and made him feel superfluous.

The St Agnes Erica had been pretty with her pastel silks and ninon, now she invariably sat opposite him wearing sophisticated black or grey.

Other men looked at her admiringly and at him with envy. She had become the sort of girl he'd always wanted, dreamed about, but it was becoming increasingly apparent that she had aspirations far beyond him.

'Do you intend to visit your parents soon?' he asked her.

'I'm not sure, why?'

'Oh, it's just that I thought I might go there to see Aunt Amelia. I'm not asking you to come with me – I'm not prepared for a second let-down.'

'I write to them, I telephone them, they know how I'm fixed and Alistair is pretty demanding at the moment.'

'You call him Alistair?'

'I do now.'

'Since when?'

'Since he's taken me out to dinner.'

'Oh, I didn't realise.'

'Sometimes he asks me to work late, we dine together and then we go home before the bombing starts. He's very nice, I like him.'

'And is that all there is?'

'He's like my father. I'm young enough to be his daughter.'

'That doesn't seem to be an impediment these days.'

'He's been a bachelor too long. I don't think he intends to change it.'

'But there must have been somebody.'

'Yes, the girl I replaced.'

'So you don't think you'll be visiting St Agnes in the immediate future?'

'I don't think so.'

244

How different it all was from what she had imagined it would be. She'd really thought that they'd be going there together, that his aunt and her parents would accept them as a pair, and that one day when the war was over she'd be the wife accompanying him when he went to work abroad.

It was late one Friday evening when Alistair came into the office to pick up his briefcase and she was just tidying her desk before going home. He came and looked down at her, at the blond hair elegantly styled, at the gentle curve of her cheek and something quite outside himself prompted him to say, 'Looking forward to the weekend, Erica?'

'I'm not doing anything special.'

'I'm spending the weekend with some friends in Hertfordshire. They've told me I may take a guest. Care to join me?'

'Are you sure?'

'Quite sure. It will be informal, country clothes and something a little more dressy for the evening. We chat, play a little bridge, walk in the country and go to church. How does that sound?'

'It sounds wonderful.'

'Then I'll pick you up at eleven in the morning and we'll drive there.'

It was a beautiful red-brick manor house they drove to and they were received warmly by the owners of the house and the other guests who arrived later.

In the afternoon as she walked with Alistair and their host Roger Evesham through the pretty village and up to the stone church on the hillside she became more relaxed so that Alistair seemed less like a father figure and she began to appreciate his sense of humour.

She wondered how many times he had taken Celia to meet his friends – Celia, who had been older and probably a more suitable companion.

They played bridge after dinner on the first evening and

245

because Erica didn't play she sat in front of the fire with Thomas, the family cat, curled up on her knee. Sitting opposite another female guest leafed through a magazine until eventually she said, 'It's nice to see Alistair emerging from his lethargy. Did you know Celia Moston?'

'No. I never met her.'

'She was too obvious, too predictable. I never thought it would come to anything.'

A bit like me and Oliver, Erica thought, but remained silent.

'She was a pretty woman, intelligent too, but somehow it went on too long, that was the mistake.'

'She married somebody else anyway.'

'Yes, I rather think in the first place that was meant to bring Alistair to heel, but it didn't. You'll be good for him, Erica.'

'He's twice my age.'

'Yes of course, but does it matter? You're evidently on the same wavelength. Would you be interested?'

'Would he?'

'Let me give you some advice, my dear. Play it cool. You're young enough to attract a bevy of men whereas Alistair has already wasted several chances. Let him see that you like him, but don't go after him.'

Erica had no intentions of going after him. She'd done it with Oliver, and in any case she wasn't sure how much she wanted from Alistair.

Another woman who had been watching her with a slight smile on her face said after a few minutes, 'Alistair is going places, Erica. He's well respected and he's clever. I have it on very good authority that very soon he'll be made a minister and a wife is what he needs. Think of the advantages, my dear.'

Erica thought of nothing else for the rest of the weekend. What would the people in St Agnes think if Erica Clarkson captured Alistair Greavson? What would her parents think and what would Oliver Denton think?

*

246

When next she met Oliver he asked questions about her weekend in the country and she sensed in him a deep frustration, the sort of frustration he had once aroused in her.

'You haven't said whether you'll visit your parents next time I go to see Aunt Amelia,' he said quietly.

'I told you I have too much to do here, Oliver.'

'But you went away for a weekend with him.'

'He's my boss.'

'Do you think your parents would approve of you going around with a man old enough to be your father?'

'I don't think they ever really approved of you, Oliver.'

'At least age didn't come into it.'

'No, but a great many other things did.'

'Well, I think you should make an effort to visit your parents. Your sister is abroad and you have so many friends in St Agnes.'

Actually Erica didn't think she had all that many friends there. She'd been a spoilt and pampered child, much sought after, but she'd been her own worst enemy and she'd made enemies.

She'd been flattered, Nancy had been liked. Now the more she thought about Alistair's future the more it intrigued her. He was handsome and charming, was the sort of man who would provide her with the right sort of house and was not too old to have children.

The prospects were mind-boggling. After the war it would be the good life, with travel here, there and everywhere, and his popularity would surely reflect on his wife.

Erica had learned a lot from her dalliance with Oliver Denton. She worked hard, she was always there when Alistair wanted her and her temperament was invariably sunny and cooperative.

Alistair liked her, but on the morning she told him she would like to visit St Agnes for her mother's birthday if it was convenient he seemed rather taken aback.

'You're going alone, Erica?' he asked.

'No. Oliver is visiting his aunt so we'll travel together.'

247

'So the romance is on again?'

'No, and it never will be.'

She wasn't sure how much he believed her, but he wished her a happy weekend as she left on the Friday afternoon and to her chagrin he appeared quite nonchalant.

Eyebrows were raised at seeing her with Oliver. His aunt received her graciously and her parents were equally gracious with Oliver, but to her amazement she was missing Alistair. Life in St Agnes seemed mundane, cloistered even, and she missed the excitement of London, even the nightly air raids and the dogfights high above which often ended in disaster.

How strange it seemed to listen to all the old gossip, and the new: the doubtful friendships between young girls and young Americans far from home; the togetherness of Grace Gantry and the Vicar; Mrs Edgebaston's American Colonel.

She felt an urgent need to talk to Mrs Edgebaston – after all she had been very kind on that terrible night she had found her in tears on the river bank.

They met at church on the Sunday morning and on this occasion Mrs Edgebaston was without the American Colonel most of the parishioners were talking about. She smiled at Erica and joined her on the church path.

They were both good at making polite conversation until Erica said quickly, 'I came here with Oliver, Mrs Edgebaston. We're friends, nothing more.'

'And are you satisfied with friendship, Erica?'

'Yes.'

'Is there somebody else?'

'I'm not sure.'

'But you were so very sure about Oliver.'

'Yes, but this time it's different. He's nearly as old as my father, he's my boss.'

'Alistair Greavson.'

'Yes.'

248

'How does he feel about you?'

'I don't know. We get along, I think he likes me. We dine out occasionally, he took me away to stay with friends of his for a weekend and I think we both enjoyed it. There's so much I need to know. He was in love with somebody else but she grew tired of waiting – she's married now. Perhaps he'll never think of me like that.'

'What do you want me to say, Erica?'

'I don't really know. Why am I like this, doubtful, insecure, wanting things out of reach? When boys came easily to me I didn't want them; when they were harder to get I agonised over them; now I'm up against a man who is cleverer than I am and much much wiser.'

'A man who is going places, a man who is capable of fulfilling every expectation you have for the future – but what about love?'

'I want love too.'

'My husband was older than I, older and wiser. Not just a lover, a friend. It was only after he died that I realised how much I had loved him; when he was alive I was never really sure. Be very sure, Erica, that is the only advice I can give you.'

Erica nodded doubtfully and Anthea said, 'Have you told your parents about him?'

'Not really, as yet there's so little to tell.'

By this time they had reached Anthea's gate and as they paused Erica said, 'I've been hearing about your American Colonel – what about your other gentlemen friends?'

Anthea laughed. 'My accountant and my solicitor, both old friends too. But Colonel Freeman is very nice, a long way from home and lonely. I know people are talking, but it doesn't bother me, it never has.'

'I'm going back to London this afternoon. Mother will write to give me all the news.'

'I'm sure she will and there is plenty of it even for sleepy St Agnes.'

At that moment Mrs Gantry and Grace passed them

249

across the road and Erica said, 'Mother told me that Grace is friendly with the Vicar. Will it ever come to anything?'

'I do hope so. She hasn't asked for my advice, but I'd readily give it.'

'I wonder what it would be.'

'Take the Vicar, he'll last longer than your mother.'

They both laughed and as if she knew what they were talking about Mrs Gantry favoured them with a long cool stare.

Chapter Twenty-Six

Nancy sat on a boulder looking out on the white sweep of the bay wishing she'd paid more attention to her history teacher.

So little really remained of Greek Alexandria and yet it was in this city where Antony and Cleopatra had played out their doomed love affair, this city where the great Alexander had been buried, this city that the Ptolemys had ruled for a thousand years.

In whatever spare time she'd been allowed she had found Pompey's Pillar and what was left of the library. She had stared entranced at all that remained of the Pharos Lighthouse and she'd followed faithfully all the stories of Nelson's Dockyard and his victory over Napoleon in the Battle of the Nile. But now, looking along the white, sickle-shaped bay, where graceful minarets towered upwards into the cloudless sky, she felt a strange feeling of regret that so little remained of events that could have changed history for ever.

Among the friends she had made very few seemed interested in the past, but were content to feel a part of a city that seemed more in keeping with the South of France than Egypt.

She reached inside her satchel and took out the letter she had received from Louise the day before. She could picture Louise sitting on the edge of her bed writing, her pretty

251

face smiling complacently, imparting news that she felt sure would interest her friend.

She had met a man she'd known briefly in distant Cheshire, he was Army, his family had pots of money which would please her mother, and she believed they were going places.

There had followed five pages about Steven Latchford; that his father was big in business and both his parents rode with the Cheshire Hunt; that their house was a bit of a show place and his brother was something in politics. Altogether Nancy thought Steven Latchford was one young man Louise would hang on to.

Her letter ended with the words: 'Saw your Commander a couple of nights ago, different girl. Perhaps not the marrying type, darling. Alexandria must be rotten with young heroes looking for a bit of respite from the trauma of Alamein.'

Nancy had met quite a few of them and they were young men clutching desperately at whatever Alexandria had in the way of entertainment, music and girls.

They crowded into the bars every evening and went to the race track, they danced the night away – and then they went back to war and shooting, to desert sunsets and the stench of death.

The fact that Julian's ship was now in the Med brought him that bit closer, even when she told herself that she was a fool to nourish ideas that were never likely to be fulfilled.

Nancy kept her friendships light-hearted. People liked her, she was pretty and a hell of a nice girl, but even with the one or two young men who considered themselves in love with her she was never more than their friend, and at night when she waved them goodbye she began to feel that life was slipping away beneath her feet.

As she drove Rear Admiral Johnson from headquarters to the dockyard she could see that a new flotilla of destroyers had arrived and yet they all looked so alike. One of them could well be Julian's.

252

Several evenings later she saw him in the company of some senior officers and one or two girls. She eyed him surreptitiously from behind a potted palm where she was sitting with a very earnest army officer who had been regaling her with the traumas of desert warfare.

He suddenly got the feeling that her attention had wandered and following her gaze he said, 'Somebody you know?'

'Actually yes. His parents live in the same town as I do.'

'Then you'll be wanting to go over to speak to him.'

'I don't think so, David, you carry on with your story.'

'I must have been boring you, Nancy, you should have shut me up.'

'No David, you haven't. Would you like to dance?'

'Yes of course, that's what we came here for. Not to listen to me going on and on about the bloody war.'

She laughed. She liked him, she liked them all, and as they walked into the dance hall he said, 'They've decided to dance too, but not your Commander, I don't think. I take it he is the one you know?'

'Yes. I'm not bothered whether he's dancing or not.'

'It strikes me the girl doth protest too loudly.'

By the time they returned to the bar Julian and the other officers had retreated to the far side of the room and David said, 'Hearty discussions are under way there, Nancy. You don't feel like interrupting them?'

'No.'

'Tomorrow may be too late.'

'For what, David? I've known Julian many years but I've seen him very seldom. I'm sure whatever they're discussing is far more important than anything I might have to say.'

Army officers never stayed long in Alex, and when David left there was nobody else she was even remotely interested in. In her innermost heart she knew it was because she didn't want to go to the places where she might see Julian

253

– Julian with some girl or girls – and she became angry with herself that she minded so much.

After Church Parade on Sunday morning some of them went off to the beach, others to bars, a great many of them back to their duties, but Nancy was not on duty until late afternoon so she decided to take the electric tram that swept along the sea front before the short journey across the desert to Aboukir.

She sat alone on the white rocks where the white surf washed up against them with the azure sea stretching away to the horizon. But for the minarets in the distance she found it hard to imagine that she was in Egypt, and she looked out to where opposite the fort lay Nelson's Island, a yellow rock, long and low.

She did not see Julian until he suddenly took his place on the rocks beside her and she felt frustrated by her swiftly beating heart, burning cheeks and his warm smile.

Unperturbed he said evenly, 'I've been wanting to come here ever since I arrived in Alex, but this is the first time I've managed it. Can you imagine it, Nancy, that glorious first of August when the French fleet lay between this island and the mainland, and yet you have to come to Aboukir to realise how daring Nelson's plan was. He turned disaster into glory and the battle of the Nile was won.'

'Oh, I wish I'd listened and understood history more,' Nancy said. 'It all seemed so long ago and far away.'

He smiled. 'So instead of swinging on your garden gate you wish you'd been indoors poring over those dusty old history books.'

'Yes, I really do.'

'And of all the places you had to come to it had to be Egypt with its overpowering sense of history.'

'Yes. Now I wish I knew more about Cleopatra and Mark Antony, why they had to die the way they did – they've never found her tomb.'

'I wonder why he listened to her, why he didn't insist they fought the Romans on the land instead of the sea.

254

Antony was a soldier; it was doomed from the outset.'

'Perhaps he loved her too much.'

'It was a love that demanded a terrible price.'

For a long moment there was silence as though they were both back in that ancient past with its terrible tragedy, then in a lighter vein Julian said, 'Why aren't you here with that young officer I saw you with the other evening?'

'I didn't know you'd seen me.'

'I hadn't until one of my officers kept looking at you.'

'I can't believe that.'

'It's true. He's been rather disappointed you haven't been there since.'

'David's no longer in Alex.'

'Was it serious?'

'No. He was nice, we got along.'

'And perhaps it isn't the time to be serious about anything outside the war.'

'So you're not serious about any of those girls I've seen you with?' She had to ask it, even though she was aware of the amused smile on his lips.

'For years I've been telling myself that sailors should never marry. I have the legacy of my parents' marriage, mostly spent many miles apart.'

'But they're together now and very happy.'

'It seems that way, doesn't it, but they're getting on in years now. I remember them when they were young and in their separate worlds, together briefly before the next separation.'

'They must have thought it was worth it. Perhaps when you meet the right girl you'll change your mind.'

'And perhaps you're suffering from a girl's romantic mind.'

He scrambled to his feet and held out his hand to help her up. 'How did you get here?' he asked.

'On the tram.'

'Oh well, I have a car down there. I'll drive you back.'

'There's really no need, Julian. I quite like the tram journey.'

'Well, suit yourself, my dear, the offer is there if you want it.'

Of course she wanted it, she wanted every precious minute she might spend with him. Silly foolish young pride shouldn't be allowed to interfere. When they reached the car he smiled. 'Do you still prefer the tram, Nancy?' he asked her.

'No. Thank you, Julian.'

They drove in silence until they reached the outskirts of the city and then he said evenly, 'Are you on duty when you get back?'

'Yes, until eleven.'

'So it's no use inviting you out to dinner. I doubt you'll be here much longer, the war in Europe is drawing to a close, I think.'

'Everybody's thinking that way. Will you be moving out?'

'There's still Japan to think about.'

Oh, why didn't he mention dinner again? Now he was driving up to the apartment she shared with three other girls and leaning across her to open the car door.

He smiled. 'So you're going to read a few more history books, even when the present might be far more exciting.'

'But it isn't exciting, Julian, it's transitory. People coming and going, most of them moving out of your life for ever. You liked them and they're gone. Don't you ever feel that?'

For a long moment he didn't speak, then he said, 'Perhaps I've tended to keep my friendships entirely light-hearted – the ones with girls, I mean. Now isn't the time for long-lasting romances.'

'Not even if you cared very deeply?'

'Perhaps I never have cared deeply. Have you?'

He was looking at her so intently she couldn't look away. It was as though that look would have the power to drag every feeling she had ever had for him into the open – but then he suddenly smiled.

'I shouldn't be asking about your love affairs, Nancy, they're none of my business.'

'There haven't been any love affairs,' she said sharply. 'I think like you do, that this isn't the time for them.'

'And now you're angry?'

'No, no I'm not. Goodbye Julian, perhaps I'll see you around.'

'Perhaps, if I'm here long enough. If I am maybe we could keep that dinner engagement one evening.'

She got out of the car closing the door behind her, and with a brief wave of his hand he was driving away. At that moment only one thought registered – there was no girl in Julian's life, no girl he wanted to marry anyway.

She saw no more of him for several days, although she knew his ship was still anchored there. There were all sorts of rumours flying around: they would soon be going home, the Army were moving out, the Navy would be sailing for the Far East. It was better to discount everything until confirmation.

On the morning she drove Rear Admiral Johnson to the dockyard she saw Julian and another officer walking towards a row of parked cars and as her passenger left the staff car she was driving they looked across and saluted; then, excusing himself from his companion Julian walked across to speak to her.

'We're moving out in a day or so, Nancy. I was wondering if I'd see you before then. You'll probably see the parents before I do so you'll be able to tell them we've met up in Alex.'

'You sound very sure about that, Julian.'

He smiled. 'I could take you out to dinner. Are you free this evening?'

'Yes. Isn't there anything more exciting on the menu?'

'There'll be enough excitement before it's all over. I would prefer to spend this evening with somebody closer to

257

home, even though I do remember your sister better than I remember you.'

'Everybody remembered Erica, I was always the kid sister.'

'But not any more, Nancy. Now you are a very pretty young lady in your own right.'

She laughed.

'I'll pick you up around seven. We'll talk about St Agnes and you shall tell me what you want from the rest of your life.'

'Suppose I don't know.'

'Then I'll encourage you, be the big brother you haven't got.'

She'd dreamed of spending an evening with Julian, in some ballroom somewhere on the English Coast, or in some of the hotels she'd visited with her parents, but never in Alexandria, looking out across a deep blue sea dotted with ships of war.

The meal over they took their drinks out onto the terrace where the night was warm and fragrant with oleander. Julian asked, 'What will you do when you get home, Nancy? As soon as the war is over in Europe you'll get your demob papers.'

'Pick up my life, I suppose, think about a job. Maybe all this has helped me to grow up.'

He didn't answer her immediately, instead he gazed pensively out to sea and when he did speak his words were not what she expected to hear.

'I'm glad I invited you to have dinner with me this evening, Nancy, you've helped me to think about normality and decency before the world went mad. Whenever I went to see the parents I thought their world was so mundane – church on Sundays and their garden, Dad's obsession with his flagpole and the comings and goings of their neighbours, even the young kid swinging on their garden gate with her cheeky grin.'

'That was me.'

258

'Yes, but I hope St Agnes hasn't changed as much as you have.'

Oh, why was her heart hammering like a wild thing? His words didn't mean anything, she was simply a girl that he knew from home, somebody he felt comfortable with. Then suddenly he smiled down at her and it was back again, all the old magic she had felt whenever she had looked at him.

'I wondered what we'd talk about tonight, Nancy, when we'd exhausted St Agnes, but there's been so much to talk about, hasn't there. Will our lives be ordinary when we meet again, do you think?'

'I don't know. I never thought about you as being ordinary.'

He smiled. 'So you did think of me, Nancy. As what, I wonder?'

'As somebody different, who turned up frequently in your naval uniform, exciting, romantic, somebody who smiled at me and promptly forgot about me.'

'Hardly gallant, Nancy.'

'Perhaps not, but I was a kid and you were a man. You noticed my sister, never me.'

'I was never charmed by your sister. She was a beautiful girl with great expectations. I was always rather relieved that they didn't concern me – so too was my father, I think.'

She laughed. 'How I wished I was like her – beautiful, ambitious – but somehow or other she never seemed to get what she wanted from life.'

'Oh, I rather think Erica will survive and very successfully, I shouldn't wonder. Where is she now?'

'Working for some MP at Westminster. I don't hear from her, but Mother tells me about her whenever her letters get through.'

'Do you ever hear from your other friend? It was tragic that her mother died the way she did. I once heard her play the piano at a concert, she had such potential.'

'Yes, Joyce Mellor. She moved away to Derbyshire, I think. I never heard from her again.'

'So you see, Nancy, perhaps St Agnes isn't so mundane after all, it's had its share of tragedy as well as glamour.'

'Glamour?'

'Well yes. Wasn't there a charming lady all the town talked about, largely I expect because they didn't really know much about her.'

'Mrs Edgebaston.'

'That's her.'

'She was nice. I'm sure you're right, nobody really knew her or anything about her. Is all that what I'm going back to?'

'Treasure it, Nancy, isn't it what we've been trying to preserve in all these long, bitter years.'

'Will it be the same, do you think?'

'Some of it perhaps, but there will be changes – whether they'll be for the better is anybody's guess.'

'You won't be looking for a change, Julian, you're happy with your life. Anything outside it doesn't interest you.'

'Did I say that?'

'Something like that. No strings, nothing that will change it.'

He laughed, then putting his arms around her he drew her close and with his cheek resting against hers he said, 'Whatever happens, my dear, I'm glad we spent this evening together. It will give me something to think about when considering what happens next.'

'But the war's almost over, you said so, Julian.'

'For you perhaps, but not for me. Until it is, there really isn't any point in thinking too closely about normality.'

Chapter Twenty-Seven

Erica wasn't sure whether she had enjoyed the evening or not.

Alistair had informed her that his elder sister and her husband were in London, he had invited them to have dinner with him that evening and hoped she would be able to join them.

His sister Meda had been pleasant, if somewhat distant, but seemed kind. Norris her husband had been more interested in the war news, his dinner and moving on to some girlie show. Meda had said she would prefer to see a play. In the end they decided to sit in the bar and chat with Meda doing most of the chatting.

Once or twice Erica had met Alistair's eyes across the table and he had smiled somewhat sympathetically, a smile of apology that she was not really enjoying herself.

He had driven her home just after eleven o'clock and had walked with her to the flat where he said, 'I should have warned you, Erica, my sister does most of the talking and Norris allows her to. They'll be here for a couple of days so obviously I have to see something of them whenever it's convenient.'

'Of course.'

'I promise I won't burden you with them again.'

'Really, I didn't mind, they were very nice. Goodnight Alistair, I'll see you in the morning.'

Now she was thinking about the questions Meda had asked her. How long had she worked at Westminster? How did she like her job? Where was her home and how had she coped living in London during the bombing? She had disclaimed all knowledge of St Agnes – never been there. Did her parents approve of her living in London? Had she made friends?

She liked Alistair – more than liked him – for his generosity, his charming dependability, and yet it wasn't exactly in an admiring way that she viewed him.

He was good-looking, whenever with him she felt that those around them were staring at them, recognising him, respecting him – but now the evening she had just spent was making her feel unsure.

His sister, her husband and his friends were all older than herself. They would probably be discussing her now, his sister commenting on her youth and her unsuitability for anything other than their working relationship. In the end it would all come to nothing, another Oliver Denton.

She never saw Oliver now. He had sulked, then she heard from one of the girls at the office that he was friendly with some other girl. Somehow the girls she worked with all seemed to know more about him than she knew herself.

It really didn't bother her – all she cared about was Alistair. If it all ended in tears she would be the loser, and yet she couldn't be sure that he cared for her anyway – there had been that other girl who had grown tired of waiting.

Back at their hotel Norris decided he was going to bed, it had been a long day and thank goodness the German bombers had too much on their plate to be bothering with them now.

Meanwhile Meda decided she would talk to her brother who she hadn't seen for some time.

'Your secretary seems a nice sort of girl, Alistair. Rather young for the job, don't you think?' she began.

'She copes very well. She worked in my constituency before coming here to replace Celia.'

'She's not exactly in Celia's league, is she?'

'What exactly do you mean by that?'

'Her youth, her inexperience. Celia'd been with you a long time – you had to admit you were devastated when she left you.'

'Perhaps for a time, but I've moved on, I had to. I'm very happy with Erica, Meda, she fits the bill admirably.'

'In what sense?'

'Meaning?'

'You were in love with Celia, at least I thought you were. You kept her hanging on until she grew tired of waiting, which was no more than you deserved. But does this young woman really take her place in every way?'

'If you mean are we lovers, the answer is no, not yet.'

'But it's going that way?'

'Meda, I don't know. Maybe she's too young, maybe I am nothing more than a father figure in her life, or perhaps I'm just her boss. I don't know. I haven't tried to find out.'

'Shall I tell you what I think?'

'You'll tell me anyway.'

'She's a beautiful girl, ambitious and materialistic. I've learned that simply talking to her. If you want something more from her, Alistair, you'll get it, but is she going to be right for you? You're going places – will she be the right woman to have beside you?'

'And what conclusion have you come to?'

'She'll enjoy every minute of it, but will it be what you want?'

'You don't think it will be?'

'I'm going to bed, darling, it's been a long day. Just think hard before you do anything stupid.'

'I don't think I'm doing a bad job in helping to run the country in these very difficult times, but my big sister doesn't even think I'm capable of running my own life.'

She laughed. 'You have a lot of help in running the

country, Alistair, you're on your own running your life. Perhaps you need some advice. I'm very concerned about you, I always have been.'

'Even when it's been totally unnecessary.'

'Even then. Look at you. You're well into your forties and you're still on your own when you close the door at night. If you died tomorrow the country would survive. But you could do more with your own life – you've been so dilatory with it so far, Alistair.'

She realised immediately that she'd said the wrong thing when he said, 'Perhaps you're right, perhaps I should think more about Erica before she does a Celia on me and moves on.'

'I wasn't meaning her, Alistair. Be very careful there.'

He laughed. 'Whenever I have anything to report, Meda, I can assure you you'll be the first to know, but right now I'm going home. Shall I see you and Norris again before you leave?'

'But of course. You could dine with us here one evening, just you, Alistair.'

'If you took the trouble to know her better, and not keep on looking for discrepancies, you might realise that I don't really need a watchdog looking over my shoulder.'

They smiled at each other and embraced before he walked out of the room.

Why did she bother? He'd never listened to her advice, like all men he thought he knew best and it had only been when things had gone awry that he'd credited her with some sense. She'd like Celia, who'd have made a good sister-in-law, but she couldn't imagine Erica Clarkson as one – she wasn't bad at summing up other women. The age difference didn't help but Erica would never be her sort of woman – beautiful and vain, always looking for the good life, and only capable of loving where she found it.

Perhaps she was being unkind, perhaps she wasn't like that at all, but at fifty-one Meda thought she knew enough of the world and the people in it to form her own judgement.

She would have to be very careful. Alistair was all she'd got left in the family and there had been many times when she'd antagonised him over something or other. She didn't intend to lose his friendship because of Erica, even when she felt sure the girl would be a worthy antagonist.

She found Norris sitting up in bed reading the paper, a whisky and soda on the table near the bed.

He smiled at her. 'I knew you'd be saying your piece, Meda. I wanted no part in it.'

'What did you think of her?'

'Pretty, young, ambitious. She's after him, you know?'

'You really thought so?'

'Oh yes. She's not sure about him though, but he shouldn't worry. When he goes for her he'll not find her wanting.'

'It could be a disaster.'

'Oh I don't know. A job some men would die for, a beautiful young wife, enough of the good things in life. Most men would think they'd got all that and heaven too.'

'But would it satisfy her?'

'Are you women ever satisfied? I've asked myself that sometimes and often.'

Alistair paused at Erica's desk the next morning and she looked up with a smile.

'Not too bored with dinner last night, Erica?' he asked her.

'Oh no, it was nice of you to invite me and to meet your sister and her husband.'

'Norris never has much to say but he's not a bad chap when you get to know him. Meda has always been very forthright – we used to argue when we were children.'

'I argued with my sister too. We were never really great friends.'

'And were you the big sister like Meda?'

'Yes.'

'Is your sister at home in St Agnes?'

'Why no. She joined the WRNS. Mother wrote to say she was in Alexandria. She keeps them posted at home but I've always been terrible at writing letters and Nancy's not much better.'

'I'd like to meet her one day when all this is over. Is she like you?'

'No, not at all. She's got light auburn hair and green eyes. She was smaller than me but I expect she's taller now. She had a terrible crush on the Commodore's son but I suppose she's over it now. Surely she'll have met a host of young naval officers where she's been.'

'Of course, and young crushes never really last. Did yours?'

'No. I've forgotten him.'

He smiled. It was the first time he'd really talked to her about her family and now with a swift nod he moved into his office leaving her staring after him.

There were so many things she wanted to know about him, so many things he needed to know about her.

Erica knew what she wanted, she wanted Alistair Greavson with all that went with him, but after last night she kept on seeing his sister's eyes assessing her, her pointed questioning and the shadow of Celia.

The girls she met at Westminster were never reluctant to talk about Celia. How much she had cared for Alistair, even when she was leaving to marry somebody else; their times together, including weekends in Paris and Lisbon and one momentous week in New York. Erica reckoned he had not forgotten her and was still missing her.

She was careful to give nothing away. She had come a long way from the girl who had worn her heart on her sleeve over Oliver Denton. This new grown-up Erica faced the world dry-eyed and confident, even when she yearned for the day Alistair showed more interest in her comings and goings and treated her less like his secretary and more like a woman.

She made constant excuses not to visit her parents, who

asked too many questions about her life in London, and about Alistair in particular. She knew they were worried in case she was falling in love with a man who would never love her. They thought there would only be tears at the end of it, but Erica knew that if he couldn't love her he would never deliberately cause her pain.

He had not asked her to meet his sister again when, several days later, she stared at the letter she'd received from her mother that morning informing her that Oliver Denton had just announced his engagement to a certain Linda Gargrave, a brigadier's daughter from Exeter.

Her mother thought she should know but still hoped she would not be too upset by the news. They all thought she was well and truly over Oliver by this time and would meet some man more worthy of her.

The news didn't upset her in the slightest as she never thought about Oliver these days, but it did surprise her. She'd never really thought he would commit himself to anyone as he was far too selfish.

The opportunity to tell Alistair came several evenings later when he invited her to have dinner with him after a particularly hectic day. With a grave smile he asked, 'Does it bother you, Erica, or have you decided to relegate him finally to the past?'

'It doesn't bother me and hasn't bothered me for some time.'

'I'm glad. So if you met him tomorrow you'd be able to wish him well and really mean it?'

'Yes. I would really mean it.'

'And you're ready to replace him?'

'With the right person, yes I am.'

His expression gave little away. He was looking at her with such grave intensity all she could feel was the fluttering of her heart. Oh why doesn't he say more? she thought desperately, now is the moment when he could tell me that he cares. Did he do this with Celia, pretend with well-chosen words, but words that meant nothing in the end?

The meal was taken largely in silence, but it was not an uncomfortable silence, simply one filled with a sense of waiting, that there was more to come.

Whenever he dropped her off at her flat she never quite knew if she should invite him in for coffee and this evening was no exception. She was therefore surprised when he said gently, 'It's quite early, Erica. Have you plans for the rest of the evening?'

'No, have you?'

'No, and I'm not much relishing the thought of going home to an empty flat. Care to keep me company for a while'

'Yes of course. I'll make coffee, or would you prefer something stronger?'

'No, coffee will do very well.'

As she busied herself in the small kitchen she was aware of him strolling round the living room looking at her photographs.

When she took the tray in he settled down in the chair nearest to the fireplace and looking towards the mantelpiece he said, 'Your photographs are all family, I suppose?'

'Yes. You've met Mum and Dad, this is my sister Nancy.'

'Pretty girl.'

'Do you think so?'

'Well, she's very young in this one, fourteen or so I should imagine. What were you like at fourteen?'

'We were never alike.'

Somehow he looked so right sitting easily chatting about this and that, happy to listen to her favourite records. Oliver had called her taste bourgeois, decidedly middle class, so that in the end she never expected to play her records when he visited her. Now she asked him diffidently, 'Do you like this kind of music?'

'Yes, I like all sorts of music. This is easy to listen to.' He was so easy to talk to – they found things to laugh at and other things to argue about, arguments that didn't hurt or make her feel inferior.

She was amazed when he consulted his watch and proclaimed it to be well after midnight.

She didn't want him to go, didn't know what she wanted but he stood up and turned towards the door. 'I've enjoyed tonight, Erica. Thanks for taking pity on a lonely old bachelor.'

'Is that really how you see yourself, Alistair?'

'I'm afraid it is these days.'

She had to say it, she had to know. 'Do you mean without Celia? You're missing her so much?'

For a long moment he stared down at her, then gently he said, 'I did miss her, Erica. I told myself that I'd been all sorts of a fool, but as each day passes I realise I'm missing her less and less. You've been good for me, Erica, spending time with you on evenings like this, but am I being fair to you?'

'I'm not sure what you mean.'

'A girl, young enough to be my daughter, getting over an unfortunate love affair – and a tired, lonely man feeling sorry for himself.'

'You never seemed like that to me.'

'I threw myself into work, thought it would solve all my problems, obliterate all the hurts and regrets, but it didn't. My dear girl, out there is some young man thirsting for life and love with someone like you – not some melancholy man seeking to recapture something he threw away so carelessly, and not so long ago.'

'Are you telling me you could never love me like you loved her?'

'Gracious no, is that what it sounded like? No, Erica, I'm telling you it would be unfair of me to make you love me. I'm more than twenty years older than you. If you were forty and I were sixty it wouldn't matter, but it matters now – it's a risk neither of us should be contemplating.'

He turned to open the door and in desperation she said, 'Oliver Denton hurt me because he couldn't love me, now you're doing the same thing, but this time you're making

269

the excuse that it's the age difference. With Oliver it was some other ridiculous excuse that was equally untrue.'

He turned to stare at her, his expression curiously haughty, and with a little cry she ran into the living room to sit crouched on the settee with her hands covering her face.

Erica well knew it would bring him to her side, anxious, repentant. It had never failed with her parents, with numerous boys, even with girlfriends. She had tried it with Oliver, but they'd been too much alike, too self-centred. Would it prove any different with Alistair?

He sat beside her with his arms around her, soothing her with gentle words, denying that he meant to hurt her, and this time she knew it was for real – he was hers whatever the years would bring. She didn't want a young man with his desires and ambitions, she wanted this wise, mature man with his secure established future and in return she would show him the joys of loving a young passionate girl, something he had never thought to experience again.

Chapter Twenty-Eight

The loud banging on the door terrified the little girl sitting on the hearthrug and brought her mother hurrying from the kitchen to go anxiously into the passage to open the door.

A large, red-faced, irate woman stood glaring at her and, pushing her to one side, she marched into the house looking round the kitchen expectantly.

'Where is he?' she demanded. 'He said he'd meet me at the top field at seven-thirty. I've been standing up there like a fool waiting for him and it's blowing a gale.'

Edith Blackstock was her husband's youngest sister, but they were all very similar, loud-mouthed and truculent. They didn't like her, had never liked her particularly after she married their brother Roger when he was invalided out of the Army.

He had recovered slowly, but even after their daughter was born they came no closer to accepting her. They thought she was uppity and too middle class, that she looked down on them and was no use on the farm, never had been, not even when she'd been their land girl.

Roger Blackstock had come back into her life after her father and his new wife had moved out of it. They had left her in the house with most of the furniture gone and with debts her father had allowed to accumulate.

They had gone to live in Scotland, she'd never heard

from them since and as far as Joyce was concerned they would never meet again.

As Roger recovered he became a constant visitor and he would arrive bringing odd pieces of furniture he had found tucked away in the attic at the farm. His three sisters deplored their friendship, didn't think much of her work and certainly didn't want her in the family.

Edith surveyed the living room with something like disdain. They had moved into one of the small cottages near the farm but the sisters still maintained that this was really their home, Joyce the interloper.

'I suppose he's still in bed,' she snapped. 'Always going on about being a farmer, the only one who knows anything about the farm, but never around when it comes to doing something useful.'

'There are still days when his war wounds trouble him, Edith. This is probably one of them.'

'Well, you can at least tell him I'm here and ask him if he intends seeing me.'

'Let me make you a cup of tea, you can drink it while I'm asking him. I'm sure you're ready for something.'

'I can make the tea. After all it's my kitchen, I know my way around.'

Joyce decided not to argue with her. In such a mood Edith could be impossible.

Her husband was already dressed but sitting on the edge of the bed with his head in his hands. As he looked up she could see the pain in his eyes and she went to sit beside him. Seeing the pity in her eyes he snapped, 'She's here, I heard her voice. I tried to get up earlier but the pain is awful this morning. I couldn't 'ave gone to meet 'er.'

'You have to tell her, Roger, make her understand.'

'She shouldn't need tellin'.'

'I'll talk to her, perhaps you should get back to bed.'

'It's no better in bed. I'll talk to her.'

She knew what was in store, hard words and shouting, her daughter's frightened face and then nothing.

272

Would they have accepted some other woman or would they have disliked any woman he'd married? He would always be their little brother, but he was the man in the family and the farm had been left to him.

His father had assumed that the girls would marry and move away – that they hadn't made matters worse. Joyce knew that in his innermost heart Roger knew he had married a woman who was totally unsuitable to be a farmer's wife.

She stayed on the edge of the bed listening to the sound of their angry voices downstairs. After a few minutes her daughter came to snuggle up beside her and she held her close.

Joyce was well aware that she had made a mess of her life. Pride and hatred, the need for revenge and too many bitter memories had all conspired to make things the way they were, and as she held her daughter's trembling body against her she remembered the last time she had seen her father.

He and his wife had stood in the hall of the old stone house, their packed suitcases waiting to be loaded into the taxi, but there had been no expression of regret in her father's cold eyes.

In cold, clipped accents he had said, 'You've disappointed me far too long, daughter, and I'll not be seeing you again. You've made your bed, now you'll lie on it. Have you anything to say?'

'Only to ask if I can have my mother's cameo brooch. She always said that one day I could have it, something to remember her by. It's the only thing I want.'

'My wife has it. Your mother never had good taste in anything. I bought her that brooch when we toured Italy with the orchestra; my new wife will appreciate it.'

It seemed to Joyce that she had moved from one sort of hatred to another. On that last morning she could willingly have killed her father, and now in this house listening to the raised voices from below there was enough hatred to incite either one of them to kill the other.

She heard something crash suddenly against the wall, then nothing but the slamming of the door. Taking hold of Jenny's hand they crept slowly down the stairs.

They were treading on broken glass where a vase had been flung against the door, the carpet wet with water from it, the broken petals of the flowers strewn around.

Roger stood at the window leaning heavily on the sill and she went immediately into the kitchen to find something to help her clear up the mess.

'Don't touch the glass, Jenny,' she cautioned her daughter, 'the pieces are very sharp, you could cut yourself.'

Roger turned away from the window and sat heavily in a chair. 'I suppose you 'eard most of that?' he said sharply.

She didn't answer and after a few minutes he said, 'What's got into them? It's not my fault Dad left the farm to me. I was the only man in the family and besides they could 'ave got married and moved away. Edith had boyfriends, so had Mary, now they're that jealous they make me feel I've no right to be livin' 'ere.'

'It won't always be like this, Roger, they'll get over it.'

'I doubt it. They ran things while I was at the war, now I'm back sooner than they expected and they don't like it.'

'It's me they don't like, Roger. To them I'm somebody who appeared out of nowhere, different, not the sort of girl they expected you to marry.'

'I shouldn't 'ave to ask them who I should wed – probably some girl from the village who they could boss about and expect her to be grateful.'

'Was there ever a girl you thought you might marry, Roger?'

'One or two, I suppose. Girls I'd always known, girls me sisters knew.'

'I can understand their resentment, can't you?'

'No. I didn't tell them who they should marry. You came along and you were different. You had style. I didn't think you'd think me good enough for you.'

274

'Oh Roger, if only you knew more about me, you'd never have thought that.'

'Well, I know you 'ad trouble with your father and you don't talk about your mother or your life afore ye got 'ere, but I know you've had a decent education by the way ye speak. And I know there's lots more I need to know about ye. One day perhaps you'll tell me.'

'Yes, one day.'

Jenny had gone to sit next to her father at the table and looking at her pretty face she thought, Does she have any talent? How shall I ever know in this environment? Yet she felt sure that perhaps one day it would surface. They'd have to wait, but how could Jenny be given the sort of chances she'd thrown away? She thought about the grand piano now residing in the concert hall and destined never to be hers.

'Do you still have a lot of pain?' she asked him. 'Would you like tea?'

'The pain's better. I was too angry to think about it. I'll 'ave that cup of tea.'

'What are you going to do about the top field?'

'I'll get up there this mornin'. So many of the lads are still at the war and some of 'em might not even be comin' back. There's too much for women to do and I'm pretty useless right now. Now that I've simmered down I suppose Edith isn't all wrong.'

'Try to make it up to her, Roger, you need each other. Don't fall out because of me.'

'Comin' back to some other job it wouldn't 'ave mattered that I'd been wounded, but to come back to farmin' ... The land's a hard taskmaster, Joyce, ye need to be fit and strong, to be out in all weathers, to see to the land and the animals, the changin' seasons and every one of 'em bringin' its share o' problems. I keep askin' myself if I'll ever be fit to do the farm justice.'

'But it's too soon, Roger. Every day you'll get stronger, you have to tell yourself that.'

He grinned. 'Believe me love, I do, and then the pain

starts up again and all me resolutions dry up. I'll get up there now and make me peace with the sisters.'

'Do you want me to come with you?'

'No. I can manage on me own and they'll not be expectin' you.'

She smiled. He was right, she was better off out of it. Perhaps in time they would be able to accept her.

She watched him walking painfully to the tractor and climb into it with the utmost difficulty. Turning to Jenny she said, 'I know what we'll do, darling, we'll find another vase and then we'll walk to the village and buy a bunch of flowers. Would you like to do that?'

The child smiled at her and ran excitedly into the passage. She picked up the daily newspaper from the hall and handed it to her mother and Joyce looked at the headlines. Where once there had been despair now there was exuberance, the Germans were being driven back, Italy was no longer on their side and France once more belonged to the French. Germany was engaged in a life and death struggle with Russia and the tide had turned. There was still Japan, but somehow it seemed so far away.

People were smiling now, on the streets and in the village shops and handing over her money for the bunch of daffodils the florist said, 'It's all goin' well, Mrs Blackstock. I 'ope your husband's feeling better these days.'

'Some days better than others, I'm afraid.'

'Ay well, it's early days. My, but your little girl's gettin' to be quite a young lady, isn't she?'

'Yes, I think she's going to be quite tall.'

'I 'opes you're quite happy at the farm, the sisters 'ave ruled the roost for a long time.'

'Yes, they managed very well.'

'They'll try to manage yer 'usband given half a chance. I went to school with Mary, I should know.'

Joyce smiled politely, but not to be put off the shopkeeper went on, 'It can be difficult when you're not from

276

these parts, everythin'll seem very strange to you, I'm sure, but the folks round 'ere are very decent and well meanin'. Why don't yet get involved with things at the church? Yer'd meet people, find an interest, somethin' outside the farm.'

'Perhaps I will when my husband's feeling better. I do need to meet people and get involved with something, but at the moment I'm taking each day as it comes.'

'Ay, I'm sure yer right, Mrs Blackstock.'

Roger patched up his quarrel with his sisters but more and more they began to take over the running of the farm because there were whole days when he was in so much pain he felt unable to move from his chair.

She was his wife and his housekeeper, she looked after Jenny but realised that she would always be the outsider, a person to be sneered at as her mother had been.

The sisters came up to the farm and meetings were held in the living room while she was expected to stay in the kitchen to serve them with food and drinks whenever they requested them. They were indifferent to Jenny and she was aware of the mockery in their eyes and sometimes their derision when she served them with food.

Roger never saw it. On the one occasion she complained about their behaviour he merely said that since she knew little about the farm and its demands why should they consult her about anything?

Her time as a land girl was discounted, but she could understand it since she'd been subjected to orders then and rightly so. How could a girl who had lived for her music be expected to know anything about the land?

She took Jenny to the village hall where the church choir and the Scouts were giving a concert in aid of the war effort and looked longingly at the upright piano in one corner of the platform with an old man playing it. The tunes were simple, and she learned that he also stood in for the organist at the church who was serving in the Air Force.

One afternoon she was the first to arrive there. Unable

to help herself she stepped onto the platform and opened the piano lid. She looked round nervously, straining her ears for any sound that people were arriving, then began to play. It all came back to her so easily, Chopin's *Nocturne*, gentle and dreamy, then Beethoven – she didn't hear the people coming into the hall and it was Jenny tugging at her skirt who brought her back to reality.

Every seat in the hall was occupied with the Scouts and choir lining the walls in absolute silence. The old man who normally played the piano stood looking down at her entranced. Embarrassed, she stared up at him before rising to her feet and saying, 'I'm so sorry. I didn't realise so many people had come in. Come, Jenny, we must try to find a place.'

'Nay Mrs Blackstock, ye surely don't expect me to play after that performance,' he said.

'Of course. I shouldn't have played, but the piano was so tempting and it's such a long time since I played one.'

'Ye'll play for us again, I hope?'

'Well, I really don't know. I'm busy at the farm, there's never enough time.'

'Oh there's time alright if I know the Blackstock girls. None of them'll be interested in music. How about this little one 'ere?'

'That's what I'm hoping for one day. We haven't got a piano. She's only a child. Perhaps by the time she's interested we'll have one.'

'Yer'd like to play like yer mother, wouldn't you?' he said smiling down at the child.

Jenny smiled shyly and nodded her head.

'Ye see, what's meant to be will be,' he said. 'Now promise me you'll play for us again.'

'If it's possible.'

Over their evening meal she told Roger about the events of the afternoon and when she'd finished he said sourly, 'Didn't ye think to tell him we were farmers, not musicians.'

'You're the farmer, Roger, you and your sisters.'

'And you're the farmer's wife with better things to do.'

'I want it for Jenny, Roger, that's if she shows any talent for it. She's young so obviously it won't surface for a while, but if it does she should be given a chance.'

'How? We don't have a piano.'

'It doesn't have to be a piano, it could be a violin, a clarinet, any instrument.'

'Joyce, I'm tired, I don't want to listen to all this talk about Jenny and music. It's what yer father wanted for you and you didn't, so what makes you think Jenny'll be any different?'

'But I did want it, Roger. I didn't want it the way my father wanted it – so obsessive that there would have been no room for anything else, friends, some sort of life, even my mother.'

'Isn't that what you want for Jenny? What about me?'

'Roger, I'm your wife, it's too late for me to make music my life because you're my life, you and Jenny, but you can't expect me to forget what it meant to me before I met you.'

'We'll talk about it some more. Tonight I'm tired and I don't want you talking about it in front of my sisters, none of them'll understand.'

'I know.'

'The farm's our livelihood, not some fanciful dream of music for Jenny. If you go on and on about it, they'll have something to say.'

'Jenny's my daughter, Roger. They wouldn't listen to me about the farm, so they shouldn't censure me about Jenny.'

'I just don't want to hear any more about it now. I'm going to bed.'

A few days later Mary Blackstock sat at the kitchen table eating her breakfast and it was obvious she had something to say.

There was a small secretive smile on her face and as she

279

helped herself to toast she said quietly, 'I've bin 'earing about your solo concert at the village hall.'

'Really, who told you?'

'Practically everybody in the village. Quite an audience you had.'

'So I heard.'

'They were sayin' they 'oped yer'd play for them again. I told them yer'd got a sick man and a child to care for so it was 'ardly likely yer'd 'ave much time.'

'You're probably right, and I'll have even less time when the new baby is born.'

Chapter Twenty-Nine

The war in Europe was over. They'd sung their patriotic songs, waved their flags and marched proudly to the strains of Elgar's music. Now they were filling the church pews and organ music was swelling out into the warmth of a May morning.

The spectacle had beaten anything the longest day could have provided and as the Vicar looked over the heads of his congregation he could almost read the minds of a great many of the people there.

There was pride and relief on so many of their faces, but he knew that for Commodore and Mrs Watson there was still anxiety for a son facing the last implacable enemy in the Far East.

The Major's face was thoughtful and no doubt thinking of all those boys he had encouraged over the years with words of pride, seeing them go off to war with all the enthusiasm they had displayed on the rugger field, and no doubt reflecting on the faces he would see no more.

The Clarksons too had a great deal to think about. Their daughter Nancy would no doubt soon be coming home, and the wedding of their elder daughter to a Minister of the Crown was the talk of the town.

The Vicar very much doubted if it would take place in his church; surely the wedding of somebody as well known as Alistair Greavson would merit something rather grander than this old Norman church, but he was glad to see that Oliver Denton and his fiancée were sitting with his aunt – he wondered if perhaps he had misjudged the young man after all.

Mrs Edgebaston had arrived late and was sharing a pew with Hilda Marks and her husband. Everybody knew the two women didn't care much for each other, and even now sharing the same pew there was a distance between them.

It was not like Grace and her mother to be late – normally they were among the first in church and he hadn't seen either of them at the war memorial.

He loved Grace, had asked her to marry him, and only the evening before they had both talked to her mother about their feelings, encouraging her to give them her blessing and saying they wanted her with them at the vicarage.

She would have her own space there, a small flat with her own sitting room and bedroom, somewhere where she could receive her friends. The old lady had said very little but had sat most of the evening with a frozen face and he had watched Grace becoming more and more distressed.

Now he feared the worst. Something had apparently gone wrong to make them miss church and it was time for the first hymn.

He would need to visit them as soon as church was over, but it wasn't going to be easy. This was not a normal Sunday and already he was beginning to feel his usual antagonism for the old lady.

He really didn't like Mrs Gantry. He had always considered her unfair to Grace, particularly after her father died. Mr Gantry had been a nice man, always kind and considerate, but his wife had never shared his popularity in the town. After his death his widow had mercilessly taken over Grace's life and now he expected the worst. If she could do anything to prevent their marriage she wouldn't hesitate to do so, and he wasn't sure that Grace would have the courage to rebel.

He delivered his sermon even though his thoughts were

282

elsewhere, and he had meant it to be one of his best. He hoped his congregation wouldn't think he had let them down.

He wasn't alone in his anxiety. Grace faced her mother across the room after urging her to hurry or they would be late for church. Mrs Gantry had merely shrugged her shoulders and stated her intention of staying at home.

Grace stared at her in amazement before saying, 'But this isn't just any Sunday, Mother, this one is special. The war in Europe is over, there'll be a parade at the war memorial and everybody will be there. We can't simply not go.'

'You go if you feel you must. The Vicar will be in his element and you want to see him perform, I don't. His poor wife hasn't been dead five minutes and you're trying to step into her place, it's unseemly. I can't think what your father would have thought about it.'

'Don't you think my father would have been happy for me?'

'I do not. He'd have agreed with me. One expects better things from a man of the cloth, not this rushing into marriage before his wife's gone cold in her grave.'

'His wife has been dead five years, Mother.'

'And he thinks he needs somebody, well I need somebody. I can't have long to live at the longest. I never expected my daughter to want to leave me in my old age.'

'Mother, I'm not leaving you. We've asked you to come with us. Paul has had architects in to see how the vicarage can be rearranged to accommodate you, so how can you possibly say I'm deserting you?'

'Well I can and I do. I don't want to end my days in a little flat at the vicarage. Who would want to come to see me there?'

'The same people who would come to see you here, Mother. You could help me with so many things, you'd come to enjoy it.'

'I would hate every minute of it. You a glorified secretary

283

and me in a manufactured flat. I'd feel like some below-stairs servant or some decrepit half-witted old woman you needed to keep out of sight.'

'That's an awful thing to say, Mother.'

'That's how I feel. If you marry him I shall stay here. I can get a housekeeper, a good kind soul who would take care of me, and I would have all my own things around me.'

'You're doing all this so that I won't marry him, aren't you, Mother? You did everything to come between us years ago. I was in love with him then, now you're doing it again.'

'How can you possibly say you loved him then. He married somebody else and if you didn't marry him now he'd quickly latch on to somebody else. That Mrs Edgebaston is still available and I've seen him chatting to her often enough.'

'I can't talk to you when you're like this, Mother.'

'Can't you see I'm trying to make you see sense. All these years you've hankered after him, even when he was married, and now you're telling yourself it was love. You were thwarted, Grace, and now you're afraid of losing him a second time.'

Grace had never felt so helpless. Paul would have missed their presence in church so no doubt he'd come to the house as soon as possible. What would he make of her mother's truculence?

'It's too late now for church, Mother. I'm making a cup of tea. Do you want one?' she asked in some desperation.

'I don't want anything. He'll be here as soon as church is over and I'm ready for him.'

Grace could only dread their meeting and its outcome. She sat alone in the kitchen drinking her tea, remembering how she cried herself to sleep on the day Paul married Molly Preston. She'd liked Molly, they'd been friends at school, but her love for Paul had never gone away and now it was all going wrong again.

*

284

The church service was over and Paul stood at the church door waiting to shake hands with his parishioners as they left. Why were they spending so much time chatting to each other? The morning had been a long one, so they should be thinking about lunch.

Anthea Edgebaston was the first to leave. She had been quick to distance herself from Hilda Marks and her husband and now she was taking his outstretched hand, saying with a smile, 'It's been a long morning, Paul, I expect you'll be glad of the break before Evensong.'

'Yes, this has been a morning to give thanks and mourn a little, I suppose.'

She nodded and smiled before moving off into the pleasant May morning.

Muttering to her husband Hilda Marks said, 'She seems in a mighty hurry, I expect she's got a mark on.'

Used to his wife's snide comments he thought it unnecessary to reply.

The civic party were leaving now and Councillor Stedman paused long enough to allow Paul to see the tears still wet on his wife's face.

Alcc had been their only son and he had lost his life when his plane had crashed over the South Coast. His young wife and her child had sat with her parents and Paul was unsure if he had adequate words to comfort any of them.

Lady Jarvis and her sister Marcia were chatting to Commodore Watson and his wife who was busy explaining to them that Sir Robert was in London and had been unable to attend.

Paul asked after Julian but they had no news to impart, and it was the Major's wife who said quietly, 'Grace and her mother were not in church, Vicar. Is Mrs Gantry unwell?'

'It's unlike them not to be here. I'll call round this afternoon to see if something is wrong.'

'It'll be the old girl,' the Major muttered, 'she's usually

the one to disrupt matters, ask my wife.'

His wife gave him a look she hoped would silence him, but he left shaking a doubtful head.

The Clarksons informed him Nancy would soon be on her way home from Egypt and hopefully a quick demob. Quite unable to stop himself the Vicar said, 'And Erica, how soon will the wedding be?'

'We really don't know, but hopefully so that Nancy can be her bridesmaid. We don't know where the wedding will take place,' was the reply.

'Of course not, and her husband to be is a very prominent man.'

One by one or in groups they walked towards the church gate and Paul hurried into the vestry to disrobe. Only the Verger remained and with a wry smile he said, 'I thought they'd never go, Vicar, but it was a good turnout. I knew it would be, but it went well, I think, the service and the parade.'

'Yes, very well, Mr Harper. I doubt if many of them will turn out for Evensong, after all that.'

He felt decidedly hungry – it had been a long time since breakfast – but he was worried about Grace so lunch could wait.

The Verger watched him hurrying out and guessed immediately where he was going. He couldn't ever remember Grace or her mother missing church, and to miss on such a morning something must indeed be wrong.

Standing at the window Grace had seen the people walking to their homes and she knew it wouldn't be long before Paul arrived, then she saw him hurrying along the road, his head bent in thought.

She went quickly to open the door and they looked at each other for a long moment in silence before he said, 'Is something wrong, Grace? You didn't come to church.'

He was instantly aware of her distress, her eyes were filled with tears and as she drew him into the house her mother's voice came to them from her sitting room. 'You can both come in here if you want to know what I have to say.'

Paul looked at Grace in silent concern and she whispered, 'Oh Paul, I don't know what's the matter with her, she's been awful all morning.'

They found Mrs Gantry sitting in her usual chair in front of the fire and she motioned them to sit opposite on the settee. Paul guessed that what she had to say had been mentally well rehearsed.

Fixing them with a stern stare she began, 'I've told Grace that I don't wish to live at the vicarage. I prefer to stay here, this is my home.'

'And are you expecting Grace to remain here with you?' Paul asked quietly.

'It would appear she has to make a choice, either to marry you or stay here to care for me. As a vicar what would you advise somebody in the same position to do?'

'I've never been asked to advise on such a matter, Mrs Gantry. Each one of us has a life to live and to make the best we can of it.'

'Even if it means hurting somebody else.'

'You know it was never our intention to hurt you, we have offered you a home with us. I have promised to make the vicarage as comfortable as possible for you so that you can retain your independence and still have your daughter with you. If that is hurting then I'm afraid I don't understand your logic.'

'Don't you see you are taking away my independence. A little flat at the vicarage, to give up this lovely old house that has been mine since the day I married, what you are offering in its place is simply unacceptable.'

'And what of Grace? You would be asking her to spend her life caring for you in this house until the time comes when she will be left alone, then what? We love each other, we have the chance to be together, hopefully for many years.'

'It doesn't seem to have taken you very long to forget your late wife.'

287

'And that remark is very unfair. Molly has been dead for five years and I tried to make her happy. She was happy with me and I know this is what she would want for both of us. Molly was a very kind and loyal woman.'

'So you tell yourself.'

'Mrs Gantry, I don't think you want happiness for Grace. Your concerns are only for yourself. Are you quite sure you could live alone in this house if Grace decides to marry me?'

'Oh yes, I could manage very well. I am not without money, money which I intended Grace to have one day. If I decide to remain here I shall need a full-time housekeeper and other help. My money will diminish, but that would be unavoidable. Grace would have to accept that.'

'Neither Grace nor I are concerned about your money, Mrs Gantry. Vicars do not amass fortunes but I am comfortably off thanks to my grandfather. Your money is the last thing I'm thinking about.'

'Then Grace will have to decide, won't she – either her mother or you. If she chooses you there are people in this town who will be amazed by the pair of you.'

'If you mean they will condemn us, I don't think so, Mrs Gantry. I think my friends in this town have far bigger hearts than to condemn us. They will find considerably more difficulty in understanding you.'

He got up from his chair and looking down at Grace he said gently, 'Well Grace, I can do no more, it's up to you now. Are you going to let her win a second time or are you going to follow your heart? I can't decide for you, my dear, it's something you have to think about very carefully until you're absolutely sure.'

Without looking at her mother again he moved towards the door and after a few minutes she followed him. He stood in the hall waiting for her to join him, then drawing her into his embrace he said, 'I'm leaving, Grace, I have to think about the service this evening and I really do need some lunch. I'm not going to persuade you about anything, it has to come from you. Looking back it's almost the same

288

conversation we had years ago, only this time I thought it would be different.'

'My mother hasn't changed, Paul.'

'No, but I'm hoping you have.'

'Oh why does it have to be like this? Why does she always have to spoil things for me? Why have I never been able to stand up to her?'

'This is your chance, Grace, it's now or never. Think about it, darling.'

For a long moment she looked at him piteously, then with a brief smile he left her and she watched him walking swiftly along the road in the direction of the vicarage. He would go home to hear Mrs Atkins tut-tutting because he was late home for lunch, and he would struggle preparing for Evensong with the memory of her mother's intransigence filling his mind.

Her mother would not change her mind; no amount of pleading from either of them would make her. She would be relying on Grace's sense of guilt and she was feeling it already.

She looked through the window at the clouds dulling the day where a breeze ruffled the river, and although it was only three o'clock she felt strangely weary.

Making up her mind suddenly she went into the hall and pulled out a mackintosh from the hall wardrobe plus some sort of covering for her head. She could no longer stay in the house – whatever the day she had to get away from her mother, and she needed to think.

The roads were strangely deserted but as she passed the newly erected war memorial, the scarlet poppy wreaths that had been placed there gave an incongruous glow to the sombre location.

Before she reached the vicarage she took the steps leading down to the river. There on the riverside walk the shower began and she was glad for it meant she was unlikely to meet anybody.

She was dismally aware of the damp feeling around her

but it did not deter her from sitting on the stone wall above the river looking down to where it flowed moodily towards the weir.

She was so immersed in her thoughts she did not see Mrs Edgebaston and her dog walking towards her. At that moment Mrs Edgebaston paused suddenly wondering why it was always her who found women sitting there alone in the depths of despair. She would have liked to have moved away unobserved but there was something about the dejected woman sitting there that brought back memories of Erica and the fear that she would suddenly decide to do something drastic.

It was the dog sniffing round her ankles that suddenly made Grace look up to find Anthea Edgebaston looking at her with a compassion that brought the tears to her eyes. Then Anthea was sitting beside her waiting for the sobs to cease.

Chapter Thirty

Grace accepted the cup of tea Anthea handed her with a grateful smile, but for a long time they sat in silence, a silence that Anthea had decided she should not be the one to break.

It was Grace who finally said, 'I'm sorry Mrs Edgebaston, what must you think of me?'

'My name is Anthea. I've often wondered why nobody ever feels they should use it.'

'I'm sorry, I didn't know it.'

'No. I think only the Major uses it. I know that your name is Grace. I certainly think of you as Grace.'

'I feel I owe you some sort of explanation, but I don't quite know how to start.'

'You really don't need to say anything, but sometimes it's good to talk about one's troubles.'

Grace smiled wistfully while Anthea sat with her dog curled up on her knee stroking his tan coat.

'He's a nice little dog,' Grace said. 'I've never had a dog. Mother didn't care for them, she always said they'd mess up the house. We never had a cat either.'

'Benjie's been a very good friend to me. Most of the time he's been all I've had.'

Grace stared at her in some surprise. 'You always seemed so at one with life, so confident. I always wished I could be like you.'

'Life makes you what you are, brings out the best and the worst in you I suppose.'

'Did you know that the Vicar has asked me to marry him?'

She had been unprepared for the suddenness of the announcement so for a moment she didn't quite know what to say, but seeing Grace's anxiety she said, 'No, I didn't know, but I'm not surprised.'

'Why? Why aren't you surprised?'

'Because I've thought for a very long time that he cared for you. Aren't you happy? Don't you want to marry him?'

'Yes I do, but we're not sure it's going to be possible.'

'Why ever not?'

'My mother. You're not surprised are you?'

'Not entirely.'

'She can be difficult, most of the neighbours are aware of it, but she is my mother, I owe her a lot.'

'And doesn't she owe you something, Grace? Do you want to marry him?'

'Yes. I've been in love with him since I was a young girl, and I'll be forty next birthday. We were in love with each other years ago and thought we would marry then but my father died and Mother was on her own and unwell. The time wasn't right and in the end Paul married somebody else. It hurt terribly at the time but we both got over it. I liked Molly, we were friends and I was sorry when she died. Now we are both being given a second chance it seems it isn't to be.'

'Your mother has said she doesn't want you to marry him?'

'Not exactly, but she won't come to live with us. She's in her eighties and wants to stay where she is with a house-keeper, if she can get one. She's not too well and I don't see how I can leave her.'

'So she's going to win again. You're letting him go out of your life for a second time – if he finds somebody else you'll be hurt again.'

'She's making me choose.'

'And the choice is the rest of your life, Grace. What sort of life have you had since your father died? A game of bridge every Tuesday, church on Sunday and two weeks at some hotel in Torquay every July. Is that really enough?'

She shook her head dolefully. 'No. I admit Paul could give me so much more, but how can I leave my mother?'

'But you had no intention of leaving her. You've both been very generous and she's turned your generosity down. She could have her own way, but aren't you entitled to have yours?'

'But how can I leave her now? She's old and far from well. We were so sure she'd be happy to live with us at the vicarage but it's not what she wants.'

'What do you want, Grace?'

'I want to marry Paul, but it isn't always possible to have what we want, is it?'

Anthea didn't know what more she could say. Grace had been conditioned for years to doing everything her mother asked of her. It had been so easy to give advice to Erica Clarkson because Erica had only listened to what she wanted to hear. It had to be the best for Erica because she'd always had the best, but it seemed that Grace had already had her mind made up for her so there was nothing more to be said.

'I'm sorry you missed the parade at the war memorial this morning,' she said in an effort to change the subject.

Grace smiled bleakly and said, 'Oh yes, I wanted to go but Mother wasn't ready in time.'

A lie, thought Anthea. Mrs Gantry would never have missed church unless something more important was in the offing, in this case her future and Grace's marriage.

'I suppose the church was full,' Grace asked.

'Yes, Mrs Prothero's nephew was there with his fiancée. It's the first time I've seen her.'

'Mrs Prothero says she's very nice – we all thought he would marry Erica.'

293

'Yes it's strange that things don't always work out as we planned, and now Erica is marrying somebody else.'

'Oh yes. I hope she gets married here and not in London. Mother seems to think it will be in London though. What do you think?'

'I really don't know. Erica has always been full of surprises.'

Talk of weddings was making Grace reflective, and Anthea said hurriedly, 'The tea's gone cold, I'll brew another pot.'

'Oh no, please Anthea, I must be getting back. Mother'll wonder what's become of me.' Consulting her watch she went on, 'Gracious, it's after five, she'll be wanting her tea. Thank you so much for listening to all my woes.'

'Are you any nearer solving them, Grace?'

'Not really. I don't think there is a solution, do you?'

'As a matter of fact I do think there is, but I doubt if my solution would be yours. I'm not going to church this evening, will you be there?'

'I don't think so. I don't think I could face Paul again today, and Mother won't want to go, I'm sure.'

'Well, you've got to meet him some time.'

'I know.'

'I take it you've already made up your mind.'

'I've had it made up for me.'

'I'll come to the door with you. Stay there Benjie, you've had your walk for one day.'

They parted at the front door and she stayed there for several minutes watching Grace cross the road and walk towards her house. Suddenly she seemed surrounded by a great loneliness, and Anthea's heart felt sad as she contemplated her future.

Grace was not going home to a happy house and Anthea thought about her as she took the tea things into the kitchen. What would mother and daughter talk about for the rest of the day? Mrs Gantry had obviously won but would their conversation be amicable? Would she be conciliatory to the

294

daughter she was robbing of a future, or would she still be truculent, reassuring her that it was all for the best?

All Grace's friends would know about Paul's proposal and would have been happy for her. Now they would find it hard to believe that it had all come to nothing. Her mother had never been a popular woman in the town – now she would be even more disliked and all their sympathies would be with the Vicar. Anthea could imagine the Major's scathing comments, which no doubt during the next few days she would be subjected to. If he felt the need to scandalise anybody he invariably made his dislikes plain to her, for the simple reason that she'd always been the butt of their snipes.

As Grace walked up the path she saw that the curtains were drawn in her mother's bedroom and wondered if she'd decided to go to bed rather than spend the evening trying to make conversation. She felt cold in spite of the rather mild temperature, and the church looked somewhat forlorn in the rain.

She knew that Paul would be busy preparing for Evensong and her heart ached with the dying of a dream and the dismal prospect of her future life.

She let herself into the house and for a moment stood listening to any sounds from upstairs. Her mother had evidently eaten since soiled crockery stood in the sink – Grace reflected grimly that the events of the day hadn't interfered with her mother's appetite.

She started to wash the crockery and then reluctantly thought it was time to go upstairs to confront her mother. Crossing the hall she was amazed to see her mother descending the stairs wearing her best outdoor clothes.

For a long moment they stared at each other then her mother said, 'I didn't know where you were, but you'd better hurry up and get changed if you're coming to church.'

Grace gaped at her in astonishment. 'You're going to church, Mother?'

'Of course I'm going to church. We missed it this morning, I've no intention of missing church this evening.'

'I'm surprised you want to go. How can you face seeing Paul after this afternoon?'

'Why shouldn't I see him? He's the Vicar doing a job of work and I'm one of his parishioners, no more, no less.'

'And he's the man who asked me to marry him.'

'I thought we'd sorted all that out, Grace. Are you coming to church with me or not?'

'No Mother I'm not, and I don't think you should go either. For one thing it's raining.'

'We've gone in such weather before.'

'I've been with you, Mother.'

'I'm quite capable of crossing the road and walking the short distance to church. Someone will see me home, I'm sure, and no doubt will wonder why my daughter has allowed me to go out alone on such a night.'

Mrs Gantry was blissfully unaware that with every word she uttered her daughter was at long last being finally convinced of the mistake she'd been about to make.

She watched her mother marching off across the road with a determined tread and then she went to sit in front of the fire. She had a lot to think about.

Mrs Gantry took her place in the pew aware that around her people were trying not to take too much notice. Hilda Marks nudged her husband and said, 'Mrs Gantry's here alone, I wonder where Grace is.'

'None of our business,' he muttered.

'I know, but you've got to admit something's evidently wrong.'

'Perhaps Grace isn't well.'

Sitting in the adjacent pew Mrs Prothero smiled and whispered, 'Isn't Grace with you?'

'No, not this evening.'

'My nephew and his fiancée have left so I'm on my own too.'

Meanwhile the Verger was informing the Vicar that the congregation was likely to be a lot less than it had been for the morning service. Paul was glad, it had been a long day.

It was a little later when he was able to view the congregation from his seat near the choir stalls and as his eyes met Mrs Gantry's he was very aware of the overconfident gleam in them – a gleam that proclaimed that she had won.

He felt ashamed of the mechanical way he had delivered his sermon. People had turned out on a rainy evening to listen to words he had penned when his mind was involved with other matters, and as a man of God he was ashamed of his feelings of dislike for the small darkly clad figure of the woman sitting alone in one of the pews.

Mrs Gantry didn't think his sermon was up to much. He wasn't nearly as good as the old vicar who had married her forty-three years before, but then nothing was as good as it used to be. She'd be able to tell Grace when she got home that she'd been wise to stay away.

Taking his outstretched hand outside the church when the service was over, no words were exchanged, and as she walked down the church path with Mrs Prothero she said, 'I didn't think much of the Vicar's sermon this evening, did you?'

'Well, I thought he seemed very preoccupied all day. He was so very good at the war memorial, but in church this morning he seemed a little distracted. It's been a very long day for him.'

'It is his job though, we all have our off days.'

She knew why he'd been distracted. Grace hadn't been in church. Mrs Gantry had no doubt in her mind that Grace would realise where her duty lay. Vicars didn't make fortunes – she'd be better off staying where she was with money at the end of it, rather than bolstering him up in a dreary vicarage living with a man whose job didn't earn him much money. She hadn't brought Grace up to be a fool.

Mrs Prothero was talking about her nephew Oliver.

'It was so kind of them to visit me today. I do like his fiancée. I was always so bothered about who he would marry, or if he would marry.'

'I thought it would be the Clarkson girl.'

'Oh so did I. She was such a pretty girl, but rather too young for him, I thought. Did you know that she's marrying Alistair Greavson?'

'She'll be far too grand for us. I wonder if she'll be married here.'

'Oh I do hope so. Her parents would like that, I'm sure.'

'But not Erica,' said Mrs Gantry. 'That little madam would surely prefer London and a bevy of prominent guests.'

'We'll have to wait and see,' she said diplomatically.

'Would you like to come in for a cup of coffee?' Mrs Prothero said with a smile.

'Well no, I really think I'd better get home to see what Grace is doing.'

'Why isn't she with you?'

'Oh, she said she had letters to write and other jobs to do. Goodnight, I do hope you'll invite me in for coffee another time.'

She found Grace sitting staring into the fire, an open notepad on her knee and a pen in her hand. When Grace looked up she said, 'Have you had something to eat? I forgot to tell you I'd already eaten.'

'I know Mother, I washed up the crockery after you'd gone to church.'

'What have you been doing with yourself? Good job you didn't go to church. The sermon wasn't very good, certainly not up to his usual standard.'

Cynically Grace thought that if his sermon had been worthy of Shakespeare her mother wouldn't have thought much of it.

'Who are you writing to?' her mother demanded.

'Nobody really. I was just scribbling one or two things

298

down in case I'd forgotten them. Do you want anything before I go out, Mother?'

'Out! Why, where are you going?'

'I'm going to the vicarage. Is it still raining?'

'Not very much. Why do you have to go to the vicarage? Can't you write to him? In any case I'm sure he knows what you've decided.'

'Not from our conversation this afternoon, Mother.'

'I thought you'd made it very plain, you had to me at any rate.'

'No Mother, it still needed a great deal of thought. I've thought of nothing else sitting here alone and I've made up my mind that I intend to marry Paul. I love him, we love each other and I need something more in my life than what I've had these last few years. Mother, think about your life when you were my age and think about mine. You had love and the companionship of a good man, what have I got?'

'You have me, and my money, all of it when I've gone.'

'It isn't enough, Mother. I'll always care for you, I'll always be there for you when you want me, but I need more. I don't want your money, spend that on yourself, on anything you need. Money doesn't make up for all the things I need.'

'You'll have no money with him.'

'But I'll have other things.'

Her mother sat down weakly on the nearest chair and Grace got up and moved towards the door. 'Mother, the offer is still there for you to live with us at the vicarage. If you decide not to then I'll still be here for you when you need me. I'll always be your daughter, that will never change.'

Her mother didn't answer her but simply stared in front of her in total disbelief.

She did not feel the pressure of Grace's hand on her shoulder, nor hear the closing of the front door as she went out into the overcast May evening.

At the vicarage door several minutes later Paul stared

299

at her in astonishment. He had been so sure that it was over. Then with a smile he reached out and drew her into his embrace. Her expression said it all, Grace had come home.

Chapter Thirty-One

The residents of St Agnes's most exclusive area were duly impressed with the sight of the large Bentley sitting on the Clarkson's driveway, particularly since it belong to a Minister of the Crown.

Alistair Greavson and Erica had arrived late on Friday evening and were apparently spending the weekend with Erica's parents, coinciding with Erica's sister Nancy's demob.

As a family they had attended an orchestral concert in the Town Hall on the Saturday evening, gone to morning service in the church on Sunday and informed their friends that Alistair had to return to his duties on Monday morning but that Erica would be staying on for several days with her family.

Alistair had been gracious, Erica perfectly charming and they had found Nancy every bit as pretty and surprisingly mature.

The engaged couple reluctantly informed the Vicar that they intended to marry in the early summer of the following year, but unfortunately the wedding would be in London because St Agnes could not be expected to accommodate the number of guests involved.

The Vicar had hardly been surprised, but Erica had been delighted to hear of his forthcoming marriage to Grace Gantry, which had been largely instrumental in glossing over their decision to marry in London.

Their friends decided they liked Alistair, he was charming and approachable, and most of the women who had thought he was too old for her changed their opinions. He was the sort of man she needed to control that rebellious streak in her.

The Clarksons stood at the gate watching him drive away on Monday morning and, putting his arm round his daughter's shoulders, David Clarkson expressed the opinion that the weekend had been a success. They liked Alistair very much and they would be proud to welcome him into the family.

Nancy sat on her sister's bed much as she had been wont to do as a schoolgirl, watching her sister flinging things out of the wardrobe onto the bed.

'Gracious, I'd no idea I had so many clothes here,' Erica said sharply. 'Most of them I don't need any more. If you want any of them feel free.'

'I'll have a look at them. After all that time in uniform most of the clothes I have here are either too big or too short.'

'Heavens yes. You were small with puppy fat, now look at you – you're as tall as I am and as slender. I never thought you'd grow up to be a beauty.' She held up a confection in white chiffon. 'This was the dress I badgered Mother to buy for the end-of-term dance at college, for all the good it did me.'

'Why?'

'Well, the boys I fancied liked somebody else and the boys I didn't fancy liked me.'

'I seem to remember that all the boys fancied you, even Oliver. The trouble was that you fancied him too much and he wasn't ready for that sort of commitment.'

'What makes you suddenly such an authority on my past life?'

'But I'm right, Erica. Admit it.'

'You're half right. What happened to you all that time in the WRNS? All those young officers – didn't you manage to capture a single one of them?'

'I met some very nice ones and others perhaps less so. I certainly wasn't looking for a permanent one.'

'Did you see anything of Julian Watson?'

'A few times. I saw him last in Alexandria.'

'You had a real crush on him, you used to blush to the roots of your hair whenever he came near you. He must have been amused by you, enough to make him give you a wide berth if he saw you in uniform.'

'You'll have a lot to learn about diplomacy when you're married to a Minister of the Crown, Erica, you never displayed much and you're not doing so now.'

'Heavens, what a little firebrand you're turning out to be. I'm quite capable of being everything Alistair asks of me and if I'm criticising you, Nancy, it's only because it's how you used to be, not how you are now.'

Nancy smiled. 'How are you proposing to spend your time here? So many of your old friends have gone.'

'I know. I have to see Jenny Stedman; it was so awful about Alec. To think if I'd married him I'd be a widow, my life ruined.'

Nancy didn't think it was an entirely good thing for her sister to call on Jenny Stedman, a young widow with a child. Erica would arrive obviously sympathetic but still unable to hide the fact that the life ahead of her would be anything but dull.

'What are we going to do for the rest of the day?' Erica asked petulantly. 'There's so much to do in London. I suppose we'll spend it visiting. It's ridiculous that I have to make apologies for having my wedding in London.'

'What about breakfast?'

Their parents were already at the breakfast table when Nancy went down. Her mother said, 'We started without you, darling. Is Erica joining us?'

'Yes, she's sorting her wardrobe out.'

'Oh well, I'm glad about that, she's left so many things here.'

Nancy picked up the letter lying on her breakfast plate

and idly scanned the postmark, then eagerly opened the envelope.

The letter from Louise was filled with enthusiasm for the things she'd grown up with – hunt meetings and pony trekking, dog and agricultural shows – and she'd kept up her friendship with Steven Latchford to the extent that they were about to announce their engagement.

Their respective families were delighted, Steven was wonderful, everything a man should be, and she wanted Nancy to travel up to Cheshire to meet him.

'I do so want you to be my bridesmaid when we marry,' she wrote. 'Steven is actually from Derbyshire but we've decided it's to take place in Chester Cathedral which suits everybody. Do please write and tell me when you can visit. We'll really give you a good time, and who knows, you might meet a friend of Steven's who is equally gorgeous.'

Nancy smiled and her mother asked, 'Is your letter from somebody interesting?'

'From Louise. We served together for some time in the WRNS. She's engaged, getting married very soon and wants me to visit.'

'Why don't you?'

'Oh, I certainly will before I have to start thinking about my future.'

'And what is it going to be?' her father asked.

'Daddy, I'm not sure. I wish I'd worked harder at school. I didn't do too badly in the WRNS but there were many times when I wished I'd known more about history and such.'

'History? When was that?'

'In Alexandria, thinking about Mark Antony and Cleopatra and how it all went wrong. I was with somebody who could talk about it as though it was yesterday.'

'And who was that somebody?'

'Oh, some officer who just happened to be there. What's for breakfast?'

'There it all is on the side table, darling. Do tell Erica, she was always the one we had to wait for.'

It was so wonderful to be a family again, thought David Clarkson, even though both girls had moved on. Erica was about to be married and somehow or other Nancy had changed the most. There was a maturity about her that he had never thought he'd see and whimsically he said, 'You should call on the Commodore and his wife, Nancy, they'll be surprised how you've grown up.'

'Mrs Watson spoke to me in church. She said she'd like me to go round to see them this afternoon.'

'I suppose Julian is still in the thick of it?'

At that moment Erica arrived at the breakfast table and with a bright smile said, 'Just like old times, isn't it?'

'Not quite, dear,' her father replied. 'This time next year you'll be a married woman and Nancy here is contemplating her future.'

'Oh, she'll still be here. I'd like to bet on what's going to happen to Nancy. She'll work in your office, Dad, and marry a local boy, somebody good and solid with a good job and impeccable parents. Don't you agree?'

Nancy's parents looked at her questioningly but she merely smiled as Erica went on lightly, 'Oh not tomorrow, but soon. Nancy won't surprise you with improbabilities like I have.'

Why is she so sure? Nancy thought to herself. Have I always been predictable? Is that what Julian thought about me?

As if her parents' thoughts were somehow or other on the same wavelength her mother said, 'I've got a book I'm sure Lois would enjoy, Nancy, we have the same taste and she often sends one of her books round.'

'I'll bet it's a slushy love story, Mother,' Erica said.

'Actually it's not, it's one of Agatha Christie's. *Death on the Nile*. I know Lois and the Commodore have spent time in Egypt, so it's bound to appeal to her.'

Commodore Watson opened the door to Nancy a little later and with a broad smile said, 'Is this the little girl who used to swing on the gate and do cartwheels across the lawn?'

Nancy smiled. 'Heavens, what a reputation,' she said.

Commodore Watson talked about the war and her service in the WRNS and then his wife talked about St Agnes and the people in it but in her heart Nancy knew what she really wanted to talk about was Julian.

Afternoon tea was served to them and it was only when the Commodore went into the hall to see if the second post had arrived that she said, 'Did you see anything at all of Julian, dear? I know you said you'd met up with him somewhere, but I mean when you went abroad?'

'I saw him in Alex several times.'

'Oh I'm so glad. Did he look well? Was he pleased to see you? Did he say anything about what he would do when the war was over? Oh I know the Navy is his career, but there are other things in life.'

'He was very well, Mrs Watson. I saw him with other officers several times, all of them wishing they could do more to bring the war to an end, restless that it wasn't happening quickly enough.'

'Ah yes, I can imagine Julian being impatient about that. He told us so little in his letters. Was he ever with a girl?'

'There were girls, of course, who came and went – it was the same for all of us.'

'But what were they like, these girls? Was there anybody special?'

'I really don't think so. He took me out to dinner in Alex before he left.'

'Did he really, dear? That was nice of him. Surely he talked to you about the future, some girl, some sort of expectation.'

'None of us talked about expectations.'

From the doorway the Commodore's voice said, 'I knew it, as soon as my back was turned she'd be on about expectations and Julian's girlfriends, if he had any.'

'Well naturally, I'm his mother, I want to know if there is anybody. You should be interested too.'

'I'm not, all I'm interested in is the end of the war and

his coming home safely. Now, young lady, did you satisfy my wife's curiosity?'

'I'm not sure. Perhaps she'd like there to be more.'

'Now tell us about that sister of yours. Marrying Greavson, isn't she? Oh well, he's been a good man at his job, the right man in the right place at the right time. He's chosen a young girl to be his wife, which is not a bad thing, perhaps.'

As Nancy walked the short distance to her home in the early evening she reflected somewhat cynically that Mrs Watson had seen no danger in the fact that her son had invited her out to dinner in distant Alexandria. In spite of her new maturity they still thought of her as the young girl swinging on the gate, the sassy young girl with the cheeky grin and back answers that came too readily to her lips.

She might have thought differently if she could have heard the Commodore and his wife's conversation at that moment.

'You say he invited Nancy out to dinner in Alex?' he said sharply.

'So she said.'

'But why Nancy? Why not some other girl when time was precious?'

'I don't know. Because he knew her as a girl from back home, because he thought it would please us, because he felt like it. Oh Andrew, how do I know?'

'Perhaps it hasn't occurred to you, Lois, that young Nancy has grown up, and very beautifully too. Think back a bit about Alex – the setting sun across that exquisite sickle-shaped bay, the white minarets and the visions of the past that never leave you. I always felt that Alexandria felt more Italian than Egyptian, except at sunset, then the past and the present seemed as one.'

She was staring at him with some amazement, then she said, 'Why Andrew, I'd forgotten you could be so roman-

307

tic. Are you thinking that perhaps Julian rather liked our little Nancy?'

'And now you're putting words into my mouth that I haven't spoken. No, I'm merely saying that a man doesn't ask a girl out because she once ran a few errands for his mother, nor am I saying he suddenly saw something in her he'd never seen before.'

'Then what are you saying?'

'That he liked her enough to ask her out to dinner, to dance with, chat with – there may never be anything more, but don't rule it out, love, go on cultivating your little Nancy.'

'Oh no Andrew, she could get hurt that way and if there's to be any cultivating it has to come from Julian. I do so wish this wretched war in the Far East was over and done with.'

Only a few days later the two atom bombs dropped on Japan brought the war in the Far East to its conclusion. It was an act that caused enormous loss of life and tragedy throughout Japan, but saved untold lives elsewhere.

Once more there was the flag-waving and the marching feet of thousands as they laid their wreaths of scarlet poppies before war memorials throughout the land, and peace returned once more to a weary, war-torn world.

It was in the Spring when Nancy journeyed north to attend her friend's engagement party at her parents' house in Chester. The city smiled under a benign sun and Nancy fell in love with the gentle meandering river which reminded her so much of St. Agnes.

She stood with Louise on the banks of the river surrounded by swans and mallards clamouring for food, and Louise said, 'There were times when I never thought I'd see all this again. Do you remember how we used to lie in the shelters listening to the planes overhead and the crunching of bombs. I never thought we'd get out alive. I thought I'd never see Steven again.'

308

'And tomorrow you're taking me to look at the new house you've found.'

'A new old house, Nancy. Oh you'll have to see it. It's really old with oak beams and a huge open fireplace and flagged floors. Mother thinks it's a disaster; she says I should have workmen in at once to renovate it but I've told her it will take all the character away. It's staying exactly as it is.'

'I'm sure it's perfect.'

'And what about you? What sort of house are you going to have and who are you going to share it with?'

'I'll think about the house when I've found the man.'

'You had a lot of affection for that naval officer. Did you ever see him again?'

'Julian. Yes I saw him in Alex a few times.'

'Nothing came of it?'

'No.'

'Oh well, now the war's over there'll be somebody. You're so pretty, Nancy, some man will think he's awfully lucky to find you.'

'And you're my friend, conditioned to see the best in me.'

'I'm going to like living in Derbyshire, Nancy, it's hilly where so much of Cheshire is flat. We're not far from Bakewell and in the middle of the Peak District. You'll love it, and we'll introduce you to dozens of Steven's friends.'

'You sound just like my sister, she's on about the men in London she's going to introduce me to.'

'Well of course, darling, some politician on the way up.'

Chapter Thirty-Two

Joyce and old Mr Compton had been conspirators for months, since he'd seen her pushing her pram accompanied by her daughter along the village street on a day when the wind defied her umbrella and made it difficult for her to keep the pram on an even keel.

'Eh luv,' he greeted her. 'Ye shouldn't be out on a day like this wi' these little uns.'

Breathlessly she had smiled at him, then taking the pram out of her hands he said, 'I'm just goin' to the village hall, ye can come with me and shelter until the rain stops. We'll 'ave a nice cup of tea.'

'I should be getting back, Mr Compton.'

'Nay lass, what's a few minutes to cheer an old man up on a day like this?'

So that was how it started, drinking tea together while Jenny stared down at the piano keyboard before venturing to press some of the keys.

The old man smiled. ''Ave ye got a piano up at the farm?'

'No. Music is the last thing they think about I'm sure.'

'I'm sure too. I've 'eard ye play, remember, and ye misses it. What about the lass there?'

'Oh I wish she would take to it but how can she? We haven't a piano and are not likely to have one.'

'How often do ye come down to the village?'

'Once or twice a week, perhaps a little more in the school holidays.'

'And the lass is in school?'

'Since last September.'

'And ye meets 'er with the pony and trap? Then why not come round 'ere on the way home? I can give ye a key and ye can give that lass some lessons. What about that?'

'But somebody is sure to see us and wonder who is playing the piano.'

'Leave it to me. I'll 'ave a word with a few people, and in return one night ye can give us a concert just as a thank ye gesture.'

She laughed. 'Oh I don't know. I'd love to try it, but I'm not sure.'

'About yerself or that family up there?'

'Not myself. I'm not sure about Roger and I know what his sisters would think about it.'

His eyes were wise and kind as he looked at her, and gently he said, 'I knows a bit about yer history, luv, but I knows the Blackstocks better. The old man was somethin' of a tyrant, and the girls take after 'im. More like men than lasses, they are. I doubt if any of 'em has 'ad a man friend and it's gettin' a bit late now. I don't know yer 'usband all that well – 'e was nobbut a lad when he went off to war. Ye were 'ardly the sort o' lass I thowt e'd marry.'

When she didn't speak he patted her hand and said, 'None of it is my business, luv, but I'm an old man with little education, a bit o' money and a luv of music. I've heard many a one play the piano and the violin when I've gone up to the big cities for a concert or two, but I recognised talent when I 'eard it. I reckon ye could a done a lot more with yours, luv.'

'I know. Anger, bitterness, resentment all played a part in the waste of it all, and now it's too late.'

'But not if there's some o' that talent in the lass yonder.'

'How will I ever know?'

'By givin' 'er a chance and I'm givin' ye the means to

311

find out. Surely yer not afraid to try?'

So that's how it had been. There were days when she had met people looking at her curiously as she drove the trap into the small square in front of the village hall, but she had seen her daughter's face alive with anticipation, her deep-blue eyes dancing with joy. Then there were the lessons, simple at first, and as Jenny demanded tunes instead of scales, the consummate ease with which she accomplished them.

In Jenny Joyce recognised herself, the eager young girl rushing home from her lessons to the piano which was far more important.

They both longed for the summer holidays when they would have more time, but it was one evening at the end of May that she came face to face with Roger's sisters in the lane outside the farm and they stood in front of the trap, arms akimbo, their faces frozen in anger. The eldest one said sharply, 'We know where you're goin' every day when ye pick Jenny up from school. Who are ye meeting down in the village?'

Jenny crouched beside her mother, frightened at their bluster as Joyce said, 'I'm not meeting anybody. I'm letting Jenny practise the piano.'

'A likely story. Why is she playing the piano? Ye 'aven't got one 'ere so what good will that do 'er.'

'I want her to have one, I want her to be what I can never be.'

'Well, we'll see what our brother has to say about that. He married a wife who'll 'elp him on the farm, not some girl who fancies 'erself teachin' music. Who told ye you could use the village hall anyway?'

'I have permission.'

'Who by?'

'I don't intend to tell you because it's really none of your business.'

'We 'elp to pay for the upkeep of the village hall, we

312

don't pay for people to go in and use the piano when they feel they have a right to it, wastin' electricity, messin' the place up.'

'Now you're being ridiculous. We don't mess the place up and we stay for a very short time. Why are you being so vindictive? Why do you mind so much?'

It was the eldest sister who answered her. 'We mind because you're our brother's wife and because yer different. Why he 'ad to marry a girl who can barely boil an egg and gives 'erself such airs and graces she makes us feel like nothin' at all we can't imagine, but yer not gettin' away with it. We 'as our rights too, ye know.'

'Dorothy, you're being ridiculous. I'm trying very hard to be a good wife, I've never wanted to hurt any of you and if you'll tell me what I've done wrong I'll never do it again, I promise, but whatever it is don't take it out on Jenny. She's done nothing to deserve it.'

'She's a farmer's daughter. Yer tryin' to turn her into somethin' she's not, you're tryin' to turn her agin 'er family.'

'But I'm not, how can you say that?'

'We'll not be lettin' ye. We'll be complainin' to the committee that sits at the village hall and that'll keep ye away from it. Playin' the piano indeed – what sort o' lark is that for a farmer's daughter?'

Joyce stared at them in disbelief, while beside her Jenny sobbed as the youngest sister snapped, 'And what about the baby then? What are ye goin' to turn 'im into?'

'A man, I hope,' Joyce said sharply, 'a decent man without the sort of bigotry you have for things you don't understand.'

'And what's that supposed to mean?'

'You don't like me because I'm different, you'll never make an effort to like me. You'd rather go on day after day wishing your brother'd never married me, perhaps even despising my children because they're mine, and in the end what will your attitude achieve? What good will it do any of us?'

313

'Well, Roger'll 'ave somethin' to say to ye when he gets 'ome, 'e'll not let ye get away with it.'

As she fed the baby and gave Jenny her meal the little girl asked, 'Why don't they like us, Mummy, why are they always so angry with you?'

'It's just the way they are, darling.'

'What is Daddy going to say when he gets home? They said he would be angry.'

'Yes dear, they've made very sure he will be angry.'

'But I don't like it when he's angry, I'm frightened.'

'You'll be in bed, darling, and in the morning it will all be over and done with.'

'But will I never be able to play the piano again?'

'Yes Jenny, I promise you will. I don't know how or when at this moment, but you will.'

She put the children to bed and then went downstairs to prepare their evening meal. She wasn't the sort of cook his mother had been or any of his sisters, but she was trying hard. She couldn't face the large meals Roger liked with roast meat and masses of vegetables every day and he laughed at the size of the food on her plate. When she said he deserved more after working out in the fields while she'd been at home doing little, he'd merely said, if she was short of something to do his sisters would find her plenty, something that might increase her appetite.

She sat in the twilight waiting for him to come home, listening to the lowing of the cows as the dogs brought them in for milking, the occasional raucous laughter from the men and the heavy tread of their feet on cobbles as they crossed the yard. Soon they would be leaving for their homes and Roger would be in the kitchen, his face a mask of anger, his voice hectoring, incensed at all his sisters had been able to tell him.

Whatever she said to him he wouldn't understand, he would never understand.

She had been a fool to ever think she would be right for Roger or she for him. She deserved that he should be angry with her – he'd fallen in love with a dream, foolishly, because she was different from his usual village girl who'd been happy to have had a romp in the hay with him and a drink in the pub when it was over.

He'd thought her a cut above all that, and he'd been conceited, the lad with a farm of his own to offer her, and she'd been fool enough to think it would be enough. Now they were both paying for their mistakes and she sat waiting for yet another taste of retribution.

She heard him come into the kitchen and went immediately to serve his meal. He didn't turn round to look at her as she went to the range and her heart sank. He stood at the kitchen sink scrubbing his hands as she said gently, 'Your meal's ready, Roger, shall I serve it?'

When he didn't answer she sighed and carried it into the room next door. It was the usual unimaginative mishmash of meat and vegetables. She wasn't a good cook and had always been grateful that Roger didn't ask much of her in that area. It was the sort of food he'd been accustomed to all his life. Now he took a few mouthfuls before pushing the plate away, and she said anxiously, 'Is something wrong with the food?'

'It's not the food, the food's right enough, it's you. What's all this about Jenny?'

'You've been talking to your sisters.'

'Never mind that, I want you to tell me. What's all this at the village hall after school, tinkerin' about on the piano. I thought yer'd left all that behind with yer father. Don't tell me 'e's surfaced again.'

'It's got nothing to do with my father. I don't know where he is, I shall never see him again.'

'Ye told me yer'd finished with music, that it was all over and done with and I believed yer.'

'Roger, I'm sorry, I can't help it. Don't you see it was something that was born in me? I don't want it for me any more but I had to know about Jenny. I had to know if there was any of my talent in her.'

315

'Just like yer father wanted it for you?'

'Yes, I suppose so, but not like him. For her to enjoy it, not to hurt anybody else.'

'Well, I'll tell ye now it's got to stop. My daughter's a farmer's lass, not some would-be concert pianist that'll take 'er away from us and all of this. I don't want to hear any more about it, just that it's got to stop, and there'll be no messin' about with the lad either. When he's old enough 'e'll be a farmer like me, not a fiddle player.'

'You married me, Roger, you don't own me. You have no right to shape my entire life.'

'I feed ye and I clothe ye. You 'ave no money, only what I puts on the table so if that's not enough then yer've got to go out and earn some. I'll tell ye this, if ye leaves this 'ouse to chase after that music then the kids stay 'ere. Yer'll not be takin' 'em with ye.'

'I never had any intention of leaving you, Roger. This is my home and you are my husband. Isn't Jenny going to be given a chance?'

'A chance for what?'

'To do something she evidently enjoys and has a talent for. Can't you see beyond this life of yours, beyond the farm, and stop listening to everything your sisters say?'

'I listen to 'em because they're right and you're wrong. They're like me, they've given their lives for this farm and we've made it what it is, p'raps them more than me. None of 'em are married, this is their life.'

'And you want it to be Jenny's life?'

'I want it to be the lad's life. I want Jenny to be one of us. One day she'll no doubt marry some farmer like me, and that's what she'll learn from us, not to tinker on the piano and think she's too good for us. Now let that be an end to it. I'm goin' out, I don't want any dinner, I'm not hungry. I'll get somethin' at the pub.'

She heard him slamming the kitchen door and was glad that he was going out. She had to think about the rest of her life if there was anything left of it other than insurmountable obstacles of breeding and class, hard-working normality and artistic temperament. In her heart there was no hatred for him like there had been for her father.

Jenny woke a little later and called to her mother, asking anxiously, 'Why didn't Daddy come in to say hello to me? Has he gone out?'

'Yes dear, for a little while.'

'Why was he so angry?'

'I didn't know he was angry.'

'Oh yes. He slams the doors and he doesn't speak to you. Or he shouts all the time.'

'Perhaps something upset him on the farm.'

'Will he come to listen to me play the piano?'

'I don't think so, darling. He isn't very musical and in any case we shan't be going to the village hall for a little while, it's needed for other things.'

'What sort of things?'

'Oh, things in the village.'

'But I will play again, Mummy, I will get to play again?'

'We'll see, darling. Now do you want me to read you a story or are you too sleepy?'

'Mummy, Miss Jenkinson has a piano at school. I told her I could play. She said one day she'd listen to me.'

'Oh, I don't know, darling, what would the other children have to say?'

Jenny shrugged her shoulders. 'I've told her I'll take the music you gave me. She won't forget, will she?'

'She's a very busy lady.'

'I know, but I'm sure she won't forget. I'll remind her anyway.'

Joyce had no doubt that her daughter would remind Miss Jenkinson. Jenny had all of her father's confidence and possibly some of her grandfather's. In the years ahead she sensed the clashing of temperaments where variance and similarity vied with each other and the years that she'd hoped would be tranquil promised to be anything but.

*

317

Roger was in a better frame of mind when he came home, sitting before the fire while he took off his boots and sinking his head in the newspaper.

'I see the Latchfords are throwin' open the gardens a week on Saturday to meet Master Steven and his fiance.'

'Shall we be going?'

'Oh ay, the whole do's for the likes of us.'

'Why is that?'

'We're landowners, not just farmers. Me grandfather bought our land from old Sir Alec Marsden when he was goin' through a bad patch. Most o' the farmers are tenants. We're a bit superior, like.'

'Do you know Steven Latchford?'

'He went in the Army durin' the war. Yeomanry like me, only he got the rank o' Captain. I reckon he'll be marrying some member o' the Cheshire set, landowners, Cheshire Hunt members. Gettin' married in Chester Cathedral it says.'

Joyce only knew that the Latchfords lived at the large stone house overlooking the village but other than that she knew nothing about them. For the first time for ages she found herself thinking about St Agnes with its professional people, retired army and naval officers, and most of them well heeled but living in an entirely different environment than the one she now found herself in.

What would Roger think of those people if he had ever met them? Probably that they were snobs with too much money, incapable of getting their hands dirty, and he wouldn't have liked them, any of them. Then she thought about Nancy, Nancy who'd been fun. Would she ever forget Julian Watson in favour of some other? Perhaps she already had, perhaps she met somebody while she was serving in the WRNS. Then there had been Erica. Perhaps Erica would have fared better with Julian but then Erica had been mercurial, really only interested in Erica.

They'd been kind to her after her mother died. She'd liked Mrs Edgebaston and Grace. The Major had treated her to bluff quirks of humour to cover his embarrassment and she'd liked his wife and Mrs Watson.

Why had it all gone so terribly wrong? She could have lived in St Agnes and loved it, been with people she could relate to. Across the hearth her eyes met Roger's and he said, 'I 'ope you've taken it in about Jenny and that piano?'

'Jenny will be disappointed, she loved it.'

'She'll get over it. Make us a cup o' tea, Joyce, we'll 'ave an early night.'

Chapter Thirty-Three

The sun shone brightly on the day of the garden fête at the Latchfords' house and everybody was in their Sunday best. Chairs had been set out on the lawns and long tables groaned under plates filled with food.

Jenny ran on ahead filled with excitement but Joyce received only a cursory glance from her three sisters-in-law.

Roger was quick to make his escape to talk to other farmers and she knew she would see little of him during the afternoon ahead.

The Latchford family had done their duty by receiving their guests and their tenants, and now as they sat with their private guests on the terrace Joyce reflected that that would be the way of things.

She wandered with the children round the gardens, the baby slept in his pram and Jenny said that she preferred the park with its swings and seesaws.

It was in the rose garden that they came across Mr Compton who smiled at them brightly, though Joyce would have preferred to have met anybody but him at that particular moment.

'Ey lass,' he greeted them, 'I've bin missin' ye at the village hall. How come yer've not bin in evidence o' late?'

'I've been busy at the farm, Mr Compton, and Jenny's been at school.'

'But didn't ye start to call in after school was over for the day? 'Ave yer fallen out with yer piano, Jenny?'

'No. Mummy said other people wanted the hall.'

'Ay well, there 'ave bin one or two things goin' on.'

Jenny ran ahead and he took his place beside Joyce as they moved back to the crowded lawns.

'Has there bin trouble with the family, lass?' he asked.

'Well, they don't like it. They don't understand it and I have to live with them.'

'I can't say I'm surprised, but it doesn't make it right. You 'ave a life too, ye know, and if that little girl's got a share o' your talent then somethin' should be done about it.'

'If only it was that simple, Mr Compton.'

'Yer one agin' four of 'em, but ye can't let 'em browbeat yer all of the time. I 'eard ye 'ad good reason to stand up to yer father.'

'Where did you hear that, Mr Compton? I thought that was my secret.'

'Oh ye know, lass, gossip never stands still and it never loses anythin'. If ye could stand up to yer father surely ye can stand up to them women and yer 'usband.'

'My father thought I was expendable; my husband thinks I'm there to obey.'

'Oh that's it, is it. Well lass, think on it. I don't think I'll be stayin' on 'ere very long. It's not really my cup o' tea but it's very kind o' the Latchfords to 'ave invited us.'

'But you'll have something to eat surely?'

'I'll 'ave a look at the table, it all looks very invitin'. Good afternoon Mrs Blackstock, and I 'opes to be seein' ye soon.'

He smiled and walked away, and from one of the tables she saw Dorothy Blackstock staring at her curiously. She felt she was living in a goldfish bowl, to be listened to and watched. At that particular moment she had no wish for food but simply to wander alone with the children where there were no crowds.

321

She took the path by the river where there was only the solitary figure of a woman strolling towards the bridge. Jenny was running on ahead when suddenly she tripped and cried out. The woman turned to look what had happened and at that moment Joyce stared into Nancy Clarkson's eyes. She uttered a little cry, then picking Jenny up she turned away dragging the child with her.

Nancy stared after her in startled surprise, at first unable to fully comprehend that she had been looking at Joyce Mellor, then she hurried after her calling, 'Joyce, Joyce, please wait.'

They stood together at last but it was an unhappy situation as all Joyce wanted to do was get away.

'Joyce, I couldn't really believe it was you. What are you doing here?' Nancy asked, and Joyce occupied herself by soothing her daughter before saying, 'I live near here, Nancy, what are you doing here?'

'I'm here for the event. I was in the WRNS with Louise – she's the one marrying Steven Latchford. Joyce, I want to know all about you, you never wrote to me, you never kept in touch in any way. I thought we'd been good friends in St Agnes.'

'I'm sorry, Nancy, it's my fault, but when I left I simply wanted to forget everything that had happened to me there. I missed you and have a different life now. I just want to forget the past.'

'Are these children yours?'

'Yes, this is Jenny, my son is called John.'

'So who did you marry? I know you were in the Land Army. Was it around here?'

'Yes, I worked on his farm but he was in the Army. He has three sisters who ran the farm then.'

'Oh Joyce, there's such a lot I have to know. Are you still playing the piano? Have you got that beautiful instrument at the farm?'

'No, we haven't room for it.'

Jenny was busy tugging at her mother's skirts saying,

322

'Tell the lady that I can play the piano, Mummy?'

'Oh that's wonderful, are you going to be as good as your mother?'

'She doesn't play. I play at the village hall.'

'Well, that's wonderful. Joyce, can I call to see you before I go back tomorrow? Just for a little while to catch up on old times. It won't be for long because I do have a long drive home, but don't you want to hear about everybody? And I do so want to hear about you.'

At that moment they both looked ahead to see Roger Blackstock walking towards them, and Joyce was quick to say, 'This is my husband coming to look for us, I must go.'

Nancy fell in step beside her and when they joined him he stared at Nancy curiously as Joyce said quickly, 'This is Nancy Clarkson, Roger, somebody I knew in St Agnes.'

He did not take her hand but said shortly, 'And what is somebody fro' St Agnes doin' in this neck o' the woods?'

'My friend is marrying Steven Latchford.'

'Is that so? So you'll be part o' the official party then. Well, we're nobbut farmers and I've come to tell ye that food's bein' served if ye wants any.'

'Oh yes, we must go, I'm sure the children are hungry It's been lovely seeing you again, Nancy, have a safe journey home.'

Nancy looked straight at Roger Blackstock and said, 'I would like to call and see Joyce before I drive home. Would that be terribly inconvenient?'

'Well, she does 'ave a home to run and farm work's not somethin' ye can lay aside.'

'I'm sure it isn't, but it won't be for long, we do have some catching up to do and I may never be this way again.'

'I don't suppose it'll do any harm just as long as yer not one of 'er old friends wantin' to push 'er back into music.'

Nancy merely smiled. Taking hold of his daughter's hand he pulled her away and Joyce prepared to follow him, pushing the baby in his pram.

'Is your farm easy to find, Joyce?' Nancy asked.

'That's it at the top of that slope yonder, there's a dirt track from the road. What time will you be calling?'

'What time do you want me?'

'Around half-past nine. I'll have taken Jenny to school and we'll have the house to ourselves.'

'Until tomorrow then,' Nancy said and then Joyce was hurrying away after her husband. Nancy followed more slowly, realising suddenly that she was not looking forward to her next meeting with Joyce. Somehow she didn't think her friend would have any good news to impart. Behind her smiles there had been a sort of sadness, of something irretrievably lost – perhaps it was wrong to go back in case there was nothing left.

Nancy found the road up to the farm without any difficulty, and as she walked across the cobbled yard she couldn't begin to imagine how the Joyce she remembered could be facing up to life in an old farmhouse surrounded by ramshackle barns and fences. Yet when she settled down in front of the fire in a room that was shabby yet strangely comforting she had to admit that there was a certain charm about it, from its faded rugs to its comfortable chairs, none of which really matched.

Joyce served tea and sandwiches saying, 'You've a long drive, Nancy. I thought you might like something to eat.'

'You shouldn't have bothered, Joyce, I did have breakfast, but these look delicious.'

'Everybody enjoyed themselves yesterday, it was so kind of the Latchfords to invite us.'

'Yes, they're nice people. I'm sure Louise is going to be very happy here one day.'

'It will be her house then?'

'Oh, one day when the older people have gone. She's setting up home near Bakewell in the immediate future. She's nice, fun to be with, now she's got all she wanted.'

'Not many of us can say that, Nancy.'

'No, perhaps not.'

'And Julian, is he still number one on your list?'

'I was obsessive about him, wasn't I?'

Joyce smiled. 'He was nice, handsome, charming, the sort of man most girls would fall for.'

'I saw him when I was in the WRNS. He actually took me out to dinner when we served in Alexandria.'

'And that was all?'

'Yes, we were just two people from back home. I knew his parents, he knew mine, the war was coming to an end in Europe, he was moving on. That's all there was, probably all there will ever be.'

'I hope not.'

'Tell me about you, Joyce. Where is your piano? Do you still play?'

'My father gave my piano away to a concert hall in Buxton where it's used whenever they have concerts. I missed it, but I can live without it.'

'And your father?'

'He married again. I never see him. I don't even know where he's living, somewhere in Scotland, I think.'

'Doesn't that worry you?'

'No. I was closer to my mother. I never forgave him for the way he treated her, and the way he treated me.'

'He was ambitious for you, Joyce.'

'I know, but it would never have worked. I wanted to play, but not the way he wanted me to. He made me feel like a slave.'

'But your little girl says she's playing.'

'Not really, although if she was given the opportunity then I think she has it in her.'

'Surely she'll be given the opportunity?'

'I don't think so. You heard Roger yesterday. He won't discuss music – it divides us, or so he thinks – and he won't hear of Jenny having anything to do with it. We haven't got a piano and he certainly won't buy one for her.'

'Do his sisters live here also?'

'No, they have an old farm on the top road. It's part and

parcel of this one and they work very hard on it. I know nothing about farming which rankles with them a bit.'

'Are you happy, Joyce?'

Joyce stared down into the fire, but when she looked up Nancy could see that her eyes were bright with tears.

She did not immediately answer, but when she did her voice trembled with uncertainty.

'I wonder sometimes if I've ever really been happy. For short periods sometimes, and then something would happen to make me doubt it.'

'But you fell in love, you got married.'

'Yes. I love my children, but I wonder sometimes why I thought marriage to Roger would work. We really have nothing in common outside our children – he could have found some girl more worthy of this sort of life.'

Nancy felt there was nothing to say. Joyce had been frank with her, and might regret her frankness after she'd gone, so to relieve the situation she said, 'What can I tell you about St Agnes?'

'Oh yes, do tell me about that. How about the longest day? Will they be having one this year?'

'Yes, they're preparing for it, and it'll be the first real one since the war started. Could you come for it?'

'Oh no, there's too much to do here. Tell me about the people I knew there. Is the Major still marching his cadets and does Commodore Watson still hoist his flag on every occasion?'

'Yes, that's all going on. The Major has a new stream of boys, but the Vicar's wife died and he's getting married again, to Grace Gantry.'

'Oh I'm so glad. I really liked her, she was always nice. What about her mother?'

'Well, I'm not sure. Mother says the old lady is staying put, but she's quite old and there's some talk about all sorts of things going on. There are times when I sense Grace is worried.'

'And Mrs Prothero and the bridge ladies. I liked most of

the people in St Agnes. There were just one or two like Mrs Marks I didn't care for, she was such a gossip.'

Nancy laughed. 'Mrs Prothero's nephew Oliver is engaged to be married. She's pleased about that.'

'And Erica?'

'Also engaged, and getting married in the summer.'

'Oh I'm glad. She was such a pretty girl. Who is she marrying?'

'She worked for him in London, he's an MP.'

'Really. I'm so glad for her. Is he nice?'

'Yes. Quite a bit older than she is but they seem happy enough.'

'All the boys wanted to be seen with Erica.'

'Yes, even when it didn't always work out for her. Who else do you want to hear about?'

'Oh, Mrs Edgebaston. I did like her, she was always so fashionable and sophisticated, and half the people didn't quite know what to make of her. I often thought she wanted to raise a few eyebrows, but I did like her.'

'Yes, she does it deliberately, I often think.'

'Will she ever marry again do you think?'

'She certainly has men friends, and Mother says she had a friendship with an American Colonel during the war, which of course couldn't last. He's probably back in the States.'

'I'm so glad we met up again, Nancy, I was prepared to run away, but now I'm glad I didn't. Will you be up this way again?'

'How can I tell? I need to get a proper job of some sorts. I'm still not sure what it's going to be but I need to think about it, I shall got to secretarial college like Erica I think.'

'Remember me to them in St Agnes, Nancy, but don't tell them too much about me. Tell them about my children, not my life as a farmer's wife, and nothing about my music – it's all in the past.'

*

As she drove away from the farm Nancy felt somehow immeasurably sad that she was feeling no deep satisfaction about her meeting with Joyce.

She felt that Joyce's life was in limbo, that she was existing in a time warp of her own making, and yet none of it had started here.

She had not promised to write, or even see her again should she ever be in the area, but then it was time she took her own life in hand and did something with it.

There were so many things buzzing through her head as she drove home that day, but when finally she parked her car in the drive she was unprepared for her mother rushing out to meet her, her face alive with smiles of welcome.

'Darling, I expected you earlier than this. Were you very late leaving?'

'Well yes, Mother. I hope you didn't delay dinner for me?'

'No, but you've had a caller. I didn't know what to tell him, except that I was sure you'd be back soon.'

'Who was the caller?'

'Commander Watson, darling. He seemed quite disappointed that you were out.'

She couldn't prevent the swift beating of her heart, and looking at her mother anxiously she said, 'Is he still here?'

'He went back home, but I expect he's still there.'

'Perhaps it's too late to call now.'

'Oh, I don't think so. Why not telephone?'

'Was he just calling to see me?'

'Well, it was a nice neighbourly gesture dear. He chatted to us about the war, the bombs on Japan, that things are getting back to normal and he's on two weeks' leave.'

'Is he staying here the entire time?'

'You'll have to ask him, darling. He's a lot like his father, a rather reserved man, so we didn't like to ask too many questions. Perhaps you'd rather leave it until the morning.'

She wanted to telephone him now, to hear his voice,

sense if there was any warmth in it or merely politeness. As she followed her mother into the house her father called out, 'Telephone Julian, Nancy, I told him you would.'

Chapter Thirty-Four

She was nervous. What would they talk about? In Alexandria it had been easy to talk about history and life's uncertainties. Now they were facing a changing world and those last dramatic scenes of war could have changed Julian even more from the man she still believed she was in love with.

Her heart was beating frantically as she waited for somebody at the other end of the telephone to lift the receiver, but there was normality in his voice, and laughter.

'I'm sorry I was out when you called, Julian. I've only just got back,' she said quickly.

'And did you enjoy your weekend in Derbyshire?'

'Yes, very much.'

'Then you must tell me all about it when we meet.'

'Yes.'

'Your parents told me you're still a free spirit which means we both have time on our hands for the next few days at least.'

'How long is your leave?'

'Two weeks. A lot can happen in two weeks.'

'I can't say that two weeks has ever made much difference to me, Julian.'

'Then we must try to alter all that. I'll pick you up around ten in the morning, if that's convenient.'

'It sounds intriguing.'

'It won't be anything like the island off Alexandria but we'll think of something. Until tomorrow, Nancy.'

'Yes, goodbye Julian.'

Her parents were both looking at her with anticipation but she was determined to show no emotion, saying blandly, 'He's calling round for me in the morning, apparently we're going off for the day.'

'Well, it's got to start somewhere,' her father said laconically.

'Oh, Dad, he's here for two weeks and doesn't know any girls to ask out. Erica's in London and he never really took up with anybody else. He's asking me because we know his parents, and we met up during the war.'

'All right, love, nobody's reading anything into anything, just go out and enjoy yourselves. We shan't ask any questions.'

Too excited to sleep she was up very early rifling through her wardrobe in search of something that would do her credit. Inspired by the sunny morning she chose a floral skirt and matching top. On arrival at the breakfast table her mother said brightly, 'You look very nice, dear. I really think you're in for a fine day.'

'Oh I do hope so, but I don't know where we're going, and I'm so nervous.'

'Why darling, you look charming and you're really very pretty. I'm sure he'll think so.'

'I've seen Julian with lots of girls, beautiful girls – there are probably one or two he's going back to.'

'And maybe there are not.'

As she helped herself to breakfast her mother reflected that if this had been Erica she would have been confident of her charms, and sure that he would approve of her. Even now, with the man she was going to marry, she was always so cocksure. Why couldn't Nancy be more like her?

He came for her promptly at ten o'clock. As she watched him walking from his car the years slipped away – this was

331

the Julian her eyes had been worshipping since she'd been a starry-eyed schoolgirl.

His smile was warm, more personal than the one she remembered when he'd merely been kind to the tomboy child from further up the road.

There was a new enchantment in the winding lanes with their tall hedges, in the rocky tors that towered over the rich red soil, and then suddenly the long silver line of the sea.

At first there was shyness at being together, that he had wanted to invite her to spend the day with him, and then between them there was laughter and comradeship, and it didn't matter that he might not in the end love her. All that was important was that this day was good, even if it might be all there would ever be.

He talked about the years he had spent at Dartmouth Naval College and his great love for his chosen profession. She encouraged him to talk about the friends he had made and then she learned a little about the uncertainty of never quite knowing when he would see either of his parents, or if they would be together when he did.

'You know where they are now,' Nancy said with a smile. 'Are they happy in St Agnes?'

'Yes, I really think they are. It's not where I thought they'd want to be, I thought Dad would want some place where he could still be really near the sea, but he's never said he doesn't like where they are.'

'And when you leave the Navy, will you want some windswept shore?'

'How can I say? It's some time away and things change.'

'But will you change?'

He was looking out across the river, his eyes strangely sombre.

'Nancy, I don't know. All my life I've told myself to live my life for me, to be hard on myself, to be realistic, but changes are often inevitable. We don't know who we're going to meet – the emotions of a boy are not necessarily

332

the emotions of a man. I tell myself that I haven't changed but how can I be sure?'

They sat in silence for several minutes and then he said more light-heartedly, 'Are you still regretting those history lessons you wish you'd taken more note of?'

'I regretted them in Alex, here it doesn't matter quite as much. I've been wondering if I should try to get back into the WRNS. I loved it, now I don't really know what I want to do.'

'Good gracious, Nancy, the war's over. Things will be vastly different now.'

'Did any of your girlfriends stay on in the service?'

'I'm not sure. We lost touch when I went out to the Far East and I really haven't bothered since then. Wartime romances are probably not meant to last.'

'So there was a wartime romance?'

He laughed. 'And how about yours? That young army officer, and the others I saw you around with.'

'Like yours. Passed into limbo and were never rekindled.'

'Well, I've got two weeks' leave so we have to think what we're going to do with it. Have you any preferences?'

'You're saying you would like to spend it with me?'

'Only if you'd really like to. We get along, we're friends and my parents would be delighted. They like you, Nancy.'

She smiled. They got along, his parents liked her, and at the end of the two weeks he would go back to his ship and she'd be left with just memories. Perhaps it would be better if some of the time she was brave enough to say, 'Today I'm not available, Julian, I have made other plans.'

Of course it wouldn't be like that, she'd be thinking about what she should wear and then be waiting for him in the front porch like a grateful puppy.

Julian's mother watched him driving past the house with Nancy towards the end of his leave with certain misgivings in her heart.

333

Only the night before she'd sat with him over a late night drink when his father had decided to go to bed and they'd talked about how Julian and Nancy had spent their day. They'd discussed the shoreline that swept across the extent of Torbay and the secluded places they'd found to eat at.

'Not many days left,' Lois had commented idly.

'No. It's gone awfully quickly.'

'And you've enjoyed it?'

'Yes Mother, I really have. Two weeks. I wondered what I'd do with myself but it's been marvellous.'

'I'm glad. And when you've gone back will you spare us a second thought, your father and me, and Nancy?'

'Well, of course I think of you, Mother. I always have.'

'You used to worry me.'

He laughed. 'Worry you! How?'

'You were always so sure. Sailors who married were foolish, you said, that you wanted no strings, no come-backs. Is it still like that, Julian?'

'What do you want me to say, Mother?'

'Is that how you're going to live your life, meeting girls, liking them, then moving on, back to what matters most? Do you never wonder how they might feel?'

'Are you telling me they all want something more?'

'I know I did. It didn't matter that your father was on a ship somewhere in the world and I was here on dry land with a child. We were together when it was possible; when it wasn't possible we were still together in our hearts.'

'I saw you lonely and frustrated many times, and thought you and I were having a raw deal while Dad was perfectly content.'

'How do you know? Don't you think he worried about us? Don't you think he wished we might be together when it wasn't possible?'

'Yes, I'm sure he did, and if he hadn't married he wouldn't have had any need to worry about you. There are two ways of looking at things, Mother.'

334

'I know. You think your way is the right way, but I don't happen to agree with you.'

'We won't argue tonight, Mother, I've had a lovely day and I don't want to spoil it. You don't have a son with a job in the city and a nice wife and children, you had a son who went to sea, a son who's been conditioned to think the way he does.'

He kissed the top of her head and with a gentle smile left her.

She was no nearer knowing how he felt about Nancy yet she knew that Nancy was in love with him. It was no use talking to Andrew. She'd tried it the day before and he'd said, 'She's young, she'll meet dozens of men and he'll meet other girls, if there isn't one already. You know what he's like and I doubt he'll change.'

'Why don't you talk to him?'

'My dear girl, he's a man in his thirties, not some schoolboy. He knows where he's going and he wouldn't thank us for interfering.'

Things were not much better at the Clarkson house.

Nancy and Julian had arrived home a little earlier than usual. She'd said they'd spent a perfect day, she didn't want anything to eat but would go to bed early as she had letters to write.

Her parents sat pondering together as to how Julian's return to his ship would affect their daughter's future. They both knew she loved him, had done so for far too long, and had now spent eleven days in his company – would she love him more, or less?

Nancy was not writing letters, instead she sat in the window looking out along the road. She watched the Vicar and Grace leave Mrs Gantry's house, walk together to the gate and stand together in each other's arms for several minutes before he left her. She saw Mrs Edgebaston and a man walking her dog, then the man drove away. Then Lady Marcia drove her open car up to the hall. All these were normal goings-on for St Agnes, but what would Julian be doing?

She'd chatted to her parents about the day they'd spent and once or twice she'd thought her mother had looked at her anxiously, unsettled in case she was going to be hurt by him.

'It's no use worrying, love,' David Clarkson had said later. 'Who knows when he'll be on leave again and she'll meet other men. She'll be thinking very seriously about the future so when he's gone back she'll have other matters to occupy her mind.'

Julian had always been able to smile about his mother's anxieties about his future. She wanted him to marry, she wanted grandchildren and she wanted him to have the right sort of future, even in a place like St Agnes with the right sort of wife. But was it for him?

He felt strangely unsettled. In a few days he'd be heading back to Plymouth and then what? He'd enjoyed his leave, Nancy'd been fun, jolly company, pretty and agreeable, and he hoped she'd be there whenever his next leave happened to be.

All right, so that made him a self-centred, selfish individual, but it also meant he wasn't expecting some poor girl to fall for him when all he'd be able to offer her was uncertainty, separation and a career that came first.

He lay on top of his bed staring through the window. A full moon illuminated the large beech tree outside and he could hear the church clock striking twelve. He'd thought it was later than that and knew he couldn't sleep. He'd told Nancy that tomorrow they'd go on the river if the day was fine, and she seemed to like the idea. No doubt they'd meet people who would give them a bright smile and begin to speculate, but they could speculate all they wanted – in three days he'd be gone.

Impatiently he decided to go downstairs and hunt for something to read. His father had a load of seafaring books

336

and no doubt there'd be something to help him pass an hour or so.

As he walked through the living room he could see that his mother was still sitting in the conservatory. He opened the door to tell her it was late but when he saw that she was asleep he decided to leave her. Somehow or other he didn't want another conversation with her – she had a one-track mind.

For some unknown reason he stepped out into the garden to find that the night was unseasonably warm and balmy and there was the scent of honeysuckle all around him. He decided it would do him good to walk, perhaps as far as the church – it was highly unlikely he'd meet anybody else at that time.

He crossed the road towards the river and he was outside Mrs Edgebaston's house when he heard her calling for her cat in the garden. He paused and when she saw him she came forward with a smile.

'Sophie wanders off if I don't watch her,' she said. 'I really don't like her staying out all night. Ah, here she is.'

A large tabby cat was crossing the lawn, looking at them sharply before hurrying inside the house, and Mrs Edgebaston laughed. 'She's not the friendliest of cats, she's rather aloof, I'm afraid.'

'I didn't realise you had a cat. I know you have a dog.'

'The cat was a stray. She adopted me, but she's rather more fond of my daily than she is of me.'

Julian laughed. 'I wasn't sleepy and it's such a lovely night I thought I'd have a walk towards the river.'

'Your leave will soon be up, won't it?'

'Yes, two more days, then one for travelling and settling in. I've enjoyed it.'

'Yes, your mother said you were enjoying it.'

'I thought my father'd never settle in St Agnes, and I didn't think there would be much for me – how wrong can you be.'

'So you like it after all?'

'Yes. The town, the people, even the eccentric ones.'

'Eccentric! Now I wonder in which category you would place me.'

'Oh, on the bright sophisticated side, but there is the other kind.'

'Yes indeed.'

'You say that most feelingly.'

'Perhaps I do. There have been times when I've been on the receiving end of eccentricity.'

'Did you mind?'

'Sometimes one develops a second skin. So when shall we see you again, or don't you know?'

'No, I really don't know. Perhaps it's the uncertainty that makes life in the Navy so interesting.'

She smiled, wanting to ask him more. What of the future? Something other than the sea and ships? But she sensed a reserve in him and turned away.

'Safe journey back,' she said, 'it's been nice for your parents having you home, and Nancy.'

As he walked towards the river he thought about Nancy. For almost two weeks they'd been an item and people had smiled at them with evident satisfaction. Nancy was popular and they seemed to like what bit they knew of him.

As he drew level with the Clarksons' house he saw that a light still glowed in one of the windows and he wondered if it was Nancy too who was unable to sleep.

There had been several times during the last few days when he'd wanted to make love to her, when he'd felt sure she wanted it too, but always something intangible had stopped him. Would it spoil the sort of friendship they had, and would she read more into it than he intended? Was it because in this small town they all knew each other too well, cared too much, expected too much? Was it not right for either of them?

He decided against the walk along the river bank. The full moon had turned the river into a long, silver, gently moving path and even as he looked down at it there was a

338

quick movement in the water. He sensed that some animal was busy in the reeds.

He looked in the conservatory but apparently his mother had gone to bed and he decided to make himself a cup of tea and take it upstairs.

Two days left. Two days to enjoy what was left and then back to the life he knew best – for the immediate future this nice, ordinary, peaceful world of St Agnes would belong to a different planet.

Chapter Thirty-Five

The talk was all of weddings – Erica's wedding in London and the Vicar's wedding to Grace Gantry. The one in London was obviously the most talked about, and Erica had invited her favourite people in St Agnes to attend the ceremony.

She had decided that her sister should be one of her bridesmaids, the other one of Alistair's god-daughters who Nancy had never met. It was Erica who decided that they should wear deep rose pink, which was not exactly the colour Nancy would have chosen to go with her light auburn hair. The Commodore and his wife had been invited as had Major Robson and his wife. Sir Robert and Lady Jarvis were also included in the guest list and Erica's father said with some doubt, 'All this has a certain snobbish element, dear. Certainly some of the people here will think so.'

'Oh no dear, Erica says it's because Alistair and Sir Robert have so much in common regarding politics.'

'Is that so,' he said dryly. 'I wonder how many of her old school friends she's invited – hardly any by the sound of it.'

'Well, I'm glad it doesn't clash with the Vicar's wedding. We should all rally round Grace.'

The people living near the church watched would-be housekeepers calling at the Gantrys' house for an interview with Grace and her mother, but somehow or other whenever they were asked about the situation, nothing had been decided.

Mrs Gantry was unimpressed by any of the women who applied for the job. They were either too young, too careless or hardly her class, so Grace decided the decision should be entirely her mother's. In her heart she believed that in the end her mother would decide to move in with them, but the old lady was certainly stretching it out. It was Major Robson as usual who said what everybody else was thinking.

'Mother not made up her mind yet, Grace?' he asked as he greeted her coming through his front gate one Tuesday afternoon.

'No, she's not been happy with any of them.'

'Why is that then?'

'Not her sort she says. Really, Desmond, I don't think she'll find anybody and the wedding is only weeks away.'

'So, what will you do? Call the wedding off because you can't leave her on her own or chivvy her into living with you?'

'I don't know.'

'And what does Paul say?'

'Very little. He's trying not to interfere, but it is a problem.'

A few minutes later the Major decided Mrs Edgebaston should be his confidant as he chatted to her over her garden wall.

'Just been talking to Grace – no nearer finding a housekeeper for the old girl.'

Anthea smiled. 'No, it must be very difficult.'

'Impossible, I'd say.'

'What is the alternative?'

'Well, I know what my alternative would be. A residential home.'

'Which she would probably decline to move into.'

'Oh she would. In which case I'd be inclined to ask Him upstairs to find a solution.'

341

Anthea laughed. She liked Desmond Robson even at his most audacious. 'And are you looking forward to Erica's wedding?'

'Well, Elspeth certainly is. I thought you might have had an invitation, Anthea.'

'Oh no. You know me and this town – I'm still the unknown quantity. With my penchant for appearing larger than life I would do little to grace such an auspicious occasion.'

'And I think you'd add to the glamour. Besides I thought you and young Erica had developed some sort of friendship.'

'Nothing that would merit a place at her wedding, Desmond.'

'Oh well, I'm off to the school to put the lads through their paces. Isn't that your telephone ringing in there?'

Laying her gardening tools down on the lawn she hurried into the house to answer it before sitting down in bewildered surprise.

She had relegated Colonel Bill Freeman to the time when all those soldiers and airmen far from home had occupied the vast camp several miles from the town – men who were homesick and generous, grateful for friendship and hospitality; and Colonel Freeman had been one of the men she had particularly liked.

He was a widower in his late forties, his home was in Vermont, he loved sailing and was a keen golfer. He'd talked to her about his boat anchored at Cape Cod, his friends and his home, and in him she sensed a loneliness. He did not have children.

She had entertained him to meals, sometimes in the company of her other male friends, and they had all got along together, particularly when he accepted they were nothing more than friends.

She had not expected to hear from him again when the war was over – after all they lived separate lives in different countries. Now he was saying, 'Sorry to be ringing out

342

of the blue, but I told you I'd be in touch whenever it was possible, Anthea, and I hope you believed me.'

'Well yes, but I also knew you'd be going home to America as soon as the war was over. It isn't always easy to keep promises.'

'This was one I intended to keep. I've been home, seen the house was still standing, seen the boat and she's there where I left her; now I'm back here to catch up with old friends. You haven't said you're glad to hear from me.'

'Well, of course I am, Bill, where exactly are you?'

'I'm in London and could get the next train to your neck of the woods. Would that be inconvenient?'

'No, I'll be very glad to see you.'

'Right, expect me sometime during the day. Have to go, honey, there's a queue outside the kiosk.'

She sauntered back into the garden feeling bemused and strangely uncertain. Of course she wanted to see him although tongues would be wagging, but then when had they ever stopped? She was a free agent, a widow for many years, and what she did with her life was nobody's business, and yet her life was here. Would he expect to stay with her, raising even more eyebrows, and after he'd left would her image be even more tarnished in the eyes of certain people who had never really accepted her?

He arrived in the early evening, handsome, bronzed and smiling. Putting his arms around her in a warm brotherly way he said, 'I've booked into the hotel, Anthea, and do you know, they remembered me, it was like coming home. You look very well, honey, things settled down to normal then?'

'Yes, more or less. We'll eat and then you can give me all your news.'

'I've booked a table for us at the hotel – didn't want you to spend time cooking when we've so much to talk about.'

'How long do you intend to stay, Bill?'

'Well, let's play it by ear, honey. Give us time to

343

discover my old memories, meet up with people I met here and spend time with you. I'm not interfering with any plans of yours, I hope.'

'You mean my time in the garden, my trip to the shops, walks with my dog and church on Sunday – it all sounds very mundane doesn't it?'

'It's what I want to see here. Now put on your most glamorous dress and set the hotel alight.'

She smiled with amusement as she dressed for dinner. Mrs Edgebaston walking down the road with her American Colonel, wearing a dress considerably more sophisticated than one her neighbours might have chosen – so what did it matter? She'd learned to live with such criticism.

The rest of the diners that evening merely saw two people were enjoying each other's company, a handsome American and a beautiful Englishwoman who had a great deal to talk about and much to laugh at.

Later they sauntered along the river bank with Anthea's terrier and the only person they met was Major Robson who extended a warm handshake and provided Anthea with an amused smile that spoke volumes.

Bill Freeman seemed in no undue hurry to leave. The people she liked most had already departed for London and Erica's wedding, and it was left to the likes of Hilda Marks to gossip to those who were left behind.

'I saw Mrs Edgebaston with her Colonel from the United States dining at the hotel,' she remarked to Mrs Prothero. 'I suppose he's got a wife way back in America.'

'Oh no Mrs Marks, I don't think so. I understand he's a widower.'

'Is that so. They're spending a lot of time together.'

'That's nice for both of them.'

'I really thought you would be at Erica Clarkson's wedding. Didn't she buy your flat in London?'

'Yes, of course, but I declined the invitation because I'm

344

going to my nephew's wedding next weekend in Yorkshire.'

'Isn't that a coincidence when he and Erica used to be together.'

Mrs Prothero decided to ignore that statement. She'd never been sure that Erica had been right for Oliver or he for her and besides, Oliver had always said there was nothing in it, just friendship.

Mrs Gantry for once was too occupied with her own problems to have any interest in other people's comings and goings. She hadn't liked the last applicant for the job as her housekeeper – she'd been too young, too cocky and asked too many questions about days off.

'I'm never going to find the right person,' she complained and inwardly Grace agreed with her.

'What shall I do when you go off on your honeymoon and I'm here with nobody to look after me? The daily woman's not enough.'

'You would have been looked after at the vicarage, Mother.'

'Oh I know, that's what you both want, but it's not going to happen. You'll have to put your marriage off.'

'We can't do that, Mother. The Bishop is conducting the ceremony and we can't put the Bishop off.'

'You can put me off.'

When Grace didn't reply her mother said sourly, 'I've outlived my usefulness, but I can't die to order.'

It was a battle of wills. Where once Grace would have had no chance against her mother, now the old lady was seeing a new Grace – Paul was behind her and she was losing ground.

She was aware that their neighbours were very much on Grace's side, even Mrs Prothero who she had always considered her ally and best friend.

'You can stay with me while Paul and Grace are away,' Mrs Prothero had said. 'I'll be back from Yorkshire, and it will only be for a week anyway.'

345

'Why should I burden you with my presence?'

'Oh I'd enjoy having you, dear. Besides it will mean Grace won't need to worry about you.'

'I don't think she's in the least worried about me. She's off with her vicar and when she comes back nothing will have changed, she'll be there with him and I'll be here on my own.'

Mrs Prothero remained silent and after a few minutes Mrs Gantry said sourly, 'You think I'm being difficult, don't you? Nobody seems prepared to see it my way.'

'Oh, I'm sure they do, dear, but nobody seems to know the answer.'

To change the subject Mrs Prothero asked, 'What is Grace wearing for her wedding? I'm sure she'll look awfully pretty.'

'She's shown me, but I was too upset about my predicament to take much notice. I think it's blue, she's far too old for the usual thing.'

'She'll look lovely in blue.'

'I'm not buying anything new, when would I ever wear it again? And clothes are expensive. I'll probably wear that navy dress and jacket I had for the longest day before the war.'

'But this is Grace's wedding, dear, surely you'll find something new. I've bought something for Oliver's wedding.'

'Well, of course you have. He's very good to you and keeps in touch.'

'And Grace doesn't?'

'Oh well, you know what I mean. I feel she's putting the Vicar before me at every hand and turn.'

Mrs Prothero gave up. She felt she was flogging a dead horse. At that moment Anthea Edgebaston and her Colonel drove down the road and Mrs Gantry said sharply, 'I wonder how long he's staying here. Wouldn't you think he had friends and family in America he'd want to be with?'

'Perhaps he has, but they seem very happy together.'

346

'Hilda Marks says he's a widower, she knows everything that woman.'

As Mrs Prothero walked home she reflected that Mrs Gantry never wasted an opportunity to chat to Hilda Marks. Both women were inveterate gossips and in the weeks ahead there would be plenty to gossip about.

She felt sorry for Grace – she wanted her to be happy, but she was unsure. Her spirits lightened as she reached her first gate. She was looking forward to Oliver's wedding. She liked his fiancée, but when she'd mentioned Erica Clarkson's wedding to him he'd been clipped, saying he was too old for her, she was too inexperienced to take on so much responsibility, and she'd have been better with somebody of her own age.

'He's really very nice,' she'd said gently.

'Well, of course, politicians are all things to all men, but I know Erica. I'll give it a couple of years.'

She hoped he was wrong, had been too scathing.

Anthea decided to enquire when Bill was thinking of returning to America. He seemed happy to drive through the countryside and explore old cities that were so much part of England's history.

He adored Exeter and they spent a long weekend in Bath. He pored over maps and circled places he wanted to visit. One evening Anthea said quietly, 'Aren't you missing your boat?'

'Oh, she'll be waiting for me when I get back. She's been the one most certain thing in my life for a long time.'

'I thought you'd have been anxious to return to her.'

'I say, Anthea, why don't we do some sailing? We could go up to the Lakes or down to the coast, find a boat I could hire. You do like sailing, don't you?'

'Well, I've never done much of your kind of sailing. Cruise boats, that's all.'

'Then I'll introduce you to it. You'll love it. A week or two to get acclimatised. What do you say?'

347

So they went to the Lakes and sailed on Coniston and Windermere, and then they went to the coast and found a yacht in Langstone harbour.

St Agnes saw little of them and people began to speculate.

They had been back in St Agnes several days when he appeared just after breakfast brandishing an envelope and saying, 'A letter from home, Anthea. My god-daughter's getting married and I'm expected to give her away. Her father died several years ago – he was my best friend.'

'You can't possibly miss that, Bill. When will you go?' she asked.

'Well, it depends on you.'

'On me!'

'I want you to come with me, Anthea. I want to show you Cape Cod and my boat. I want you to meet my friends, discover America.'

'Bill, I don't know. What about my house, my dog, my cat. I have commitments here.'

'Bricks and mortar, Anthea. Arrangements can be made for Benjie and your cat. Come for a while to see if you like it, if you can exchange this place for it. Until you've seen it how will you know?'

'How long are you expecting me to visit, Bill?'

'Long enough to see how you like it, if you could ever live there, whether you would be prepared to give up living here. I'm asking you to marry me, Anthea.'

She stared at him incredulously. She liked him, more than liked him, they were good together, and yet it was the biggest commitment she had ever been asked to make. With John it had been here, with Bill it would be a new world, probably a very different world.

Urgently he said, 'Anthea we're not so very different, are we? My roots were here, this is the country my grandparents came from, we speak the same language, we're closer than any other people on earth – and if you're not

348

happy there then I'll come back with you to England. I know I can be happy here.'

She looked at him helplessly, then said, 'A visit, Bill, then we'll see how we go on from there.'

'That's enough for me, darling. A visit and we'll go on from there.'

That night she telephoned Nigel and Gordon, and although it was almost midnight she knew they would come. They listened to all she had to say and it was Gordon, the more thoughtful of the two, who said, 'Do you want to marry him, Anthea?'

'I hadn't thought so far. I don't know, I'm happy with him, but you know how long I've been on my own. I've never thought of marrying again.'

'There's a lot to think about.'

'You mean my husband's family?'

'Where your money is concerned, how it will affect them if you live in America.'

'Then what do you think? That's the reason I telephoned you.'

It was Nigel who said, 'Why not have your visit decide after that. Give it a month, by that time surely you'll know if you would rather not live with each other, or if your destiny's together.'

'For a man who's never married, you think it's that easy?'

He smiled and shrugged his shoulders. 'What do you think, Gordon?'

'It seems a good idea to me. We'll miss you, Anthea.'

'You're so sure that I'm going?'

They both smiled. At that moment there was nothing more to say.

Chapter Thirty-Six

It was undoubtedly the wedding of the year when the popular Minister of the Crown married the beautiful sparkling girl young enough to be his daughter. The church was crowded with guests, nobility and politicians from both sides of the House, and to those who had come from St Agnes, Erica had never looked more beautiful.

Janet Clarkson wept a little, but not just for Erica, but for her younger daughter too, who had been receiving admiring glances from everybody they met.

As she had done so many times in the past Nancy had sat on her sister's bed watching her pout and preen before her mirror and as always she'd thought her the most beautiful girl she was ever likely to see.

Finally satisfied Erica said, 'Well, will I do?'

'You look wonderful, Erica.'

'Stand up, let me look at you. I always found something wrong with you, but not this morning,' she added after spinning Nancy round and viewing her with satisfaction tinged with some sort of disbelief.

'I never thought you'd grow up this pretty, Nancy, and yet you still didn't manage to capture Julian Watson.'

'What made you think I'd tried?'

'I know how much you fancied him.'

'And I knew he was not the marrying sort. He's dedicated to his career and only his career.'

350

'Oh well, there are other fish in the sea. I'll look around at the reception and pick one or two out for you.'

'You needn't bother, I really wouldn't be interested. Why don't we go downstairs and let Mother see what she thinks of us?'

After that it had all moved so fast, and then after the ceremony they seemed to be caught up in a whirlpool of people that seemed neverending.

There were people there who knew the Commodore, naval men who remembered him, and Major Robson remarked to his wife, 'Well this is some do and no mistake. We'll have a lot to tell them back home.'

'He's really very nice,' Elspeth said with a smile. 'He doesn't look so much older than her. What do you think?'

'Well preserved, my dear. I've never thought politicians live in the real world, they're cloistered.'

The toasts had been drunk, the speeches had been said, and Alistair and Erica were leaving for their honeymoon in America. Erica embraced her parents, exquisite in pale grey and a sheen of silver fox, and as they ran down the stairs to their waiting car Alistair's sister remarked grimly to her husband, 'I hope he's done the right thing. It's all been so quick.'

'Well, it's no use worrying about it now, old girl, the deed's done.'

'Aren't you in the least concerned?'

'He's old enough to know what he's doing.'

'It's not him I'm worrying about, it's her.'

'She'll be fine, love. Enough money, enough prestige to suit most women and Alistair isn't exactly in his dotage – there's plenty of mileage left in him yet.'

After favouring him with a long withering look she turned away. Men could be so insensitive, Norris in particular. Surely he must see that it was natural for her to be worried.

Across the room David Clarkson could see that his younger daughter was in the company of a young man who

351

was looking down at her with obvious admiration so out of curiosity he decided to join them.

Nancy introduced him as Nathan Worsely, Alistair's friend and colleague, and after a few minutes she was glad to leave him in the company of her father, with the excuse that she needed to freshen up.

Nathan was nice, he talked about his job, his expectations, and more about his job. After a few minutes in his company David began to wonder how his elder daughter would cope with people like Nathan Worsely, the sort of people who made up Alistair's life and in the foreseeable future her own.

Back at their hotel the Watsons reassured the Clarksons that they had had a wonderful day and enjoyed every moment of it. Lois Watson said rather wistfully, 'At least you've still got Nancy's wedding to look forward to – we've got no chance with Julian.'

'Got an aversion to marriage, has he?' the Major asked.

'Marriage is not for sailors,' she replied.

'Well, you married his father.'

'That's the point – the long absences, the times we spent apart, right from his schooldays he had doubts about it.'

'I'm sure he'll change his mind when he meets the right girl,' Elspeth said consolingly, but as they moved away the Major said quickly, 'I thought he'd found it in Nancy when he was home on leave. It would seem I was wrong.'

The Clarksons had listened to the conversation without taking part in it and as Nancy left them to go to her room her mother said, 'Do you think she minds when they talk about Julian like that?'

'I don't know, love. If it had been Erica she'd have been bemoaning her fate, driving us all mad by her tantrums and histrionics. If Nancy does mind then I dare say she'll suffer in silence.'

*

352

They all decided that as long as they were in London they'd make the most of it. They went to shows and enjoyed all the other diversions the capital could offer.

It was the Commodore who was the first to say he'd had enough. Then the Major was saying he'd better get back to his cadets and the women were missing their bridge afternoon and all that would be going on in St Agnes, including Grace's wedding and the problem of her mother.

Here we are, Lois thought, enjoying ourselves and we're concerned with trivialities, and yet here in London we're birds of passage – what we're going back to is home.

The Watsons were the first to arrive back in St Agnes. As they drove into their drive they could see lights shining in the house and another car parked there. Turning to his wife the Commodore said, 'What have we here, that's Julian's car, isn't it?'

'Yes. Stop the car here, Andrew. I'll go and see what it's all about.'

Before she reached the door it opened and Julian stood there smiling. 'I wondered when you'd be coming back,' he exclaimed. 'Mrs Edgebaston said you were in London for some wedding or other.'

'Erica Clarkson's wedding, Julian. We told you about it.'

'I didn't know you'd be invited.'

'Darling, what are you doing here? Another leave so soon?'

'The last for some time, Mother. Don't tell me you're surprised – you should know the Navy by now.'

He went out to bring their luggage in then while his mother made coffee he sat with his father demanding to know about the wedding. But his father said, 'Never mind about the wedding, what about your news?'

'Wait until Mother's here, I'll tell you both together.'

So they talked of other things until she served the coffee, then his father said, 'Now, out with it, we've waited long enough.'

353

'Command of a new ship, Dad, and the Far East. It's been on the cards some time, I didn't want to say anything before, not until things were more certain, at least.'

'So how long are you here for?'

'A few days, but I'm not sailing for some weeks.'

There were tears in his mother's eyes as she said, 'Oh Julian, all those years when the war was on and now this. It might be what your father wanted, but it's not what I wanted.'

Julian put his arms round her shoulders, saying gently, 'I know, Mother. You wanted me round the corner, some nice girl, the park on Sunday, holidays near the beach. Dad's proud of me, but I've disappointed you terribly.'

'Oh no, dear, you're everything I can be proud of, it's just that I wanted so much more.'

'I know, grandchildren to spoil and me round the corner when the lights fused and Dad couldn't start the car. It was never destined to be like that, Mother.'

She smiled sadly, 'I know that now, dear. So all we've got are the next few days then we don't know when we'll see you again. Or will you get more leave before you go?'

He smiled ruefully. 'The world's getting smaller, Mother, even the Far East isn't so far away these days. I'll always be your son.'

'I know, dear.'

There was nothing more to say – she'd been there with his father and expected it from Julian. That didn't mean that it didn't hurt, but wasn't that how it had always been? The men sailed away while the women waited for them to come back.

'So what are you going to do with the next few days?' his father asked evenly.

'Help in the garden, vegetate, perhaps I'll ask Nancy if she'd like to drive off somewhere.'

'She looked very beautiful at her sister's wedding.'

'I'm sure she did. Did you enjoy it?'

'Oh yes, very much. Nancy will tell you all about it.'

Lois was worried. Julian would take up with Nancy as easily as he had discarded her and she would be hurt because he would be going out of her life, possibly for ever. By the time they saw each other again she would have met somebody else and he would be a hardened old bachelor in love with the sea.

She did not know what arrangements Julian had made with Nancy, only that the following day she saw them driving off together and as her eyes followed them doubtfully all she received in return was a wave from both of them.

Julian told Nancy his news which she received with a calm smile and no hint of how her heart sank. They walked together along the river path after morning service the following Sunday, both of them in nostalgic moods, in Julian's case for the life he was leaving behind. Young men and girls were boating on the river and the sun shone out of a clear blue sky, while all around them was laughter and the peaceful normality of a typical Sunday afternoon in an old English town. Children were feeding the swans and the mallards near the weir, and swallows swooped lazily over cottage gardens.

'I wonder if you'll miss all this,' Nancy mused, 'and what you'll be exchanging it for.'

'Pagodas and rickshaws, the squalor of Aberdeen Harbour and orchids instead of roses, different culture, different people.'

'What will you miss most, I wonder?'

'Parents, friends ... you, Nancy.'

'You'll miss me?'

'Yes, does that surprise you?'

She paused, then, turning away, went to stand looking over the wall into the depths below where it was suddenly quiet and even the sound of laughter seemed to have faded away. Julian followed her and stood looking down at her. She was accustomed to the amusement in his eyes, the teasing banter of a man who was so sure of his destiny, but when she looked up at him his eyes were strangely grave, the teasing amusement gone.

Uncertainly she said, 'I didn't expect you to say you'd miss me.'

'Why shouldn't I, Nancy? Doesn't the time we've spent together mean as much to you as it's meant to me?'

'It's meant a lot to me, I've enjoyed being with you.'

'Is that all?'

'What more do you want me to say to a man who needs to be fancy free, a man who isn't looking for anything beyond the here and now?'

'It's true, Nancy. That's how I wanted it to be. Fate's a rotten listener, isn't he?'

'Are you telling me you don't feel that way any more?'

'I thought that way ever since my schooldays, then when I went back off leave I began to see my life differently. For years I've listened to old salts telling me that sailors should never marry. They were so sure and I saw them going off into retirement to their golf clubs, their solitary existence somewhere near the sea and I thought that was what I wanted. Then I thought about what my father had – Mother and occasionally me.'

'Which is best for you, Julian?'

'Well, that rather depends on you, Nancy.'

Could she really believe it? All those long years when she'd cared about him, now was he really saying he needed her in his life? With a huge smile he reached out and drew her into his arms. 'I'm asking you to marry me, Nancy. You might think I'm a hopeless case, but if you don't you might think of saying you will.'

She had never believed that one day Julian would kiss her like that, and now he was saying, 'Shouldn't I be asking your father's permission?'

She laughed. 'Oh yes, I'm sure you should. Instead of driving off somewhere perhaps we should go back there.'

So they drove back to St Agnes and David looked up in surprise from his chair in the garden.

'Back already?' he called out. 'I thought you were off for the day.'

He realised there was something different about them, walking hand in hand and smiling as if the world had become a more wonderful place. And then Nancy was running into the house and Julian was asking his permission to marry his daughter.

There was so much happiness that afternoon as they drank their toasts, but it was Julian who said at last, 'Perhaps we should tell my parents. Why don't we all go?'

So the four of them set off down the road. To the Major chatting to Anthea Edgebaston in her front garden it resembled something like a victory parade.

'Something's afoot there,' he said with a smile, 'what do you think?'

'Like what, Desmond?'

'Well, the Clarksons are beaming and Nancy and Julian are hand in hand. I'd say we need to watch this space, wouldn't you?'

Her eyes followed them as they entered the Watsons' garden and saw the way Julian was looking down at the girl next to him, and his tender smile as their eyes met.

'You could be right,' she said softly.

'Oh well, I'll give them my blessing. I've never been too sure about some of the so-called romances. I've always known where Nancy's affections lay even when I never thought they'd be realised. If they're now going that way then I'm delighted.'

'You're quite a romantic at heart, Desmond.'

'My wife wouldn't agree with you, she says I'm a materialistic cynic who sees everything in black and white.'

'Then you've conditioned Elspeth to think that about you.'

'Probably – to save me from the gossips she surrounds herself with.'

Anthea laughed while they both imagined what might be

357

happening at the Commodore's house.

As Lois reached for the wine glasses she could feel the salty tears rolling down her cheeks, but at least they were tears of happiness. This was the day she'd dreamed about, when her son would bring home the girl he wanted to marry. But there was an added bonus – the girl was somebody they knew and liked.

What did it matter that they would spend time apart? Nancy would understand as she'd been in the Navy herself, and when they came together the time would be doubly precious.

Now she could think about grandchildren, about young voices in school holidays – life at last was taking on a new meaning.

It was Julian's father who suddenly brought them all down to earth by saying, 'Are you intending to marry before you go off to the Far East? I hope the wedding will be here.'

'I'm sure that's what Nancy would like. There's a few weeks yet, possibly a few months. If its weeks we'll have to get a special licence.'

As Nancy's parents looked at each other doubtfully Lois said, 'I know what you're thinking, the same as my parents thought. When do we see them? How can they bear to be apart?'

'Well, Nancy will come out to Hong Kong. I'll get shore leave whenever possible and she'll love it. Hong Kong is very civilised and besides, isn't this what you and Dad did most of the time, Mother?'

'Well yes, whenever it was possible.'

But then there had been Julian and school in England. Nancy would face the same predicament.

Julian smiled. 'Mother, for years you've been telling me that nothing mattered except your promise to each other. I thought I was right and you were wrong – now I've changed my mind and you're having doubts.'

Lois smiled. 'No Julian, I'm glad you've changed your mind and you're right to have done so. Andrew, do pour the champagne and let us all drink to Nancy and Julian and their future happiness.'

The toasts were duly drunk in spite of the conflicting emotions of the six people lifting their glasses.

Nancy and Julian were ecstatic, his parents proud and delighted, Nancy's parents facing for the first time the prospect that their younger daughter would be moving away from them to a new and different world.

Later that evening when Nancy sat with her parents mulling over the events of the day, her father said, 'It's only just beginning to register that you'll be moving away from us, darling, and such a long way away.'

'But I'll always be your daughter, Daddy. If ever you need me I'll be here.'

'I know you will, love.'

'I'm sorry I've fallen in love with a sailor instead of some boy who works nine to five and spends his weekends in the garden. I do love Julian, you know. I always have.'

'We know, love, and we're happy for you, but we're thinking about us, not you, so we just hope you'll forgive us.'

She smiled. 'Well of course I do. It would have been awful if you'd been glad to see me go.'

Chapter Thirty-Seven

Joyce Blackstock drove the pony and trap into the stable yard and met several of the men setting off into the fields. They doffed their caps and smiled, but even now after several years they still regarded her as not quite one of them.

She picked up the post from behind the kitchen door as she went in and started to leaf through it. It consisted mostly of bills and catalogues but there was one letter addressed to her, written in handwriting she recognised, Nancy Clarkson's.

Hurriedly she slit it open and pulled out several pages of notepaper and a photograph of Nancy with her arm linked in that of a smiling naval officer, Julian Watson.

She sat down at the kitchen table and started to read:

This is a photograph of Julian and me at our engagement party last Saturday evening. I know it will surprise you, Joyce, but I can tell you that I am happy and very much in love – but then you will know that because you know how much I always wanted Julian. I still need to pinch myself that he has actually decided he wants me.

We are getting married in three weeks at the church in St Agnes and I'd love you to be there, so you'll be getting an invitation. I'll understand if you can't make it, however.

Julian is going out to the Far East, perhaps only a few days later and I'm to join him there. Julian will be on his ship but we'll have a house there and spend as much time together as the Navy allows.

Before I join him I shall try to get up to Derbyshire to see you and Louise. It will be a very brief and hurried visit but I want to see you, Joyce. There's so much to tell you about old times and old friends. I hope your husband and the children are well and that the farm is prospering.

I can't really believe that in a few months I'll be on the other side of the world. I'll miss my parents and my dear familiar world, but whatever life throws at me I've got Julian, he's all I've ever wanted.

Joyce put the letter down and sat for several minutes thinking about the life that she believed had gone for ever. She remembered that first long summer in St Agnes, filled with the warmth of new friends, and laughter, as they had walked home from school along the banks of the wide sparkling river.

She and her mother had loved the house with its lawns and rockeries filled with alpines. She could remember Edith's dry humour and her mother's smiles. They had been contented before her father's arrival after that happy Christmas when she had entertained the audience at the school concert – the praise, the excitement – then nothing.

She couldn't go back to St Agnes, not to see people who would remember the trauma and the heartache before they'd moved away. She had a new life now – why revive memories she'd struggled to forget for so long.

She slipped the letter and the photograph into a drawer as she didn't want Roger to see it. Roger would be non-committal, snide even. Nancy was part of her life before he came into it. Nancy with her naval officer husband, her home in Hong Kong – rich people, he'd say, not his sort or hers either if she had any sense.

361

She seldom went into the village now, just a quick visit to the shops every Friday, but never to the village hall; and she hurried on quickly whenever she met people who remembered her playing the piano that afternoon months ago.

Jenny had not forgotten that she wanted to play the piano, but she never spoke of it when her father was around. She associated the piano with the rows between her parents, and young as she was she had learned when to keep silent.

In some strange way Joyce felt that she had betrayed both herself and her daughter. She felt that her entire life was in limbo, her memories sad, her future something that should never have been.

She looked again at the photograph Nancy had sent her. Two happy smiling people in love, and although she felt glad for her friend, there was an element of regret for a life that could have been hers and which she was trying to forget.

A few days later Nancy read her letter of congratulation, that she was happy for her, but unfortunately she would not be able to attend her wedding. The letter went on:

This is our busiest time of year, what with the harvest and everything. Jenny is only just back at school after the summer holidays and there is so much to do on the farm I never seem to have a moment to myself.

Lies, all lies. She was simply a housewife cooking meals for her husband and children – anything remotely needed on the farm was done by Roger, an army of farm labourers and his three sisters. If she walked out tomorrow only the children would miss her. Roger would soon find somebody else if he hadn't already done so.

Nancy passed her letter over to her mother across the breakfast table and after reading it Janet said thoughtfully,

'Did you really think she'd come to your wedding, dear?'

Nancy shook her head. 'I had to ask her, though. I'll call to see her when Julian's gone back to his ship, and I'll be able to show her the wedding photographs.'

'D'you think she's happy?'

'I don't really know. Joyce was always so good at hiding her feelings, even when she must have been very unhappy – particularly after her mother died. Mother, have you thought what you will do with the piano when I'm away. I love music and always wanted to play, but I simply didn't want to practise. When I heard Joyce play I realised how much money you'd wasted on Erica and me, and on this instrument.'

'But you both played very nicely, dear.'

Nancy smiled. 'And that's all we did, Mother. Now here you'll be with a piano nobody plays and I know very well you'd much rather have Granny's walnut bureau down here instead of hiding it away in the loft.'

'Granny was very proud of it; it's a beautiful piece of furniture, Nancy. She'd be horrified to see where we've had to put it.'

'Then why not get rid of the piano, Mother?'

'You mean sell it?'

'I know somebody who would like it.'

'Would they want to buy it? It cost a great deal of money, love.'

'Leave it with me, Mother. We'll talk about it again.'

She spoke to Julian about it and he thought it was a hair-brained scheme. 'Darling, her husband's dead against anything to do with music. You could have a revolution on your hands. Besides, have they the money to pay for it even if he allowed them to have it?'

When she didn't immediately answer he said, 'You're thinking of giving it to them, Nancy. Can you really afford to do that?'

'Well, we can't take it to Hong Kong, can we? Perhaps Joyce could persuade her husband to buy it.'

'And perhaps pigs might fly, my dear. Besides, shouldn't Erica have a say in it?'

'Erica hardly ever played, but of course I'll mention it to her.'

'My dear, it's your piano, you must do as you think fit. But not before you've really thought it through.'

The days at the end of September were truly the last blazing days of a perfect summer before the days shortened and the chill of autumn crept into the air.

Nancy and Julian's wedding was a truly naval affair and as the congregation took their places in the pews it seemed that all around them was a sense of inevitability. This was one wedding that was meant to be.

Both Julian's father and the Major had elected to wear their uniforms and Julian and his brother officers looked predictably handsome. Alistair Greavson stood with his wife's parents, smiling proudly as he waited for his wife to follow her sister down the aisle, his expression one of a man well blessed.

To Grace Gantry sitting with her mother she could only think that in a week's time she too would be a bride and once more the church would be crowded to see the Bishop tie the knot.

There was still the agonising question of her mother to be dealt with, and one more would-be housekeeper to interview, but at least for today they could try to forget the problems of the last few months.

Gerald Marks was wishing his wife would shut up in case those sitting nearest to them heard her more caustic remarks. He knew that she was regarded as a gossip and that events such as this one gave her full rein to say her piece, but even so people didn't always agree with her.

'I thought Anthea Edgebaston would have to outdo the bride's mother,' she commented sharply. 'Isn't that that American Colonel she's with?'

'Do be quiet, Hilda, people will hear you.'

She bit her lip angrily while her husband glanced at Mrs Edgebaston's offending outfit. As always she looked attractive in a pale lilac dress with a large matching hat; the man sitting next to her was obviously delighted with her company.

He knew that from the moment she had arrived in St Agnes there had been women who talked about her, her clothes, her style, her obvious money, but he'd always thought she was rather nice, and certainly a match for all the busybodies.

His wife said, 'I don't suppose Grace Gantry's wedding will attract the crowds this one has.'

The woman sitting next to her said sharply, 'He's the Vicar, Hilda, and the Bishop himself is marrying them.'

'Well of course, but her mother is still a problem, you know.'

He was heartily relieved when the organ announced the arrival of the bride as Julian and his best man took their places in front of the altar.

Here were two sisters who had grown up in St Agnes and there were tears in a few eyes as they walked slowly down the aisle, both of them beautiful, both smiling. As they passed Julian's parents' pew the Commodore found it hard to believe that his future daughter-in-law was the same girl as the one who had grinned at him cheekily across the gate and performed cartwheels across his lawn.

This beautiful girl in her parchment satin gown was now taking her place beside his son, who was looking down at her with loving admiration, the son who they had thought would never marry, a fact born out of the legacy his parents had left him with.

It had been a beautiful wedding on a beautiful day and as the guests made their way home they were of one accord that this had been a day to remember.

'That was a good do,' the Major remarked heartily to his wife. 'Can't think I've ever enjoyed a wedding quite so much.'

'Yes, it was wonderful,' Elspeth said softly. 'I couldn't help thinking however that in three days Julian will be off to Hong Kong, and Nancy not very long afterwards.'

'Well, distances are shortening and they're not a lifetime away. Your mother always had a lot to say when I served overseas, but we managed, didn't we, old girl.'

'We did, and I wish you wouldn't keep calling me your old girl, I'm hardly in my dotage.'

He grinned. 'What about Anthea Edgebaston and the American Colonel then?'

'What about it? He's probably only here for a short time. He might even have a wife back in the States.'

'He hasn't, and you can pass that on to Hilda Marks when she starts saying her piece.'

'She's particularly vitriolic about Anthea. I really don't know why.'

'Probably because she's prettier, richer and because she's an unknown quantity.'

'Do you think we'll enjoy Grace's wedding as much as this one?'

'Well, her mother's face will be predictably glum, Grace will be worried and Paul resigned. Maybe the Bishop will liven things up.'

'Nancy and Julian looked so happy. Did you ever think that schoolgirl crush would come to anything?'

'God moves in mysterious ways, my dear. Now we'll just have a word with Andrew and Lois, then we'll get off home.'

Erica was reflecting on the difference between her own wedding and her sister's. Hers had been all formality, too many people she didn't know, most of the women thinking she was too young, and an awful lot of men wishing they were in Alistair's shoes. Today had been a huge family affair with half the neighbourhood regarding it as their wedding too.

*

As the Major and his wife strolled down the road they found Mrs Edgebaston and her Colonel walking alongside them. Anthea introduced him to Elspeth saying, 'It has been a lovely day, hasn't it. The first English wedding Bill has ever attended.'

'And you enjoyed it?' Elspeth asked.

'Very much. You do things in a different way to us. In the States, for example, the bridesmaids precede the bride, here they follow on.'

The Major laughed. 'Yes, a bit like our use of the language – same language, different way of using it.'

'Well, I'm trying to encourage Anthea to visit my home in Vermont to see if she enjoys it. I do a lot of sailing which she isn't familiar with – perhaps you can encourage her too.'

'I'll certainly try.'

When they had parted company the Major said feelingly, 'Now you can inform Hilda Marks that he isn't married and that she's off on a visit to America – that should shut her up.'

'He's rather nice. I wonder if there's another wedding in the offing.'

'Maybe, but not here.'

'Why ever not?'

'Because some of them have made it hard for her – she'll want to put it all behind her.'

'What happened to the other two men I've seen her with?'

'One's her solicitor, the other her accountant; one a confirmed bachelor, the other dodgy about women.'

'Oh Desmond, why do you know so much about her and me hardly at all?'

'Because I took the trouble to find out, dear. Hello, there's Grace and her mother with Mrs Prothero. I wonder what they made of it all?'

'Mrs Prothero was loving every minute of it, but I stayed well clear of Mrs Gantry.'

*

It had been a happy day but even so there had been so many undercurrents regardless of the sunshine, the unfurling love story and the delight of loving parents. Human nature would always create difficulties – somehow or other it was in the scheme of things.

In her bedroom Nancy was changing into her going-away outfit. Even if it was only for three days her mother had insisted on the pale-blue dress and jacket which Erica was eyeing with a doubtful smile.

'I suppose you'll get to wear it in Hong Kong,' she said.

'I suppose so. I told Mother I didn't need it, not for three days, but she insisted.'

'You can't get very far in three days. Somewhere within sight of the sea, I suppose?'

'I don't much care.'

'Well of course not, you've got Julian. What more could you want?'

'Was I always so obvious?'

'Why worry? He's yours now.'

'Erica, there might not be time to ask you later, but Mother wants to put Granny's bureau where the piano is. You know neither of us were very good at playing it and I know somebody who may wish to buy it.'

'You can get money for it?'

'Well, it was quite expensive. Mother says I can sell it but you will be entitled to half the money.'

'I suppose it would buy a few ball gowns, but I'm really not all that bothered. I have enough money, Alistair is very generous.'

'Then it really wouldn't bother you if I gave it away?'

'Gave it, who on earth to?'

'Joyce Mellor, for her little girl.'

'I didn't even know you were in touch with her. Why can't she afford a piano? Besides, what happened to that super piano she had here?'

'Erica, it's a long story and I haven't time to tell you now. Her father gave that piano away; she's married to a farmer and has two children. She's a very different Joyce from the one we knew – if she'll accept the piano, would you be happy for me to give it to her?'

'Well I think it's a bit of an ostentatious gift, don't you?'

'Perhaps, but one day I can tell you more about it.'

At that moment the door opened and their mother was saying, 'Darling, aren't you ready? They're all downstairs waiting to wave you off.'

'Go on,' Erica hissed, 'we'll talk about the piano some other time.'

So after many embraces and farewells Julian and Nancy were driving down the road through a crowd of well-wishers and into a future Nancy had never believed would be hers.

Three days were all they had before Julian sailed to Hong Kong – in the month before she followed him there would be time to worry about the piano.

Chapter Thirty-Eight

Another would-be housekeeper, another disaster as far as Mrs Gantry was concerned, and only five days to go before Grace's wedding.

'You didn't like her, did you Mother?' Grace asked quietly.

'Well, she was foreign, wasn't she?'

'She was half Italian, Mother, her father is married to an Italian but they live in England.'

'But weren't the Italians against us during the war? Why would I want to employ one of them?'

'Mother, the war is over and the Italians were on our side in the end. Shouldn't we forgive and forget?'

'Not when it comes to somebody living in my house.'

'Mother, we've interviewed a great many women and none of them have been suitable, that was the last one and there are only five days left. What is it to be?'

'What choice is there?'

'With us at the vicarage or a residential home.'

'I can stay here with our daily and get another woman in to help her.'

'So we start interviewing daily women, is that it?'

'I can interview them. You needn't bother yourself.'

'No Mother, this can't go on. You have to decide, and another daily is not the answer. Let Paul go ahead with the flat at the vicarage or think about a place at Berkeley Park.

It's very nice there with people of your age, they say the food is very good and your friends could visit whenever they felt like it.'

'It's expensive.'

'Well, it's your money, Mother. I don't want any of it.'

'You can say that now but wait 'til he's retired and his pension's not up to much. You'll have to leave the vicarage to make room for somebody else and it's then you'll find yourself thinking about my money.'

'Mother, are we any nearer a solution?'

'Who's going to give you away? You've no uncles or cousins and you need to be thinking about it.'

'You could give me away, Mother, you're all I've got.'

'You're asking me to give something away when I'm dead against it?'

'Mother, I don't know what to say, but this much I do know. I am going to marry Paul but I shall not desert you. Whatever you want to do I'll be behind you whether it be coming to live with us or something else, and if you don't want to give me away I'd better start thinking of somebody else. Have you any suggestions?'

'None.'

Grace looked at her sadly before saying, 'Then I'll ask Major Robson. Elspeth won't mind, there will be plenty of her friends she can sit with in church until he can join her.'

'Why Major Robson? He will be flattered. I've always thought he had a roving eye.'

Grace gave up. If she'd told her mother she'd ask another bishop to give her away she'd find fault with it and him.

She was doubtful about asking the Major, but he'd been the first person she'd thought of. Most of the men were no more than acquaintances. She thought the Commodore nice but distant, David Clarkson too was nice as was Hilda Marks's husband, but she decided the Major could be relied upon to bring a bit of light relief into the uncertainties surrounding them.

*

371

Two days before the wedding Mrs Gantry decided she would take a look at Berkeley Park. Grace knew she would find untold things wrong with the place – even as they walked up the drive they could see groups of people sitting in chairs across the lawns and her mother said, 'I wonder if they expect you to sit out in all weathers?'

'Today's a beautiful day, Mother, they seem to be enjoying it.'

'They probably want to get people out of the house.'

'I'm sure they don't force them to go out, they probably want to enjoy the sunshine.'

Her mother remained non-committal as one of the housekeepers took them round and Grace couldn't resist saying, 'There are people sitting in the lounges, Mother, so evidently they didn't want to go outside.'

'I've got all my faculties. Some of them were fast asleep and some of them looked a bit vacant. What did you think of the bedrooms?'

'Well, Mother, you could bring some of your own furniture, they seem roomy enough.'

'At least you won't want any of it, the vicarage is overcrowded with furniture as it is.'

'What you don't need you can sell – it will help to pay your bill here.'

'It's very expensive.'

'You have an alternative, Mother?'

'You'd like him to win, wouldn't you?'

'There are no winners, Mother, not even you.'

Right until the moment they were ready to leave the home her mother gave no indication of what she wanted to do, and they were actually at the door when she said, 'I have to think about it. I'm not sure. When can I move in if I decide to come?'

'Well, I can only say that you should make up your mind fairly quickly. We get so many requests and there are only two bedrooms available in the immediate future,' the matron said.

As they walked away her mother said sharply, 'They always say that, it's the same whenever you buy a house or a car – make up your mind quickly or somebody else will grab it.'

'Have you made up your mind?'

'I'd like to see what Amelia Prothero thinks. She's my best friend after all, and even if she'll never have to move into a place like that she'll have her own ideas about things.'

'I would think that is exactly the sort of place Mrs Prothero might move into one day. Why do you say she wouldn't?'

'Because she's got a caring nephew and Edith Pinder.'

Grace gave up the argument. Amelia Prothero's nephew did not figure very highly in her estimation and Edith Pinder was getting older too.

As her mother had predicted the Major was flattered when Grace asked if he would give her away. She added diffidently, 'I hope Elspeth won't mind that she will have to go to the church on her own.'

'Not at all, she'll be glad to be rid of me. She always says I'm more interested in the girl guides than I am in the sermon.'

Grace laughed and with a sigh of relief said, 'Well, that's one less problem at any rate.'

'Have you got your mother sorted out, Grace?'

'I hope we're getting there.'

'Where, I'd like to know?'

'Berkeley Park with a bit of luck. She doesn't want to live with us at the vicarage in case Paul thinks he's won.'

Grace's eyes filled with tears as she welcomed visitors bearing wedding gifts but it was Janet Clarkson who said, 'This is from Mrs Edgebaston, Grace, she was sorry she couldn't attend your wedding but she hopes you will like her present. We're all dying to see what it is.'

'Where is she off to that she can't come to the wedding?' Hilda Marks asked.

'Didn't you know, Hilda?' Elspeth said with a smile. 'She's gone to America with the Colonel.'

'How long for?'

'I really don't know, but several weeks, I dare say.'

'Do you think anything will come of it?'

'Well, one hopes so.'

'How about the other two men?'

Nobody knew anything about them or if they did they were saying nothing.

They stood around watching Grace take off the silver wrapping paper then they all gasped with admiration at the large Royal Worcester vase that Anthea had treasured and been generous enough to give away.

It was a different sort of wedding from so many others in the old Norman church as the congregation consisted of a mixture of guests, everyday churchgoers, girl guides and scouts, as well as visiting clergy from other parishes. The younger element would have preferred to see the bride in traditional white but most people agreed that Grace had never looked prettier as the Major proudly escorted her down the aisle.

The pale-blue dress emphasised her graceful slender figure and her pretty face under the wide-brimmed pale-blue hat did much to appease those who had had doubts about the wedding, even when they saw her mother standing unsmiling in her pew. This was Grace's day and nobody was going to take it away from her.

It was inevitable that the Clarksons should be thinking about two other weddings, Erica's in London, and Nancy's in the same church.

Sitting with her sister Edith Pinder said quietly, 'There'll be a few missing faces at the next longest day. There's been some changes.'

'Ay well, the Vicar needed a wife, that's one good thing,

374

and think back, our Edith, changes or not the longest day's allus been a success, some more than others, I'll grant ye.'

'I wonder if Mrs Edgebaston'll marry her American?'

'What if she does?'

'I'll miss her with her style, and them towering heels she favoured, plus the fact that she didn't give a toss what the gossips thought about her.'

Edith was thinking about the clothes Mrs Edgebaston had passed on to her and which had been greedily taken by her nieces, plus the handbags and the shoes, even ornaments some of which her sister had removed while she was still wondering where to put them.

'Not many smiles from Mrs Gantry,' her sister whispered.

'No, and she's movin' in with Mrs Prothero for a few days. I'm not looking forward to that.'

'How long will the Vicar be away?'

'Only a week. There's the house to sell and the furniture to see to. No doubt the old lady will be taking some of it with her to the Home.'

'It would 'ave easily furnished the flat.'

'I know, but she didn't want it, did she?'

It was agreed by everyone that the repast in the Church Hall was of the highest standard and they all did justice to it. Even Mrs Gantry had little to complain about.

Sitting with Mrs Prothero she said, 'I'm glad they got some decent caterers in, it must have cost plenty.'

'It's been a lovely wedding, surely you must have enjoyed it.'

Mrs Gantry didn't speak and wisely Mrs Prothero asked no more questions but gladly welcomed other guests who paused on their way to their tables.

The Bishop made a delightful speech followed by the Major who had been preparing his for days. It was witty, flattering and aimed at raising everybody's spirits, so much so that when he sat down his wife whispered, 'Very good,

Desmond, I'm glad you kept it reasonably short.'

'I've enjoyed the day and I'm glad she asked me to give her away – she needed somebody like me.'

'Why you, I wonder?'

'Well, David Clarkson's already given two girls away, I don't think he'd have relished a third, and the Commodore could have been decidedly flamboyant.'

Sitting beside Grace, Paul's thoughts had gone back many years, to the time when he had been a young curate in the parish and had first set eyes on her. They'd been so right for each other, but then with her father's death everything changed and in time he'd met Molly.

Molly had been a good sort, a tower of strength in his work and they'd been happy enough. Now fate had given them a second chance and her mother mustn't be allowed to spoil things this time.

Meeting the Bishop's steady gaze he thought they were sentiments a great number of their guests would agree with.

Turning towards his bride he murmured, 'Happy, darling?'

'Yes Paul, very. It has been a lovely day. I just keep wondering if Mother's enjoyed it.'

'Well, she's chatting to the Major. If anybody can raise her spirits, he can. Look, she's actually smiling.'

The Major was holding out her glass for the waiter to refill followed by his own, and Grace said, 'I hope he's prepared to look after her if she's unsteady on her feet. She normally doesn't drink.'

He laughed. Grace's sense of humour was returning. For years it had been restrained, so much so that he'd often wondered if he'd imagined that she'd ever had one. Now the old Grace he'd known and loved was coming back, and all around them was laughter and cheerful conversation.

It was late that evening when Edith Pinder served Mrs Prothero and her guest with the usual cocoa, and Mrs Gantry said, 'If I could have found somebody like you,

376

Edith, I wouldn't be leaving to go into that Home. The ones I saw were either too young or too inexperienced, not one of them was anything like you.'

'Well, I was young and inexperienced when I first came to work for Mrs Prothero. I've grown up here.'

'And I've grown up too,' Mrs Prothero agreed. 'I was a young bride who could barely peel a potato. We were two novices together, but it worked out, we learned from each other, and now here we still are and never a cross word between us.'

'They say Mrs Edgebaston's going to marry that American. She's over there visiting and if she does marry him what's going to happen to Margaret Jones? She seems to fit in very well there – she might have been all right for me.'

'Margaret Jones told me months ago that she suspected Mrs Edgebaston might not stay in the area after all she's bin talked about – usually by gossips like that Mrs Marks. But Margaret likes her and has said workin' for somebody else was somethin' she wouldn't want.'

'Didn't you work for her? Why did you come back here if she's so wonderful to work for?' Mrs Gantry asked sharply.

'I came back to be with Mrs Prothero. I'd never known anythin' else and Mrs Edgebaston said she understood. But I liked her, I liked workin' for her and if she does go to America I for one'll be wishing 'er well.'

'You're probably very tolerant, Edith. You liked working for the Mellors too, didn't you?'

'I liked 'er, I never liked 'im.'

'Whatever happened to them?'

'Well, if she was going to be a concert pianist ye never 'ear of 'er. I reckon all that's gone.'

Mrs Prothero sighed. 'That is sad. She was such a beautiful girl and so talented. Right from that first day Mrs Mellor never really fitted in but Joyce did. She was not like either of her parents.'

'I wonder what became of Joyce and her father after they left here.'

None of them knew, and after clearing the table Edith said, 'Is there anything else you want before I go to bed, Mrs Prothero? Mrs Gantry's room's ready for her and we usually eat breakfast around nine-thirty.'

Mrs Prothero looked at her guest to see if she agreed and Mrs Gantry said, 'Oh yes, we often ate earlier than that but nine-thirty will do very well.'

Mrs Gantry couldn't sleep; her thoughts kept going back to the wedding and what she persisted in calling her own uncertain future. She doubted if Grace and her husband would be giving her a single thought, but there was much to think about.

Who would want to buy her house and how much would they be prepared to pay for it? Would they like the garden or would they start uprooting her roses and shrubs, and what about the furniture?

She would take her bed and favourite easy chair, but what about the nest of walnut tables that had been her mother's, and the solid oak bureau which was something you couldn't buy these days?

The man from the sales rooms who had come to view the furniture said pictures were going out of fashion and young people were thinking more in terms of teak and pine rather than walnut and mahogany which was hard to get and very expensive.

'Doesn't your daughter want any of this stuff?' he'd asked.

'Not really. The vicarage is fully furnished.'

'Well, I'll certainly do the best I can for you, Mrs Gantry,' he'd said, 'but times are changing. What was once somebody's pride and joy means nothing to the next person.'

The woman at the Berkeley had said, 'We really haven't room for your big stuff, Mrs Gantry. A bureau, a few small tables perhaps, one or two of your favourite pictures and ornaments. I'm sure you'll have no difficulty in disposing of the rest.'

378

Nobody cared any more. They all lived in lookalike semis, bungalows or small terraced houses that didn't have room for decent stuff, so how could they be expected to know anything about real furniture?

Everybody was on Grace's side and on the Vicar's side, purely and simply because he was the Vicar. Well, they all knew now that she wasn't going to be pushed around into doing what they wanted. Her own flat in the vicarage indeed – she was going to live at the Berkeley, that would show them.

Chapter Thirty-Nine

Nancy parked her car on a ridge overlooking the grey stone village surrounded by the Pennine hills. It seemed so different from Louise's where she had spent the last four days. Nancy parked her car on a ridge overlooking the grey stone village surrounded by the Pennine hills. She had spent the last four days in Louise's house with its oak beams and open fireplaces and the beauty of the area has not seemed too rugged. Now the outstanding scenery of the Peak district strangely overwhelemed her by its beauty.

As she climbed the hill towards the farm set against a cluster of rocks she thought about her time with Louise. They had talked endlessly about their time together in Scotland during the war, the formidable and traumatic crossing of the Pentland Firth in a Force Nine gale, and their reception from a stern petty officer who'd had little patience with the group of sick and weary girls.

How different her meeting with Joyce was going to be, and for the first time she began to feel that she had been unwise to come here. Louise had a husband who idolised her, sufficiently well off to satisfy even Louise's exacting standards, and as she crossed the cobbled farmyard she couldn't help but compare their standards of living.

A slightly flustered Joyce opened the door to her, and in answer to Nancy's smile she said hurriedly, 'Oh goodness, I'm still wearing my apron. Everything that could go wrong went wrong this morning. Jenny had toothache and I had to take her to the dentist, then she didn't want to go to school. She's upstairs – I decided to keep her at home.'

'Don't worry, Joyce, it's lovely to see you.'

As they embraced Joyce said, 'I want to hear all about your wedding, Nancy. Oh, I wish I'd been there, but it simply wasn't possible.'

So Nancy brought out the wedding photographs and at last Joyce said, 'You look so beautiful, Nancy, and Julian is very handsome. I always thought so. When will you see him again?'

'In a few weeks, hopefully. He'll find a house for us, and then I'll see him whenever it's possible.'

'And everybody else? What else has changed in St Agnes?'

'Grace Gantry has married the Vicar and her mother has decided to go into a residential home. I think she made it rather difficult for them. Grace seemed so happy – I hope things work out well for them. Mrs Edgebaston is in America with her Colonel and there are all sorts of rumours that she might marry him.'

'But that would be wonderful. I liked her, she was very kind to me.'

'I liked her too. I hope she does marry him.'

'The house is awfully untidy, Nancy. I haven't washed the breakfast things yet or tidied up. What must you think of me?'

'Joyce, I've come to see you and hear all about what you've been doing with yourself. Is Jenny playing the piano?'

'Well, not at the village hall. Her teacher has allowed her to play after school for a little while. She's very impressed with her.'

'And what about you?'

'Nancy, I don't know. I haven't told Roger about Jenny – he'd be dead against it.'

'Why is he so difficult? Most fathers would be proud of her.'

381

'Not Roger. Nancy, he's a farmer. He doesn't want a musician in the family, he wants a normal daughter who will love the farm, stay close to us, be the sort of wife I've never been – he listens to his sisters too much.'

'You say he doesn't want a musician in the family – why then did he marry you?'

'Because he thought I'd come to hate music like I hated my father. We were both fooling ourselves and now we're trapped in a marriage neither of us want.'

'But you loved him once surely?'

'I couldn't have done. I had nowhere to go, nobody to go to. My father remarried and they were going away, neither of them wanted me in their lives and Roger was there thinking he loved me – perhaps he did for a time. I was so different from other girls he'd known, but now like me we're both wandering around in a marriage neither of us understands.'

'Have you thought of divorce?'

'He won't divorce me, he says it's unheard of in his way of life and I don't have any money of my own – my father saw to that. Roger isn't a bad man, Nancy, he's good with the children and we always have good food on the table. I daren't tell him about Jenny, I daren't mention music of any kind, he'd never condone it.'

'And will Jenny conform like you? Will she keep silent about her piano playing? Will her teacher? And if they don't what will be the outcome?'

'Oh, but she must.'

'Did you, with your father?'

For a long time Joyce sat staring in front of her without speaking until at last she said, 'I'm trapped Nancy, it's always going to be like this. I can't see anything else for me.'

'I thought I might have some good news for you.'

'Good news, for me!'

'I want to give you our piano. I can play a few pretty pieces and so can Erica but we'd never be in your class.

382

The piano was an expensive luxury because my parents wanted us to be the best and had enough money to indulge us. Now Erica lives in London and doesn't want it and I'll soon be in the Far East. I've mentioned it to my mother and she has no objections, in fact I have the feeling that she would prefer to put something else in its place.'

Joyce stared at her with incredulity written large in her eyes, then weakly said, 'Oh Nancy, I want to say thank you, thank you for this but I can't. Roger would never allow it.'

'Can you be sure without asking him?'

'I would stake my life on it. For one thing he'd hate anything musical to come into our home, and he'd call it charity. Whenever it was played there'd be an awful row – he's that bitter about it.'

'And what about Jenny?'

'She mustn't know.'

'Then you're both letting her down. Could I talk to him?'

'He doesn't even know you're coming here this morning. I didn't show him your letter because I knew he'd be out in the fields and you'd be gone before he got back.'

'I was so looking forward to telling you, thinking you'd be thrilled and excited, now I feel I've filled your heart with pictures of what might have been, only to have them swept away.'

'But I'll always remember your gesture, Nancy, I'll always know that if things had been different we'd all have been so grateful. Now come into the living room and I'll make tea. Tell me about your wedding and what everybody was wearing. Tell me about Julian.'

So they talked.

Nancy had always been able to talk about Julian, even when he was only a romantic dream, but somehow on this occasion she felt that she was merely making conversation, that Joyce spoke in the right places, with the right sentiments, but that her mind was miles away.

She was becoming desperate – surely they had exhausted

every last moment of the wedding, the guests, what they'd worn; and then had come Erica's wedding and Grace and her vicar.

'I was hoping to take you out to lunch,' she said at last, 'but of course it isn't possible with Jenny at home.'

'No. She'll feel better tomorrow, I'm sure, but she hates dentists.'

'Perhaps I should be getting off now, Joyce. I've left the car down the road and I do have a long journey. It's been lovely seeing you again.'

'Oh yes it has, Nancy. Do write to me from Hong Kong, won't you. I'm never likely to get there and Jenny will treasure any postcards you can send her.'

Joyce looked away in some confusion as she met Nancy's eyes. Jenny could have had so much more – what were a few picture postcards to a child who would never know what her mother had thrown away?

They embraced each other on the doorstep and Joyce stood there until Nancy waved to her from the gate. She stood for a long moment looking across the expanse of pastureland with cows and sheep standing peacefully under the trees, then she saw Roger with another man standing near the stile, turned away quickly and hurried on. He had not seen her, but then she saw the other man walk away towards the farm and she stood hesitantly near the car. At that moment Roger turned and saw her and some strange compulsion drew her towards him. He stood staring at her while she walked down the road.

For a long moment they stared at each other. He did not attempt to shake her hand and she sensed the hostility in him even before he said, 'So, what brings ye to Derbyshire?'

'I called to see Joyce. I'm on my way home now.'

'Oh ay, a meetin' with the upper crust, like as not the Latchfords.'

'Yes, for a few days.'

'And can we expect these meetings to be a regular occurrence?'

384

'No. I'm joining my husband in the Far East in a few weeks. This meeting was to say goodbye.'

'Army is he?'

'No, Navy.'

'Well, me wife wouldn't 'ave much news for ye, she 'ardly ever goes out.'

'Doesn't that bother you?'

'No, why should it? It's her own fault. I invites 'er down to the pub to mix with the folks I've grown up with, but I reckon she thinks herself too good for 'em, or she's still yearnin' after that music 'er father dug into 'er.'

'It's a pity she hasn't got a piano, she could indulge herself a little.'

He laughed loudly. 'A piano! Not likely.'

'Why is that? Surely you're not afraid of a piano – it would be a very harmless pastime.'

Glowering at her he snapped, 'It's not 'armless to me.'

'Don't you like music, Mr Blackstock?'

'Not 'er kind of music, I don't.'

'Joyce didn't know anything about farming but she's trying very hard. I learned to play the piano but I was never anything but mediocre, my sister too. Our parents would have been so proud of us if we'd been only half as good as Joyce'

'Ay well, your folks probably 'ad the money to want all sorts o' things for ye. I want a wife and daughter who live in the real world.'

'You know, Mr Blackstock, I've never spoken to a bigot before. I've married a man who listens to me, and even if we don't always agree at least he's prepared to see my point of view.'

'So what's that supposed to mean?'

'I came here this morning hoping to fill Joyce's heart with delight because I've offered to give her my piano. I shall be going away and my sister's in London, but I thought it would give Joyce so much pleasure and Jenny too, but I can see now why she refused it. She knows you

385

would hate it, and she's put you first. I'm really very sorry. She'll never tell Jenny what might have been, but I'm telling you. If you have a conscience, Mr Blackstock, perhaps it's not too late.'

With a brief smile she turned and left him and she knew that he was watching her all the way back to the car. She never turned round.

Her parents would be amazed that Joyce had refused the piano – neither of them would understand a man like Roger Blackstock. She hoped she hadn't made things worse by speaking out at him, although they probably couldn't be worse anyway. Perhaps one day Jenny would rebel, but by that time it would be too late for music.

Roger sat down to his evening meal with a dour expression which Joyce was used to. Trouble on the farm, the animals, his sisters, one of the tractors, any number of things could bring that expression of gloom onto his face.

She'd cooked his favourite roast beef, and she believed she'd made a very good job of it on this occasion, so while he ate it she told him about Jenny and the dentist and that she'd kept her off school.

'Was Jenny 'ere when your visitor arrived?' he asked suddenly.

'How did you know I'd had a visitor?'

'Well, you didn't tell me and that's for sure. I saw 'er goin' to 'er car.'

'It was Nancy. She'd been visiting her friend near Bakewell.'

'Did she bring anything with her?'

'Her wedding photographs, and she's going out to the Far East. Her husband's in the Navy.'

'Officer, I suppose?'

'Commander in the Navy.'

She watched him pushing the food around his plate and she began to feel apprehensive.

'We had a light lunch as she had a long journey home.'

386

'I asked if Jenny saw her?'

'No. I told you I put her to bed, she wasn't very well.'

'Nothin' else to tell me?'

'Not really. We talked about St Agnes and the people we both know. But we've grown apart, it's inevitable.'

He pushed his plate away and she asked anxiously, 'Haven't you enjoyed your meal?'

'The meal's all right.'

'There's apple pie if you'd like some.'

'No. I've 'ad enough. Yer not tellin' me everythin', are ye?'

'About what?'

'About why she came 'ere. It wasn't just 'er weddin' photographs, was it. No, it was somethin' else and I'm waitin' for yer to tell me what it was.'

Joyce sat down weakly on the chair opposite him and from the sardonic smile on his lips he appeared to be enjoying her discomfort.

After a few minutes she said softly, 'I don't know what you want me to tell you.'

'Well, ye can start by tellin' me about the piano.'

'Why did she have to tell you about that? I told her I didn't want it. She had no right to tell you about that.'

'Why did ye tell 'er ye didn't want it?'

'Because I didn't think you'd want it. You've always been difficult about music. Nancy wanted to give it to Jenny, but I knew you'd never let her play it, or even learn to play it. I knew what would happen if it came here.'

'What exactly?'

'You'd make me get rid of it, you and your sisters between you.'

'You think I'm a bigot.'

She didn't speak, and after a few minutes he said, 'Well, don't ye?'

'About some things, yes.'

'What things?'

'Music. You know it's the truth.'

387

'Ay, that's what she said.'

'Well, it's not coming here so we can forget about it.'

'And 'ow much was she chargin' ye for this piano?'

'I told you, she wanted to give it to Jenny for her to have lessons, for me to teach her if you like.'

'So ye could both play it?'

'I suppose so. I knew how much that would anger you – it was a risk I wasn't prepared to take.'

'So there was to be no charge, and 'ow did she propose to get it 'ere?'

'I've no idea. Nancy would take care of it.'

''Ow much would a piano like that cost?'

'A lot of money, more than we could ever afford.'

'And most folk would think we'd be fools to refuse it, I suppose.'

'Under normal circumstances, yes.'

'Ye mean if I weren't such a bigot?'

She didn't answer him, and for what seemed like an eternity he sat looking down at his hands resting on the table. At last she rose to her feet saying, 'I'll see to the dishes. Will you be going out later?'

'Maybe.'

He was still sitting there when she returned to the room twenty minutes later. Looking up he said, 'One day when our Jenny marries some uneducated farm labourer or the like, yer goin' to blame me. Ye'll tell me she was capable o' better things, she could 'ave bin a musician like yer father and married a fella who could give 'er everythin'. Well, I'll not 'ave ye blamin' me for everything. Ye can tell yer friend Nancy that Jenny can 'ave 'er bloody piano and everythin' that goes with it. I'll allus be a bigot. I'll never know what it's all about, but I could see what she thought about me in 'er eyes. She thought I was your worst enemy, yours and Jenny's. Well I'll tell ye this, I think it'll be you Jenny disappoints, not me. I still maintain she's a farmer's lass, not a jumped-up musician.'

'And will you have the grace to apologise if she proves you wrong, Roger?'

'No. Because I know darned well she won't.'

She heard his footsteps marching away across the cobbled yard and at that moment she didn't care where he was going or to whom. Jenny was to have her piano and their lives would be different. Searching in a drawer for writing paper and envelopes, she began to compose her letter to Nancy.

Chapter Forty

There was much speculation as to when Mrs Edgebaston would return to her house and if she would be accompanied by her American. Did he have a wife in America? Children? If they married would she go to America or would he come here? The talk was endless so that when they both returned five weeks later Elspeth urged her husband to find out as much as he could.

'Why me?' he demanded.

'Well, you talked to her more than anyone.'

'That's because I took the trouble. Right nice lady she was.'

'But of course, we got to like her.'

'Not all of you. Maybe they've come back to tie the knot here.'

'Do try to find out, dear, in the nicest possible way of course.'

The opportunity came that afternoon when he found them walking Benjie along the river path.

'So how was America?' he greeted them.

It was left to Anthea to enthuse about the beauty of the New England scenery, her introduction to sailing and her meeting with Bill's friends. Not a little frustrated Desmond soon realised none of this was what Elspeth would want to hear about.

Turning to Bill he asked, 'How long are you here for this time?'

'Oh, we'll be going back when things are sorted out,' he replied.

'Is that so. May one enquire what sort of things?'

They both laughed, and Anthea said quickly, 'Oh Desmond, you're dying to ask questions, and yes, we are married, so things here do need sorting out. Then and only then will we be thinking of going back.'

'So you'll be leaving St Agnes for good, Anthea?'

'I'm afraid so, Desmond.'

'Will you be sorry?'

'In many respects, yes, in others perhaps not. Things have changed here while I've been away!'

'Well yes. Nancy's in Hong Kong, the Vicar and Grace are married and her mother's in a residential home. I don't really think we've heard the end of that saga.'

'You mean she isn't happy there?'

'I very much doubt if she'll be happy anywhere, just as long as she doesn't upset things for them.'

'And Elspeth still has her Tuesday bridge four?'

'Yes. Grace is often busy with other things now but I believe they've got their eyes on somebody else willing to join them. Friend of Hilda Marks.'

'Then I'm sure they'll never be short of something or somebody to talk about.'

'No, that's what I've been saying. Well, it's nice to have you back if only for a little while, you too Bill. Mind if I pass the news along?'

'Whether we mind or not, Desmond, I'm sure that's what you'll be doing.'

They all laughed and he made his way quickly to his house.

He felt sure that that evening the telephone would be very busy. Elspeth was genuinely pleased with his news. She had come to like Anthea and she would be missed.

In many ways when they had got to know her Anthea had

391

seemed like a breath of fresh air – her style, her generosity, even when they had thought her a little too different, and had never quite made up their minds about her gentlemen callers.

Decisions had now to be made about her life and her money. Her stake in the firm would have to be resolved and when she talked to Bill about it he said, 'Does it still hurt so much after all these years, Anthea? You'll be a long way away so perhaps now is the time to put that money back into the firm.'

'I'll have to see what Gordon thinks about it.'

Over the years she had given money generously to the town in her husband's name – new playing fields, new library, hospital wards, although the family had objected saying the money should have been ploughed back into the mills. Gordon thought that now was the time.

'Do the mills need it?' she asked resentfully.

'Well, trade hasn't been all that good over the last few years, but they've survived where a great many firms have had to close. I know you have little time for Colin Edgebaston, but surely you got him out of your system a long time ago.'

She didn't answer. She had loved him and she had hated him and she still blamed him for the fact that she could have loved John more. She had married John in an act of revenge on his family, whilst still loving his nephew, but now looking back she realised that when the love turned to anger she had made Colin Edgebaston pay dearly for what he had done to her.

'I shall need to meet members of the Board, Gordon. Perhaps you or Nigel will come with me.'

'Of course, Anthea. I will arrange the meeting and most certainly I will be with you.'

So it was on a dark dismal day at the beginning of November that she faced all those who were left of the

Edgebaston family, and she asked herself how she could ever have loved Colin Edgebaston.

Now Chairman of the Board he sat at the head of the table larger than she remembered him, and with a bloated red face that she found repulsive.

Sitting opposite her was his son John, a tall gangling young man who played with the paperweight in front of him and constantly allowed his eyes to rest curiously on her. She knew none of the new Board members, although the Company Secretary greeted her with sycophantic regard.

Gordon briefly stated the reasons for the meeting then called upon Anthea to tell them what she proposed to do. Her words were brief.

She informed them that she had remarried and would be going to live in America. She had invited the Town Council to state if they knew of any project that she might be expected to donate to – after that any of the money remaining in the fund would belong to the firm.

'How much money is that likely to be?' Colin Edgebaston asked, and Anthea smiled. 'You will need to consult my accountant about that. Your uncle left his private fortune in my hands, as well as this money I have spent over the years and am now returning to you. Have you any other questions before we leave?'

There were no other questions. This was not the same woman he had dallied with, some little girl in the office, some girl he felt he could pick up and drop at his convenience. The woman he now faced was sophisticated and adult, with his uncle's money behind her, and the contempt she still had for him showed plainly in her eyes.

Conversation was minimal as they drove home in the early afternoon and Gordon said quietly, 'Well, that wasn't too bad, was it, Anthea?'

'No, but I'm glad it's over and done with.'

'Did you find him very strange?'

'Well, he's certainly fatter and more bloated.'

393

'Rumour has it that he drinks rather heavily and his marriage is none too happy. His wife and daughter spend most of their time in France; her father had a villa in Antibes.'

She didn't answer, but she was thinking that this was the man she would have done anything for. She had loved him and believed he loved her – now all that was left were memories of her stupidity, her pathetic naivety.

Squeezing her hand Gordon said wryly, 'You can afford to put it all behind you now, Anthea – a dream that went wrong. Bill will make you happy, I'm sure – a new life, a new country. I'll miss you, Anthea.'

She smiled. 'And I'll miss you, Gordon. All those nights when you listened to me, dried my tears, told me that one day none of it would matter, and I never really believed you. Now it's all true. I've had my revenge too, and although they say it is sweet somehow it doesn't seem so.'

'Leave it in the past where it belongs, my dear. Sufficient unto the day is the evil thereof, a very true saying. Only the future is important now.'

'I've got people looking at the house next week, Gordon. The sooner I sell it the better I shall like it. My cat is going to my daily, who always made more fuss of her than she has of me, but Benjie is coming with us. Will you come out to see us, Gordon?'

'I'll make an effort, Anthea, although I've never been much of a one for foreign travel. Give me the Scottish highlands or the Yorkshire Dales.'

She smiled. 'I was walking up the road yesterday when I saw them taking the piano out of the Clarksons' house. Do you suppose it was going to Erica?'

'Ask the Major, my dear. I'm sure he'll be able to tell you.'

It was not the Major but David Clarkson who told her the next day that the piano had gone north to Derbyshire. Meeting her astonished gaze he added, 'The piano, the stool and the music. It was Nancy's idea to give it to Joyce Mellor's little girl, who apparently has an aptitude for music.'

'That was very kind, David.'

'She's in Hong Kong and Erica didn't want it. I hope it does some good.'

'So where is Joyce Mellor?'

'Somewhere in Derbyshire, married to a farmer and with two children.'

'And the piano's for her daughter, not for Joyce?'

'Apparently not. She's given it up.'

Meeting Anthea's surprised gaze he shrugged his shoulders. 'I know, it doesn't make sense, does it, but we didn't ask too many questions. Nancy seemed rather anxious not to talk about it.'

'And is Nancy happy in Hong Kong?'

'Very happy. They've found themselves a very nice house overlooking the sea and she sees Julian whenever possible. She's made friends, other naval wives, and she's very much in love with the man she always wanted.'

'Oh yes, that's the best bit, isn't it. Not many of us marry our first love.'

'So you're going to live in America?' David asked her.

'Yes. I'm selling the house as soon as possible, then St Agnes will see me no more.'

'We'll miss you, Anthea.'

'Particularly if the people moving in here are terribly circumspect, then you'll miss me.'

He laughed. 'Well, you have to admit we've had our fair share of upsets. At least things are pretty quiet at the moment, I'm glad to say.'

'Yes, let's hope they stay that way.'

Only a few minutes later as he passed the vicarage he saw Grace parking her car on the drive, and although he smiled at her it was evident her mind was on other things.

Grace's visit to her mother at the Berkeley had been the

395

usual mishmash of complaints – about the food, the staff, her companions – and wearily Grace had said, 'Mother, it's lovely here, you have a very comfortable room and every-body else is saying how good the food is.'

'Well, it's not to my taste.'

'Why is that?'

'Twice this week we've had chicken, hot for lunch, cold for tea. Oh, I'll admit not both on the same day, but twice in one week. It's lacking in imagination.'

'Have you complained?'

'They don't take any notice.'

'I don't know what to say, Mother. Everybody else says how much they like being here, you're in the minority.'

'Perhaps their standards are not as high as mine.'

'I'm sure they are, Mother. They've come from similar homes and similar backgrounds. Hearing you complain all the time will antagonise them.'

'The library came round yesterday but they didn't have any books that I wanted, the newspaper's depressing and there's too much of it, I can hardly hold it in my hands.'

'You'd grumble if there wasn't enough of it, Mother.'

'Have you nothing to tell me about St Agnes?'

'Well yes. Mrs Edgebaston has married her American and she's going to live in New England. Her house is up for sale.'

'I wonder what sort of neighbours you'll be getting.'

'We'll have to wait and see, Mother.'

'Has he any money, this American?'

'I don't know, Mother, but evidently enough for a boat which he sails at Cape Cod. Anthea says it's beautiful.'

'Oh, she'll embroider that one, I've no doubt.'

'I like her, she'll be missed.'

'Oh, no doubt, by all the men, particularly Major Robson. I've seen them chatting together at every opportun-ity. I don't suppose his wife knows much about that.'

'Mother, Desmond likes women, he's plenty to say to them, and he chats to me.'

396

'Well, you're the Vicar's wife, so you'd do well to limit your conversation with the Major.'

'Mrs Prothero is going to be a great aunt – Oliver's wife is expecting a baby.'

'Perhaps it's just as well he didn't marry Erica Clarkson, I don't think she'll ever want children.'

'You don't know that, Mother.'

'And how about the other one?'

'Nancy has joined her husband in Hong Kong. Her parents say they've found a nice house and are very happy.'

'I thought he was on a ship.'

'They don't allow wives to live on board, Mother, and he does get shore leave.'

'I don't much hold with women marrying sailors and then following them around. Mrs Watson once told me that she was often here with Julian while her husband was on the other side of the world.'

'Perhaps if Nancy has children that is what will happen to her.'

'Give me a man who works nine 'til five and you know where he is.'

'Well, Paul doesn't work nine 'til five, but I know where he is.'

'Busy is he?'

'Very.'

'Trying to make ends meet?'

'We're very happy, Mother. We've renovated the vicarage and it's really very nice. You've only visited us once.'

'I know.'

'But you visit Mrs Prothero.'

'She comes for me.'

'I would come for you.'

'You've always so much on, and he's none too fond of me.'

'Look, I have to go now. Paul has to go to a meeting tonight, something to do with the church roof – there's always something.'

'And not much money from the collection, I suppose.'

'We get by, Mother. I'll see you next week but I'm not sure at the moment what day.'

'Well, you know where I am. It's like being in prison, just ask for the warder.'

As Grace drove home she hoped their meal was already on the table. She was later than usual, but it was always like this when she went to see her mother – grumbles, sly digs at their insufficient income and when she changed the subject, there was her mother's avid curiosity about the neighbours she had left behind.

Paul opened the door for her and smiled. She loved his smile, it was warm and tender, and even when they hadn't been together he had never been able to disguise what he felt for her.

'Mother all right?' he asked.

'The usual, Paul.'

He grinned. 'Don't worry, darling, she'll never change.'

'I'm sorry you have to go out, Paul, it's starting to rain and the mist is hovering over the river.'

'I won't be late and I haven't far to go.'

He never asked what she and her mother had talked about. It was as though he knew the general gist of it and as they ate their meal he seemed totally engrossed with the notes he had prepared for the evening ahead. What would they have talked about if her mother had moved in with them? Grace wondered.

Her mother had asked her a lot of questions about her role as vicar's wife, saying caustically, 'Molly must be a hard act to follow. She was very businesslike, very efficient.'

'I hope I'm coping as well, Mother,' she'd answered.

'Don't you know? But then nobody's likely to tell you, are they. I'll ask Amelia Prothero, she'll tell me.'

Whenever Grace met Mrs Prothero she sensed sympathy in the older woman's eyes. If anybody knew her mother's shortcomings it was Amelia Prothero.

After Paul had gone out she settled down in front of the fire with Thomas, Paul's black cat, purring on her knee.

She'd never had a cat, or a dog, and she was glad that Thomas liked her. When she told her mother about him all the old lady could say was, 'I've never liked cats, supercilious creatures they are.'

When she told Paul what her mother had said he'd simply said, 'Good job she didn't come to live with us then, we'd have had two of them to put up with.'

Chapter Forty-One

If you were to ask any of the older residents of St Agnes what sort of weather they might expect for the longest day they would tell you that they could only ever remember it raining on one or two occasions. And in the year 1947 the sun rose in golden splendour on a town expecting nothing less.

As always the gardens were bright with flowers, the air laden with the scent of roses and long before breakfast the sound of innumerable lorries could be heard making their way to the Cricket Club, the residence of Sir Robert and Lady Jarvis and to other venues destined to supply goods and refreshments to all who asked for them.

Days before fairy lights had been affixed to the trees and all along the river bank the cobbles had been cleaned, the stonework whitened and even the ducks and swans seemed to know that something was afoot from their noisy clattering.

Major Robson donned his uniform thinking that it was becoming a little tight around his midriff, but after he had waxed his moustache and set his cap jauntily on his head he walked into the breakfast room to seek his wife's approval.

'Well, what do you think,' he asked. 'Not bad for a man getting on for sixty?'

'You've put weight on since you started to wear that. You'll get indigestion before the day's out.'

'Oh, I'll go and see to the cadets, and I've got a junior officer in tow. Then I'll saunter down to the Cricket Club. Are you going to join me there?'

'I'm not sure.'

'It's Wednesday so you've no bridge.'

'I'll think about it, Desmond.'

'Well, I think you ought to set a good example to the new people in the town, let them see that we're all together in this, make them feel welcome.'

'I should think they'll wonder what it's all about.'

'They'll be very glad they're here – boating on the river, cricket and refreshments in the pavilion, the gardens at the Hall and the usual concert this evening. Can you think of another town laying on so much?'

'I remember feeling thoroughly bemused about it when first we came to live here.'

'And then we entered into the spirit of things and came to enjoy it all.'

'I'll admit it was a lifesaver for you, Desmond, a touch of the Army with all that marching and discipline.'

He was busy looking through the window and after a few minutes he said, 'There he is, the flag's going up, Elspeth.'

'What did you expect?'

'I can't think why he doesn't wear his uniform. It would add credence to the ensign. Ah, there are one or two of my lads on their way to the school.'

'Then you mustn't keep them waiting, Desmond.'

'No. I wish I hadn't eaten breakfast – like you said I'll probably have indigestion before the day's out.'

She stood at the window watching him strut down the road, thinking he was still a fine figure of a man, even when his walk was a little slower than it had been last year.

He paused to chat to the Commodore saying, 'You've got the flag up in good time, Andrew?'

'Well yes, it's looking a bit wind-blown, but I reckon it'll last a few more years.'

'Going to the Cricket Club later?'

'Probably.'

'I've told Elspeth she should go. Will Lois be there?'

'I'm not sure. She doesn't care for cricket, says it'll rain if she goes and the match will be abandoned.'

'Shame on her.'

The postman arrived and as he handed his mail to the Commodore the Major said, 'I hear Erica and her husband are visiting. No doubt they'll go to some of the highlights. Trust an MP to look to the future and grab as many votes as possible.'

The Commodore laughed. 'He's quite a nice chap – the Clarksons seem to think so at any rate.'

After the Major had left Andrew went to stand at the gate where he could look up the wide road towards the church with a feeling of nostalgia that refused to go away. There'd been so many changes – it was true that nothing ever stayed the same.

There was a new family in Mrs Edgebaston's house, a man, his wife and two children, both of them girls. They seemed nice enough, the man taught English at the school and his wife gave piano lessons. He'd only ever acknowledged them across the garden but Lois said she'd spoken to the wife and found her perfectly nice, but shy.

Then at Mrs Gantry's house there was a young couple. He worked in the city and went off every morning in a new Austin, while she sat in a sun lounger wearing something that left little to the imagination. He could imagine Mrs Gantry's comments if she knew the sort of young woman who inhabited her front garden.

He looked up the road towards the Clarksons' house where a large grey car was parked and where once he'd been treated to a cheeky smile from the schoolgirl swinging on the gate. Never in a million years had he thought that one day that same girl would be married to his only son, and in a few months the mother of his grandchild.

Lois had been the first to read Nancy's letter and impart her news. She'd been delighted because she'd never thought

402

she'd be a grandmother with Julian's views on marriage, and Andrew had said gently, 'That's when it all starts, isn't it Lois – long separation, he's there, she's here, sometimes they're together and the child's here. There's nothing anybody can do about it.'

'Oh Andrew, we coped and they will too.'

When he listened to Lois and Nancy's parents talking about the good things he hoped that that was how they would always see it.

The Clarksons were sitting down to a rather late breakfast and Erica was saying, 'I told Alistair he'd be bored to death by it all but he still wanted to come.'

'Why will he be bored? The day's never bored me.'

'Well no, Daddy, because you had your cricket match and the thrill of watching me perform in the school concert.'

'You haven't told me what you did in the school concert,' Alistair said with a smile.

'I sang, I danced, I acted in some of the sketches. I was good, wasn't I, Daddy?'

'Very good.'

'Did you always get the leads?'

'Always, then when I left they got Joyce Mellor. She played the piano, but not for long. By the way, Mother, did you ever hear anything about our piano?'

'Yes. I got a long letter from Joyce thanking me for letting her have it for her daughter. She says she loves it and they hope she'll do well. She said she'd let me know how well things go – but that was several months ago.'

'You mean Nancy simply gave her piano away?' Alistair asked.

'Well yes. It was my piano too but I never really took to it – I was in London and Nancy was going to the Far East. Nancy always liked Joyce. I didn't really know her very well.'

'Well, I must say it was a wonderful present to give away.'

'There'd been a lot of tragedy. I think Nancy felt sorry for her.'

Thinking some explanation was due David said, 'Her mother committed suicide here. Her father was a well-known musician with some philharmonic orchestra. I rather think their life together was very unhappy; it was a great pity for the girl.'

'I think I read something about it in the paper. Wasn't the daughter destined for a musical career?'

'Yes, but apparently it came to nothing. She's married, living in Derbyshire, a farmer's wife, so it would appear she's abandoned her music career.'

Erica had had enough of Joyce and to change the subject she said, 'Does anybody ever hear anything from Mrs Edgebaston?'

'I don't think so, dear,' her mother answered, 'at least we never hear, but then she wasn't terribly close to anybody except Elspeth and her husband.'

'I liked her. She was so stylish and very worldly.'

'That's a funny thing to say, Erica. I'll admit she was stylish, but what makes you think she was worldly?'

'I don't really know, except that she had that look about her.'

Erica remained quiet while the others talked. She knew very well why she considered Anthea Edgebaston worldly.

She never thought about Oliver Denton now, but this particular morning she remembered the mist on the river, the cold dank feeling of it in her hair, her damp skirts clinging to her legs and the mud stains on her satin slippers. How close had she been to flinging herself into the deep dark depths of the icy river?

Anthea had been kind and very discreet. There were other women who would have had a lot to say about finding her alone on the wall above the river, with tears streaming down her face and despair in her heart.

Anthea had brought her out of despair into reality, made her see that her life didn't end with Oliver Denton's departure from her life, that there would be a new beginning, other men, other reasons to go on living, and in Anthea she had sensed that she too had once felt the same things she was feeling.

They were talking of other things, but suddenly Erica said, 'I hope she's happy with her American. I'm glad she found him.'

Her mother looked at her uncertainly before saying, 'Oh, so are we, dear. It's just that we never really knew her.'

'I hear Oliver Denton got married,' she said carelessly.

'Oh yes dear, I believe they've had a baby, a little girl.'

'And his aunt Amelia will be thrilled, I'm sure. Does St Agnes see much of them?'

'Oh, they visit Amelia. Edith Pinder tells us that she dotes on the baby and is constantly buying presents. She's already left some money to her, if Edith is to be believed.'

'Well of course, Mother, isn't money what Oliver is always interested in. He cultivated Aunt Amelia to his own advantage.'

'Oh, I think he was very fond of her, dear,' her mother said.

Her father thought it was time to change the subject but Erica simply laughed. 'Daddy, Alistair and I have no secrets. He knows all about Oliver and he knows I got over him a long time ago.'

While her parents and Alistair chatted she went to look out of the window. Nothing in St Agnes seemed to change, even the new people still grew the same flowers their predecessors had grown. She thought back on all the longest days she'd hated and enjoyed. Days when she was top of the heap and others that had disappointed her. Well now she didn't have to worry about them any more. She had Alistair and a way of life this pristine old town could never have given her.

She smiled at the sight of an elegant figure on horseback riding past the house and, turning to the others, she said, 'I see Lady Marcia's here again. She'll make the Major's day.

How many husbands at the last count?'

'We don't discuss such things,' her mother said primly.

'Of course you do, Mother. Behind the curtains along this road there used to be enough gossip to fill a dozen newspapers.'

'Of course there wasn't. Really, Erica, what is Alistair going to think?'

'Nancy and I listened to a lot of it. By the way, how is that sister of mine and when is the new arrival expected?'

'Late September or October, I think. We're so thrilled about it and you'll be an aunt, Erica.'

'Heavens yes. From a distance, I'm glad to say.'

'You mean you're not as thrilled as we are?'

'I suppose so, Mother. I just don't talk about it all the time.'

Somehow Janet didn't think Erica would ever have children. Children would change her way of life too much, interfere with what she called 'living' and perhaps the age difference in them might have something to do with it.

'And how exactly do we spend the day, David?' Alistair asked.

'We all please ourselves, of course. Erica likes boating on the river, I go to watch the cricket. I'm not playing this year – I've had a bit of gout unfortunately.'

'You've been living it up too much, Daddy,' Erica said.

'So what are we going to do, darling?' Alistair asked.

'What do you want to do?'

'I prefer cricket to boating.'

She smiled. Once, a long time ago, a boy she had liked had preferred cricket and she'd fallen out with him. Poor Alec, she hoped he was playing cricket somewhere in heaven.

'There's Grace running down the road,' she said, 'looking younger and a lot more fashionable. I suppose she'll be kept busy the rest of the day.'

'Of course dear, she's making a very good vicar's wife.'

Grace was on her way to see her mother who she

406

intended to bring back to take part in the celebrations. She knew very well that the old lady would make all sorts of excuses but Paul had said, 'I expect she'll give you a hundred and one reasons why she shouldn't come, but she should be backing you up, darling, whatever she thinks about me.'

Grace found her sitting in her usual chair in front of the window but she was wearing her best navy-blue dress and on the table beside her chair rested her copious handbag and large straw hat.

'I'm glad to see you're ready, Mother, the town is getting busy already and we don't want to miss anything.'

'I haven't said I'm going anywhere,' her mother replied.

'But you're evidently dressed for it.'

'I'm dressed for sitting out in the garden as it looks like being a nice day.'

'You mean you're not coming to the fête?'

'I don't know. Lot of fuss about nothing, and the same every year.'

'Not this year, Mother, there are new people in the town.'

'Is Mrs Prothero's nephew visiting?'

'I really don't know, but Alistair Greavson and Erica are here.'

'Then it's just as well if Oliver stays away, it would be an embarrassment for all of them.'

'I don't think so, Mother, they are adult people and time has moved on.'

'I suppose there will be hats,' her mother said.

'Oh, I'm sure there will.'

'Well, Mrs Edgebaston could always be relied on – terribly flamboyant they were, but then so was she.'

'Come along, Mother, I promised Paul we wouldn't be late and there's a lot to do today. I didn't bring the car, Miss Byers says we're all going back in a taxi.'

'Oh surely not, it's too much like a Sunday School outing.'

407

At that moment Miss Byers came rushing into the room saying, 'We're ready to leave now, Mrs Gantry. We'll drop your daughter off at the vicarage then we'll take the rest of you up to the Hall. There's to be a walk around the gardens for those who can manage it, then there will be refreshments laid on in the conservatories. If you want to go into the vicarage with your daughter, Mrs Gantry, no doubt you'll be able to visit the Hall later.'

'I'll stay with the others,' Mrs Gantry said shortly.

It was too soon for Paul to think she had forgiven him for taking her daughter away from her – all in good time. Besides, she wasn't altogether happy with the Berkeley – there had to be something better for the amount of money she was paying for it.

Paul came out of the vicarage to greet them. He was a popular vicar and much to Mrs Gantry's chagrin the fact that she didn't greet him any too warmly hardly registered with any of them.

He stood with Grace to wave them off and with a wry smile said, 'So the battle is still on.'

'It would seem so, Paul.'

'Not to worry, love, we've a busy day ahead of us. First there's the regatta, then the cricket, then the Hall followed by the concert. By the time the day's over we'll be too exhausted to spare your mother a thought.'

Later in the day Lois Watson joined Janet Clarkson in the window of the cricket pavilion and Janet greeted her warmly saying, 'So you decided to come after all, Lois.'

'Yes, I sat in the garden feeling quite happy there, then I realised everybody else was out and about, and there would be no Nancy to come waltzing through the gate. I suppose I'm too late to help with the refreshments.'

Janet laughed. 'Much too late.'

'How is the match going?'

'Very well. We've got a new batsman, a young man who's moved into Mrs Edgebaston's house.'

'That's nice.'

As they looked out across the rows of deckchairs towards the pristine green of the field Janet gave a little sigh. There was something missing – Anthea Edgebaston's presence under the trees with her coterie of admiring men, decked out in her colourful silk dress, her smiling face beautiful under the matching hat, and wearing the sunglasses most people had considered quite inappropriate for the longest day.